BERANDIZIUM VILLAM
(Brading Villa)

By

JAN HARPER-WHALE

This historical novel is the second, in the Wihtwara trilogy, shining a light on new insights of the life and civilizations of our Ancestors on Wihtland (Isle of Wight) in the 3rd century A.D.

Based on two years of intensive research, uncovering archaeological evidence and ancient spiritual Codex, Jan Harper Whale continues the narrative not only of the Wihtwara, but extends it to exciting discoveries along the Silk Road.

The Romans extended their Empire to the hinterland of Britannia. They constructed roads that connected the Silk Road for East to meet West. And with that eastern trade came ancient wisdom, different cultures. Britannia became multicultural.

Yet the "might" of Rome became too unwieldy, burgeoning with too many elites hungry for power. Within the opulence and wealth, there lay embedded into the culture extreme brutality and cruelty. They expressed this cruelty through their religion.

Rome, through the Roman Catholic church, lay a curse on all humanity: religious fundamentalism and punitive reprisals.

It is the truth behind the massacre in 686AD of a whole race of peaceful pagan people on Wihtland, the Wihtwara.

<u>Berandinzium Villam</u>

The 2nd book of the Wihtwara Trilogy

Copyright © 2019 Jan Harper-Whale

Cover Design and illustrations by Jan Harper-Whale

http://www.waking-the-dragon.co.uk

ANCIENT GODS

Zoroaster · Ahura Mazda

Mithras
Leo degree

Abrasax

FORWARD

Just occasionally you come across a work of fiction that can only be described as an astonishing, page-turning tour de force. Just such a work is this second in Jan Harper-Whale's trilogy featuring her beloved Wihtland, which the Romans called Vectis and we today know as the Isle of Wight.

The depth and breadth of research is highly extensive and although presented as a work of fiction, there is a rich bed of fact underpinning the plots and sub-plots of the storylines.

So great is Jan's attention to detail that phrases in Greek, Latin, Anglo-Saxon and even a latter-day version of the language of the Ancient Britons are peppered throughout the book.

A big motivation for Jan to write this trilogy must have been her ancestors, the Wihtwara and the Warinni. Dagrun Wahl has a surname clearly like Jan's Whale. But she is also very deeply concerned with the care and preservation of the earth, our 'Great Mother.'

There is fantastic and fascinating detail of ceremonies to several pagan deities, including Zoroaster, Mithras and Abrasax.

It is not always a particularly 'comfortable' read. It has several dark corners in which the main character, Eyvindr Wahl is subjected to deep trauma. But these dark elements are very much in keeping with the tenor of the main story and help to underscore the major sociological events and adventures within the narrative. And there is a message of hope and love in the epilogue to the story.

It is a book that is extraordinarily difficult to put down, once begun. A big read that sets you thinking and makes you yearn for the next set of events.

With someone so powerfully attached to the Wihtland of the past, the Isle of Wight of today, it might seem a little strange to spend a while dwelling on Antioch, the Silk Road, Byzantium. But these often emotionally intense passages are critical to the development of some of the key characters and their eventual connection to the Island.

All the while, Jan is careful to keep the feminine very much to the fore, as indeed it was in ancient times in these lands.

All who live on and/or love this special Island of ours will be fascinated and beguiled by this extra-special volume. And even those without a connection will find it a tour de force indeed, whether reading purely as the novel it is presented to be or with one eye on the spiritual history of ancient Eastern religions, that comes to meet the Northern Pagan spirituality.

Music for the soul!

Maurice Paul Bower
Wight Druids, Newport,
Isle of Wight. 2019

Acknowledgements

And in deep appreciation to the researchers, archaeologists and writers whose incredible work has fuelled the passion to complete this work.

Stephen Oppenheimer: The origins of the British.

Stephen Pollington: The Elder Gods.

Tylluan Penry: The Magical World of the Anglo-Saxons.

J.N. Margham: Anglo-Saxon Charter Boundaries.

D.Jason Cooper: Mithras; Mysteries and Initiation Rediscovered.

And, the painstaking work of Malcolm Lyne and the Hampshire archaeology team who unearthed and presented that special "key", the clue to Gnostic rituals practised on Wihtland in the 3rd century A.D: The erudite treatise: Roman Wight.

A heartfelt thank you to Maurice Bower, whose friendship and patience is boundless. This book would never have reached the printed page without his diligent editing, and to island archaeologist, Alan Phillips, whose knowledge began my search.

And to my husband Mitch who is my Rock. And very a talented technological genius.

Thank you Merry, whose proof reading and moral support has sustained me throughout. "This book is the knot that ties the other two books together."

Whilst the scholars and friends have provided the inspiration for this work, I should like to make clear that any interpretations in this fictional account are purely my own.

Bletsunga Beorhte, Bright Blessings
Jan Harper whale

ANCIENT (OLD ENGLISH) NAMES ON WIHTLAND

Old English	Modern	Old English	Modern	Old English	Modern
Affetūn	Afton	*Carisbroc*	Carisbrooke	*Rānadūn*	Renham down
Ēastūn	East Afton	*Chestebeorg*	Chessell	*Rægecumb*	Roe deer valley
Sūdtūn	South Afton	*Ceorfdūn Scyte*	Cheverton Shute	*Slācum*	Rowborough bottom
Westtūn	West Afton	*Dēawcumb*	Dew Valley	*Rūhbeorg*	Rowborough Farm
Nordtūn	North Afton	*Fōrdūn*	Foredown	*Rungge*	Rowridge
Meolodūn	Ashey down	*Froggalónd*	Frogland farm	*Senclinz*	Shanklin
Pypacumb	Assembly valley	*Forsterswelle*	Frosthils	*Scorawella*	Shorwell
Beaddingabuman	Bathingbourne	*Gemot Beorg*	Galibury Hump	*Smerdūn*	St Martin's down
Adolfeshylle	Bathingbourne	*Lāfadūn*	Garston Down	*Gārdūn*	St. Catherine's down
Ōrhāmm	Bembridge	*Gārclif*	Gore Cliff	*Stiepel*	Steep Hill Cove
Bicandoene	Bigbury farm	*Heldewaye*	Hillway. Bembridge	*Summorbeorg*	Summerbury
Hūfeinga	Blackwater	*Loewerceadūn*	Lark hill - Lordon Copse	*Idelcumb*	uncultivated valley
Etdredecumb	Bowcombe	*Lucleah broc*	Lukely Brook	*Wæter Geat*	Watergate
Breredingas	Brading	*Moterestān*	Mottistone	*Westōferdūn*	Westover down
Berandinzium Hus	Brading Villa	*Mōtstāndūn*	Mottistone Down	*Westiggedūn*	Westridge down
Wykendeshylle	Brighstone	*Stithes ffeots heafod*	Newtown	*Walpenneclinz*	Whale Chine
Brocbeorg	Brook down	*Plæsc Bearu*	Plaish Copse	*Everlant ēalond*	Yar/Bembridge
		Rægehris	Rains Grove		

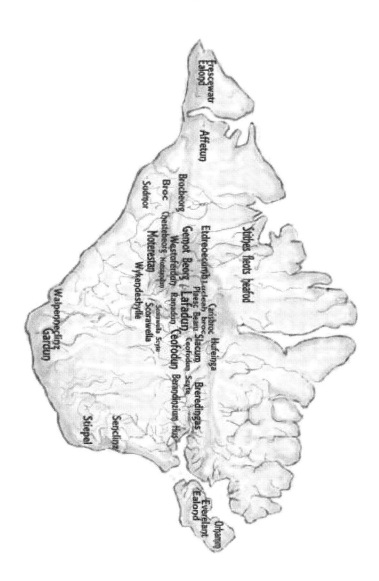

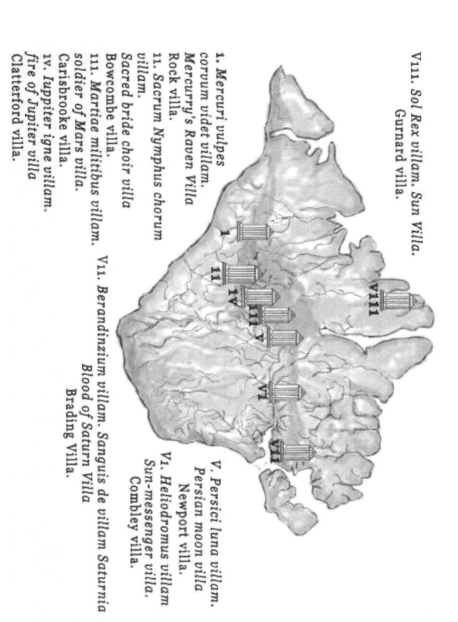

VIII. *Sol Rex villam. Sun Villa.*
Gurnard villa.

I. *Mercuri vulpes*
corvum videt villam.
Mercurry's Raven Villa
Rock villa.

II. *Sacrum Nymphus chorum*
villam.
Sacred bride choir villa
Bowcombe villa.

III. *Martiae militibus villam.*
soldier of Mars villa.
Carisbrooke villa.

IV. *Iuppiter igne villam.*
fire of Jupiter villa
Clatterford villa.

VII. *Berandinzium villam. Sanguis de villam Saturnia*
Blood of Saturn Villa
Brading Villa.

V. *Persici luna villam.*
Persian moon villa
Newport villa.

VI. *Heliodromus villam*
Sun-messenger villa.
Combley villa.

CHARACTERS Real and Fictional.

Real characters. (Roman)

Gallienus-Emperor with Valerian.

(both ruled the Eastern and Western halves of the Roman Empire.)

Saloninus...son of Gallienus

Silvanus...Prætorian Prefect to Saloninus.

(Both murdered by Postumus)

Marcus Cassianus Latinius Postumus

Established and ruled over the Gallic Empire until murdered by his own soldiers

Honoratianus...Consul and adviser to Postumus.

Constantius Chlorus... Emperor with Maximian.

Helena...Consort to Constantius.

She was a devout Christian who helped create Roman Catholicism.

Octavious Sabinus: Governor of Britannia Inferior.

Titus Desticuis Juba: Governor of Britannia superior.

Censorinus... Roman writer and grammarian. (Influence of the stars & genii, religious rites and astronomy)

Antoninus Liberalis... Greek grammarian: A collection of Transformations

The Usurpers:

Lælianus: Governor of Germania superior.

Victorinus: Gallic governor.

Carausius: declared himself Emperor of Gallic Empire.

Allectus: finance officer (rationalis) to Carausius.

Fictional Characters.

The Wihtwara:

Dagrun Wahl.........Day Rune.... Guardian of the stones.

Eileifer.... forever heir... Husband

Gudrun.... divine rune... Mother

Folkvarthr.... Guardian of the people... Father

Eystein....... island stone... Brother

Eyvindr.... island wind... Brother2

Cahal: Eyvindr's son

Ealdmōdor: Grandmother

Cæna: Dagrun Wahl's son

Lāfa...Love......Dagrun Wahl's daughter

Arkyn...Eternal King's Son.... Lāfa's Husband

Lifa...life... Close friend to Dagrun

Aslaug.... god-betrothed woman... Priestess
Eastmund... eastern protection... Adopted boy to Eileifer
Eardwūlf... land wolf... Eastmund's father: Rōmānisc
Hild... Dagrun's servant
Bjartr... oath sworn to Eyvindr

Durotrige Characters:
Blāthnat... Cahal's girlfriend
Aife... Eyvindr's wife
Andraste... slave girl
Agrona... warrior woman
Aodhan... Husband to Agrona

Greek characters:
Berandinzium Villa Greco/roman family
Vrittakos Eluskonios... The owner of Berandinzium villa
Venitouta Quadrunia... His Wife
Aia Duxtir Quadrunia... Daughter
Quintina... Slave woman
Tullia... Slave girl

Antioch
Achaikos Metaxas... High priest to Abrasax, Silk Trade
entrepreneur

Amyntas Argyis... Greek friend to Achaikos

Kiana.. Sogdian Queen, Zoroastrian High priestess

Tahmineh... Kiana's daughter "Tamina" (worshipper of Ahura Mazda)

Cleisthenes Raptis... slave owner

Alcæus Pachis... slave owner

Andreas... rescued vagabond.

Roman characters

Albanus Antonius Cogidubnus... 3rd generation "client" king overseeing Villam Regis (Fishbourne Palace)

Agrippa Aquilla.. Wife to Albanus

Aurelius Cæsar Cogidubnus... Eldest son

Crispus Flavius Cogidubnus... Middle son

Balbus Decimus Cogidubnus... Youngest son

BOOK ONE
Chapters

BOOK TWO

BOOK THREE

BOOK FOUR

BOOK FIVE

BOOK ONE

BERANDINZIUM VILLAM
258 A.D.
PREFACE.

Aelius squinted at the distorted reflection glaring back at him, from the polished copper mirror hanging on the lime-washed wall of his small *cubiculum*. It was his only privilege for the "royal hostage" status awarded him. A double-edged sword. He was forever set apart from both the slaves and the Roman elite, who had started to arrive at the Villam.

But this small, private, living space set in the outer buildings, and near the hypocaust was a luxury and as his face relaxed into the idea of a bath in the warm waters, later, when his day's work was done, Aelius straightened his spine, pulling on his leather subligaculum over the tunica. "Eyvindr you lissan būc!" he chided in his native tongue, "let this anger drive into your work. Make them gasp at your talent!"

But he boiled with frustration. It was after all a barely disguised slave status. The truth gnawed at his guts. He was their prisoner, truly, made to work on this day of grief for all the Suevii. His own sister bent double with the grief he could not ease, nor could he wrap her in his arms, as she had done for him, when his soul was shattered and broken.

The king of Wihtland was in the *deaō-gerihte*. Eileifer had died suddenly, the king of peace, the hearth-king who had never raised a sword. He had kept a wonderful harmony on the sacred isle.

Aelius murmured gently to the gods, "He has honoured the Ancestors and will be nestling in the warmth of *Neorxenawang* as soon as flame licks the oak"

The altar he kept hidden would come out this twilight. His prayers would be sung like a *nigt-gala*, to Nerthus and Wōden, Frèyja and Thunor.

Aelius was a broken man, but he had glued the fractured parts together as best he could. He was a man of many sides. He was a Roman in public life. He had joined the men of Mithras to touch the gods. He was an apprentice to the bull-slayer god, Mithras. To feel the power of spirit course through him in their underground temple, was as essential to him as the air flooding his lungs.

Yet he remained Eyvindr, his Warinni spirit rose, in private, with his family around him, to sing, cry and weep for Nerthus and the island he rarely travelled through. The newly appointed overseer to control the final stages of construction, was a tyrant. The Villam was lamentably behind schedule. The news travelled far enough to reach the ears of Emperor Decius whose edict travelled back with more speed.

Wihtland, called Vecta, by the Romans was a sacred isle. The power brokers had invested heavily in the construction of temple Villams to accommodate the ever-burgeoning cult of Mithras. There was no better island in Britannia that could provide the energy, and beautiful landscape for the seven Mithræum required for all the initiation grades. Berandinzium Villam was by far the most lavish and decorated of them all. It was the final Villam, offering the last initiation of Pater. The culmination of trials and tests to prove devotion to Mithras.

But Berandinzium Villam was created with far more complexity. It was really the creation of Vrittakos Eluskonios, the middle-aged Greek gnostic, who worshiped Abrasax. The ancient archetypal god, whose home was the cosmos and whose encoded name created sheer magic in the hands of adepts. He lived above ground in the Villam, to the equally powerful lion-headed god of Mithras, whose subterranean home released adepts into the Roman army and beyond with stunning regularity. Two very similar gods shared the space within Berandinzium Villam.

Vrittakos even welcomed the occasional honouring and subsequent over-indulgence to Bacchus. The priestess from Lundinuim would arrive with her party of priestesses and hangers-on to celebrate. They consumed more than a fair share of the island wine. It was renowned.

Vrittakos was an adept in his own right. He juggled these three powerful balls in the air for many years, without dropping any of them. It was a consummate feat of skill, both spiritual and temporal. He was mercurial in his skill for debate, compromise and peaceful resolutions.

But now, even these skills were inadequate to the storm brewing in Rome, explosively communicated by the new overseer, who, it seemed had a mandate. He discharged this with little courtesy to the Greek family and much less to the workers, both *libertus* and slave alike. Lashings and screamed orders that left a trail of spittle disappearing into his flabby chin, were a daily occurrence.

And he was the reason Aelius was absent from his brother's *Deaō-gerihte*. Aelius, whose muscle in his cheek always twitched when fury caught him, his teeth clenching, made his way to the servants' hall on the north side of the Villam. He could hear the overseer shriek into the early morning mist at some slave, whose agonising scream made a duet of horror to start his day.

Vrittakos, who was a close friend to the Warinni, had been overruled. Aelius was reduced to imploring sentiments to the overseer, the day before. Aelius' own spirit had been crushed long ago, and now, his feelings were spat out in pieces by this burly overseer and lay on the ground before them.

Aelius saw Vrittakos walk towards him, on this murky and misty morning.

"Such a dour and dank day for a royal death-rite," he muttered, looking to the ground. Vrittakos came up and extended his arm in a Suevii greeting. He looked pinched and pale. He was of indeterminate age and his body seemed ever youthful, yet the stress of his present circumstances needled away at his soul.

"Eyvindr, my dear friend," he said softly, extending his arm to gently embrace him, "I will explain all of this to Dagrun and Lãfa. They will know you are with them in spirit".

"Tell me how Dagrun fares, please!" Aelius replied, choking back tears. "And tell me everything when you can spare the time."

Vrittakos turned to re-join his family, waiting by the covered wagon that would take them to the Ancestor stone, the *Cenningstãn.*

"Ahh," Aelius shouted, "I forgot. I have something you need to give Dagrun. She will know what to do with it." He turned and ran back to his *cubiculum*. Within the hardened leather case tucked under his bed, that held his movable altar, wrapped in deerskin, was the jewelled and decorated *seax* Eileifer had gifted him after his escape from Cantium. It was a mark of oath-sworn fealty. This was a part of Aelius that needed to be returned. Dagrun would know.

He ran over to the wagon, Venitouta, Vrittakos' wife, extended her delicate arm out to Aelius, and gently stroked his cheek.

"Stay strong, Eyvindr," she spoke, looking deep into his anguished soul, "Do not allow that *veneficus exsceo* to rile you, or overcome you. He is nothing!" She spat on the ground and cursed him some more in Latin. She took the *seax,* holding it to her heart, nodding imperceptibly.

The oxen moved on, encouraged by the sharp lick of the driver's whip and the wagon lumbered off into the mist.

"*Aelius!*" came the high-pitched scream from the overseer, "You piece of shit, you have dawdled long enough. Breaking your fast is but a dream. Get to the floor and finish that mosaic!"

Aelius almost stood to attention, straightened, spun around and smiled. As he turned on his heel, the only giveaway to his true state of mind was that tic in his cheek. And that was how he carried himself in the back-breaking work at Berandinzium Villam, always, like the royal swan gliding effortlessly upstream, no one seeing the fury of feet and tired legs underwater.

Aelius's brain rarely gave him rest, only the hard labour of the day leaving him exhausted, afforded him dreamless sleep. Sometimes. He would travel the length and breadth of Wihtland, in his mind, when the work was so repetitive, it gave his mind that chance to wander. He prayed diligently to the gods and goddesses of his natural world. The pagan gods that meant so much to him. He fashioned *drycræft* metal fixings, swords and *seax*, in his fertile mind.

As Aelius strode over to the *atrium*, where the most intricate mosaic was developing, his mind skipped over the past. The day Vrittakos threw his arms around fragile shoulders and welcomed him with an open-heart to his family, to his villam. How he was given unofficial *libertus* almost instantly and was permitted to design, create in whatever medium he felt challenged to do. He developed his skill as a smithy, in fine jewellery and domestic *seax*. Vrittakos encouraged him to design some of the border mosaics, and when he joined the Mithras elite, he was asked to design for the gods.

But more than all these gifts bundled together in a joy re-discovered, was the re-union with his family, with Dagrun, who visited the Villam frequently. She loved it here, he thought, along with the teachings of Abrasax, the ancient god whose celestial wisdom of the stars and planets simply saw her open-mouthed and hungry for more. His last memory of her, before life became intolerable, was her talking excitedly to Aia, Vrittakos' daughter, about some point of celestial mystery, or earth wisdom, her arms flowing theatrically and Aia laughing and shrieking a *Giese!* They both inter-changed tongues between old Saxon and Roman, at will, leaving Aelius flustered. He prided himself as being multi-lingual. The river of Wyrd had sent him to foreign lands that required he learned the tongues quickly or died. The Roman tongue was a grudging task, in his time in Cantium, whereas the Durotrige tongue turned into a joy, when he lived on Frescewætr èalond.

But these two *cwèns* had bested him!

He turned to gaze at the path leading down to the estuary, where he last saw her, and willed a silent prayer to Nerthus, sent on the taut nerve-endings of his heart.

"Nerthus, Foldè *Mōdor, Sendan Eald Mōdor on þæt feðer-homa fram Hragra æt fæðm mín dèore sweostor on hiè ofðyncan. Sendan hiè ðryð. Und......!*"

Nerthus, Earth Mother, send grandmother on the wings of Heron to embrace my dear sister in her grief. Give her strength. And......!"

Aelius growled and hissed as the vine rod swished with such force, it broke through the thin linen of his tunica and hit the skin, bloodying his back. The overseer lashed at him even harder, the welts meeting each other sending small rivulets of blood down his spine.

"*Aelius!!!* Take that and that, you lazy toe-rag of useless bones!" screamed the overseer, in sheer twisted joy, able to let loose with Vrittakos gone. He had been patient. He had waited for this moment and now it had arrived.

Aelius' knees sagged as the next vicious thwack hit him. But he straightened with a low hiss through gritted teeth, he would not succumb, he would not give this evil pile of *veneficus exsceo* any victory. Yet more lashes of the rod came to test his will, weaving a now bloody tapestry on his skin. Every hit became more intense, it was a battle of strength and with nothing to hold him, Aelius' whole body was trembling in trauma. Still he remained upright. He could see through tangled, bloodied hair, that work had stopped. Everyone was looking on in horrified silence, in warped fascination or total disgust. Empaths felt his agony and crumpled with each hit. Fractured and damaged souls grinned with each new spray of blood.

The brother to the King of Wihtland was being badly beaten for virtually no crime, by a squat and ugly Roman, whose measly claim to power urged him to create more for himself, through fear. If he could floor this royal giant, then everyone would obey him. So, he thought.

But his soul was moribund and did not know the royal soul of Eileifer was looking on, screaming at the pain being inflicted on his brother, then flying with speed to the All Father, Wōden himself. Justice would be served this day.

The next hit saw Aelius crumple, with the ground, thankfully, coming up to meet his bloodied face, as he sank into blackness.

… … … … … … … … …

Aelius willed his mind to hold the dream. He began to feel his body in an arch of terrible pain he had never experienced before. He drifted back into unconsciousness.

He was observing that exquisitely creative moment at the forge, when the cast was set aside, delicately pulled open to reveal the *drycræft* formed in metal, still warm, rough, but unmistakably a potential beauty. Sunni was gifting her rays to make the bronze glint in places, and it made Aelius' heart open. His mind saw it completed. So, it suddenly morphed into the finished sword hilt, with filigree twining in silver and some gold to represent the eternal serpent embrace of Wōden and Nerthus. A garnet was placed at the head to show the Wōden spirit eye and a jet, for his earth eye. A ring hung from the hilt. It was, in its magnificence, a ring sword, to be cherished by the kings and handed down through the years. Aelius, went to scratch his head and realized he had the long locks of his youth, and his hair tied in the Suevii knot. He was Eyvindr, and he was home. His shattered heart burst open.

Eyvindr, Eyvindr, he kept hearing his Warinni name.

"Eyvindr, please wake up!" Lífa stroked his head, gently calling his name with more insistence. Slowly his mind connected with his body, and he groaned, long and low, trying to twist away from the excruciating pain that flooded his consciousness. He was lying on his stomach, with his arms laying down either side of a cot packed with furs. His head lay to one side, and he forced one grit-caked eye to open. The blurred image of his friend, Lífa, came into focus. He lifted his arm to touch her worried face.

"You should not be here!" he uttered, "You should be at the *Deo-Gerihte* of our King!"

"Eyvindr, sweet man, you have been floating on the river of Wyrd for two twilights now. Agrippa and Aurelius rescued you after that overseer had finished. One of the tribunes pulled him away, saying he had rarely seen such dripping hatred from a man. And he has seen some terrible acts committed in his time away on the killing fields of Gaul. They brought you here to this room next to the kitchen and near the apothecary, so we may heal you."

"Why," croaked Aelius, "What made him do this? I have done nothing wrong!" He fought back a choking torrent of tears. He was, in his soul, a peacemaker, a *scōp* and an artist. If he been made for violence, he would be on the killing fields now, in some godforsaken part of the Empire. They had named him Aelius, against the will of Vrittakos, whose ownership of the Villam had now become tenuous. But his spirit screamed within, for his Libertus status to be honoured again.

"I am nothing more than a slave now!" he cried.

"*Giese*," Lífa whispered, "But know this, Eyvindr, your *sweostor* and Aslaug are, at this very moment, working up a whirlwind of *galdor-cræft* to ease your pain. Nerthus and the gods have been summoned."

"My sister should be grieving!" Aelius replied, a shocked expression taking over his pinched and aching face.

"She is, but Dagrun took your attack with great anger. She is incandescent with rage. She is the guardian and a Warinni. The anger has helped her, in fact, to face another day."

"Hmm," Aelius conceded, "She has the power of Wōden and Nerthus with her. Woe betide her adversaries is all I can say"

"Now hold your tongue while I refresh your dressings and bathe your wounds" Lífa admonished. She had collected many herbs to make the poultices. They would draw out poisons and help seal up the broken skin. But they were anything but easy, when herb contacted the bloody skin, Aelius felt every lash all over again. He became tired and exhausted, drifting back into unconsciousness once more, releasing him from pain.

··· ··· ··· ··· ··· ··· ··· ··· ···

CHAPTER 1

Proiectus corpore separari
Body and Soul cast Asunder

Vrittakos arrived back at the Villam from a deeply heart-wrenching death rite for his close companion, Eileifer, king of Wihtland. Venitouta and his daughter Aia wept quietly and persistently throughout the long ceremony. The Suevi host had gathered at the *Cenningstãn* from every corner of Wihtland. Together with Druid and Durotrige from both *Frescewætr Èalond* and *Everlant Èalond,* many people paid tribute to a kind and popular king. The energy and atmosphere were leaden with sorrow. Dagrun Wahl, who had aged quickly, needed the support of her *Fæder,* as she put the heavy torch, alight with flames flickering and dancing in the wind that had suddenly blown in, to the funeral pyre. The torch shook, her father grabbed it with her, and together they lit the pile of tinder laid carefully around the shroud of her husband. A wail issued from his daughter Lãfa. And she sank to the ground.

The *nigt-galas* began the lament, the song for the dead. To Vrittakos, it meant it was time for him and his family to withdraw. It signalled the private mourning for the Warinni, and he was not familiar with these pagan ways. His was the way of Abrasax, the worship of that ancient celestial god, the ultimate overseer of all. Yet he could not honour him, and the overwhelming urge and need to do just that, after these grief-stricken days on Wihtland, was overpowering him. Frustration set in at the thought of the elite Romans arriving to welcome the newly created adepts in their worship of Mithras, the bull-slayer. And Berandinzium villam had benefited in the most lavish adornments these days, from a seemingly bottomless money bag of *sestertii* and lately *denarius*. It was their preferred place of worship. They paid him and his workers handsomely. But they were ever the harsh task masters.

He began to feel nervous, as the oxen lurched their covered wagon home, down rutted and steep pathways until they reached the valley floor and meandered through pasture and thicket. The dawn was overcast and misty. Little sunshine would greet these elites. They would be coming all the way from Rome. And the Emperor Gallienus would expect a full report.

Vrittakos broke into a sweat. He looked over to his wife and daughter, hoping for some diverting conversation. Both were utterly silent, deep in their respective grief. The death of Eileifer had left a big hole in their hearts. Venitouta loved him like a brother, as Dagrun had become a sister to her. Both women were at times inseparable and they loved each other.

Aia loved Eastmund, the adopted son to the king. He had stood by her all through the rite, when by rights he should have been with the Wahl family. His tousled hair fell about his face, as he stood stock still, his head rammed into his chest. At one point, Vrittakos caught his daughter reach out to hold his hand. He clasped it tight, as his shoulders began to shake.

"Oh, that poor, poor *puer*," he thought.

As they turned into the approach to the Villam, Vrittakos realised something was clearly amiss. He has expected a completion of sorts, a tidy approach to the Atrium. There were small huddles of slave workers secreted around corners, and when they saw the master had at last returned, broke away and assumed work. The overseer was nowhere to be heard. That was highly unusual.

"Something is amiss, my dears," Vrittakos looked across to his wife and daughter, both deeply saddened and quiet, staring at nothing. "I want you both to go and rest, bathe and get warm in the far rooms. I will discover what has happened here in my absence." He looked down to notice an area of gravel darkened and scraped. It was clean when he had left, he thought. He watched them both go, for a moment, making their way past the *peristylium* whose beautifully created fountain was bone dry.

"*Per omnis Hades!*" he muttered, "What has happened here? The elites will have me flayed!"

Vrittakos, with growing concern etched on his sculptured face, walked into the *Atrium* and looked upon, in the far room, intended to honour his guests, piles of the black tiles from Durotrige lands, and the red tiles from Wihtland clay lay jumbled together with white chalk tiles from the downs. The mosaic, that highly sacred and important honouring to the gods, lay unfinished. The elites would be arriving, expecting perfection for their ceremonies and would be greeted by this chaos, this mess.

His hands balled into tight white-knuckled fists, as he rounded on the workers who were brushing, cleaning, but certainly not finishing that mosaic.

"Where is Aelius!" he shouted, "You," he pointed to a young lad, whose head was bending down studiously counting the hairs on his broom, "Get him, *Now!*"

"He cannot do that Vrittakos," came a soft voice from the *ala*, set aside from the *Atrium*, you need to go to him".

Vrittakos spun round to see Lífa standing with arms crossed, head to one side.

"What in Hades are you doing here?" he asked.

She waited for him to join her, swung on her heels and marched briskly across the *peristylium*, gesticulating wildly, as she told him all the sequence of events, especially how he had lain unattended for hours until she could be fetched, taking Eileifer's stallion to speed the journey.

"I had no time to alert you, Vrittakos," she apologized, "I just sped away, cursing that venomous shit, all the way. It does seem that the Warinni have their own curse upon them, that brings these vile specimens to do their worst with those gentler souls of the tribes!"

"Agh, yes, you are talking of the evil Gandãlfr" he muttered. "How is Eyvindr?" Vrittakos never alluded to Aelius' false name before his Warinni kindred.

"As I said, it was the worst thrashing I have witnessed. It seems the overseer kept on, even after Eyvindr had collapsed. You could award Agrippa and young Aetius, if you feel so inclined. Between them they halted the onslaught, pulled the "shit" off Aelius, who had thankfully passed into unconsciousness. I believe he may have died, so he owes them his life."

Throughout this grim retelling, Vrittakos kept shaking his head in disbelief. Then he suddenly stopped, just before the archway to the northern Villam, where Aelius lay, in one of the *cubicula* reserved for guests.

"You will see for yourself," Lífa said gently, knowing the great affection Vrittakos held for Eyvindr. He had been instrumental in securing his future and teaching him trade and skills that would enrich his life and that of his family.

"Why has this happened. Eyvindr is a model worker, diligent and creative!" he asked

"Both Aslaug and Dagrun are in *drycræft* now, entering the flow of Wyrd, to find the answer to that, Vrittakos," Lífa replied, "Here, you go in, I need to collect fresh binding and poultices."

Vrittakos opened the door to see Aelius, sitting up with his feet to the floor, and facing away from him, Vrittakos grimaced and sucked in his breath to see the bloody ridges and welts that was once smooth skin. Discarded poultices lay on the floor and puss and fleshy detritus intermingled with the soiled linen. Anger grew within him. It was a savage attack on his friend. "He is like the son I never had," he thought wistfully.

"Eyvindr," he spoke gently as he moved round to see the face of his friend. "I am so profoundly sorry. Words are not enough. I am seething with anger to pour it out on that *venenatus spuo*. But I cannot hear him or see him. So, where is he?"

"In hell!" growled Aelius, "the darkest hole possible!"

"Do you have any inkling why this should have happened?" Vrittakos said, scratching his dense, greying curls, hoping an answer might spring out of that tight mass.

"I was but two minutes late for breaking my fast. And he gave no chance for me to take food. Oh, and I rushed back to get the *seax* for Eileifer's *deaō-gerihte*. He waited until you were all far enough away." Aelius tried to shift his weight, sucking in air at the pain.

"You must rest Eyvindr," Vrittakos took his arm and rubbed it, trying to sooth the pain, both physical and emotional. It was, he thought, a most terrible trauma to a man who had already suffered at the hands of twisted Roman generals in Cantium. Then a thought struck him.

"Did this overseer arrive from Rome, on the Legate's boat, that docked first at Cantium?"

Aelius shrugged, "I try not to make conversation with the shit!"

"I will find out all I can. And if I catch him first, I will personally flog the answer out of him!" Vrittakos heaved his weight up on arthritic legs, his own personal and daily pain level afforded him an empaths approach to Aelius.

"Justice will be done, Eyvindr. You have my word" he smiled down on Aelius, and quietly left, nearly bumping into Lífa, who had an armful of linen and herbs to dress those awful wounds.

"Come and see me, my dear, if you please, afterwards, and before you head back to *Lãfadūn*" Vrittakos said, "I need to know what Dagrun and Aslaug may have planned".

"*Vrittakos!*" Aelius shouted from within, "tomorrow, I will get that mosaic finished".

"You will *not,*" Lífa and Vrittakos both insisted together, as he charged back into the *cubiculum*. "*Impossibilis*! You remain here," Vrittakos barked an order, not to be countermanded.

"Look," Aelius insisted, looking up with a stubborn, fixed expression, "You need that mosaic completed in a short time. There is no-one else here who knows the configuration of colours, and though I may be training two men to help me, they cannot take it over in my absence! I will be present tomorrow, on a couch if needs be, to direct the work. But that mosaic will be finished on time. You have *my* word on that!"

Vrittakos knew he had been bested, and grumbled quietly as he left the room, although a smile etched its way onto his tired face, there to remain.

Lífa settled herself down and began the slow healing process, that still created the pain of every lash on Eyvindr's back. He concentrated all his thoughts on the frescos of this elaborate and intensely colourful *hospes cubiculum*. Deep ochre and red had been painted around the figures that glided gracefully with silks swirling around the women, as men watched in the background, adoring the beauty before them. A perfect dream-like scene, full of serenity, with alluring, carnal imagery laying subtly beneath the near-transparent silks, all pastel colours of blues and yellows. No expense had been spared gaining these intense colours. The minerals extracted from deep within the earth, rendered and powdered, mixed with egg-white and some with lime, glowed with a fluorescence that was unworldly.

Aelius wished himself lost within those images, creating Vanaheim in his mind, and travelled there, feeling no pain at all. Lífa continued in silence, carefully, slowly mending his back. The scars would remain for the rest of his life. She caught a sob in her throat and chased it down. After nearly an hour, she was reaching the lower part of his back, and a particularly vicious lash had caught the bones of his spine, exposing them. She worried continually about infection. If his blood became infected, especially here, near the nerves, he might still die. She placed the All-heal herbs of Wōden here, quietly invoking the song of the runes and the spirits of the herbs to enter the poultice.

Her chanting brought Aelius gently back to the present.

"What is my sister and Aslaug doing?" he said, "Dagrun is in mourning!"

"Dagrun is doing what she does well, Eyvindr," Lífa retorted, "She is mightily angry as you must acknowledge. And it is necessary."

"You have not answered my question!" he shot back.

"That is because I do not know. They are in deep trance. In *seiðr*. They are asking the Nornia for help, Wōden and Thunor. There will be justice. Our kind of justice, Eyvindr!"

"And here is *my* question to you!" Lífa leant forward to look intently into Aelius' eyes, to catch his soul, "Why are you insisting on staying with this Roman Mithras god? The bull-slayer. Why are you Roman? Eyvindr! You were rescued, by us, your family. We love you and wish you back with us!"

Aelius, very slowly turned. A deep, black look entered his eyes, as he stared intently at Lífa, pupils enlarged with emotion. He spoke so softly, Lífa had to lean into him.

"You have been treating the decimation and ruin of my physical body. That is what Romans do, with gusto, with satisfaction. But they are not at all satisfied with that. It is nothing to them. They yearn to crumple your spirit. Your soul is for bartering to the next Roman. And they will do a more complete job in rendering you an empty shell. And there comes a day when all the splintered and fractured parts of you are laying at your feet. You suddenly realise with total clarity that you are forever someone's property. You will never be able to put all those pieces back.

Has that answered *your* question?"

"*Giese,*" Lífa whispered, and with head down, she quickly gathered the soiled linen, and herbs. She left, glancing back at her dear friend and silently wept.

… … … … … … … … …

Chapter 2

Si enim hortus et in bibliothecam, quae est opus ves-
trum!
If you have a garden and library, you have everything
you need!
(Marcus Tullius Cicero. 106 BC -43 BC)

The sun's rays filtered in through the fine glass that had been cut into rectangles and fitted into the window frames, only just completed the previous day. The shafts of muted green light shone onto the mosaic floor, warming the backs of the craftsmen, as they deftly layered the tesserae in patterned sequences. Aelius looked on, from the couch Vrittakos had fetched from the *triclinium*. He sat straight and rigid for as long as he could stand it, then shifted onto the pile of pillows brought by a slave girl to relieve his aching body.

He was giving almost continuous instructions to his team of apprentices. His eyes darting from one feature to the next, always insisting on yet faster placement, smoother cement and meticulous laying of the coloured tiles. It was a masterful design, intricate with deep symbiology. This floor was the showpiece. It contained layers of the Mysteries from the ancient worlds, gathered together in an interlaced design, that only the adepts would understand. Aelius, whose world was pagan, whose spirit lay in nature's embrace, saw another world here, one that Vrittakos knew. It was his triumph. He was creating his own miracle. The most ancient gods and goddesses lived in this mosaic, together, understanding each other's value to humanity, and each living in the sacred diversity that this design was applauding. Mithras met Abrasax, and celebrated Bacchus. The cockerel twinned with the lion and the griffin. A trinity of pure magic. The power that brought the leaders and the governors to this villam, Berandinzium Villam, lay in these mosaics.

"Have a care with the tesserae forming the *Ablanathanlba* hanging round the neck of our god in disguise," shouted Vrittakos, who refused to leave his stricken friend, in case the *venenatus spuo* reappeared. His absence from the villam fuelled suspicions for Vrittakos, which he was determined to resolve.

"My god is Abrasax," Vrittakos suddenly called out, "The cockerel-headed one, who is half-man, half-serpent. He who rules the 365 heavens, and is the great guardian of the cosmos, whose last heaven, the material world, is this one. That is why we have 365 parts in our bodies. It links us directly to Abrasax, and we have 365 days to our yearly calendar, so our physical world is connected to him also"

Aelius smiled up to his benefactor. The first smile Vrittakos witnessed since the attack, and he beamed back, his grizzled face disappearing in a feast of wrinkles.

"You are the most devout Gnostic Basilidean I will ever encounter!" Aelius smiled, eyebrow raised, "but I really doubt you will succeed in converting that lot over there!"

Two apprentices glanced over, grinning. The others were concentrating on the work, pressurized by Aelius to finish the black, red and grey border design, which required precision, to hold the red and grey in circular formation, while the other apprentice was laying the black border.

"I honour sacred diversity in my advancing years, Aelius," Vrittakos murmured sadly, "Those young men see only Mithras".

"And Bacchus," Aelius grinned back, "They seriously honour the God of wine. And" he added, "don't you let the tribunes hear your heretical talk, when they do arrive!"

"Careful young man, you overstep yourself!" Vrittakos growled, grinning at the clever and subtle way he was besting those arrogant, Roman elites.

His villam had mosaics to rival the best in Gaul, even Rome itself, but hidden within, was the magic. They honoured the Greek classical myths. Yet the symbiology was carefully laid out to hide the magical formulae within. He was very proud of all the craft-work and the frescos. Each room now vibrated with art, with life. And today the sun welcomed that energy and brought the whole villam into vibrant life. The colours danced out to him, and he rejoiced.

The dark shadow of the last few days receded for a while, and both owner and apprentice relaxed and appreciated the world they had created.

They worked for several more hours, until hunger overcame them and the call for food was announced. It was mid-afternoon when they all made their way along the wide colonnaded corridor to the *culina* and eating area.

The sun cast long shadows of the colonnade onto the garden, creating a patchwork of dark green pillars, amongst the foliage and flowers. The slaves had been busy planting the garden with the deep reds of poppy, just beginning to bloom, and many rose bushes, expertly arranged in graduated colours. The contrast was stunning.

Vrittakos was very pleased, nodding in appreciation "Albinus, give these workers here a bonus, they have earned it. Increased rations for the weeks ahead I think" Several faces looked up from their work, smiling, giving thanks to their master, and they each thanked their own gods for this. Vrittakos was a caring governor.

"How is your body?" he asked Aelius, who was hunched over with the effort of walking just a few yards.

"I would appreciate a change of linen dressings," he replied, "But do not think it is an excuse to withdraw. I mean to continue through this twilight. Everything will be completed on time.

"There are the red tesserae of medusa's head to complete, and the green limestone is running out. We need to get more supplies in very quickly, Vrittakos."

"Ah! Absolutely. I will go and see the messenger now and arrange his travel to Durnovaria. How much *sestertii* should accompany him?" Vrittakos raised an eyebrow.

"Hmmm, I would find *denarii*, Vrittakos, if possible. We need to cover all eventualities. He needs to collect tesserae from our clay foundries here, for the white chalk base, and the black must be bought also from Durnovaria. To complete everything.... say 100 denarii?"

Oh! Far-shooting Apollo, you will bankrupt this poor Greek merchant!" Vrittakos exclaimed, throwing his hands up in mock exasperation. He turned and grinned at Aelius, who had suddenly straightened to his full height, expecting a verbal backlash.

"Hah! I knew it. You are faking the hunch back, young Aelius. Look at you now!" Vrittakos threw his arm around his friend, who winced but smiled back. He was truly beginning to relax now the day had nearly gone and he was free of the overseer. Vrittakos had another surprise waiting for his chief apprentice.

"There should be someone waiting in your *cubiculum* to dress your wounds," Vrittakos said over his shoulder, grinning, as he carried on to the dining area.

Aelius opened the door to see her lovely face again, as a delighted exclamation shot from him. Aife, his wife jumped up from the bed and ran to kiss him and hug him. He shook with joy and with pain. He backed off to hold her at arm's length.

"Aife, you are my delight, but have a care, this is not the Aelius you left" He gingerly lifted his tunica, marred still with some blood stains, and turned to hear the gasp of horror from his wife. She led him to the stool, made him sit, as she fought back her tears.

"This will take an hour or more, and you must be starving, my husband. Shall I ask for food to be brought here?"

He shook his head, "my appetite has left me. This is going to hurt me," as he shut his eyes to travel again to block out the pain. And Aife felt every shudder as if she, herself, had been put to the lash. Her anger grew to a tight ball. She thought she might explode. She would kill this overseer, if ever she caught him. He deserves a slow death, she thought silently.

After she had finished, and Aelius had carefully laid his body down to rest, she went out to find a slave girl to bring food to the cubiculum.

"My master has ordered me to freshen a new cubiculum for you both" the slave girl pointed over to a door along the ala, and very near to the peristylium. "He said you and your husband needed the healing of flower scent carried on fresh air".

"Ah, what a lovely gesture," Aife commented, "And what is your name, I feel we will be seeing you often?" The girl looked more native than Roman.

"Andraste," she replied, looking to the floor, "I was taken in Durnovaria, as just a small child, parted from my mother. I have no idea where she may be. I have been here at this villam, since the first foundation stones for the new block were laid."

"Hah, I knew it," Aife exclaimed, "You are Durotrige, like me! Now I am stationed here with my husband, Aelius, or should I say Eyvindr, a royal of the Wihtwara, I shall petition Vrittakos for your *Libertus*. You can be childminder for my brood. Would that be to your liking? You can then travel to find your real family".

Andraste gasped with shock. "Dare I believe this! Master Eluskonios is kind and caring but he has never even thought of offering me *Libertus* before. Why would he agree now?" she asked.

"Hmm, there can be no harm in asking. After all I like your honesty and I trust you. You are Durotrige. Of my people. Andraste, I will speak for you." Aife had a feeling, an intuition that lives were about to change, that Wyrd was flowing through this villam and touching everyone. But what she touched was in truth, a torrent, only just invoked, the first ripple in the tidal wave lying in wait.

The twilight was enveloping the broad colours splashed around all corners of the villam. A line of slaves proceeded along the *alas*, carrying the torches to set in brackets lining all the walls. The flames danced and weaved in the night breeze, creating a shadow display on the frescoed images, that brought them to life. Colourful birds and animals seemed to gyrate to mysterious music unheard by human ear. The subtle carnal poses of the women in sheer silks, became more tantalizing as flesh seemed to come alive in the weave of the amber flames. Moths and insects danced their way to the flames, to a death.

Aelius stubbornly rose from his bed when he heard the march of the torches. Aife became exasperated with her stubborn husband, clattered all the dishes and plates together, herself, and marched off to the *culina*. He made a promise to her, as he hobbled out of the door, that he would be only an hour of two at the very most. This, she doubted.

... ...

The *onus scapha* barged unceremoniously into the landing stage, weighed anchor, scraping the worn timbers that supported the wide walkway of old-seasoned oak, now embedded in the turf and roughened grass that led up to emporium. This jewel of size and design was newly built and very impressive. It was a stark contrast to the mess of dirt and deep ruts which formed the approach. A team of oxen spent their life dragging cargo to the wide double-door entrance. Today, they were hauling the large consignment of tesserae.

The villam would be completed. The pressure Vrittakos was feeling around his old heart, made him wince.

"Abraxas, give this old heart strength I beg you!" he muttered to the sky, looking up, imploring the god for help, "This has all the makings of a full Triumph, but with no crowds of admirers, only the damn crows!"

Seagulls vied with the crows, always expecting a food consignment. They would be disappointed this day, but Vrittakos and Aelius were jubilant, but very tired. They both entered the shadowed interior, dust permanently rising in the shafts of sunlight that filtered down from gaps in the timber and the open shutters. At the far end, huge tables had been placed to sort and mark the goods, before sending them on their way. A small team of slaves from the villam were already piling the coloured tiles into separate boxes, packed with straw. By evening, and all the following day, everyone would be on their knees, arranging and finishing the incredible mosaics.

Artists would be lined up against the limed walls, outlining the figures, animals that would grace the villam with magical life. Gardeners would be barking orders to yet more slaves, on their knees, planting the remainder of the flower garden that would delight the elites. The atmosphere crackled with the deep concentration of all the residents of Berandinzium Villam. It created such a levelling process, an equality of communal effort, that slave and master became indistinguishable from each other.

"I have reached a decision, Eyvindr," Vrittakos commented, as he leant forward to fix four more tesserae in place, creating the interlocking guilloche that surrounded the medallion honouring Orpheus, "I have always sought to be fair minded when dealing with my slaves. But I am not just Greek, I am an old Greek. I want to make my mark here, before I join my Ancestors somewhere in the 365 heavens. I had already reached the decision to press for your permanent *Libertus* status with the elites, that is only right. But I wish to make all these people here, free. Look around you, Eyvindr, how much better they work, when fear of a beating does not stalk their every move."

"Oh, I will applaud that," Aelius said with feeling, "Have you discovered more of the whereabouts of the *venenatus spuo*?"

"Nothing, I'm afraid. I have a growing suspicion that he was placed here on the behest of those blood-thirsty generals in Cantium. The reward of money would never have been enough and their need for revenge has festered for all these years"

"I agree," growled Aelius, "but it will never be proved. Never!"

He continued to give instruction as the mosaic showing Orpheus neared completion and his bitterness took a deeper hold. He suddenly decided that sitting just giving instruction was not enough. His precarious state of mind might just unhinge him. Pulling on his stick he hoisted himself upright and limped over to that part of the Orpheus medallion that needed his attention. He needed to get lost.

Aelius sank to his knees, pulling a selection of tesserae made on Wihtland, his spirit instantly travelling to the sparkling waves, sea lapping by his feet, as the cooling breezes washed the pain from his tortured mind.

Vrittakos looked on silently, as he too travelled back to his homeland in Greece. Would he ever see those Cyprus fir trees sway in the high heat of summer, as he ate black olives and drank Greek wine? His spirit screamed out silently. "Legions of the lost, you trampled souls, rise up in your thousands to squash the true usurpers, these Romans whose lust for land and power has vanquished so many. Abrasax, by the spirit of all that is true, reach down to embrace us, enfold us with your strength. Let justice start here, now" Vrittakos heaved a deep sigh, his chin hitting his ample chest, as he continued to silently pray to his God for help.

... ...

The evening sun was drifting slowly to the underworld, creating a splash of iridescent hues across a cloudless sky. The flowers now in bloom, matched nature's colours and became vibrant, alive, as they swayed in the gentle breeze.

Vrittakos, sitting on one of several stone benches placed around the completed *peristylium,* revelled in not a single bloom. Usually so adroit in not only naming the species, but holding and caressing them, talking to them, he was above all, a man of nature. Not this evening. His whole attention lay in the scroll before him. It had arrived, altogether ceremoniously, by a messenger of the Governor of Britannia Superior, Titus Desticius Juba. The scroll was long. It named in elegant style, the list of luminaries and elites that would descend upon the villam with Titus Desticius in a few months' time.

Vrittakos' hand shook as he read the list for the tenth time. He mentally toted up the legates, at least six, the governors of Britannia Inferior, Nonius Phillipus and from Gaul, Octavius Sabinus, a man of great reputation. Aurelius Arpagius, who was aspiring to power, and therefore probably ingratiating, was coming with someone Vrittakos had not heard of, a man named Pacatianus. He must be of consular status, Vrittakos reasoned. He was listed amongst the high and mighty.

He continued to scan the scroll, and stopped, missing a heart-beat, eye popping, as he re-read the name to make sure wishful thinking had not taken hold of him.

"Censorinus!" he bellowed to anyone in earshot, "Oh Abrasax, you heard me! "We will gift an honouring ceremony to you to sur-pass all others."

"As soon as the Mithras celebrants have departed," he added as an afterthought.

He looked over to a slave picking the remaining dead heads and tidying the few weeds that were defying the quick hands and eyes of the gardening workers.

"Aeliana, fetch my wife. Be quick girl!" He suddenly screwed his tired eyes to face the sun. With a huge outtake of breath, he felt the strain of these last weeksop finally leave him.

"Censorinus," he whispered, "how many nights did we debate and argue till the torches dwindled to puffs of arid smoke? How many theories were tossed about and brought back with new light shining upon them? Ahh, dear friend, we solved the mysteries of the cosmos and found they had confounded us and wrapped us up in exquisite circles of formulae still to be solved" Then Vrit-takos saw the name below his mentor and friend. Quintus Caerellius.

"By Apollo, but news of our villam is stretching all the way to Rome!"

Venitouta was stretching over the last coverings to complete the last of the guest beds. She enjoyed this servant's work. Her ever-busy mind could wander happily within the menial work, and her slaves loved her for it. She hardly ever snapped orders at them, and she hoped these coming days of intense activity, would not see her anxious and complaining.

Venitouta heard Aeliana before her head popped around the door. Her hardened leather sandals were never tightened enough and flapped against the completed tesserae floors offering a beat to everyone in the Villam.

"Aeliana, you are an embarrassment!" she said, twisting her head round from the final smoothing of the fine linen bed covering, " Go immediately to Valerius and instruct him, with my permission, to give you soft-soled sandals and fit you with a longer tunica, and also I think it is time for a stola, of a colour to match those eyes of yours," she smiled as she watched the girl's eyes widen and her beautiful curled hair bobbed as she nodded in excitement.

"Oh, mistress," Aeliana replied, "Master wants you. He is in the *peristylium*. He seemed agitated."

Whenever was he not! she thought, these days he is like Atlas holding the universe on his shoulders alone! She straightened and made her way into the sunshine, the day fecund with fragrance and bees, colours and petals from so many flowers. She loved her creation, for this *peristylium* was hers. The lilies were her great love, next to the roses. Acanthus rose above the beds of pansy, bobbing their heads in the breeze, just sprung up from a sweltering midday.

She glanced to the herb garden, mentally noting the additions needed to the culinary section, if they were to impress the elites and the equites.

"*Maritus, quid anxietas tu*?" She bent her head to kiss him lightly on his crown, as he sat bent over this official scroll.

Vrittakos looked up and smiled at his wife

"Hmm, I am hardly worried at this moment, Touta. My heart is exploding with joy, my dear"

"Your heart is in danger of stopping beating altogether, my love!" Venitouta retorted, tapping his chest. "what is so wonderful?"

"Simply this...Do you remember back in those sun-kissed days in our homeland, two hunched figures, forever debating, always arguing the whole universe into our tiny minds?"

She thought for a moment, then gasped. "You are surely not talking of the master mathematician, philosopher and altogether pain in the head!" she feigned amazement, "Censorinus, if I'm not mistaken."

She sat next her husband, for whom love had never dwindled. "I sent a messenger over to him in Southern Gaul, where he lives now. Rome has become unbearable for him and his family. He will tell you. I believe you need, no deserve, a boost, a happy encounter amidst this nonsense about to descend on us".

"Rite and ceremony, honouring the gods is never nonsense, Venitouta!" he admonished.

"No, I mean the battling ego that always seem to accompany them" she replied, "I know our villam serves a very special purpose. All the villams on Vecta honour our Gods and Goddesses, but the men and even some of the women grate on my nerves."

"Ditto," Vrittakos echoed. "But we must accommodate them. For now," he said cryptically.

"And look who is coming with him…. Quintus Caerellius!"

Venitouta nodded, scanning the rest of the scroll. Her quick mind taking in the high-level of elites and equites from both Britannia superior and inferior. Consuls and aspiring generals, even a potential Caesar.

"They are not just coming to take part in the Mithras initiation levels, that is the smokescreen. This is a high-level political gathering. Politics and plotting!"

"Agreed," Vrittakos said, pointing to two names in particular, "Valerian and his son Gallienus. And where there is Gallienus, his "shadow" Aureolus will surely follow"

"Valerian holds extreme views, *Maritus*," Venitouta ventured, holding her hand to her mouth, "You can be sure the darkest energy of the Decian persecution will be surrounding him. I have heard from Censorinus that high level Christians have been forced, under pain of execution, to perform blood sacrifice, in public, written and recorded.

"We will, all of us, in these coming days be inspected, judged and recorded. It will turn our ceremony into farce, a performance!

"We are of the Illumination. We are of Abraxas! How will we honour our Gods and Goddesses now?"

"As we have always done, my love," answered Vrittakos carefully, "This villam is the final initiation of the Mithraic stages. Sacrifices are part of our rite. We have created this temple, it is open and accepting of all religions, even the new Christianity if it comes without judgment on its lips. I will not force anyone under my roof to deny their faith. And I will speak out."

"I will not have you isolated, *Maritus*," Venitouta declared, clapping her hands in a decision, "My messenger must fly like the wind to reach those great minds who can assist us. Balance is everything."

And with that, Venitouta rushed off to write a new scroll to be given to four wise men in Gaul and Achaikos in Antioch, who, together with Censorinus, might bring a level of spiritual integrity to a potential political blood bath.

"Not in my home!" Venitouta whispered, as she rushed out of their tablinum to find her most trusted messenger, Agrippa.

... ...

Chapter 3

Non tam pura voluptas sit anxietas perpetuo.

There is no such thing as pure pleasure: some anxiety always goes with it.

(Publius Ovidius Naso (43 BC- 17 AD))

Vrittakos swept from his *tablinum*, a flurry of robes and flapping sandals, waving the scroll in the vacant air, until it unravelled very nearly to his feet.

"Hades be damned," he roared to the bust of Juno sheltering in the alcove of the exedra, where slaves and freedmen were bustling, carrying plants to be placed on pedestals beside the indoor pool. Men swerved. Vrittakos surged through them.

"Aelius, attend me," he shouted at the prone figure reaching out to place more tesserae in place around the pool.

Aelius sensed his fury and jumped up with his back muscles rippling along the barely healed welts. He winced.

"I am being commanded," Vrittakos spluttered, continuing to flap the offensive papyrus in front of Aelius, who looked amazed. He had never seen Vrittakos lose his sense of spiritual serenity. He turned to command the nearest slave to fetch wine.

"I am, it seems, the overseer for the entire island! *Venenatus spuo* has slunk back from whence he came, the gutters of Cantium, spreading all manner of lies in his wake, I do not doubt! I am commanded to inspect all the villams of Mithras, the Mithraisms and the guest quarters, hypocausts, baths and surrounding gardens. Six villams, Aelius! And all within one, just two months."

"I thought these elites were coming here in several months' time," Aelius pondered, rubbing his back and looking over to the sea to momentarily find some peace.

"Ah, there we might have a slight silver lining to these dark clouds," Vrittakos gave a thin-lipped smile, "I have to compile a full report on the state of our villams, then sail over the small water to Clausentum, then onto Noviomagus Reginorum to meet with all the equites and elites. They say the Villam Regis there is now so outstanding, it surpasses the Caesar's palace on the Palatine Hill. This is where the politicking and back-stabbing will take place. Then they will wish to visit our sacred island to scourge their battered souls with flagellation and sacrifice. All part of the road back to Rome!"

After several moments' silence, where they each sought to find some balance, Vrittakos continued, shedding some of his tension, "Aelius, I am inviting you to this palace. Believe me, the last time I visited, it drew breath from my body. Now I am told it is near completion. It is several times the size of Berandinzium itself!"

"I am your royal hostage, Vrittakos. Where you go, I am bound to follow," replied Aelius drily, giving a brief sideways grin at his friend and *patronus*.

"Ah and on that subject," Vrittakos replied, bouncing back on his heels, back to the jovial giant, "I have today drawn up your *Libertus* papers, Eyvindr. We will perform *manumissio* for you and others, after the initiations and the ceremonies."

"Does that mean I can go over to Cantium and kill that bastard!" Aelius shot back with feeling.

"You may do what you wish, young friend, but I would advise against it. It will diminish you, trust me!"

"Joking, Vrittakos, you have temporarily lost your humour" Aelius wrapped his arm about the big Greek, who smiled into his chest, nodding as they walked back to the Atrium.

The consignment of box shrubs had just arrived from the boat, docked in the estuary. Bobbing happily in the cart like so many freed green elves, they rolled into the *peristylium*. Venitouta arrived, clapping her hands in sheer anticipation of making the final touches to her creation. She strode over to Vrittakos holding out her drawings for his approval.

She swept her hair back that had caught in the growing breeze, looking over to the wonderful expanse of land encircling the villam. All around her, was burgeoning with life. She knew the honouring and thanksgiving rite to Dona Dea and Hōræ ãrum was close. She would bring her ladies together. She felt sad not inviting Dagrun, who had taken part previously, before Eileifer had travelled to *Neorxenawang*. Dagrun was neither able nor permitted to attend celebratory rite. Venitouta missed her company and sighed deeply.

"*Problemata* Touta?" Vrittakos queried, as he caught the reflective look on his wife's face.

"I am missing Dagrun, *Maritus*," she confided, linking arms, and looking up gave a thin smile, "We are close to the *Maius* rite of *Ver*. She always comes, as I attend her *Drímeolce Þægweorþwa* in return".

She shrugged to push the sadness away, "Here, would you accept my designs for the laying of the box trees?" she said passing the drawings over.

They were beautiful, and brought a smile to Vrittakos, who sorely needed some lightness in his day.

"These are accomplished, my dear! The sketch of the *Nymphaeum* is exquisite. On this subject of overseeing work, I have every faith in you to keep all in order while I am away."

"Excuse me, *Maritus*?" She shot him a look of pure alarm.

"I have asked Aelius to join me in the inspection of the villams," he said simply, "He has a great need to be free of this place for a while. He needs to see his Wihtland Isle again. And the weather is clement. It is perfect...."

"The mosaics!" Aelius burst in, "I cannot just leave them, Vrittakos".

"Ah, yes, the gods have heard me, Aelius, all has been taken care of. I have been in communication with a master tesserae designer. He is fleeing the plague that has be-devilled much of the Eastern Empire. Gallus is struggling. Politically all is insecure. The very fabric of Rome is ripping apart. With us on edge of Empire, in the hinterland, we are watchers, as it were. And Britannia is ripe for the picking when the rest of Rome is fighting amongst itself.

And so, my dear friend and theologian, Achaikos Metaxas will be arriving any day. He will be our new overseer. He fled Antioch, not just from plague but the building hostilities in the region that made his work near impossible. He has no love of Rome either. He is of the illumination. His is a rare and beautiful talent in the honouring of the cosmos and Abraxas. Along with Censorinus and Quintus, beloved thanks to my wife! we will plant the seed of Alexandria and water it daily here at Berandinzium Villam!"

... ...

BOOK TWO

Chapter 4
Antioch

Achaikos gripped his jaw tight, until his bones ached to be freed. Holding a linen rag to his nose, allowing shallow breaths, he raced down the colonnade through the rubble and smoke which stung his eyes in great billows of caustic poison, his eyes searching for the citadel. His toga was unravelling, and he made the final effort to keep hold of it by flinging the spun silk over his left shoulder.

"I should jettison this luxury," he thought, "but it holds most of my Pater's life in these threads. Every mile of the Silk Road is woven through them."

The gods were again furious. This latest assault on Antioch, the stomach-wrenching tremble, as the city shook for the third time, had made him retch. This felt close to the end, a hell which he did not, and would not, subscribe to.

Achaikos has spent the last months in silent retreat, urging his soul through deep thought and philosophy to a place above good and evil. To illumination. He had written the promised treatise. He had experienced the shedding of so many parts of his spirit, that had been tangled in the material quagmire. He believed he had reached transcendental unity. And the lack of feeling, of detachment, brought a peace he had never experienced. He wanted to stay in that mindless place, but it became sterile in a way he had not anticipated. Achaikos then discovered a fundamental Law. That Oneness must alienate itself in Nature, to reach Absolute Knowledge and then return to itself on a higher understanding, indeed the ultimate level: The Omega point. It alienates itself to undergo the process of completion.

That was just two weeks ago, and now Nature was testing him to the very point of destruction, of death!

"This fall from grace is extreme!" he thought, as he stumbled over fallen masonry, leaping now, over a demolished partition wall which caught his precious silk toga, claiming it, devouring it as a gift, to the earthquake. Achaikos let it all unravel. A shining ivory snake of luxury, of wounded Id, lay motionless behind him. With just his Tunica and his courage, Achaikos loped on, forever keeping the Citadel in his clouded vision. It hung like a sky lantern, internally brilliant against the night sky. It was his reclaimed soul hanging there, amidst this destruction and he simply had to get there. Abrasax awaited him there.

Another tremor shook the city. He braced himself as the ground beneath him shook. He dived for cover, instantly realising there was no cover. A human and stupid idea to guarantee survival. Missiles came from above. It was a conditioned response. The screaming of dying people that he had tried to block, assaulted his ears now.

Darkness, overwhelming blackness commanded his attention, as did the hand that reached out and grabbed his foot.

"Help me! *Mūfam sa attanaddaru a-ia-a-mu-ur*" came the strangled plea from a trapped victim laying under the rubble that Achaikos was stumbling over. He bent down without hesitation and began heaving the boulders away, until he saw her face, bloody and bruised. She heaved a great intake of air and began shuddering in shock. He increased his efforts until most of her body was free. She was a native, not Greek nor Roman but Syrian. She spoke in Akkadian.

He pulled her out from her grave and sat cradling her in his arms until the shaking ceased. No words were spoken. He could see plainly; she was a slave. The crinkled welts on her back showed she was not a passive slave either, and that her master was a cruel and shameful man.

"Your name, please," he said softly.

"Alba," she replied, heaving more lungsful of air.

"That is a Roman name, a slave name," he replied, "you are Persian are you not?"

"Yes. I am," she looked up at him for the first time, and smiled, "Thank you for saving me. My true name is Katayoun, Kiana, it means elements of the earth"

Achaikos suddenly felt laughter bubble up from deep within, a reaction that caused his shoulders to shake, as he buried his head in his chest. It was catching, as Kiana, at first puzzled, realised the pun.

As the destruction of the fabled city of Antioch subsided, two survivors, fated to meet, laughed in relief until their rib bones ached.

… … … … … … … … …

Achaikos and Kiana held each other up as they stumbled forward, Achaikos thinking how neatly she nestled in the hollow of his chest, and this felt surprisingly nice. Her hair was stiff with mortar dust and chips of shattered brick, but he could see plainly, as he looked down on her diminutive frame, that her hair was raven black with hints of blue.

That final quake had seen part of the Citadel disappear.

"It has been foolish to even contemplate making for the shrine. This is the final stroke of an angered god: whose *diamones* abound." Achaikos stated in a low tone, barely heard by Kiana.

"*Anaku kí gallã kuní rí bãnè lal-mur.* I am too young to know of earthquakes," Kiana said, looking over what remained of a city that had been her prison. She began to feel truly liberated, yet fear, her constant companion, nullified the feeling before it could take root. She fought it. This was her moment. She was alive and most certainly her tormenter was not.

"I have experienced them, well one, when I was around your age," Achaikos remembered it well. His mater had been caught in the destruction. His pater had never truly recovered from the loss and spent many more years travelling the silk road, attempting to run from his grief whilst creating a huge fortune. That wealth was bitter for Achaikos growing up with little love around him. And it was the driving force that propelled him to the spiritual world he now inhabited.

"We need to leave the city," he stated plainly. Grounded now in common sense, he felt drawn to the earth. "In more ways than one," he thought looking over to Kiana. "It is a long walk, through this rubble, but we need to reach the temple of Apollo. The forest is more secure and will give us safe shelter."

Survivors, like themselves, chose to remain and help the injured. Meritocracy, and the belief, so strong in this sacred city of Antioch, that Abrasax was within them all, made search and rescue obligatory, until finally exhaustion set in, and everyone joined in a walking group of wounded towards the temple of Apollo.

They passed scenes that would imbed within their memory, only to re-surface in the small hours of night to torment them. Achaikos began to realise his treatise was only part-completed. His arrogance had been called. He knew it. He was living the Fall and he was being drawn to the darker gods to live a primary experience of evil.

Nature is neutral and invites both divine and base energies to draw on its power. The small child before him sitting in the rubble, bloody, and shaking the limp and dead hand of his mother, keening relentlessly for her to wake up, was frozen for him to remember, always. Kiana made to leap over and pick him up. Achaikos restrained her, "Look, his older sibling is alive. Leave him. Just remember that evil has visited here, and she is goodness. She has rescued him from them," he pointed to scavengers pulling and snatching from the dead bodies, all they could find in gold and silver.

"*Venio atque coniungo noster corona!*" Achaikos shouted over to the children, "Come and join us, we are heading for the temple of Apollo and safety"

So, the small group became larger as the trek continued. Achaikos delivered a soul-deep prayer to Abrasax, within and without, promising a libation for their lives, as soon as he found an appropriate altar.

It was approaching dawn, the faint silvered light of the sun, welcoming a new day, saw the bedraggled survivors reach their safety, and soft green turf to lie on, warm fires welcoming them with the promise of food and slumber. So many people had made this exodus to Apollo and Daphne, their Far-reaching God and loving Goddess. They were like children seeking out their parents for succour. And remarkably the temple had been spared. It sat in protected woodland. Ancient trees, all exclusively chosen, creating an irrigated forest, surrounded the immense temple. A complete circumference of deep interlocking roots holding the fragile earth in a tight grip that would completely disallow it to fall.

No-one had been spared the horrors of the night. So many faces, lit by flickering shadows of the firelight, stared into the flames to find some redemption, some ease to the images that assaulted their minds. There was little talk. The immense and darkened columns of Apollo's temple, stretching back into the remains of the night, bore down on them, accusing, threatening. Angry gods.

"*Nese sū-un-ga dan-na sahuiqta,*" Kiana whispered to Achaikos, "*muskènu-ta-a-a-ra-tim sa Samas i-ta-am-ru.* This city will experience destruction. But the people will experience a reconciliation with the Gods"

Achaikos nodded silently, for he knew a cleansing had occurred.

"*Babaru babbanítu,*" She smiled and nodded over to the trees, "The forest is a beautiful woman. We must go there."

Chapter 5

Babaru babbanitu
The forest is a beautiful woman

They walked together into the deep green foliage, leaving behind the boy and his sister, safe within the comforting circle of neighbours and friends who had rediscovered each other, and vowed never to leave.

Achaikos allowed Kiana to lead, for it was the feminine power that oversaw the forest. And leading by pure instinct was the prerogative of woman. Besides, Achaikos had begun to feel diminished. Purely physical, he told himself, looking down at a torn and muddy tunica. Yet the bolt of pain that thrust itself into his solar plexus spoke of something much deeper. He had lost everything, as the image of his toga snaking back to his residence flashed into his mind.

"Ego facio non habeo franktus myrrhtus pro meus libation ut Abrasax, I do not have Frankincense or Myrrh for my libation to Abrasax" Achaikos said, holding his arms heavenwards in supplication.

"Would Abrasax punish you further, after losing all you possess, would the all-seeing One even expect you to magic incense? I think not!" Kiana stated, "Come with me."

She began striding into the forest as if it were her real home. "How does this slave girl know so much?" Achaikos thought, as he followed her, dipping under low-lying branches and breathing in the smell of crushed leaves, damp earth and tree resin! Yes! tree resin. Kiana had halted before the trunk of a truly enormous tree that thrust heavenwards to reach the light, twisting and turning in its way up. The grooved bark issued bubbles of sticky resin that gifted an exquisite perfume.

"Your libation, I believe," Kiana smiled, pulling a globule of resin and holding it to Achaikos' nose.

"*Magnificus!*" Achaikos exclaimed, "The name of this tree?"

"I know nothing of names," she gave a sideways smile, and tossed her head, emitting a small shower of dust to grace the forest floor. "What is the use of that! I know the spirit of this tree, what she enjoys, what she despises. And how she gifts. And she gifts *this*," Kiana held up a palmful of resin, smelling the aroma, drinking it in. "This magnificent gift will bring peace of mind. And from that, will come the libation you seek to give. Use it with the greatest care, however, for all and any intentions are magnified. It is extremely potent."

Kiana looked up to him, studying his reaction and decided it was all in the hands of Goddess now anyway. She knelt quickly to pick up an oval-shaped stone nestling in the fine strands of russet coloured tufty grass, laying around this tree like a swaying skirt. It had a significant indent, like a "worry" stone. The sparkle of quartz inclusions created a milky way in miniature.

"I believe we have been gifted your altar," she held out the stone to Achaikos, whose pinched face, grooved with pain and exhaustion, broke into a full radiant smile, the light reaching his tired eyes, and it lit up his whole face, tension being released instantly.

"*Formosus,*" he muttered, caressing the stone and reaching in to feel its spirit. "Will this tree gift her blood to us? It would be the very best libation to Abrasax we could offer."

"*Finis!*" Kiana halted and turned to face Achaikos, eyes wide, searching his soul. He stopped to stare back, looking down with his head slanted, questioning.

"Let me be clear," she stated, "I worship differently from you. There is no 'We.' Your Abrasax is the All-seeing One. He is above all and looks down with benevolent eyes from his 365 domains. He is in acceptance. I, on the other hand, worship the Goddess in all her aspects. Names for her differ, but she is our Earth Mother, and our Water dragon, giver of life. And she can take it from us."

"We are walking towards her now. A very sacred shrine has been created to her, in the underground. Dark and primal. She is the dark goddess here. Her name is Hecate."

So very suddenly, Achaikos felt a shrinking in his heart. Unexpected indeed. And he felt the faint trembling of fear enter him again.

"Be very careful what you wish for, priest," Kiana continued in a level voice, looking straight ahead, and walking with purpose.

"Who is this diminutive woman?" He questioned silently, as he felt attracted to her greatly and repelled in equal measure.

"Hecate will see your essence of intent," she continued, "She will see your dark aspect and it will open you up like a stranded fish. There will be no escape."

Achaikos emitted a long-protracted sigh of resignation. "I am about to experience the Fall" he stated flatly, starring down at the crown of her dark raven hair, as it bobbed rhythmically forward. He caught up with her stride and let go of all expectations.

"Yes, priest. You are."

... ...

Chapter 6

In animo elato, alioque renascitur
The soul emptied, is reborn.

Within this deep, almost virgin forest, deep sultry leaf-greens overlapped each other creating half-formed shadowy creatures. Amongst them there lay an intensely black opening. It beckoned and repelled, leaving Achaikos suddenly trembling like the small boy of his childhood, feeling cruelty and witnessing worse, leaving scars that were about to be scraped open to ooze pain again. His priestly vestments, like his silk toga, were about to be ripped from him. Any masculine bravado he wore in his youth was about to be tested.

They silently entered the cave, which gently sloped down, dry earth leaving their faint footprints. The walls were lit by tapers, set far apart leaving extended shadows to dance exotically as they passed. Kiana held her hands forward, holding the glittering stone before her. She had placed the magical resin in the indent and carried them ceremoniously.

"You will make your first libation to my Goddess," she announced, without turning to face him. It was a command. *She* was in command.

"*Ita est*," he said in Latin, forging the power within to hold him. Words of any kind suddenly became superfluous.

They walked in total silence, so much so, his ears caught faint sounds floating towards him from deep within the cave. Human sounds, animal sounds in the full spectrum of experience from joy to anguish, faintly intermingling with each other. Fatal attraction and revulsion dancing on the level playing field of life.

He followed Kiana, who veered to the left, a divergence in the path and as they walked on, the sounds left them, and they were in total silence. The tapers which had dimly lit their way forward ended abruptly.

"You have now entered the womb of your Mother," she announced, "Please remove your sandals and your tunica."

As she said these words, she began to untie her own shoulder bindings, slowly, with delicate care, until her tunica with her stola gently fluttered to the dry dirt floor. Achaikos knew she was naked. The thought made him stir. He fought it. And concentrated on obeying her command. In the total darkness now encompassing him, he heard rather than saw, the stone altar being placed before him.

"Kneel," came the command. He heard a scraping of metal. Suddenly the flare of light shook his senses, the flame being put to the resinous incense. He saw her naked body lean forward towards him, her breasts, small but so well formed almost brushing his arm. The front of her was so perfect, yet knowing her back was a terrible mess, his heart opened, and his loins suddenly burned for her. "So here it is," he thought, "the first test."

His hands now resting over his throbbing *pènis*, he tackled those thoughts and pushed them away. He relaxed. She saw him and grinned quietly saying, "Offer up your prayers, priest, then breath our Goddess into yourself and see what magic she will gift you...or otherwise," she finished grimly.

He prayed for his mother. Hoping her soul was at peace. Instantly images flooded his mind. The incense was already at work, he thought distractedly, trying to erase the horror before him. Those images only became more intense.

"Resistance is futile," came the disembodied voice of Kiana, sounding like the Goddess herself. With a rush of recognition, Achaikos realised she was exactly that. She was seeing inside his mind, guiding him.

He saw his mother now, as the small boy, with his father, before the quake that had swallowed up his mother like a hungry monster. This was a buried memory, and he was being forced to confront the horror of it. He was hiding behind the tall chair in the *culina,* his Pater's hairy bunched hand was raised to deliver the third bone crushing blow to his mother's bleeding and bruised face. She put her arm to deflect that blow which hurtled her body over to land near him. Her shoulder hit the chair and he shook with fear, eyes bulging, screaming silently for the battering to stop. She held his gaze for a second, her expression spoke to him of the most profound love and terrible shame all intermingled. "Run!" was her only strangled word, as she was hauled by her foot across the floor.

Achaikos came to, with bile lurching upwards in his throat. He gagged and vomited on the dirt floor before him, just missing the stone altar. Hatred now boiled in him for his Pater whom he had never loved, now knowing why, and prayed he was in the darkest hell imaginable. He knew he needed to release that memory, now and forever, but the equanimity needed had escaped him. He was suffocating in intense anger. Fury overcame him and he leaned over to breath in the incense and fill his lungs, hoping to escape.

Images now swirled before him, intense and real, like the waking dream, all vying for his attention to live *in* them. He was now, thankfully, separate from himself, looking on, in an amber and russet coloured world. It was dusk, but the business of the day had not receded. If anything, it was more bustling with life. He was looking on at the Silk Road, at a pit-stop of ramshackle *popinas*, the leaning slate roofs barely covering the interior where cheap wine flowed and slopped on the floor as the bare bottoms of captured women, bent over tables, clutching onto anything, tunicae bunched up into matted hair, were being pumped by drunken men, slapping their vulnerable shaking bottoms and gyrating their great weight into the women, who cried and writhed in pain. Grunts and howls rent the air.

Then, Achaikos came upon himself and his Pater, who was drunk and slurping back wine as it missed his mouth and dribbled down a dirty grizzled cheek, then onto his dirty and sweat-ridden tunica. The money pouch dangling from his leather belt swung as he lurched towards an available slave woman, who had taken his eye. But she was not for him. This one was for Achaikos. As a young man in that amber light, he looked dishevelled, with deep shadows cast about his eyes. Those eyes seemed dulled as if life had been sucked from him and he was but a shadow. Within him, stirred a welter of anger that was about to be fed.

The Pater dug a chubby, grimy hand into his pouch to pull out a few *sestertii,* banging them onto the slimy table now littered with abandoned mugs. He grabbed his young son roughly by the shoulder, pulling him forward, into the slave woman's face.

"Pound this slave with your *pènis* till she screams," he growled, "Show me you are a man at least, that I can take you with me to get silk! Earn your keep!"

The young man, whose head was bowed, in deep shadow, slowly, with calculated intent, raised intense malevolent eyes to star deeply into the slave women's eyes, and growled low. She, who was little more than a child, grown old with years of abuse behind her, keened, and tried to turn her face away. Eyes white with terror. He pulled her around and slammed her little body over, grabbing her tunica and her hair, pulling it backwards in a strong lock as he thrust himself into her, great stabbing thrusts that hurled her forwards, bashing her body against a table. He grinned at the pain he knew he was causing, but his anger had diminished. He was in control. He was at last on a level with his Pater. Now he would have his respect.

"Noooo!" came the strangled yell from Achaikos, thrusting his balled hands into the earth, as his face hit the dirt, his scream sending the dust flying. The horrific scene faded from his mind and he connected again with the present moment. His lungs contracted and expanded sending protracted cries through the darkened cave. As he reached to breathe in more incense, the nightmare became even more horrific. Before him in the intense blackness there arose a figure, floating yet growing into malevolent form. The shifting weight of this figure was coming for him. He sensed the essence of this evil. It was potent. Swaying fronds of dark energy formed into long arms, with grasping elongated fingers. They were reaching for him, to capture and own him.

"*Hecate!*" he screamed, as a face formed, as black wrinkled jaws began moving, a cavernous mouth opening, ready to devour him. This was the very blackest aspect of the dark goddess at her most furious.

Μεετ τηε δαρκ ασπεχτ οφ ψουρσελφ, ΦΟΟΛ!. ψΟΥ ΩΙΛΛ ΧΟ ΜΕ ΤΟ με! She screamed. "Meet the dark aspect of yourself, you fool. You will come to ME!"

Achaikos crumpled to the ground, his whole body wracked with sobs as his soul broke and splintered into so many pieces. With each convulsion, his mind relived those embittered days of his youth, that he had simply locked away and forgotten. That blank part of his life, the one that somehow, in its total absence from his consciousness, had forged a link to spiritual life and his love for Abrasax, was now hideously claiming him. He was made worthless. The empty shell of Achaikos shook with tormented sobs, until his lungs ached, and his throat became bloodied. Spittle streaked with his blood dribbled onto the stone. The incense hissed, releasing steam, as profane met the divine and sacred alchemy was born. As the steam grew and wafted around Achaikos, he felt the atmosphere alter, he knew his burden was lifting from him. The energy became neutral, neither good nor evil inhabited this cave. Abrasax was here.

He forced open one eye, caked with mucus and dried tears, to see before him, not the spectre of the dark goddess, but simply Kiana, kneeling before him, gently holding his outstretched hand, that was pleading for mercy, for forgiveness.

"Mercy for your tormented soul is a given, Achaikos," she said gently, rubbing his soiled hand, looking down at the remains of the incense, now a damp globule resting in the gentle cup of the stone.

"But finding forgiveness for yourself, truly, is the hardest task ahead for you. Your soul has been fractured and sent reeling into the hinterlands for many moons, and you, in your intense searching in the spiritual world for what has been lost, yet not even knowing of its loss, has been a monumentally fruitless labour."

Achaikos gasped in this sudden realisation. His gaze had never left the stone, as if Abrasax might suddenly emanate from the crystal. But now with both eyes fixed on Kiana, he knew the awful truth.

She smiled briefly, with compassion, "All your years of meditation on the divine, the scrolls written to prove your wisdom are nothing but a hardened walnut shell hiding a withered and sour nut!"

Now he arched up, straightening his aching back. He was truly feeling like that empty useless shell.

"What must I do?" he implored this young slave woman, who was possibly half his age, yet immeasurable old. She had an indefinable wisdom about her, that he felt bereft of now, scrapped down to the bone.

Now it was her time to react. She retrieved her hand and stood up, arching her spine in indignation. She rounded on him, "Are you completely stupid, old man!" she exclaimed, bunching her hands on her hips, "You have just experienced the Fall, have been granted the highest mercy, and you ask me! I cannot answer for you in any way. It is not my place to weaken you. I am here to accompany you...." she had begun pacing the dirt cave, scuffing the floor, creating small eruptions of dust that caught in the light. She stopped suddenly and turned to stare at him, "If you want me to come that is?"

"Yes," Achaikos replied simply, "I do. But where?"

"There you go again!" she retorted, "Look, let us find our way back to the forest, yes? *Babaru Babbanítu*. You need a new beginning, what better place to begin. *Eddesu* constantly renewing."

They dressed quickly, with what few clothes they had.

They both bade their farewells and offered gratitude to the Goddess and Abrasax, within the womb-cave, each in their own way, quietly and with deep solemnity. For it had been an intense and extreme Fall, which, for Achaikos, still reeling, would doubtless engender a long and unknown journey hauling his way out of this bottomless pit. Yet he felt lighter than for many a year. And for reasons he could not fathom, let alone own.

He reached out, quite spontaneously, to catch the hand of Kiana, as she strode from the cave. She did not falter, and held his, warmly, giving a half smile through her raven black hair, which spilt curling locks over her face. As they moved towards the entrance, he heard again those faint sounds of beguiling human- ity, shouts and laughter, moans of ecstasy amidst cries of fear. All intermingled with each other.

They prompted him to ask her.

"I can hear those sounds again. What is that place from which they come?"

"Oh, not necessary" she replied enigmatically, pausing for a moment, then turned to him, "It is a place you may have run to, had you so desired, your soul demanding this of you. It would have meant a much longer stay within the temple of Hecate. As it is, you have reached the limit of the Fall, and your own dark side, without the need to experience more".

"By the gods, I thank the Goddess for that!" Achaikos ex- claimed, realising at least some part of the divine design to it all. He was, he realised, at the extreme end of fatigue and sought a place to lie down and sink into unconsciousness.

The tunnel narrowed and his tall frame bent as his head scrapped the low ceiling. He was forced to look askance, and sud- denly noticed an extensive line of symbols, petroglyphs, incised onto the wall. The light from the tapers gave an eerie shadowed detail to a story, by the ancestors that might offer clues to his sal- vation. He slowed his pace to peer at them, seeing monstrous faces with large gaping mouths, and arms that looked not too dis- similar to Hecate at her most furious. Yet he swiftly took in yet another series, showing the constellations, Venus, in relation to the moon. The phialides hovered over a crescent moon and a swan, with its long neck and wings spreading along a horizon of sea and land. The edge of the physical world, symbolising the gateway to the spirit world.

He reached out to stop Kiana, only to see her shadowed form disappear around the bend in the tunnel. He sighed and commit- ted those glyphs to memory and hurried after her. He had been unaware of the stale, musty and fetid air that had fed his sore lungs until now, as the first breath of fresh forest air wafted towards him. They were near the entrance. He took a huge intake of that powerful sultry air, full of forest aromas and perfumes. Achaikos experienced it as one reborn: all new. Kiana stood close by his side, and for her part, released a long outtake of breath, releasing from her, the whole experience. She had played her part with consummate skill. Now it was time for a new chapter to begin.

She led him deeper into the forest. She knew her way, and he allowed her to find the rightful place. He knew he wanted her. He knew there was love growing between them and this was to be the birthing of a relationship he would treasure as a healing and a wonderful gift. It would come to mark the beginning of his journey to reclaim the fragments of his spirit sent asunder.

She had chosen the darkest place, with even older trees towering above them, but within this fecund glade held intoxicating perfumes, that intensified as they threw each other's garments to the bushes. And against the widest trunk, they nestled, exploring hidden places in a sensuous slow and loving way, gently releasing the pain and tension both their lives had been scarred with. He kissed each welt on her back, drawing his tongue down to heal with love each scar, releasing memories held within. And she gently massaged him, until he entered her, and they pulsated to the rhythm of the warm Antioch night.

They lay wrapped in each other arms, soft moss caressing their legs, and slept deeply, without dreams, until at the earliest soft yellow light, shafting though the trees, they both heard distinctively and quite miraculously the sound of a cock crowing.

They both sat up, a look of amazement mirrored in each other's faces.

"'Tis Abrasax, my love," Kiana said softly, "Come to welcome you to your new life. A new day dawns. What shall we do with it?"

After a few moments thought, Achaikos made a decision that would change their lives for good.

"If my soul has been residing in the hinterland all these past years, then it is to the hinterland we must go to retrieve it." He stated, grabbing both her hands in his and smiling for the first time since the earthquake had rent their lives apart.

"Where is that," she asked, looking intently into those aging eyes.

"The very hinterland of the Roman empire," he replied, "Britannia, my love, Britannia."

... ...

Chapter 7

Non vereor ne nudati satiari hominum, sed in vultus pal-

let, et esuriit

It is not the well-fed long-haired men that I fear, but the

pale and hungry looking!

Julius Caesar

Achaikos found himself shifting his weight, repeatedly, as they made their way from the heavy and magical energy of this sacred forest. He suddenly became aware of his advancing years, of his mortality, now that he had experienced the Fall to utter humanness. His bones ached in a deep and painful way. And from this came an even more worrying realisation. He was older than Kiana. She had called him "old man" in her exasperation of his witless ways.

He glanced down at her. Her head was nestling in that same hollow beneath his shoulder, that seemed natural and comfortable as they walked in unison towards bright sunlight, whose shafts, angled and brilliant, lit up tunnels of colour, flower-heads leaning to the heat, and faint dust mites dancing in the glow.

For Kiana, her ear rested by his heart for it seemed both natural and necessary. She could read so much into the rhythm and her love and concern for this "old man" was deep and genuine. He would not know this, for his journey was by its nature fraught with discoveries both benign and malignant. He would be self-absorbed at best, treacherous at worst. When a man loses his moral compass, all things are possible. And she was determined to steer him through the worst of it.

The scene that greeted them was one of burgeoning, restless and hungry humanity. Panic lay just beneath the surface of fragile civility, fear bubbling to the surface.

It knocked this spiritually attuned couple back upon themselves, almost instantly.

Achaikos leaned to whisper in Kiana's ear, "Have a care, my love. Look to your left, slowly, if you please. Those Antiochian thugs are seeing you as meat, fair game, choosing as you do, to couple with this ancient old man"

"Hmm," murmured Kiana under her breath, "We will see, Achaikos. We will see."

There were three of them. She assessed their skill or otherwise, as she unlocked herself from Achaikos, hearing him gasp with horror at her recklessness.

She moved towards the leader, as she guessed rightly that his skill dominated the other two. He was lean and sinewy, bones protruding sharply from obvious malnourishment. He was now crouching, a dishevelled head moving rhythmically from side to side, animalistic, grinning at her with an intensity that spoke of what he would do to her, very soon.

Kiana replicated his every move, moving with more subtlety, springing on the balls of her feet.

Achaikos stood immobile, rooted to the ground, feeling frozen in time. Not only did he feel old, he felt impotent. He hugged his chest, that was beginning to hurt, his heart racing, as he waited for the inevitable.

It all happened so quickly, with the speed of light: he recalled afterwards. Kiana sprang forward, jumping up with such precision that her outstretched leg rammed into the boy's chest with such force, Achaikos was sure he heard bones crack. The youth crumpled into the dirt, groaning and crying with equal measure, arms hugging his chest, aping Achaikos, who immediately released his arms to hang dormant by his side.

She twisted in the air to land perfectly on both feet, swung round and down to land on top of the groaning boy, who was now in a foetal position, wishing for his mother. Kiana most definitely was not his mother. She was Hecate in her fury and proceeded to punch the boy senseless. When she was sure that unconsciousness had claimed him, she stood to challenge the other two. They gave one petrified look towards her, stared at each other and gave a mutual nod, before running away, appearing as ungainly loping shadows against the sharp, strong sun.

Kiana searched the dormant form and found both coins and some handy weaponry.

"We shall be needing both," she commented as she continued the search. A particularly nasty looking double-edged curved sword came to light, hidden beneath his ragged leggings. "Hmm, I say this rascal has found his way here from Africa, Namibia I might guess."

"Hide it about your person if you please, Achaikos," she looked up to see him simply staring at her, just shaking his head, grey curls bouncing, mirroring his disbelief.

Kiana, now sitting on her heels, stopped her search, satisfied the lout carried nothing more of value, and putting her hands on her hips, smiled at her partner, slowly and kindly.

"Before I was captured and made a slave to a very cruel master, I was a warrior amongst my people. I grew up fighting, Achaikos. I was taught by the best masters we had. I was taught to kill inside a minute, effectively, using the least effort. So, my inferior strength was best used.

"I went into many battles, honing my skill. Those young idiots held no concern for me, believe me, I have tackled men twice their size and come away from them, all sent to the ground."

Achaikos moved towards her, hearing his knee joints crack, and wincing, bent to put his arms around her. She in turn, swivelled, putting her tousled head into his ample chest. He kissed her crown and they remained for a while, each with their own thoughts.

Then a surprising thought rose in his exhausted mind, demanding an answer.

"Kiana," he pulled back so she must look up to him, "If you are so adept at killing, why did you not dispatch the evil master who ruined your beautiful back?"

Kiana seemed to hunch and bend inwards, as if an invisible punch has just been landed in her solar plexus. Silence.

She drew breath slowly and carefully as if measuring her words. Kiana was fighting a scream that dared to escape.

"Quite simply, my master held my daughter hostage. If anything should happen to him, his relatives, where my daughter is held prisoner, would kill her. Now he is dead. His home is nothing, just rubble and he was inside it. I escaped. You rescued me."

"Where was your daughter held captive?" Achaikos shot back, eyes immediately scanning the multitude of survivors still milling around the temple of Apollo and Daphne.

He heard a low groan and turned to see Kiana crumple to the ground in a foetal heap, her small body shuddering rhythmically with each strangled cry.

"Kiana," he muttered and reached down, sinking ungracefully and painfully to his knees, holding her silently as she rent her grief into the earth. He marvelled at her selfless courage in securing their survival in the human jungle that had once been soporific, elegant Antioch. He has no idea she was a mother. She had hidden it completely. Now he felt her vulnerability with each shudder.

"We will find her," he said into her ear. If she lives, he thought.

After many minutes, the sobbing ebbed away, leaving a shell of a woman who had shown heroism beyond anything he had ever witnessed. The sorrow of a mother lost to her child defeats everything there is. Defeats life itself.

Now it was his turn to shoulder the burden, find in himself a kind of hero's energy. He had no issue with that. His old and crusty heart had opened, like a fledgling bird, and he offered it to her. A sacrificial gift he was overjoyed to experience, as he had nearly forgotten that gift and indeed never expected it to visit him.

Kiana's lungs filled with air, and the earthy pungent perfume of wet earth and turf, fed her blood. She heaved herself up to sitting, cradling in his lap, looking outward, her eyes desperately seeking the face that would give her life meaning again.

"We start here," Achaikos said, "it is as good a place as any, unless you know where she might be in the city and it still stands," he added, wishing he had not.

Silence.

"She lives," Kiana whispered, "I would know it if it were otherwise."

"They took her to the household of Alcæus Pachis, a relative of my master, Cleisthenes Raptis. She heard a soft whistle come from Achaikos, and then he stopped.

"You know him?" Kiana said, quizzically looking askance at him.

"Yeees," he replied slowly, measuring his response, "Unfortunately I do. In the lucrative business of my Pater, along the Silk Road, I became enmeshed into it as a young man..."

"I know," interrupted Kiana, leaving any more explanations to be guessed upon. Achaikos already knew her spiritual gifts to be impressive

"He was a few years older than myself," he continued, looking into the distance, scanning for stray children, "And he was learning the tailors trade from his pater, as I was learning trading with mine. My pater struck deals with cloth; they made a wealthy pair. Together, the clothing trade blossomed in Antioch.

"I did not like him, by the way. Now I positively loath him. Glad he has gone from us." he concluded, setting his jaw in unexpressed anger. "Now, your daughter. Her name?"

"She has two," Kiana looked up to him, pain etched upon her face, adding years to her. Achaikos had suppressed the urge to think upon her age. Now it was surfacing despite his wishes to the contrary.

"Charmion is the name given to her by my master. And yes, she is his." Kiana kicked the dust before her into the air.

"And I came to love her completely. She does not look like him, thankfully. Everyone says she bears her mother's looks.

"Her true Persian name, and one that is most secret to us both, is Tahmineh, Tamina for short. A worshipper of Ahura Mazda. If she gives that name, she will receive honourable hospitality in my homeland," she added.

"May I ask why?" Achaikos was beginning to feel the sure ground beneath him was being shaken with each new revelation.

"Because she is of royal blood....as am I," she concluded simply, as if this statement would explain everything. It did not. Life just got more complex for Achaikos; whose spiritual seclusion had not served him at all adequately.

"And her age?" he added, "So I may know accurately who we seek amongst this throng of survivors."

"She has passed fourteen summers gone," Kiana gave a brief smile, as if one memory had surfaced that gave her lasting joy.

Achaikos looked to the ground, making a mental calculation of years against the look of Kiana, and drew a blank. It did not make sense, he looked askance her yet again in puzzlement.

"I am older than my looks, old man," she said, her mouth inching into a brief, dimpled smile, "I come from a Sogdian tribe whose women are gifted with youthful looks well into their middle years. Royal blood may have something to do with that. Then suddenly, we wrinkle and crumple everywhere in a matter of a year. I am in my 27th year," she stated, "Now may we start hunting for my child?"

She strode forward, releasing herself from his ample chest. He followed, as they both started shouting the girl's Sogdian name so Kiana's daughter would know immediately her real mother was near.

··· ··· ··· ··· ··· ··· ··· ··· ···

Chapter 8

Est melius creare, quam discere. Procreatio, inquam,

essentia vitae!

It is better to create than to learn. Creating is the es-

sence of Life!

Julius Caesar

The temples of both Apollo and Daphne had lost their revered sacredness and had become instead pure sanctuaries for the discarded and homeless Antiochians, now all levelled in stature. Both highborn and slave occupied the same space. But they clustered in groups, making their own separations from the mass of people, forever milling about in between the sky-born classic columns.

Achaikos noted sardonically, that the men clustered around the columns supporting the huge sculptured edifice of Apollo. So, he reasoned, the women would, by this naturally made division, be within the sanctuary of the highest Goddess Daphne.

"Kiana, I suggest we separate and pool our efforts," he turned to her, placing his hand gently on her shoulder. She was tensed like a coiled spring.

"I will go yonder, and enquire amongst those men there of your daughter's master, Umm his name again please?"

"Alcæus Pachis," she growled, "He is Plebeian who has wormed his way up to become acknowledged as a theologian, he tutors at the Agora when he is not acting as Prætor."

"An ambitious man then," Achaikos remarked, flexing the digits of his left hand, a sure sign his mind was churning.

"If he is still alive, they will know of him," she replied, "He bathes in glory, all think of him as a dignified and special Antiochian. My daughter will give you another story, if she ever comes to trust you that is."

Achaikos felt his stomach leap, emotions entered him, rare and unformed, hinting of the hidden barbaric world of which he knew far too much and had buried deep within.

"Where did they live exactly," he remarked, trying to focus on the practical.

"In an apartment by the Orontes, the Murus Seleucia," she answered, her gaze never still, hoping she would alight on the precious face of her daughter, "It is the older part of Antioch," she added, "I am going now. We meet back here when the sun has melted to the pillars of Daphne." She was already striding off, finishing her sentence, head turned backwards, looking at the patriarchal man who for one fleeting moment looked bereft. The love she felt for Achaikos had shrunken to a wrinkled walnut, for her mother's love now swamped all other feelings.

"And we have only just cemented this flimsy love for one night," she sighed briefly and returned to scanning the groups of women clustered in the temple of Daphne.

"Tamina!" she called, loud enough for several women to look directly at her, but only for them to stare blandly back at this stricken mother. *"Tamina, Tamina!"*

She began to run in between the pillars, shouting her daughter's name, her sandals flapping on the marbled floor. Further and further into deep shade of the temple interior, until she almost fell upon the altar, sacred and untouchable. She ground to a halt and sunk to the floor. Resting her cheek on the cool floor, she let her tears flow and soak into the rivulets of patterned grey and blue marble

It was breathlessly silent. Kiana looked up at the elegant, benign face of the goddess Daphne and prayed to her. Her mouth moved in hurried words, so much to express, to hope for and to apologise for. She was kin to the Goddess in her dark aspect. She had gained her strength to carry on in her hard life. She aligned with those sharp choices; the sometimes-belligerent courage of black and white with no greys to confuse.

But now, she needed a different focus. Besides, she was now free, no slave women, she, anymore. She thanked the Goddess for that miracle. That she was still breathing after the anger of the Gods had crumpled the city into shame. And in truth she knew, as did many others, that Antioch had become labile in nature. Superficial and frivolous. The city had been gifted with the most glorious good fortune, temperate climate, bountiful harvests of rare and delicious food. The Gods watched on, as their favoured children set about spoiling it all.

Why, she thought, even the hallowed Agora had sunk to sessions of irreverent jokes and scandalous gossip that diminished those who were meant to be lifted. Look how they scandalized the new Christians, their name had become a pun, a joke word used to ridicule. And Tamina's master was amongst the worst of them!

Tamina!

Kiana pulled herself up, straightened her back and looked up. The towering pink marble columns rose to a neck-wrenching height. She marvelled at the sheer might of them. None of these had been created in sections. The famous marble from Mons Claudianus was regarded as a wonder of the Roman world. Whole intact columns were teased and coaxed out of the quarry. The dry wooden pegs that were driven in, were soaked and expanded to crack the marble in one magnificent piece. Legions of men suffered the arid desert climate to achieve the impossible.

She put her hand to feel the coolness of the marble and became riveted to the ground. She felt a powerful energy entering her body, coursing through her muscles and her veins. It spoke of the courage and determination of the men, in their hundreds, who had worked to produce this wonder, and their spirit had remained in the marbled column. Kiana suddenly realised the power invested in the temples had come from the men who toiled to create them. The Gods were the celebration of humanity's creativity. And she knew the Goddess Daphne had heard her prayers and had answered her in a marvellous way. She felt strengthened now and knew she would find Tamina.

... ...

Chapter 9

Nese sū-un-ga dan-na sahuiqta muskènu-ta-a-a ra tim

sa samas i-ta-am-ru.

The city will experience destruction. But the people
will experience a reconciliation with the gods.
(Akkadian saying)

The sun was indeed melting into the pillars of the temple to
Daphne, as Achaikos trudged wearily to their previous meeting
place, thankfully finding a warming fire that had been caressed
and blown into life by needy survivors. The wind had picked up.
Sparks joined in a spiral dance towards the moon. The fire, oblivious of the pain and suffering around it, rejoiced at being alive.
The survivors were grateful for its warmth. And some gave thanks
to their Gods and Goddesses. Others simply stared mindlessly
into the flames, looking for everything undeniably lost to them.

Achaikos numbered himself amongst the second group. His
spirit had clamped down and resisted the urge to examine recent
events. All he *could* do was simply observe, to pocket his observations, sending them to the back of his mind.

He stood bent towards the fire, palms stretched outwards,
hoping the heat would travel to his aging, aching joints. Achaikos
scanned the landscape. Standing on the midway ascent to Mount
Silpuis, he saw, even in this fading light, devastation that surpassed his memory of the earlier earthquake. Children remember
differently, he chided to himself. He had lost his mother and that
was all that mattered then. His mind swung immediately to Tamina. Was she alive? He suddenly realised Kiana's desperation to
find her daughter had swallowed whole, any love she may have
held for him. He sagged. And then wholly accepted the situation.

The benevolent, giving river Orontes had been used by the Gods to erupt into vicious anger. It had always supplied in a constant flow; food for the vines, olives groves, dwarf oak, sycamore and fruit trees planted by its banks. Orontes had uprooted, flattened and laid waste most of the vegetation as it had surged upwards, in a tidal wave of huge dimensions. Thick debris swayed on its surface, now trapped within the ruins of the city, as the tidal reach ebbed and flowed. Darkened by silt, it looked almost black. Like an indolent sea monster basking in the evening light, oranges and ochres highlighting its scaly body.

Achaikos shuddered, knowing the body count would be immense. This was the worst earthquake for Antioch. He almost stopped breathing as he realised the damage to Murus Seleucia district, where Tamina had lived, was almost total. Orontes had swept through the harbour homes taking whole apartments with it and leaving many with just a bare wall remaining.

It had swallowed the island, now cut off completely from main Antioch. It was simply no more. Achaikos could just make out the tip of stadium arch, centrepiece to the chariot's races. The palatium was submerged.

The water petered out just before the Agora and the amphitheatre. Would Tamina have fled there? He sensed she would have made a desperate flight to reach the high observatory of the Agora. He began to stamp his feet, not just for warmth, but impatience. Where was Kiana? he thought, as he scanned the crowds around him.

His enquires of the despicable Alcæus Pachis achieved a full descriptive of a high ranking Antiochian Roman. But no evidence of where he and his family, including his slave, Tamina, might have been yesterday. The men of Antioch either loved him or despised him, depending on whether they took bribes or resisted the corruption. Those who resisted seemed wish him dead. He was an evil and violent man.

The men had huddled in ethnically kindred groups. It was a mirror of their lives in Antioch. Jews, Christians, Assyrians and Greeks all had their designated, residential areas in the city. They were walled in ostensibly for their protection against flood from the Orontes. But it was really apartheid. Yet it worked, Achaikos thought. There was very little violence sponsored by racial or religious hatred. No, our enemy is our own Gods!

He was too deep in thought to converse with the men around him now. Indeed, they were morosely silent, in their own personal hell. There was no joining together of the disparate groups either. Culturally it was too difficult to break that wall, for it was both physical and emotional. And it had governed their lives from birth.

It was in this moment of stark realisation that Achaikos knew the people here were doomed. Not because of the earthquake itself, but their reaction to it. They had become truly labile. Soft Greeks and the growing Christian community butted heads. The beginnings of serious dissent between animism and plurality of many Gods worship against monotheism was taking root here.

Achaikos decided it was time to leave for good. As if this decision had suddenly rent open a gap in Time for them to walk through, Kiana appeared, striding towards him, eyes fixed on her goal. And she would not countenance any delay, for food or sleep. Achaikos pulled in as much air into his lungs as he could. For he knew that would be all that could be feeding him for the foreseeable future.

... ...

Chapter 10

Quantus multus maior volo pn oservo me descend

Abrasax!

How much further would you have me descend

Abrasax!

"Do you mean the Goddess Daphne actually spoke to you?" Achaikos panted, as he fought to keep up with her lengthening shadow which was, as she walked into the fading sun, gyrating at his flapping sandals, offering him a rhythm that matched his pounding heart.

"Yes, in a manner of speaking," she tossed her raven hair aside, as she looked back at him, "She showed me the making of the pillars at Mons Claudianus. How the creativity of the craftsmen there, gave life to the marble and how that is its power. It is us, raw humanity, who create the awesome energy in our temples. The Gods and Goddesses revel in it. They don't create or even empower it. We are the co-creators, Achaikos!"

"Hmph!" he replied, "They have lost it now!"

"It will be the followers of Christ who will re-build Antioch, Achaikos," Kiana replied, "the Nazarenes will band together."

"The Christians!" he retorted, "They are a joke"

"Only because they have been lampooned by ignorant men in the Agora," she countered, balling her hand to hit her thigh in exasperation. Thoughts of Tamina were flooding her mind. She would kill Alcæus with her bare hands, if the Orontes had not claimed him.

"We go to the apartment first," she said, "Then anywhere else and everywhere else until we find her!"

"The Agora," Achaikos replied quietly, "She will make for there. It still stands."

Kiana suddenly halted in her downward descent, causing Achaikos to collide into her. Instinct made her perform a sideways swirl, spinning on her heel and ducking his impact completely. He tumbled forward, losing his balance. He landed badly, old bones scraping the hard earth, littered as it was with stones. He lay for a moment, his soiled and torn tunica bunched up to his stomach, revealing veined legs and lumpy muscle. With his head bowed low, he muttered to his god, "*Quantus multus maior volo pn oservo me descend Abrasax!*" Kiana reached out and smoothed his tunica down and held his head up, so he was forced to see her.

"It is entirely up to you," she gently stroked his face with her hand, pulling the tangles and dirty strands of matted hair away from his face, which had been scraped and oozed fresh blood, "You should be proud that your "fall" is so very great, for it means your ascent to the higher levels of spirit and wisdom was tremendous. Focus on that old man. Be part of the solution and not the problem."

They sat together for a while, both lost in their own private thoughts. Kiana was silently keening for her daughter; only huge self-control prevented an outward display. The veins on her neck were bulging, inward panic pumping her heart to impossible levels.

Achaikos looked over the landscape before them. The escarpment down which they were travelling had not been destroyed. Vegetation and crops were being systemically stripped to the bare stalks by locusts in human form. Hunched figures, whose hands were feverishly pulling at the olive crop, the orange and lemon trees, then bundling the fruit into *tunicas*, pulled from their bodies to make makeshift bags. The sun's evening shadows stretched their forms into a grotesque tableau showing a baser, harsher instinct.

"And we should be joining them," Achaikos muttered.

"Yes, we should," Kiana replied, jumping up as if an invisible hand had flicked a switch in her, leaving Achaikos to stumble along behind, as she diminished into a dot before he had taken only two intakes of laboured breath.

After the fruit gathering and the thankful filling of empty stomachs, they took the narrow, winding pathway down to the city. Achaikos could clearly see which parts of the beautiful city had been ravaged, and which had stood firm against the wrath of the Gods. As they came within the temenos of those sacred buildings that remained, the elongated shadows started to creep around them, chilling their hearts to the core. The spirits now darkened, and malevolence seemed to suck at their souls.

The brackish water was lapping Emperor Commodus' Xystus, giving the strong feeling that a full *Cohors Prima* of soldiers commanded by the Emperor himself, had stood in spiritual *Testudo*, stopping the fury of the Orontes from despoiling his work of art. The famed walkway that stretched nearly the full length of Antioch central to the Forum Valentis arch, still glittered in the remaining shafts of sunlight. Light against dark, evil against goodness.

"And all is neutral in the eyes of the Great One," Achaikos thought, "and how this sight before me, lays open my own soul. My fall is the city's fall. I am the city and the city is me."

"Your Goddess Daphne spoke true to you, Kiana," he shouted to the scurrying form stretching the distance between them with each second, "We are the creative force that shapes both worlds. We are indivisible from our Gods"

"She is not my Goddess, old man!" came the furious reply, "I have told you this already, and already you have forgotten!"

"If Tamina is anything like her mother, she will have fought to find a way for her survival," Achaikos shouted back, "you give yourself little credit and you demean her too!"

She stopped, turned to look at him, as he blundered his way forward to reach her. She held out her hand to grasp his. He looked surprised, then beamed down at her, a full Greek smile, full of teeth, which were proudly still his own.

"Good Achaikos," she said tenderly, using his name properly, with respect in her voice, "You are now part of the solution. Together we will succeed and yes, we will find Tamina."

… … … … … … … … …

As they moved further down to the lower reaches of Mons Silpius, Kiana fought to take in every detail of the devastation, keeping her from imploding into hysterical panic. She detached. Her training as a martial arts fighter took over. Evening was fast descending; her eyes were peeled back.

They needed to find a boat. In this event, it was not difficult as they waded into the dirty water lapping the treasured walkway. There were several small boats, unmoored and banging rhythmically against fallen masonry. Kiana lifted her arm and pointing to a reasonably descent *scapha*, as she proceeded to lift legs and arms to wade towards it. It had no oars, so she looked frantically amongst the floating detritus. Remarkably, a rough-hewn spade floated nearby. She hauled herself into the boat, signalling for Achaikos to join her.

She saw the Agora as she turned her head, and sent out a prayer, deep and urging for her daughter to hear her. She sensed now that she was alive. Her heart beat faster and chided Achaikos for his slowness, as he reached the little *scapha* with a long blowing out of his lungs. He swung his leg over, and she caught him to pull his body in, as he flopped into the hull.

They needed to check the apartment first, so she oared with a rhythmical speed that impressed Achaikos, who had guessed she had never seen water, let alone become skilled upon it. Again, she had managed to mystify him.

He saw her back begin to tremble, muscles vibrating. Suddenly she bent over the side and vomited, her meal of oranges and olives mixing in a swirl with blackened wood and rubbish. And it met with the swollen and bloated body of a young girl, face up, whose expression in rictus was horrific. The cadaver banged against the *scapha* as if the soul had not departed.

"Tamina?" Achaikos croaked, feeling his own bile make its way upwards.

Kiana simply shook her head, speechless, acknowledging that it could have been.

She crashed the oar into the water and hurled the boat forward towards the Murus Seleucia apartments, inadvertently slamming into more dead bodies and drowned dogs, cats and several donkeys. It was a memory fixed, to be re-visited at unguarded moments, to haunt them both. Kiana discovered that she was holding her breath, not daring to live this moment. She heaved the fetid air into her starving lungs, for the rot had tainted the air, and she felt more nauseous.

The tidal wave from the Orontes had crashed through the green tiled-glass windows, leaving gaping mouths in derelict buildings. Walls had caved in and the water level had reach upper floors on those apartments nearest to the river. It was possibly fortuitous that Tamina was held captive in a building to the rear of the block. Kiana pointed to the apartment.

"She would have had time enough to escape this," Achaikos commented, touching Kiana's back gently. She had been struck dumb, and silently nodded.

"I need to check," she whispered, as she steered the boat to the entrance, where the door had gone, and the water lapped the ceiling. Without giving any signal, she dived into the fetid mess and swam underwater to reach the stairs, where Achaikos saw her soaked body clamber up to the floor above. He, meanwhile, had to secure the *scapha* with nothing but his hands holding fast to a piece of masonry wall. After scraping his knuckles repeatedly, he decided that hugging the lump of jagged stone was preferable.

He heaved a sigh of relief as he saw her submerged body snake towards him, after many minutes. She shook her head violently, spraying him with water, as she climbed back into the boat.

"*Bussu, Bussu, sahuiqta!*" she spat in Assyrian, "I will kill that *malus excrementum* Alcæus. Please Hecate, let me find him!"

"I suggest you find Tamina first, then you can kill him together," Achaikos replied dryly, eyebrow raised to meet his hairline.

Kiana stared straight into his eyes, "He kept her chained to her bed, and she must have been terrified when Orontes burst. She escaped, bless the Goddess, she got away. I found her chains still clamped to the post, but she had somehow broken them.

I know now she lives!"

... ...

Chapter 11

Puer matrem perdidit ut ea quae vincit et dolorem de illo sit.

The sorrow of a mother lost to her child defeats everything that is.

The light was fading, the sun melting into the water of a flaccid, turgid Orontes. But the walkway seemed to radiate an internal light all its own that led clearly to the Agora. That building was created to shine, in white marble with pink Mons Claudianus columns to offset the brilliance. Achaikos walked beside Kiana, not daring to hold her in any way. She was like a stretched bow, yet in respect, had slowed her march to his step. He realised the discipline of that was needed. They walked together, twin shadows in a failing light. He felt a conflict emerging. He hoped with all his soul, that mother and daughter would be reunited. That was one side of the conflict. A beautiful one at that, yet, the Agora invited another energy altogether. It attracted the highest minds in Antioch, the free thinkers and the prejudiced together. This was not a place for the plebeian masses. Who and what would they meet there in the aftermath of this disaster?

There was only one solitary thought occupying Kiana's mind: was her daughter there?

They made their way up the steps, in unison, looking up to the immense entrance of the Agora. The benign statues of Apollo and Daphne looked down on them, muted and silent. In fact, Achaikos reminisced; this part of the Agora was always bustling, noisy in debate and exchange. He heard their echoes now, unquiet spirits locked forever in a deathly rictus of swallowed time. The huge doors were locked and barred to them. Understandable, he thought.

"I know another way in," he turned to Kiana, who was about to break her fists in frustration on the sculptured door. "We used to use this other door as an escape from burgeoning, ignorant and bigoted men who frequented this temple of eloquence far too often!"

"In your esteemed opinion," Kiana replied, "who are you to say?"

"Oh, and you believe the likes of Alcæus and his ilk to be reasonable men, philosophers and humanitarians! Think on this, Kiana, he values his hide very much and it is here he will come, along with others who are corrupt in thought and deed."

"Good," she retorted, "Then killing him will be quick and soon!"

They crept around the outside of the Agora until they met a side door, almost indistinguishable from the façade. It was like a secret door, and it opened readily for them. Inside was intensely black, musty with old odours languishing in the still air. No-one had used this exit, no-one needed to. The Agora was silent. Scrolls and papyri were secreted here, in a room off-set from the tiny corridor they were now walking along, feeling their way in the darkness.

Achaikos halted and turned to Kiana.

"I believe this is your journey, Kiana. The last thing I wish is to scare your daughter. I am a strange man to her. She will not be with any male survivors in the debating hall, which is where I think I will be of most use. If anyone is there," he added, "She will be in any one of the smaller rooms and spaces, above. I feel she has climbed to the highest point, not knowing if the Orontes would hurl more destruction."

"Agreed," Kiana replied, "but describe to me the most likely hideaways."

… … … … … … … … …

Kiana would not have believed the sheer number of rooms secreted away in the upper level of the Agora, had her own voice now croaking her daughter's name, not shown her. Yet nothing. She was crumpling silently, relentlessly, to the forbidden fear that her precious Tamina, who carried her royal blood, destined for greatness within her extended family, was dead.

Now she was climbing to the last level, a spiral staircase taking her to the topmost area, where only devotees were permitted. A sanctified space to come and pray. It was purposefully designed to be close to their Gods and Goddesses. She turned the corner onto a landing that led into a suite of rooms, each one dedicated to a religion. Antioch was famed for its diversity and this claimed it and celebrated it. Secretly with no pomp or glamour. It just existed above, closer to heaven.

She called. Nothing. She slumped to the ground, her head clasped in her hands, now losing all hope, as it leached from her spirit, hope that had held her all this time. Hope.

"Tamina, my beautiful sweet child," she gasped in air and let out a keening howl. It lasted forever, until she had no air in her lungs and wished she could die now, in this moment.

A shaft of moonlight lit up her grieving form, sitting as she was, in the centre of an elaborate circle of symbols, numbers and glyphs. Above a full moon shone directly onto this circle from a circular hole in the high ceiling, the moon gifting the symbols, her rays to shimmer delicately in gold.

Suddenly she felt a hand touch her head. She shot bolt upright, to see the most beautiful apparition in her entire life.

"Tamina," she whispered, "*You*, is it really you?""

"Mama, tis I, I am alive. Oh, thank the Goddess, you have found me!" As Kiana wrapped her arms around her daughter, tighter and tighter, for if she let her go, she would vanish. They huddled together releasing in shuddered tears, some of the fears and terror. Until both were soaked with each other's tears, they released and finally stared and smiled, then laughed with more hugs, now comfortable and full of hope.

Releasing her daughter, Kiana asked, "Why did you run to here, daughter?"

"Oh Mama, but isn't it obvious?" Tamina replied, mildly shocked, "It is as you have always taught me. Find the place where Ahura Mazda lives, and you will be protected. After I knew for certain that the venomous turd was drowned, and I did see him floating away, eyes bulging in terror for he must have witnessed his own evil and resides now in Hades. I fled to the Agora. I knew he could not follow me, and it had become a safe place. I just climbed upwards till I could go no further. We are sitting in the circle of Abrasax, as he looks to the heavens. The Zoroastrian room is yonder," she pointed towards the dark enclave.

Stretching back, Kiana held her at arm's length, studying Tamina, for she had not seen her in so long. Many months had slipped by, each unable to contact the other. She could only see her in the moonlight, but she had altered so much from the static memory which was held in the treasured place of her heart. Tamina was a younger version of herself, with only vague similarities in physiognomy to the father. She was of slight build, her raven hair tumbling over her shoulders with the same blue tints glinting dully in the moonlight. Then Kiana noticed the scars on her wrists, one overlaying the other in persistent chafing on the skin. She had been tied up many times. Tamina watched Kiana examine her with a growing expression of horror. She turned her head, pulling her hair away to show a deep and ugly laceration, badly healed over and still suppurating puss.

"My reward for fighting back," she said simply.

"The God's anger has released us both, Tamina," Kiana explained her freedom to her daughter. "I was rescued from the rubble which claimed Cleisthenes Raptis, by Achaikos. We are travelling together. He is a kind and generous man, if a little long in the tooth! He is a high priest to Abrasax."

"Does he know who we are, Mama?" Tamina looked questioning at her mother.

"Hmm, not yet" she replied enigmatically, "he knows we are of royal blood, yet nothing of our dedication to Ahura Mazda. He is experiencing the Fall. And believe me it is a mighty fall! So, it will complicate matters to give him our full story."

"Mama," Tamina looked questioning, a frown building, "What are you planning?"

"Nothing yet. It is too soon, but we have become lovers, of a sort. He wishes to travel far away from here. That is all to the good. I wish to start afresh in new lands. I would hate to lose you again, my daughter, but it is your decision entirely whether you come with us or return home".

Tamina leant forward to kiss her mother. It was a generous loving kiss that spoke more than words. She did not want to lose her again, either.

... ...

Chapter 12

Iuvenes audire ad senem senex cui voci cum viris erat puer

Young men, hear an old man to whom old men harkened

when he was young

(Augustus 63BC- 14AD)

Achaikos prided himself that his knowledge of the Agora was exemplary. He knew every nook and cranny. Therefore, darkness presented no problem to him, as he felt his way down pitch-black corridors, through empty rooms to finally reach the destination of the main assembly hall, where, he was gratified to see a positive flickering of light beneath the door.

There was a discussion taking place within. Well, he thought, a few of the elite managed to find their way here. He paused for a moment, cocked his ear, to see if he recognised a voice or two.

Achaikos skipped a small dance in the shadows when he recognised a familiar voice booming across the hall, famed for its echo.

ωε νεεδ το ασσεμβλε αλλ ουρ ωεαλτη το βεγιν τηε ρε–βυιλδι νγ οφ Αντιοχη!

"We need to assemble all our wealth to begin re-building Antioch," shouted his old friend, Amyntas Argyris, "Allow a joining of faith ways, bury old resentments and bring the tetra polis back to glory. We cannot wait for Rome to come to our assistance. Rome is riddled with intrigue and plotting. We write to the Caesar one day and the message arrives to another Caesar altogether. The first being assassinated by the second!"

Shouts of protest or agreement drowned out further comment.

"Not much changed there," Achaikos muttered, sighing and shifting forward.

He lumbered into the hall and stopped. What greeted him was truly astonishing. He had expected to see the old gathering of recumbent philosophers, astronomers, and Roman merchant class that had frequented the Agora just two days previously. What met his astonished gaze was a hall full of the Christians, with just a minor group of Greeks and one or two Romans.

"Have the Gods favoured these Christians?" he asked himself, looking to see those people gathered in a tight group, and who believed their God to have done just that. They were young Christians, for the most part, exuding a passionate energy that rippled through the Agora like a freshening wind. The cobwebs of old wisdom sitting with old men were being unceremoniously swept away.

He suddenly remembered what Kiana had said to him. Was she a seer too? He was taken back to their journey deep into the earth's womb of Hecate, and he reeled as the flashing images took hold of his soul and fragmented it some more.

"Achaikos!" came the booming voice, shattering his imagery and rudely bringing him back to the present, "You survived, my brilliant old fellow. So very heartening to see you intact," Amyntas reached him and encased Achaikos in flowing robes, and stifling body odour. Always a man for indulgent eating, his body rippled with a fatty overload, and Achaikos held his breath. Amyntas had not washed.

"Welcome to the new and entirely unforeseen council of "elders," he whispered in his ear, "Though for the love of Apollo I know not where it is all going!"

"It would seem the Nazarene followers of Christ have an innovative idea," Achaikos ventured, looking more closely at this group of newcomers.

"More to point, they have money, lots of it. Their talent is in creating coin, Achaikos," Amyntas turned to speak, as he led Achaikos towards the circle of muttering men that held Antioch and its future, in their grip. "Rome will not be coming to our aid, yet!"

These young men, for all their wealth, and the families held all their money in communal trust, were essentially as homeless as everyone else. Yet their passion and clear-sightedness were evident as if they were desperate to prove their worth to Antiochians. They had become the butt of jokes, ridicule and gossip, the hallmark of Antiochian society. Achaikos detested it and felt a definite birthing of compassion towards these Christians. Their sector was now submerged under the Orontes and without doubt, they would be residing here at the Agora for the foreseeable future. How Rome would welcome them was a different matter. Political upheaval was rife in Rome and if persecution of the one-god Christians was a means for an aspiring Caesar to gain the senate, they were entirely expendable no matter how they re-built Antioch.

They sat together, listening to the debate of ideas and re-construction.

"I will be leaving Antioch, old Friend," Achaikos turned to Amyntas, who suddenly lent right back, folds of fat wobbling under his toga, eying his friend in astonishment.

"Why ever are you doing this!" he replied, "Your wealth is here, your business has thrived and will do again. You are a pillar of our society. Leave and you will have nothing, *nothing* I say!"

Achaikos paused before replying, gathering his words carefully, succinctly, so he may own them.

"I am living the Fall, Amyntas. Abrasax demands this of me. My whole spiritual journey to The One has insisted I experience the Fall. And it is horrific, my soul shattered into many fragments. I must find those pieces and bring them back to wholeness. The earthquake began the process. Watching my silk toga unravel behind me as Antioch fell initiated the process. I rescued a lovely woman who is supporting me. We go together, hopefully, to the hinterland, where my soul resides."

"Where in all creation is that?" Amyntas asked, slamming his pudgy hands on his knees in a gesture of protest.

"Britannia," Achaikos said simply, looking deeply into his friend's eyes.

A whistling long outtake of breath greeted this statement.

"Then you have lost your brains with your damn toga!" came the reply, as Amyntas turned away to watch the debate.

The air in the assembly arena had become stifling and hot. All exits had been closed, save those to the interior of the Agora. Achaikos wriggled in discomfort as he felt drops of sweat reach the hem of his tunica. He suddenly became self-aware, for the first time since the destruction. He was, to others, no more than an aging vagrant, dishevelled and sitting there in the future council of Antioch, wearing only his underclothes. They were dirty and torn at that. He dismissed it all, and focused on the assembly, as Amyntas had chosen to ignore him.

The groups had quite naturally clustered into their chosen racial and religious denominations, as they lived, so they debated. By far, the most prevalent collective voice was that of the Christians, who had a singularly committed approach to governance. Young minds had created solutions that were both practical and possible within the confines of a city part-destroyed and the population decimated.

Their priorities were sound. Disposal of the floating and dead bodies immediately, with the construction of pyres for burning them, outside the city walls, regardless of religious preferences. Crews assembled with skills in building and the wages for them increased immediately. Messages sent to Rome immediately and money released directly to merchants dealing in building materials. Everyone in the population able to walk would be conscripted to remove rubble and clear the city.

There were few objections and Achaikos felt a chill creep down his spine to rest irrevocably in his bowels. These Christians had a hidden power, latent and now emerging. They had withstood the parodies of "Christians" or "Nazarenes" with a quiet resentment. They were the followers of Christ, their saviour. They knew exactly who they were.

He also knew that Rome feared them already as their monotheist religion summarily dismissed Rome's pagan Gods. This

Christian movement would become a monumental force as dev-astating as the Orontes tidal wave. And they were very clever, taking full advantage of the physical destruction to take command for their own growth.

Elders, invisible to this assembly stood behind the youngsters, moneybags at the ready.

Achaikos turned slowly to gaze at his old friend, thinking.

"Old friend," Amyntas said, without turning his head, "your brain is too noisy. Best tell me your thoughts before everyone here will know what you are thinking!"

"Away from here," Achaikos replied, "I am sodden and dirty, hungry and so very tired".

"Where are you staying?"

"Safe, as high as one poor mortal can go."

"Ah, the *Divas, Diva Sacrarium*. Well you can talk to your God Abrasax to your heart's content up there. But the climb will be bad for your bones, old man!" Amyntas joked, slapping Achaikos hard on his back.

They left, Achaikos turning briefly to view, for the last time, his beloved debating chamber transforming before his eyes into something he could not name and would never again be part of.

He stopped suddenly, taking hold of Amyntas's arm, "A *virgo et eam Mater* may be hiding up there. Both have been violated, both are scarred, so have a care. They trust men as they would a rampant tiger!"

The climb exhausted Achaikos, now severely malnourished and with lack of sleep, every sinew and every bone now ached. The air was singularly fetid, and it was only when they both crept into the *Sacrarium*, did air reach their nostrils. The open ceiling brought in wafts of warm but fresh air.

Achaikos just had time see two sleeping forms huddled to each other in a corner, before one leaped forward and he felt the tip end of a knife biting into his trachea. He stopped breathing. Kiana, just as suddenly, pulled the razor-sharp knife away from his neck and slid it back into its sheath hidden under her tunica.

"You must *never* come into a darkened room, silently like that ever *again!*" she commanded, peering closely at the stranger, deciding, like Achaikos, that he was harmless enough.

"Kiana, allow me to introduce my old friend, philosopher and council member, Amyntas."

"Greetings. How can you help us?" she asked bluntly. "I assume that is why you have trundled up these stairs. Not just out of curiosity, and certainly not to take advantage of us, I would kill you instantly if you harm one hair of my daughter's head!"

"I am here to assist my dear friend of countless years, to get the hell out of here!" Amyntas shot back, eyebrows joining together, as he contained his anger, "But seeing as he has chosen to take you and your daughter, it will take three times as long to gather supplies. I will find what decent food I can now, a change of clothes and bedding, if I am fortunate. All these are becoming hard currency"

"How long?"

"Luckily for you, quite soon for the food that is, as my apartment escaped considerable damage, as did my immediate neighbours'. I would offer you hospitality. But I think it may be too dangerous. You are safer here. The Christians will never climb these stairs. Their Yahweh is not honoured in this *Sacrarium*. You will be safe. Sleep, for you will be needing all your energy to leave Antioch and reach your "hinterland".

"Achaikos, come!" Amyntas commanded.

They disappeared into the darkness, along the dim corridor from *the Sacrarium*.

"Why in name of Apollo and Daphne, have you got inveigled with that female *assassin?*" he squeaked in staccato, forcing himself not to shout. His body was wobbling in barely contained rage, obviously in care for his friend, and needing to voice his fears.

Achaikos took hold of his shoulders, forcibly, to stop the shaking.

"I rescued her....and she is rescuing me!" he replied calmly. "And I think I might actually love her"

"*What!*" Amyntas hissed back, reverting to Greek, "ψου χραζψ μαδ ολδ πηισοπηερ! Δαμν ψου!"

Achaikos slid quietly back into the room, and curled up with his women, too tired and too empty to even acknowledge them. Yet when he spread his arm around Kiana and held her hand gently, she smiled before sleep overtook her.

... ...

Chapter 13

Omne initium novum alio initio est ab aliquo fine est.
Every new beginning comes from some other beginning's end.
(Senaca the Elder 54BC-39AD)

"Shall we tell him?" Tamina whispered to her Mater.

"Tell him what exactly?" Kiana had turned to get very close to Tamina's ear. She smelt her hair, breathing in forgotten body perfumes. Kiana's soul had meshed together, her focus now clear and whole. It was an exquisite feeling. She watched the hunched form of Achaikos, as he knelt preparing his intricate and powerful invocation to the Sun god and to Abrasax. She really felt his tortured soul acutely, like her own, until recently. Her heart bled for him.

"If you mean you are the next queen of Sogdiana, consort to Persia and I am the guardian to that queen, absolutely *not!*" She watched her daughter's face transform as this news claimed her and slowly owned her. It was early morning and still dark, so Kiana smiled as she caught the whites of Tamina's eyes, glowing iridescently in the shadows of the *Sacrarium*. She felt a growing tension enter the young body of her daughter. She had had no preparation, no training. She was captured when little more than a baby. Now one more year and she would be at the gate of her womanhood and entitled to claim the throne.

"But," Kiana kissed her gently on the cheek, "Your true father would probably resist, and being the pragmatist, would have installed your other sister on the throne. The fact you are a slave master's child matters not. Our royal line runs through the female, and that is me, my dear."

She shut her eyes tightly to block out those amber and brown memories, of glinting swishing sabres and blood spraying around her, on her, blinding her. So much blood. And the screams. Then her screams as she witnessed her baby torn from her, disappearing from her sight.

She opened them to watch Tamina, regretting the missing years.

"Look Mama," Tamina said sadly, "look at him. He is so very lonely, and we should ask permission to join him in the invocation? After all we are joined in this endeavour. We need guarding too!"

Kiana studied the lonely figure before her, exuding sorrow, yet still holding a solid fixed stance of determination. It was obvious. His devotion to Abrasax remained the fixed point in his life. No diversions. She was sure they could yet meld together on a spiritual level. He had to be opened to that. But not now, not this dawn. This dawn was his and his alone.

"No," she replied quietly, "It is too soon. Give him the respect of his owned wisdom." She leaned forward to grab her sandals and nodded to Tamina to do likewise.

"We go to the *Sacrarium* of Ahura Mazda, through there," she pointed to the cavernous dark opening at the far end of the temple of Abraxas. Achaikos paused momentarily in his preparations, tilting his head slightly in their direction, as they tip-toed from his hunched form before the engraved and gilded circle that held the magical power of Abrasax, to whom he was intent on calling up for their protection.

He said nothing, he understood. "But soon," he thought, "They will join."

Tamina followed her mother through a black mass of darkness, with no point of light, no direction reference to lead them through. Kiana stretched her hand backwards to guide Tamina. Her hand was damp with sweat, tension broiled inside her. Tamina had a low tolerance to the unknown, her young life peppered with cruelty and Kiana knew that only too well. She was asking for her trust. It was a new feeling for Tamina, and she was unsure she should trust that feeling, even though it was her mother offering it to her. Kiana reached out to find the door to the *Sacrarium*. A low golden light flooded their vision that had just become accustomed to the pitch blackness. Tamina squinted her way into a large room adorned with exquisite wall murals. Before them in the centre stood a circular plinth inlaid in gold. Figures of Gods were etched and painted in dark copper surrounding the entire column. Upon it sat a large circular bowl, its metal blackened to highlight the brilliance of the eternal flame.

Tamina heard Kiana gasp, softly, as she strode over to a huge pile of logs laying in the corner. The eternal flame was going out! No one had attended it since the earthquake. Only the physical light in this temporal world symbolising her god Ahura Mazda, would stop the onslaught of darkness and the evil of Angra Mainyu from entering her world.

She immediately pulled her borrowed stola briskly over her head and covered her face, using the tassels to tie behind her head. Tamina just stared in fascination. Kiana went over to take several logs, and chanting quietly in an ancient language, she lovingly placed the logs on the eternal fire.

Tamina surveyed the *Sacrarium*. And her attention was simply riveted to the huge embossed and deeply coloured sculpture that covered the end wall entirely. It was the first spiritual presence you saw as you entered the room but then she had temporarily lost her vision.

The God had expansive long wings that reached and touched each end of the hall. It was as though he was contained within the hall yet holding the *Sacrarium* intact. The duality was evident. A willingly trapped God set to serve humankind yet could easily fly away. His crown sat firmly on his curling locks. And his beard extended to his chest, which was clothed in sumptuous silks, richly patterned in an intricate design of the eternal flame embossed in gold set against rich amber and framed with dark indigo borders. A circle of pure gold surrounded his body with feet extending to the base of the sculpture. He held a smaller circle in his hand, tightly, in ownership if its power. The ouroboros, the snake eating its tail was the holy seal.

Kiana completed her libation. Reaching inside her leather pouch she gifted a small knob of frankincense to the fire. A calming smoke hit her senses and she moved to beckon Tamina sit with her in this centre of peace. She hugged her gently, kissing her on the cheek.

"My precious daughter," she began, "We were lost to each other so long ago. You were a small child then, and you have a vacuum in your life that needs filling with our truth, so your soul may grow. You know nothing of your heritage, your bloodline, your family and your real home. Let us use this time, before our journey west, to mend your fractured spirit, just as Achaikos is mending his right now, in the temple next to us.

Kiana watched as her daughter's ebony eyes flooded with unspent tears, she felt her body begin to shake. Rasping, aching agony suddenly overcame Tamina. She was releasing those years of unspeakable torment, vicious cruelty from an evil man. She was just fourteen summers old, and her childhood had been obliterated. Kiana could only hold her tightly, caressing her back, on which she felt the same wheals of a vicious whipping, she herself had endured for *novem annus,* nine whole years!

"Who...Am...I?" gasped Tamina, fighting to bring air into her aching lungs.

"You are a Sogdian. You are born into the nobility class. Even my master was part Sogdian, so with my blood you are a Sogdian Princess.," Kiana hurtled those precious words forward to hover in the still air. They had stayed trapped in her deep memory. She had released any feeling that she might someday say them out loud. And now finding her voice to utter them, had left her breathless, as if part of her spirit had flooded out with them. For a moment, she had to heave in the frankincense-laden air.

"Let me tell you, Tamina how it all happened, how you were ripped away from your family.

... ...

"Our true home is in Sogdia. And in the second most favoured country created by Ahura Mazda. Set amidst searing desert there is an oasis, our main city Samarkand is a true heaven. I remember, as a child, with my nursing attendants walking through the merchant section of the city, on hot, stifling days, we would disappear into the shade of the traders' stalls. If you can imagine, Tamina, a city built to be the pulsating heart of the Silk Road itself. We Sogdians are master traders. It is because we have artistic perfection in our very blood. Our skills made us famous, and our bartering for the best profit, unequalled.

The trading domes, with their earthen concave walls, and hot-air conduits, funnelling the searing heat upwards to escape holes in the high ceiling, these were my haunts. It was cool. And as I grew, I made trusting alliances with some merchants, who taught me valuable trading skills.

My nursing attendants risked much to give me this freedom. But I rewarded them with never bringing trouble to myself and I never spoke of our adventures to my father, who would have had them killed!

I saw the caravanserais arrive, twin-humped camels laden with silks, pottery ware, gold and silver statues, baskets and most of all carpets, beautiful rolled lengths of woven silk and wool, that took over a year to complete by a score of women. And these treasures were sure to reach our palace. The carpets were especially treasured by us, as they held the symbol of the eternal flame of Zoroaster over their whole surface.

Samarkand held a mystery. It held power within its walls and burgeoning, exotic gardens. Everyone of noble class, and of the higher merchant class, who ran the silk road, wore silk. Our clothes draped to the floor in pleats of shimmering shot silk. As a princess, I had a dress for every occasion.

We believed our power and our protection was always delivered by Ahura Mazda. We kept the eternal flame in our temple safe and burning.

As I grew into womanhood, I felt the pull to learn Zoroastrian, devote my soul to Ahura Mazda.

Both my father and mother were appalled. My path had been destined from birth and it was in the palace as a Sogdian princess, I would remain. A prisoner in my eyes!"

Kiana stopped for moment, bringing her soul back to the present, looking at her daughter, as if seeing her for the first time. She saw herself. In her years of freedom amongst the bazaars, before she rebelled and changed her life forever.

"Tamina," she stroked her hair, as the eternal flames sent shadows dancing over the murals, "I am so very sorry. My gift to you has been a lesson in evil. Of cruelty and pain."

"How so?" Tamina questioned, "Mama, you gave me the gift of courage to live through it, and the spirit to be who I am despite it! I am damaged goods. So are you! But we are feisty, wilful, beautiful damaged goods nonetheless!"

"I made a faulty choice back then, Tamina," Kiana insisted, "I will hold that as a dark evil against my soul, from Angra Mainyu, I was neither strong enough to resist nor able to transmute. I am, after all a Zoroastrian high priestess. Whatever earthly good is that? I experienced the fall into darkness at the tender age of sixteen years. Achaikos, for all his advanced years, is now at this present moment, suffering the same, for the first time. Angra is no respecter of innocence or wisdom."

"Tell me then," Tamina queried. "What happened to change your life so terribly?" She considered her mother's eyes and saw her soul twist at the memory.

"I remember," Kiana continued, snuggling into her daughter's warmth and pulling her stola tighter around her shoulders, *"stealing the slave girl's clothes that evening. Her sandals barely kept their shape as I forced them around my ample feet. The thongs cut into my skin straight away. My first lesson in the life of a slave!*

I had planned my escape for several weeks. Waiting for the dark moon, taking money in portions, so it would not be missed. Sewing my heirlooms into a saggy old jacket, for bartering in any unforeseen emergency. I needed to reach Bukhara, the next city on the Silk Road. My father's power did not pulsate that far. I hoped to prostrate myself to the priests at the temple. They were duty bound to offer sanctuary. I knew the back alleys of Samarkand so well, and I silently thanked my nurse attendants for their free-giving courage. I did not even need a flame to guide me. I felt like a wraith, a ghost, creeping through my city in the dead of night.

And I thanked my nurses also for giving me the freedom to sit and talk with friendly merchants for many hours, sipping their spiced milk, and discovering the wealth of beauty our people created in metal, ceramic and cloth. Weapons too, I handled many a sabre and sword, beautifully engraved in symbols of the Gods. I had been taught how to handle them, fight with them to save my very life!

There is a craft of my people, your people, Tamina, that I want to find, and bring with me to the west. It is Sogdian artistry of the highest kind. Metal objects from vases to delicate buckets are painted in oxides, sky blue overlaid with white intricate designs, then fired in an oven to make them strong. Some have the Termeh Boteh, Flame of Zoroaster. That is the vase I would find.

My heart was burning with passion to gift my soul to Ahura Mazda, as Zoroaster had done aeons before me. I saw my path forward so clearly; I did not give my family one more thought. I was headstrong and totally selfish."

Kiana stared at her beautiful, found daughter and expelled angry air to mingle with the sanctified air of the *Sacrarium*. In the glowing darkness, she saw her daughter's eyes wide with fascination as her own story unfolded. And she felt small still vague growing pieces slowly slot into place within the barren landscape of Tamina's soul.

"The conceit of youth, Tamina," she sighed, "And you were never given the chance to own, even for a small time, that heady intoxicating feeling."

Tamina was resting her head on her knees, drawn up for warmth.

"Well, Mama, there is time yet! But you have gifted me freedom and for now that is more than enough. What happened to you after you escaped your "royal bondage," did you find your fire temple?"

"Yes, I did" Kiana replied, her eyes glazing over as she remembered and tried to shield her spirit, "And it cost me the tortuous shedding of my wealth and birth right I had chosen to toss away so easily!"

"I had made good friends amongst the merchants who were always travelling but always kept Samarkand as their long-stay base. And they were protective of this wayward royal, who in rebellion, had not a care for her own safety. They elected to be my protectors.

They secured a camel for my travel, which was waiting for me in the outskirts, tied to a pole and resting, chewing laboriously, dipping his large head into the food bag left for him. Dawn was clearly arriving on this my day of escape. It was a huge dawning too, and I saw this as a sign from Ahura Mazda that I had become, in his eyes, an adherent.

That brilliant sun welcomed me and my day, in a way I shall remember all my life. It was very large, sending rays of light to adorn the sky, still a dark blue. All colours were sent upward. I fell to my knees and chanted what I had learnt from a priestcome-merchant, of the revered ancient Sogdian text in Avestan, the Yasna. It is the first ceremony in worship of Ahura Mazda and Zoroaster. It made my heart sing and my body tremble, and it was living this worship that overcame all else to become, if I was allowed, a priestess of the fire temple."

Kiana, lost within her story began to chant, softly, in old Avestan, the first liturgy of the Yasna. Spoken by Zoroaster to Ahura

Mazda, it formed the initial part of the Avesta. Kiana's heart opened as she remembered every word and intonation.

"I approach you with good thought, O Mazda Ahura, so that you may grant us the blessing of two existences, the material and that of thought, the blessing emanating from Truth, from which we can put your support in comfort."

Kiana gave a long outtake of breath. Tamina was now staring at her, nonplussed. For the first time, in their short re-union, she viewed her mother as a separate individual. That her mother was truly a *Daèna*. In all her years of slavery, in captivity, she had held a frozen, beautiful and tender image of a mother she never knew. This woman, her mother had splintered that illusion into a thousand pieces. Kiana sensed the tension, suddenly growing between them.

"Oh daughter, my dear love! Know this. Every single prayer and invocation I sent to Mazda; it was with you by my side! It was never "I," always "We." I summoned your spirit. You may never have realised but sometimes I was so sure you came. It was my burden and my joy to release you from your slavery. You may view this as too little, too late, but it was the best I could do.

"And it was my supreme faith in Ahura Mazda that sustained me in all the dark years of my slavery. We believe the battle with darkness is ever present. That is why we walked through the dark hall to reach here, our temple of fire.

"I must tell you the rest of our story, before Achaikos completes his libations to Abrasax. Maybe, Tamina," Kiana spoke hesitantly, "You may feel you might join me in our ceremony? Your name Tamina means "follower of Ahura Mazda"

"Hmmmm," Tamina looked to the floor, "Please finish your story, Mama. Then I will decide."

Kiana stiffened, momentarily, gathering her thoughts.

"The camel is an obnoxious creature. Bad-tempered and obstinate. They will spit their awful saliva at you for no good reason. And they are consummately lazy. The two-humped kind see themselves as superior and the very worst to handle. So, it was, that in the shadows of the emerging day, stood a friend, a

Sogdian, whom I believed was quite fond of me, and he had elected himself to be my guardian, against camels and all else!

Niyoz hoisted me onto the sitting and very languid camel. A hardened leather water sack hung from its ample girth. And there were baskets of food and merchant goods for barter. I felt cared for and I smiled in appreciation at Niyoz, who summarily wacked the camel hard on the rump, instilling a movement that rocked me violently sideways as he got his balance. Niyoz gave me a whip commanding its use. We needed to move fast before the day got underway. Niyoz was risking his own life in helping me. I remember him turning to look so very sadly at his utopia, his Samarkand, knowing he would never see it again.

The dust swirling upwards from the camel's hooves burrowed into every crevice imaginable. I was rhythmically hurled from side to side, sucking in the rough cloth mask that protected my lungs. I could not recall any part of that first day's journey. I had my eyes shut. Thankfully, come dusk, we reached the first ganat which was honoured by a small round of vegetation and a shading tree. The caravanserai was near, the clay dome basic, but very tall with a welcome wind hole. My heat-seared lungs rejoiced at that cool water, which hit my stomach like a symphony of flutes. Time stopped as my body came alive again.

Niyoz watched me but said very little. After a meal of olives, cow meat and naan bread, we settled in the dome, the last memory of him, before I slept, was a hunched figure, wrapped in rugs, watching. I don't believe he slept. Niyoz was my guardian in the truest sense of that word.

Days followed in identical fashion. I lost count of them entirely, then on a windy morning, threatening a dust storm, we encountered the thin line of camels, stretching back, a caravan of merchants, heading towards Bukhara, the bustling city, a crossroads to all ports and trade routes.

"We are near Bukhara," Niyoz spoke, in his deep husky voice, "City of the mind. I will bring you safely to your Fire Temple today, then I must depart.

We must travel with these merchants. It will be safer."

We blended in easily, I counted twenty or more camels, heavily laden with goods from China. And huge baskets carrying meenakari, heavenly art. The merchants were mostly Sogdians. I prayed none recognised me but travelling as a slave peasant girl in ragged clothes, masked from the dust, I was anonymous.

I will never forget my first sight of Bukhara "the crossroads" on the silk road trail. Huge clay domes, the bazaars, dotted the landscape with narrow walkways in between. There was just enough space for a single camel train to move through. The noise of so many different tongues, bartering for the deal, assaulted my ears. Arms flaying widely and shouts accompanying the sale of so many goods, made my mind carousel in confusion. There was too much to absorb. I believed I had become accustomed to the merchant culture in Samarkand, but I had not met with so many foreigners before. I was relieved when the Temple appeared, rising above this humanity like a cool, serene bird in lime-washed white, the immense walls rising to the sky.

Niyoz bent my camel's foreleg and helped me down. I felt shaken and looking to the high, embossed door, suddenly nervous.

"I must leave you," Niyoz said slowly, carefully, as if those words pained him. I hugged him. I would miss his care and compassion. He never faltered. I had already unpicked the hem of my "coat of many treasures" and pulled out a little figurine of Ferohar, our guardian spirit. I brought his hand to mine, and I placed it carefully in his palm, gently closing his fingers around it.

"To remember our time together. May he always protect you." I stated simply.

I turned and knocked on the door of the Temple of Fire.

... ...

Chapter 14

Quod mundus sit mutatio; vita, opinio.

The Universe is transformation: life is opinion.

Marcus Aurelius 121AD-180AD

Tamina was sitting hugging her knees, her eyes distant, taking in every word, inflection that was building a picture for her to keep. The pieces were steadily, carefully nudging into place. The tension had eased. Kiana breathed more easily. They both heard Achaikos. He had begun the long liturgy. The cadence of his chanting was both powerful yet supplicating.

"He is asking Abrasax for his beneficence. To cloak him in goodness so he may climb up from his Fall," Kiana rubbed her neck, and shuffled her legs to gain more comfort. They had been sitting for some time and the room was bare, save for the consecrated *haoma,* and bowls kept in the corner under a silk cover. Caught now in the present moment, Kiana tied her stola around her face, and padded over to the wood pile, taking two good sized chunks, began chanting in Avestan, and placed them ceremoniously on the eternal flame.

"Why do you cover your face?" Tamina asked.

"There are two important principles of creation you must take in and cherish them both in your soul, Tamina," Kiana knelt and stroked her daughter's hair, which she found wayward, and luscious like her own.

"The elements of water and fire are Creation's tools. Water weaves around and underpins our earth. Fire simply creates us! We protect that fire. And we humans can be corrupt. Zoroaster believed we will contaminate the waters of the Earth. So, our Ab-Zohr ceremony purifies and empowers the water.

"Will you assist me in the Ab-Zohr, before we leave Antioch for good?"

Kiana found she was holding her breath. Moments passed. The chanting to Abrasax had become much louder.

"You know Achaikos has achieved a prominent level of wisdom. He is an adept," Kiana found herself talking to fill the silence, "We are in essence backside to front, we two unlikely partners," she smiled at the notice now given, that she was also an adept.

"His Fall has occurred at his ripened age, a perfectly awful time to re-create yourself. Mine happened before I reached my twentieth season. Shall I continue with our story?" she asked, not waiting for the important answer to her previous question.

Tamina looked askance, then nodded.

"I was reluctantly allowed into the Temple. The old Daèna Magi examined me coldly. I only remember his hooked nose protruding from his large cowl hood, travelling in a vertical line up and down, while he examined me in silence.

"A brief nod, and I was led away to the women's quarters where I stayed, miserably, for a very long time. It seemed I had changed one prison for another. I was conscripted to do the most menial work, from floor scrubbing to emptying the sluice holes.

"I knew I was being watched so no complaint ever passed my lips! They knew I was nobility. I was Sogdian royalty and that was not viewed favourably. There were many different dialects spoken, when not in ceremony. But my language, Avestan was always honoured then. I tried so many times to peek through tapestries and curtains to see the ceremonies. And I became so proficient that by the end of my second season there, I could recite nearly the whole Yasna, including the Gathas.

"It was that passion which got me caught, and which altered my life. I would rise, pre-dawn and perform my own ceremony to the rising sun, in our courtyard which lay open to the East. In dark shadow my voice would whisper the Yasna to Ahura Mazda. One day, as the first rays filtered towards our temple, and my voice, hoarse from passion, uttered those last words, a booming voice thundered across the courtyard, where I stood alone in the centre.

Footsteps came towards me, clacking on the stones, as this shadow moved forward. I knew who it was. The Magi bristled under his hooded robe.

I froze, as the men came for me. They grabbed my arms, roughly. I fought hard. They marched me forward to face the Daèna.

"Girl-child," he hissed, stepping closer so I smelt his rancid breath, and caught an extra whiff of a strange odour. It was permeating his whole body. I knew then his spirit was in readiness to leave this diseased physical body.

"You assume so much self-importance here, in this sacred temple. Is it your royalty that demands this of you?"

I struggled even more, as anger overtook me.

"No," I shouted back, "It is my love for Zoroaster, the love of the land, our Ahura Mazda that ignites my spirit!"

"And it is most definitely not you!" I added, instantly regretting this outburst. The priests gasped behind me, one smacked me hard against my face. I screamed, while the other pinned my arms behind my back so hard, I felt my bones crack.

"Enough," shouted the Magi, "There will be no violence within these walls, ever! If you feel justified in this," his bony hand shot out, prodding the priest behind me, "to a girl," he shrieked, "then shame on you! Join the Parthian army to vent your new-found skills. Child come with me. Your name?"

"Kiana," I replied, flexing my arms to feel the blood rush to pinched muscles.

"And you are Sogdian royalty. That is obvious for your natural command of Avestan. I now give permission for you to train for navjote and become a Daèna." The old Magi stated to me, a girl frozen in her step, as her heart opened with joy. I was instantly elevated, given silk robes and coloured head scarves. I bathed often and prayed relentlessly.

"I also learnt, very quickly, from acquired skill in watching and listening well, that politics and plotting had entered the temple. There were priests who had fallen in with the army. They were held in high esteem. Their predictions and augury could

change the course of a terrible war that was so close, it put a fearful strain on our days.

"Our daily liturgy of Humata, Hukta, Huvarshta had a hollow ring.

"The Parthian empire was crumbling and in the hollowness of several defeats came the spectre of pure evil driven by Angra Mainyu, the Sassanid army.

War was coming."

... ...

Chapter 15

Āli lawiat nawúta i-mar

The town we besiege will be destoyed

Assyrian quote

"My days melded into each other in a blissful routine of prayer. Now made more intense as I was joined with others. My spirit soared to a higher level and stayed there. Together, in the early dawn liturgy of the Vasna, I truly felt union with Zoroaster as we communed with Ahura Mazda. I felt, then, in my naïve youthfulness, that I had indeed reached the Omega.

"We did not lead a monastic life at all, secluded from humanity. We were commanded to join with the merchants and their families. So, after breaking our fast, the giant doors were opened and out we were disgorged upon a community eager to learn Mazdayasna.

"We travelled in couples for safety, especially the women, and mingled with buyers and sellers in the bazaar. It was a sheer delight for me, and the women from my temple always jostled for my companionship because I was the native girl of the merchant domes.

"We carried a heavy leather sack with our clay tablet to write the names of the righteous. We had scrolls describing the Ab-Zohr daily ritual of creating and keeping the eternal flame and purifying the water. We always re-visited a week hence to those who had kept the fire burning and the parahaoma kept safe. And it was these families that were recorded.

"We observed the Ab-Zohr ourselves, daily, at the qanat."

Kiana stopped for a moment, gathering her thoughts, for now came the crux of their story. Tamina's disreputable father. Should I tell her the full truth? she thought. As if her daughter read her mind, she turned and spoke to her mother quietly, as she, herself shifted, stood up, and bound her own stola over her face as an adept would do.

"This answers your first question, Mama," as she gracefully entered the sacred area, and in her own words spoken to the spirit, quietly placed more wood on the fire.

"And this is not just from watching you," she added, "I understand the need for purity to engage with the Eternal Flame. And my answer to your unspoken question," she continued as she snuggled up to Kiana, and with a look much older than her years, she added, "you are about to experience your Fall, and it has something to do with my father, no?"

"Yes," Kiana replied; an astonished look frozen on her face.

"I was aware he had been following us for several days. But it was on that second day I felt his energy and knew it to be predatory. But I did not know which one of us he was after. I knew it had to be me, by the fourth day, as I had chosen an ugly girl to be my companion. He followed even closer that day as if he was playing with me.

"Your father was a mixed breed. Half Sogdian, the best half, I like to believe. The rest, quarter Arab, some Assyrian, I think, but also Sassanid. His motives were as twisted as his birthright. The name you know him by is not his real name. He introduced himself to me on that terrible bloody day as Javad Esfahani.

"Whatever else he was, Mama, he was my father and I would like to know," Tamina said, a strong inflection in her voice told Kiana; she was ready.

"*That awful day dawned like all the others in my sheltered life at Bukhara. The city thrummed with business, commerce and money; my heart thrummed with the exultation of the Divine Host. That combined beating pulse hardly noticed the change. But the camels did. We were at the ganat finishing the Ab-Zohr, when we noticed the cluster of dormant twin-humped camels suddenly became restless. The day was sweltering and usually they remained totally dormant in the haze that rippled before our eyes. It was edging towards mid-day, the sun at its highest. All of Bukhara would be closing to hibernate from the* heat. Dusk would see the city come alive again and the millions of lights flood the bazaars into the night. But that city would not come alive again for many moons.

We stood in a huddle, eyes to the horizon, feeling a faint shudder in the ground.

Farideh, my closest friend and ally spoke first,

"It is not a sandstorm."

"Feel the ground, it is shaking sisters!" Goli uttered, the first to feel the fear.

"We had no concept of war, of how it began, grow, then bury us in blood, carnage and bits of limbs for carrion to pick at. We just looked in amazement, in awe almost, as the ground beneath us throbbed to an unknown beat. The sand jumped around us, giving its own dance of death.

"The camels shrieked in a tormented grappling of limbs and ropes. And it was then that our eyes caught up with their instinct. The wind generated by thousands of men on horseback hit us first.

"We screamed, high-pitched in a terror song that instantly defeated our exultation to Ahura Mazda.

"Hold hands," Laleh shouted, "Do not let go. We go back to the temple!"

"But I was wrested from my friends, captured from behind, and brought kicking and screaming to be hurled against the wall of the caravanserai. My face hit the curved wall and bled. It was a vicious rescue. I blinked through the blood pouring down my face to see Javad for the first time, his face contorted with lust.

"He took me right then, as he had always planned obsessively to achieve, even before the Sassanid soldiers has even entered Bukhara.

"You will not die this day," he growled, as he pounded into me, as I lay gripping the sides of the metal chest, "But you are now my slave, priestess of the temple." And he laughed at his victory and my shame!"

Kiana began shaking, a tremble that threatened to overtake her iron control. The memory was in sharp focus, so real, she could close her eyes and be there, yet again. The vilest of nightmares that haunted her nights for years afterwards. And as she turned to see Tamina, the young child grown old by vicious men, she saw the tears cascade down her face. A twin horror shared by mother and daughter.

They held each other for a long time, an infinity of love surrounding their pain. She knew now that they would heal, and she silently rejoiced.

She breathed in,

"Twin events were created that day by Javad Esfahani," Kiana stated, hoping to embed a different image to the hatred Tamina held at that moment,

"He saved my life and he began yours".

... ...

Kiana was listening acutely to the ritual being performed to Abrasax. It was reaching an elevated level of invocation, some parts to the liturgy reaching high cadence, signalling a completion. She knew her time was short, and the completion of their story must be realised. She did not intend episodically any re-telling.

"*I was bundled into that metal chest, with Javad seated on top when the iron warriors arrived. I heard them; their clanking was terrible. I saw in the gap of the chest, brief images of metal feet, embossed breast plates and one soldier threw his helmet just inches from my vision and I studied it, while Javad saved our skins in fluent Sassanidese. The helmet was curiously conical, like these warriors had deformed skulls. I deduced they were skilled and permanent warriors as this helmet was battered and had been mended many times.*

"*They left. And so, did we, on the twin humped camel Javad had bargained in exchange for coin. I soon discovered he had a tongue coated in silver!*

"We made for his home territory, Esfahan. That is how I learnt he was half-Sogdian. It was a several days hard galloping over scorching desert and high mountain passes. After a full day crushed between him and hump of this irascible beast, I was taken by him, and endured the pain, even though I was exhausted and hurting in every muscle of my body. My determination not to show any weakness, broke that night. I huddled in the thin rug he had thrown at me, and I shed many tears.

Something in him rose to the surface, I think it was his Sogdian spirit, for he relented, showed some care for me. From that following day, as we came nearer to his home, he softened, and we even had a conversation of sorts. On my part, I had accepted this reality. No-one was coming to rescue me. He had already done that, and I was his. We settled in Esfahan. He learnt his trade, dealing in the Silk Road cloth and became a tailor. He became very wealthy. It was not difficult in Esfahan, called "Half the World" by traders who flocked there."

"You were born there Tamina," Kiana looked to see her daughter's eyebrows raise in astonishment, "Your true birth name, your Sogdian name, is Sumaya, Soul of flowers!"

"But our life of relative peace did not last. The Sassanids were relentless in their war. Determined to overthrow the Parthians, they cut the bloodiest swathe through city and village until they reached the jewel, Esfahan.

"I was not sheltered this time. We had no time. They came in the dead of night. A coward's way. Blood is black at nightfall. I squelched through many a puddle of someone's lifeblood coursing through my bare feet as we fought to escape.

"You were three seasons old and very able to scream. I had to bury my fist in your little face to drown your cries. Then you became silent, in terror. Your saw so much, but I doubt you remember.

"We raced through the bazaars, onto a hill that leads out of Esfahan. We were joined by Javad's friend, a Greek by the name of Alcæus Pachis!"

"NO!" cried Tamina, "you are saying he was there in my birth-place!"

"Yes I am. He had a horse, a fast one, he had just purchased to speed his journeys to Antioch. Javad tore you from my arms amidst the blood and screams of hundreds of dying. He gave you to Alcæus. He saved your life. We both believed death awaited us. The very last I saw of you was your little face pinned against Alchæus' shoulder, screaming for me until you were out of my sight."

Silence prevailed, the story nearly told, and as if to underscore the telling, Achaikos had reduced the incantations to a murmur.

"We did not die that day," Kiana concluded, sitting back straight, looking at the eternal flame, "we made it to Antioch, the city of peace! Except Javad became bitter and resentful. He never did regain the immense wealth he amassed in Esfahan. And of course, he took his anger out on me, just like Alcæus did you."

"No," retorted Tamina, "He was not resentful. His life was one of constant privileges. He was a monster, Mama. A pure evil monster."

As if on cue, silence was established in the neighbouring room. Kiana could hear shuffling, as Achaikos gathered his ritual instruments.

"Time to go, Tamina," Kiana eased herself up, finding a certain numbness had captured both her legs. She giggled.

"Oh my, daughter, but your mother is getting old!"

… … … … … … … …

Chapter 16

Και ο Θεός Αμπράραξ χαμογέλασε.

And the god Abrasax smiled

Kiana and Tamina stood silently, watching Achaikos complete the long and arduous invocation to his God. Kiana had felt a shift, saw his shoulders straighten and his spine stretch to his real height. She had not realised his true height, and smiled, thinking of the hunched form of an older man.

He turned and smiled. A rich smile that creased his face, and entered his eyes, which sparkled with a joy she had not seen. They came to each other in a warm embrace, as he looked over to see Tamina staring intently at them both, a fixed expression that spoke of feelings repressed. So, he tenderly kissed her mother's crown and made his way over to Tamina. He did not embrace her at all. He tenderly held her hand encased in a loving grasp, saying quietly,

"It is nearing our time to leave Antioch. You may never see the sight of it again in your lifetime. Are you prepared and content to go with your mother and take this old wreck of a man as your friend?" Achaikos smiled and kept that look just for her. It may have achieved a small dent in her armour, but he did not believe she held any trust. He knew he was too close in looks to her sadistic tormentor. That Greek had sullied and defamed his people in her eyes, forever.

"Yes," she replied, shuffling her feet and looking down in some embarrassment. It will take Herculean patience and the strength of Atlas to win this poor fractured soul, he sighed inwardly. He felt immeasurably stronger now.

"Your soul has some edges now Achaikos," Kiana murmured, as they left the temple rooms, "You are stronger now."

Achaikos chuckled, "Hmm I have been a consummate fool, Kiana, and an arrogant bloody fool at that. But I have moved out of that skin. I am comfortable in the skin I am wearing now."

"Good," she smiled, and in reaching to give him the kiss he had longed for, whispered in his ear, "And I love and respect that skin that now houses such a beautiful spirit."

··· ··· ··· ··· ··· ··· ··· ··· ···

Chapter 17

Stultus est sicut stultus Est vetus
There is no fool like and old fool

The dawn came slowly, almost sneaking subtle colours across a cloudless sky, so typical of Antioch, lulled into lazy living. But to Achaikos and his new family, walking slowly behind their wagon piled with their worldly goods, they felt utterly estranged from the surreal sights before them as they took, for the very last time, the white, glistening walk of the Xystus.

The ceremonial triumphal walk had now become a makeshift marketplace. Survivors, both slave and nobleman, had a commonality of purpose. At least the pretence of normality showed itself, yet the persistent odour of burning flesh and the twisting spiral of smoke, of flesh meeting so many spirits that had long since fled, simply eclipsed any thought of normality. Antioch was still a living nightmare.

Kiana turned to see the devastation of Murus Seleucia, her daughter's residence, her prison, now disjointed rubble, tide marked and stinking. The angry Orontes had receded to lapping the foreshore once more. And she smiled, wearily and cynically at the surreal sight of hunched men in togas, *ordo* and *novus homo* rubbing shoulders with slaves in their ragged and torn homespun tunica, picking, scraping and tossing out the remains of their domesticity. The Gods had levelled Antioch.

Achaikos had, the previous day, found his silk toga. He had insisted on taking this last pilgrimage to his home, alone. He found the end piece lying, twisted around plaster blocks. He thought hard on this. Should he leave his damned past where it lay? "A fitting grave for a fragmented life," he thought. But it was an elegant roll of ivory silk, the best from the silk road, which ended in the ancient Chang'an province. As he painstakingly picked away the rubble and eased the silk out, he travelled back in time, along that Silk Road, a route taken so many times, with his father. Those tortured memories had been faced and eased, nullified, sent away. He could trace a better memory now. He felt the huge sway of that irascible camel, laden so heavily with silks and rugs, Achaikos believed the camel's long legs would buckle. The sunsets within the valley escarpments, a fire to ease aching bones and torn feet, as he walked that day along sharp rock fragments in an unforgiving land. Home to unforgiving people, tribal nomads of Mongol origin.

And the banter between the merchants to relieve the strain. Sogdians were the best storytellers and the funniest. It was as if they held dominion along the Silk Road for many generations and they were comfortable in their skins, and more so for the wealth they had accumulated.

As he picked up the last of the silk toga, his memory became sharp. It was the change in air, in energy, as they passed the invisible borders between cultures. China held a magic uniquely to herself. The high mountain passes only served to make Achaikos feel that he was walking along the roof of the world. The energy there sucked the air from your lungs and your eyes widened in the sheer glory of it.

He held the toga, remarkably in good condition, to his heart, for it was as scrunched and weary as he was. Yet silk is indestructible, the toughest of fibres from the lowly worm, a miracle of nature. And it was this thought that gave him the decision to treasure it. He would give it to his women, for they were the toughest, most indestructible women he had ever met, and it would mark their *libertus* from slavery, their *manumissio*. Both were diminutive in stature, and with trimmings, this silk would make two togas for each of them. He saw them both in his mind's eye, fully adorned in the shimmering silk, with the sun glowing behind them and he smiled.

Achaikos reached his home and stopped. He blinked twice to convince himself the vision before him was real.

His home stood untouched by the God's anger. It still had the ornamental lantern hanging from the doorpost. He gingerly walked forward, holding out his hand to touch the door. It resisted his touch. He had enough money hidden inside, though not his full wealth. That was kept secure in Byzantium. But enough to warrant the making of locks. His shoulders gyrated in that silent laugh of his. The key was long buried somewhere, and he would have to break into his own home.

The windows had been lavishly fitted in Roman green-glass. He reluctantly picked up a stone and threw it against the largest window. It shattered into thousands of shards and picking his way through, eased himself up into his *vestibulum*. He immediately saw cracks running the length of the room. There was dust laying on his silk road furniture. But no one had broken in before him.

He was engulfed in a sense of unreality, of feeling spared and sheltered by the Gods: by Abrasax?

He felt his knees give way. Hunched in the dust, Achaikos pummelled his chest in-between sobs that wracked his body, as he gulped out his invocation to the supreme, all-forgiving God.

"AEEIOUO
AEEIOU
AEEIO
AEE
AE
A

I thank you ABRASAX
Lord of whole Earth and the Heavens
I thank you O Great One, the second of the first
Whose are the restraints with which the abyss is bound
I thank you O god of the Sun."

He knelt there for an unknown time. The rays of light slanting through the shards of remaining glass, deepening as the sun descended into the underworld. Dust mites danced in the breeze. Achaikos shifted his weight at last, realising both knees now ached terribly, and his foot had lost all feeling. He reached out and collapsed into the nearby chair, head shrunken deep into his chest. He was deep in thought.

He was home. It had been saved; it was intact. He felt an overwhelming sense of peace, warming every part of his being. This was his awarded shelter. He did not want to leave it.

The only sound was his deep breathing through gritted teeth as he fought conflicting passions. He knew indefatigably that he was being given a choice. He could stay here and re-build his life. But would Kiana and Tamina choose to join him. He thought not.

Theirs was a shattered life here that held no attraction. But oh! by the gods, he was getting too old for adventuring across the world. He felt Abrasax was surely offering him a haven of peace, earned, here, in his own home. As his conviction grew, a welter of noise from intruders, broke through his reverie, for that was all it was, an illusion, as gaunt men in rags heaved into his room, through the shattered window.

Achaikos bellowed, picked up a weighty ornament from the nearby plinth and aimed well, hitting one intruder square across the head. He crumpled in a heap, leaving the other vagrants to falter, then deciding to escape, leaving the groaning man on the floor at Achaikos' feet. His anger was consuming him. For a second, he felt utterly betrayed. Then he realised he was being tested. The Fall had not finished. He had spent the last days in deep prayer, invoking Abrasax and eventually realising his presence had grown into the wisdom he had sought so willingly in his spiritual journey. The god's anger had shattered that illusion, felling Antioch like a diseased tree.

And now, he pondered, as he looked down on his assailant, what now?

"Live IN the Now," came an urgent voice in his battered mind. What Kiana, in all her youthful years, had told him, was true. "There is no fool like an old fool," he chided himself, as he bent down to see the damage his ornament, of considerable value, had inflicted on this poor ragtag of a man. He was unmistakably Greek, with similar olive skin, and black wavy hair with only slight tinges of grey. His face was puckered with three scars, pulling one down eclipsing useful vision and scarring both cheeks. A soldier or a criminal then? Achaikos thought, alarmed at the realisation this man could easily overcome him, injured or not.

He instantly decided not to find out, rushed to his *culina* for rope, returning so fast he scraped his elbow on a jutting corner of a table unit. He roughly tied the man's hand behind his back. The man was recovering consciousness and began a faint struggle to release his arms. Groaning and shaking his head to dispel the pain he now felt, uttered garbled profound swear words in Greek.

"ψοπυ φυχκινγ πιλε οφ σηιτ! μοτηερ φυχκερ, πισσ ποτ!"

"ψουρ ναμε, ιμβεχιλε!" Achaikos growled,

"your name, Imbecile!"

"Andreas, "he croaked back, "Andreas Simonides. Let me go!"

"Well, son of Simon, you break into my home with intent to rob. Why should I let you go? Why should I not wreak my vengeance on you eh!" Achaikos found himself at odds. He really did not care. His only intention was to retrieve his money, his gold and requisite papers for the main horde in Byzantium. This opportunist had seen an easy entry. He was obviously starving like the rest of Antiochians.

Andreas glared at Achaikos intently, with his one good eye, which suddenly rolled up into his head, and he lost consciousness again. Achaikos rolled back on his heels, contemplating this man who had suddenly burst into his life.

He heaved his prone body over to cushions laid on the *triclinium* and covered him with a woven thick linen sheet. He peered at his head wound, which was coagulating. Going back to the *culina* an idea literally gently touched his mind and buried itself quietly. He took linen bandages and a water jug. It held old water, so he flapped out to the *exedra* where the well was situated. Achaikos suddenly realised his own thirst and drank freely, gulping the chilly water into a strained stomach. He felt more level and calmer after his body was nourished. The idea had been watered.

He found an old earthenware jar of healing poultice. He sniffed it and found it good. Yarrow and thick olive oil would mend Andreas' head, for sure, he thought. As an afterthought, he picked up a jar of honey to take with him, and all other poultices that lay unused in his cabinet. He saw a journey ahead full of unknowns and every kind of apothecaries would be useful.

He stretched over to clean away the dirt and old blood from the wound and found a deep gash in need of the poultice. He pressed it into the wound and began to wind the linen around Andreas' head, lifting it rhythmically as he wound.

It was during this process that the idea suddenly flowered and sat before him.

"Well! Indeed!" he exclaimed quietly, in a whisper, "What if?"

He would have to question this man, intently, to find his soul. If any darkness lay there, he would throw him out on the street. But if, just if, this Andreas proved worthy, what a wonderful guard, a protector, he might make on this momentous, long, frightening journey into the unknown.

Achaikos was harbouring a deep nagging worry. He was not young anymore. Unfit in the ways of fighting, in defence or otherwise. He was a man of peace.

Kiana was an adept in defence. She was the only warrior he had met who was female. But even her prowess might prove insufficient. He knew they all needed guarding. An extra set of fists would indeed be welcome.

So, he stayed watching.

... ...

It took a full night of tending Andreas. Achaikos eventually fell asleep as a weak sun began to filter into his house. He was pulled awake by an instinctive need to breathe. A weight was laying across his chest. As he opened his eyes, he found himself looking at the one good eye of Andreas, at very close quarters. It was a very rude awakening.

"Untie me! flabby old man!" came the growl through gritted teeth, "Or I will head-butt you so hard your nasal passages will smell your backside"

"Ahh dah!" Achaikos shouted, "Is that all the thanks I get for tending to your head wound!"

"Who inflicted it in the first place!" Andreas shrieked, immediately regretting the volume and the passion, as lights flashed before him and his head began to spin again in excruciating pain.

"I will untie you," Achaikos replied, keeping his voice level, "But only after you have listened to what I have to say." He wriggled out from the heavy grip of Andreas and pulled this heavy weight man upright, so he was sitting opposite him, on the floor. He noticed in an abstract fashion that blood had congealed on his exquisite Sogdian rug. "Oh, by the gods, how the carousel turns!" he thought.

And so, it was, that Achaikos explained the situation to Andreas. He watched his expressions, trying to gauge the true spirit of the man. It was proving difficult. All expressions on this craggy face were distorted and his one good eye was totally inscrutable. His body language gave nothing away. Achaikos purposely did not mention either Kiana or Tamina, nor did he speak of his huge wealth. To all intents and purposes, he was asking for a bodyguard for himself on this journey to Britannia. He was taking an incredible risk, but some instinct deep within him told of a noble character lying behind the front of a bandit, a robber, or a soldier.

"νοω ιτ ισ ψουρ τυρν το τελλ με ψουρ στορψ. βεσυρε το τελλ τηε τρυητ!" Now it is your turn to tell your story. Make sure it is the truth!" Achaikos spoke plainly.

Andreas silently stared back at him. After a long pause, he spoke.

"I am son of Simon," Andreas spoke quietly but clearly, he had a timbre in his voice of an educated man, "but no silken rugs and beautiful pottery adorned my childhood," he added, looking around with his sharp-focused eye at Achaikos' obvious wealth.

"My pater never really recovered from the earthquake, past.

Achaikos nodded silently, remembering his own fractured past.

"The burden we carry of this lascivious, contemptable city of sin greets us, suddenly, a statement from the gods," he continued quietly, considering some memory from his past.

"I grew up, as a starving child, foraging, pinching, fighting my way into a dubious adulthood, while my two sisters, were sold into slavery. My mater died of grief, so it was just my pater and me, broken men. Antioch has a hidden sin. Our very lives were shameful.

And so, I ran, straight into the arms of the Roman army. A *peditatus* is only one degree above a slave, if that. And I soon learnt the acute art of survival on the slopping sands of blood and entrails, mashed-in skulls and severed limbs.

My face will show how I sometimes failed. But I am, if nothing more, a survivor with some skill."

"And you are educated to a degree," Achaikos added, "where did you learn and with whom?"

There was a prolonged silence, filled with the sounds of a sweltering day, the strong light lit up the incessant buzzing of midges and flies now infesting the choked city air. The alarming signature of disease was dancing amid the dust motes within the blazing rays of the sun, as it hit the rugs, illuminating in sharp relief beautiful colours and the eternal flame of Zoroaster.

"I am an eternal opportunist," Andreas continued, "so in return for being "a pastime" to the *Legatus legionis,* and as a conscious appeaser, he became my tutor in all things classical."

Andreas twisted his hands violently, the bindings showing blood begin to ooze around reddened skin, and stared at Achaikos, slit-eyed and angry.

"When are you going to decide I am not going to slit your flabby throat?" he hissed, gyrating his shoulders to ease the cramp in his arms.

Achaikos ignored him.

"Is your soul comfortable in your skin, this time around?" he asked, head tilted, staring intently at his prisoner.

"If my blood, from this skin, lands on the Zoroaster's eternal flame," he replied dryly, staring down at the illuminated symbol on the Sogdian rug, "I shall be mortified, damned. So, untie me!" He noticed the flash of recognition pass Achaikos' still features and knew he had hit a note.

Achaikos slowly leant forward, his eyes not leaving Andreas, looking for the slightest hesitation in his eyes. There was none. He slowly untied him and folded the rope neatly on the ground before them.

"Should you decide to accompany me on this long and dangerous journey, you will meet me at dawn in two days' time, at the Forum Valentis. You will be driving the donkey wagon. We will be going to Byzantium overland, by the quickest but dangerous route. Should you prove worthy you will be paid well. In fact, upon reaching Byzantium, where my wealth resides, I will give you a hefty award that may see you begin your own new journey in merchandizing, like my family did, along the Silk Road."

Achaikos had not taken his eyes from Andreas. Both were adept at freezing expression, but both had the sight. He knew he had chosen well.

Andreas barely nodded. Eased himself up, rubbing aching calf muscles and swollen wrists. He turned, a complete circle, absorbing slowly every item that lay in Achaikos' *vestibulum*, and for a moment, Achaikos thought he was taking an inventory. Then he saw a smile reach that battered face, and a slight nod of appreciation was given.

Andreas was seeing his future.

… … … … … … … … …

Chapter 18

Libenter homines id quod volunt credunt
Men freely belief that which they desire
Julius Caesar

Achaikos, Tamina and Kiana had all chosen to walk the Xystus, this last time, as if in ceremony. Amyntas had charge of the wagon and the donkeys, who loped along in easy fashion. Achaikos had described the events at his home to Amyntas, who had then organised the hiding of his fortune he had kept hidden in the villam, both onto his person and hidden cleverly within his baggage of worldly goods. Amyntas had joined him the previous last two days in Antioch, sparing no criticism of the whole venture, as they both worked hard embedding the small ingots in secret pockets, and sestertii and denarii coins within hems of togas, even tunica.

Agape, Amyntas's wife, along with two of her trusted slaves spent all those hours, except for a brief few, where they snatched some sleep, sewing in the treasure to a limited wardrobe for three people. Both Tamina and Kiana had been spared this task. Achaikos ordered that they spend these last hours in each other's company, leaving behind them a few treasured memories of Antioch that had been both prison and torture to them both.

Kiana's feelings deepened for her Greek lover. The sensitivity touched them both.

Camels had been purchased, with some difficulty from a passing merchant on his way east to Bukhara, where, with the overinflated price of purchase, he would invest in at least three more to expand his caravan.

Bleary-eyed and hardly rested, Agape handed over the weighted wardrobe to Achaikos, who took them from her and instantly bent under the imposing weight of them.

"By the gods, my dear woman!" he exclaimed looking down on them, stretched along the ground before him, "What exceptional handy work".

He leapt over this pile to come and hug her, deeply and kissed her crown, wisps of unkempt curls fluttering in the breeze.

"You will be sorely missed, Achaikos, you old fool," she whispered, "remember us while you jangle away on your journey. May the gods go with you."

"Oh! And we have put the lighter sestertii coins in the *tunica* and *stolæ* and *palla*. Your women can then use these to barter to buy simple ladies' things. The denarii coins are secreted in the togas, and then all the woollen *Pallas*.

"Most important of all, Achaikos, that larger ingot. I had two slaves grind it down to gold powder in manageable bundles, to exchange without causing concern. They are hidden in all the *subligaria* where no one would think of looking. Don't foul yourself or become bladder-weak that is all I ask!"

Achaikos stared wide-eyed at this woman, his friend, and had burst out laughing, for the first time since the earthquake, his voice rumbled out like an oncoming herd of camels. It was infectious and soon all three ladies provided an octave higher chorus, until they were all breathless.

"Well if there is one thing guaranteed to halt my flow, it is several *uncia* of gold nestling around these old balls of mine!" he muttered after he had caught his breath.

"Well old man," whispered Kiana softly, reaching up to kiss his lobe, "I shall enjoy wresting them for you, shan't I?"

"Come my friend," said Amyntas jovially, clapping Achaikos on the back, "Let us have supper. Our Last Supper, eh?"

… … … … … … … … …

The two days before their rendezvous with Amyntas and his wife Agape, Tamina and Kiana had luxuriated in a rare privacy together. Kiana first took her daughter to her old domicile, the broken villa, where Achaikos had first discovered her that terrible night. They hooked arms and held hands, chatting easily to each other, blind to the devastation, as they hopped and strode through rubble and detritus that still lay on the once pristine walkways of Antioch. The sun was rising in a clear cerulean sky, cloudless and shimmering hot. Their thin sandals began to bake the soles of their feet.

"I would like to take you to the temple of Daphne and Apollo," Kiana turned to Tamina and searched for a reply. Tamina had been quiet, in her own thoughts as they wove their way through debris, scattered in piles along the streets. After all, Kiana thought, my daughter's view on life in Antioch has been desperately limited and I want to give her a precious glimpse of the wonder of Antioch before we leave for ever.

"As you wish," came the quiet reply.

"Tamina, my daughter," Kiana sensed a deep worry, "Talk to me. What troubles you?"

A ragtag of street urchins, parentless and homeless, screeched into view, hurtling past them cursing in Greek and was after the leader, who was holding a stolen treasure they ardently felt was not his to own!

Skipping effortlessly over the rubble, they disappeared into the dark depths of lawless Antioch.

"My spirit is like those urchins," she replied, "I have no base, no past to fall back on, and I envy you, Mama. Somehow you have not become fractured. Yet your life in slavery has been like mine!"

"No," Kiana retorted, "no two lives are ever identical. I am in awe of you, daughter. For I believe your life was the harder. Your punishments greater because you did not have the power inside your soul to know your true bloodline, your royalty. So now," she patted Tamina's hand and held it tight to her, "Now I want to give it back to you. Will you open your heart and accept my gift to you?"

"What do you plan, Mama," Tamina looked at her mother searching for some clue.

"Well, let us get out of this hell hole!" she said decisively, "if we start now, we will arrive at the temple of Daphne by later afternoon. We can spend the night in the forest, then my beautiful child, I would be so honoured if you would assist me in the Ab-Zohr ritual, for the cleansing of the Orontes, before we leave this city forever."

As they walked briskly westward down the Commodus' Xystus, away from the *ad hoc* market stalls, the air cleared for their tired lungs. So much of this tainted city still lay in ruins, festering with clumps of detritus that stank, and always the pall of smoke at various points, where the dead lay burning. The young Christians though, had proved good their word, in organising gangs of men in clearing the city. They would rule Antioch. It was plain to see.

Kiana took Tamina right to begin the walk up those slender, gentle slopes of Mons Silpius where the olive trees stood bare for their fruit, picked clean by hungry survivors.

She spoke quietly to Tamina of the Zoroastrian faith, that had kept her strong. How Zoroaster, the great One had lived through suffering to reach higher states of understanding and how his visions had empowered all who came after him. His belief is that humanity will poison the waters. The very water of all life. How we, as humans are created with water and it is our most sacred medium to be cleansed and cared for always. That fire is the creator. How that cleanses and re-births so many parts of the Earth and it is why the eternal flame is kept alight.

Kiana watched Tamina closely, she looked so intense, her breath shallow, as she hung onto every word like a drowning man holding a life-saving rope. And her heart just broke, seeing her young daughter tentatively reach in and open the door to her spirit she had kept closed for most of her life. Kiana heaved back the shuddering tears that threatened their walk of peace together.

… … … … … … … … …

Chapter 19

The Babaru is a Babbanitu
The Forest is a beautiful woman

They reached the temple of Daphne as the sun was sinking behind the magnificent pillars of pink marble. This is the same time, Kiana thought, that I came to plead with her, my white Goddess, to end up sinking my tears into the floor at her feet. Yet, she heard me!

She suddenly turned and hugged Tamina, tightly, her body wracked with shudders as the tears fell again. Both mother and daughter cried, leaning against the Mons Claudianus marble pillar. There was so much pain and sorrow to be bled away in tears.

"Each drop is a healing for your soul, Tamina," Kiana brushed the tears from her daughter's cheeks with her hands and rubbed them down her tunica. "you will feel stronger."

"Like this magnificent pink marble, so feminine and gentle, to honour our Goddess. It was created, in one solid chunk by hundreds of men, conscripted into work at Mons Claudianus, sweat rolling down their bodies and their lungs seared in the heat. Yet they dedicated their souls to its creation. It is perfect. Don't you think?"

"Yes, your point?" Tamina shrugged and looked to the floor.

"Daughter, listen. When I ran to here, I was sure I would find you, or that someone knew where you were. I lost all my faith when no miracle appeared. And I watered that marble in a torrent. My heart broke here!" she pointed with a grimy finger at the spot where she lay in desolation.

"Yet a miracle of sorts did happen as I prayed. The sheer power of this marble coursed through my body, so suddenly it nearly stopped my heart. It stopped my tears. In a rush of warm cascading light, I saw the creation of this temple did not come from the Gods and Goddesses at all. It came from the men who created it all. Their power collectively surpassed the Gods and honoured me in my sorrow. I knew then that we are sacred. We have created ourselves as sacred beings. And I knew you would live. I would find you as I had willed it."

"And here we are!" exclaimed Tamina, "with no home, no security, no clothes, food or even warmth!"

"And aren't you happy at the release of false things?" Kiana demanded, "We have ourselves, just us. And a good man at last, to care for us. Come, we will go to the forest for the night. Then you will realise surely that you have comfort and safety! The *Babaru* is a *babbanitu*. That is what I taught Achaikos and is what you too will learn."

The two women, who looked like sisters from the back, strolled into the dark pulsating forest and disappeared into the arms of the Goddess.

... ...

Chapter 20

Humata, Hukhta, Huvarshta
Good Thoughts, Good words, Good Deeds.
Zoroastrian pledge

The same two women appeared, at dawn, as the sky threatened with dark clouds to soak the ground. There was no breeze, a stillness hung in the air, and both women held a different energy to the evening before. They had, in the dense green darkness surrendered their souls to the forest spirits, who had come, gently yet with deep care, to sooth, blow and caress away their fear with love. It was the most peaceful and nourishing night Tamina had known. And it changed her as Kiana had prayed it would.

Now the big question hung on her lips as she looked at her daughter, who held a serene expression she had never seen before.

"Daughter," Kiana searched Tamina's soul, "Are you ready now? Will you join me in Ab-Zohr?"

Tamina was looking to the ground, the gathering clouds creating a moving dance at her feet, against the intense morning sun.

Then she looked up to that sun, feeling the warmth enter her after the damp and seductive night in the forest of magic and forgotten dreams.

"Yes," she replied, turning to give her mother the most natural full-bodied smile Kiana had ever seen. Eyes absolutely level, they each entered the other's soul and rejoiced at the true reunion at last.

... ...

Kiana led Tamina to the welcome shelter of shade created by the Mons Claudianus pink pillars rising majestically above them in the noonday sun. They had a small respite of dried food. But Kiana felt little need. Her whole body was thrumming with the energy from those pillars, even to her nerve endings, as her fingers twitched restlessly with the grizzly food. She was, she suddenly realised, entering again the world of Azura Mazda, after nearly two decades. And with that joy, coupled after her long drawn out prayer recited so many times, came her beloved daughter, here in physical from, ready and willing to join.

She began slowly, and clearly, to tell Tamina how the Ab-Zohr was performed and why.

"I believe Zoroaster was alive to witness the huge expansion of the Roman Empire," she began, slowly twisting a lock of Tamina's raven black hair, as if to ground herself in the reality that Tamina was not going to vanish in a puff of smoke, as before, to the tune of screams and bloody muck at her feet.

"He saw with growing horror the mess these Romans were making of the Earth mother. The columns behind us were gouged out of sacred mountains. They cared little about that. They just saw the glory in their skill.

"I believe Zoroaster fled to the desert, as Jesus has done after him. To seek guidance, knowledge and comfort from his God. He re-entered the world with a liturgy called the Yasna, a long service of dedication to Azura Mazda, the Angels, Fire, Water and Earth. And, the most powerful alchemical rite to protect, cleanse and purify the waters. He believed humanity, in this case Romans, will poison the waters of the world.

"We go at dawn, Tamina," Kiana continued, "To prepare the first part of the rite at the Orontes. The water has receded now so there will be a foreshore. It will stink. Have no doubt. Detritus and cadavers will still occupy space there. We will need parts of the Haoma tree, twigs. Then leaves and twigs from the Pomegranate tree, pure water and cow's milk. Bowls and two pestles. We can gather the tree parts down on the slopes, the pestle will be at the Agora, as will pure water. Cow's milk, however, might be hard to find. The fire we make when we have found the correct place for this ceremony."

Kiana paused. Tamina was silently looking to the ground, running her finger gently over the still green turf.

"And how do I, Tamina, reach this God?" she asked, head slightly cocked to one side, "or am I just an observer, set to breathe in the filth and see the destruction."

Kiana inhaled deeply, "I will teach you the Yasna liturgy now. Its meaning and power will be yours; I promise you."

She sat silently for a moment, realising just how long it had been since she recited the Yasna, every sunrise, in her private, sacred space within the haloed walls of the fire temple. "Too long ago!" she thought, as her tired brain reached deep within to pull the chant forward, in Avestan.

"I will need to sing this to you in the old tongue," she said, "And then God willing, in translation, so you may fully understand. Try and learn, Tamina for come the dawn tomorrow, I will be calling to Azura Mazda in Avestan."

She began quietly, tentatively, missing inflections and pausing for too long. She stopped and tapped the ground before her, in frustration. Tamina stretched her arm around the shoulders of her mother and smiled, hugging her gently, giving her support. She knew the reunion with her spirit world mattered almost as much as finding her daughter again.

Kiana began again, more loudly, feeling her way into the worship. She had straightened her back, instinctively as the words flowed from her to her God. Inflections and pauses now came naturally. Invocations became powerful, increasing in depth until, at the ending, her body was shaking with emotion. Devotion emanated from her in a halo of light. Tamina gasped, quietly, as she herself saw the fluctuating energy coming from her mother, as it entered her. It was an exquisite feeling of boundless, selfless Love. Mother and daughter were now truly united.

They both walked down to the slopes, holding hands in the afternoon sun, intent on gathering the haoma twigs and the pomegranate leaves, both nestling in a shady cove past the decimated and bare olive trees. No metal was used. They searched to find and ask permission for, a variety of twigs, all of which fell into their hands.

"Achaikos needs to know our intentions," Kiana remarked, thinking of him for the first time since their quest began, and felt a tinge of guilt. "We will need another day, or at the very least, a morning."

They found him waiting at the Agora. He was sitting hunched on a wall outside the hidden door, their private entrance to the Agora. He looked up, hearing the flapping of their sandals. A great smile transformed his face, and if his young mind thought him still youthful, his body denied the dream, as he creaked his old bones to stand up, shrugging balefully at his two beautiful women. He had been there a long time, patiently waiting. Kiana reached up to kiss his smiling lips and hugged him warmly.

"You dear lovely fool!" she exclaimed, "Have you been waiting here so long your body melted into stone!"

"So, it would seem," he replied, "I am at peace. It has been a warm day, and it has been an excellent time spent, thinking, making more plans."

"I am teaching Tamina the Yasna liturgy," Kiana told him, "We will be making an offering to the waters before we leave. It must be done at dawn, and preparations are necessary taking today at least. Will this be possible?" Kiana searched into his eyes and saw only affection and love coming from them. Achaikos gently cupped his large warm hands around her head, kissing her forehead.

"It is an act of supreme devotion and total stupidity! You are aware that the river is stinking! The dead have not all been removed. Disease is finding its home there. I want to forbid you both from even entertaining the notion. But I know it would be resisted. Allow me at least to create a safe place for you both." He stood firmly on the pavement before them, and Kiana knew he would not be moved.

"Yes," she said simply, "Thank you." As she led Tamina away to enter the Agora for her initiation, her daughter swivelled round to give Achaikos the biggest smile he had yet seen, and his old heart fluttered helplessly with joy.

The musty, cobweb-decorated corridors that led forever upwards to the heavens was a welcoming home. They meant safety in the darkness. It was a comfort blanket amidst the horror. Even the sanctuary to honour Abrasax held an allure to Kiana, who pledged silently to learn beside her guardian and her lover.

Mother and daughter held hands as they traversed the deep black of the outer room, only letting go when the eternal flame and the huge sculpture of Azura Mazda greeted them into warmth and safety.

Tamina chose to cover her head and face with her stola as she confidently walked over to the wood pile and picked frankincense to offer as libation to the flame. Bowing her head so close to the flame, Kiana heard her prayers, so softly spoken, yet from the heart, not in her true native language Avestan but in her adopted Greek.

"οη μαρϖελλουσ ονε ετερναλ φραμε οφ Αζυηα Μαζδα. Τραϖελ νοω το μψ ηεαρτ–κεεπ ιτ αφλαμε ωιτη ψουρ λοϖε φορ ηυμανιτψ – τηε γοοδ σουλσ. Προτεχτ υσ φρομ δαρκνεσσ ανδ εϖιλ. κεεπ ψο υρ σηινινγ λιγητ οϖερ μψ μοτηερ.

Oh, marvellous One-Eternal Flame of Ahura Mazda-travel now to my heart, keep it aflame with your love of Humanity, the good souls. Protect us from darkness and evil. Keep your shining Light over my Mother."

Tamina retreated slowly keeping her eyes on the flame, and now fed, was sparking and swaying in rhythm to her breath. It was myopic, hypnotising and calming. She turned and came back to her mother, sliding gently beside her, leaning her warm head on Kiana's shoulder. Seated comfortably next to each other, Kiana began the translation of the Yasna.

"Daughter, I can feel Ahura Mazda has entered your soul, your heart is singing. That miracle most certainly should not be explained nor described. Suffice it to say, the Great One had entered my soul too and took my life in a different direction I have never regretted.

"Can you then imagine now, the revelation that Zoroaster experienced, how his life was transformed into becoming a prophet and a great thinker? How his teachings, so bound in love for humanity and courageous against the dark ones bent on evil, made it grow and travel by word of mouth to many different villages, cities and other nations too! He is the first prophet to bring the land and water we are made of and love, into his worship. The Shining One, Ahura Mazda, made the miracle of Fire, his son. So, this Eternal Flame is Him, and we must never forget. Zoroaster was told that the dark ones of humanity would poison the waters of our world. Well, Tamina," Kiana stretched her arm to the Orontes and the destruction of Antioch, "Is it not true, now?" Tamina nodded, saying nothing.

Kiana lowered her head in sadness, a keening came into her soul, that was crushed, instantly.

"The language, my native tongue is diminishing," she uttered so low, Tamina had to lean in to hear her at all,

"Avestan was created to show the magnificence of The Shining One. Every syllable was made in his honour. And it travels straight to the heart, so much, it becomes a hymn. A song. It cannot be spoken like Akkadian, which is a lyrical language most surely."

"*Girru ed-de-su-u-nur ilāni kajānu. Eddesu!*

Ever brilliant Fire-God. Steady light of the Gods. Renewing, ever brilliant!"

"Is that Avestan?" Tamina queried, looking intently to her mother.

"Ah, no," Kiana replied, "It is Akkadian, the language of Persia. Avestan is Sogdiana, and it is our Royal tongue. Both belong to us. I can teach you, as we travel those many miles to Britannia. Then, if you decide to return, your lack of knowledge will not hamper you at all!"

"What is this Britannia like?"

"Ahh, I have been told it is both wet and cold much of the time! Even the Birrus Brittannicus does not keep out the chill!" Kiana smiled apologetically, "I am sorry daughter, but my love for this man has robbed me of any common sense!"

"Mama, he is kind. I like him," Tamina replied, watching her mother's face transform into a brilliant smile. Kiana nodded and bent over to kiss her daughter on the cheek.

"I have the Zoroastrian creed," Kiana said, detaching from Tamina, spiritual focus to the fore. She padded over to a small ornate chest that lay quietly, unobtrusively, at the base of the bass-relief that stretched magnificently from corner to corner of their temple to Ahura Mazda. Lifting the lid, which creaked from disuse, she retrieved a silken vellum, pure goat skin, upon which was inscribed the Avestan invocation, a pledge for all the incumbent's life, to the worship of Ahura Mazda, the Shining One.

"I will translate for you and you must agree with a declaration to each invocation," Kiana said gently, as she re-positioned herself next to Tamina, snuggling up to her, as they were before.

"I curse the Dævas!
I declare myself a Mazda-worshipper,
A Supporter of Zarathustra, hostile to the Dævas,
fond of Ahura's teaching,
a praiser of The Amesha Spentas.
I ascribe all good to Ahura Mazda, "and all the best,"
Asha-Endowed, splendid, xwarena-endowed,
Whose is the cow, whose is Asha, whose is the light,
may those blissful areas be Filled with light".
"I so declare!"

came Tamina's strong, confident first declaration. Kiana smiled as she looked to the following part.

"I choose the good Spenta Armaiti for myself: let her be mine. I renounce the theft and robbery of the cow, and the Damaging and plundering of the Mazdayasnian settlements."

"I so choose the good Spenta Armaiti," came the reply.

Kiana continued: "I want freedom of movement and Freedom of dwelling for those with homesteads to those who dwell upon the earth with their cattle. With reference for Asha, and offerings, offered up, I vow This: I shall nevermore damage or plunder the Mazdayasnian settlements, even if I must risk life and limb."

"I swear," Tamina smiled, thinking mildly that she may never see a Mazdayasnian settlement, let alone want to plunder one!

Kiana read her thoughts, "It may come to pass Tamina, in future times, if you do decide, or if *we* decide, to return to our homeland. Then you may remember these words and be thankful."

"I reject the authority of the Dævas," Kiana continued,

"the wicked, no-good, lawless, evil-knowing,
The most druj-like of beings
The foulest of beings, the most damaging of Beings.

I reject the Dævas and their comrades, I reject the demons Yatu and their comrades: I reject any who harm beings. I reject them with my thought's words, and deeds. I reject them publicly Evan as I reject the head Authorities, so too do I reject the hostile Followers of the druj."

"*I so fervently swear with all my heart to the reject these demons and to do so publicly!*" Tamina hissed this through clenched teeth. Kiana felt her fury, knowing she was, in her mind, bringing her tormentor to justice in a public arena. And she knew it would be repeated many times, until it no longer gripped her.

"As Ahura Mazda taught Zarathustra at all discussions, at all Meetings, at which Mazda and Zarathustra Conversed even as Zarathustra rejected the authority Of the Dævas, so I also reject, as Mazda Worshipper and supporter of Zarathustra, the authority of the Dævas, even as he, the Asha-endowed Zarathustra, has rejected them."

"I reject the Dævas, and all authority of them!" declared Tamina, now in the full stream of the creed's meaning and its loving claim on her injured soul.

"As the belief of the waters, the Belief of the plants, the belief of the well Made original Cow: as the belief of Ahura Mazda who created the cow and the Asha-endowed Man: as the belief of Zarathustra, the belief of Kavi Vishtaspa, The belief of both

Frashaostra and Jamaspa: As the belief of each of the Saoshyants Saviours - fulfilling destiny and Asha-endowed - So, I am a Mazda-worshipper of this belief And teaching."

"I profess myself a Mazda-worshipper A Zoroastrian, having vowed it and professed it. I pledge myself to the Well-thought thought, I pledge myself to the Well-spoken word, I pledge myself to the well-done action."

"I pledge myself to the Mazdayasnian religion, which caused the Attack to be put off and weapons put down: Which upholds khvætvadatha, Asha-endowed: Which of all religions that exist or shall be, is the greatest, the best, and the Most beautiful: Ahuric, Zoroastrian. I ascribe all good to Ahura Mazda. This is the creed of the Mazdayasnian religion"

A silence fell, the gentle crackle of wood flame dancing up into the spirit world to be taken and held by Ahura. Kiana found she was holding her breath. Her daughter had yet to complete her initiation. Tamina's head was bowed, leaving her face curtained by her blue-black hair, stretching almost to her knees. Then Kiana saw the drops hit her tunica, and spread, followed by many more.

"Your vows, my sweet daughter, you need to complete," she whispered gently.

A void of silence met her and her felt a deep sorrow waft over to her. She waited. There were no more words except those important ones to come only from Tamina's mouth. And they must be heart felt.

Tamina suddenly drew a huge intake of breath, as if her life had ebbed away from her.

"I *profess myself a Mazda-worshipper and I pledge myself to the Mazdayasnian religion,*" came the final utterance, clear and strong.

Kiana, let her own breath escape, the one that she had been holding. In relief and joy her beloved daughter's spirit came to greet her at last.

… … … … … … … … …

Chapter 21

Να είσαι ένας από αυτούς που ανανεώνουν τον κόσμο

Be amongst those who renew the world.

Zoroastrian pledge.

Ab-Zohr
The Parahaoma rite

The women discovered that Achaikos had laboured long while they were in the Temple. He had scoured the foreshore of the Orontes to find a small safe area for them to fulfil their Ab-Zohr without contracting diseases now rampant along the festering shoreline. He insisted they reach it by boat, which he secured from a former sailor who maintained one of his own vessels. Kiana became even more intrigued and impressed by this benefactor who held a fortune in Byzantium.

The pre-dawn sky shed a faint glow across the murky waters of the Orontes. Ripples from the small boat that held, crammed into each other, Tamina, Kiana, Achaikos and his rower, caught that glow, making a gentle pattern across the water. It was peaceful, yet seductive, as those same ripples eased around the bloated and stinking cadavers that bumped against their little vessel.

"*I curse the Daevas!*" Tamina hissed, holding her sacred bundle close to her chest.

"And so, it is, dear heart," Kiana whispered, as she halted in her precis translation of the Ab-Zohr. Tamina's mind was still full of the creed. Kiana knew too much knowledge too soon would collapse in on itself, leaving a void filled with miserable confusion.

"And so," she continued, softly giving Tamina some knowledge of the ancient Avestan rite, "After the first pressing is done, the second begins with a certain part of the Yasna chanting, this time using milk, "We present these Zaothras to the beneficial Creator, Ahura Mazda, the resplendent, the glorious, and for that of the Bountiful Immortals, I desire to approach this Haoma with my praise, offered, as it is, with punctilious sanctity, for a blessing. And this fresh milk, and this plant Hadhanaepata. And, as an act of worship to the beneficent waters, I desire to approach these Zaothras, with my praise offered with punctilious sanctity, having the Haoma with them, and the flesh, with the Hadhanaepata. And I desire to approach the Haoma-water with my praise for the beneficent waters; and I desire to approach this plant for the barsman with my praise, and the well-timed prayer for blessings, that which has approached to accept our homage, and the memorized recital and the fulfilment of the good Mazdayasnian Faith, and the heard recital of the Gathas, and the well-timed and successful prayer for blessings, that of the holy lord of the ritual order. And I desire to approach these wood-billets and their perfume with praise - thine, the Fire's O Ahura Mazda's son! Yea, I desire to approach all good things with my praise, those Which Mazda made, and which have the seed of sanctity (from within) for the propitiation of Ahura Mazda, and of the Bountiful Immortals, and of Sraosha the blessed and of Ahura Mazda's Fire, the lofty ritual lord!"

Achaikos was just a shadow, head bent to his chest, in the pre-dawn inky blackness, as his oarsman deftly swept them along the Orontes. But his old heart was pounding in his chest, as he looked up occasionally to catch a nuanced phrase from Kiana, teaching her daughter. He was hanging onto every word, as the truth slowly dawned on him. Not only was she a Sogdian princess of royal blood, but a Zoroastrian priestess of the highest acclaim. He desperately wanted to stretch his arms out to her in deep love and passion, but desisted, as they would all have been tossed overboard to taste the poison waters of the Orontes.

"Oh! Sacred river," he shouted silently to his god Abrasax, "When will she be healed?"

"Patience and Time," came the silent answer back to him, "and the good works of good men, whomever they are and under whose Name they praise and pray to!"

Achaikos smiled, bent his head to his chest, and listened.

"Now Tamina, the mortar having been pounded, is mixed with milk and pounded a lot more. I am giving you this task, my love. Then you place it down until Yasna 31 when you pound for a last time, and strain the liquid into the bowl, putting the mortar next to the fire to dry, as with the first pressing. Then we make the offering. First to the Fire, then to the water holding Ahura Mazda always in the forefront.

"I offer my sacrifice and homage to thee, the Fire, as a good offering, and an offering with our hail of salvation, even as an offering of praise with benedictions, to thee, the Fire, Oh Ahura Mazda's son! Meet for sacrifice art thou and worthy of our homage, may'st thou be in the houses of men, who worship Mazda. Salvation be to this man who worships thee in verity and truth, with wood on hand, and Barsman ready, with flesh in hand, and holding too, the mortar. And may'st thou be ever fed with wood as the prescription orders. Be thou aflame, be forever without fail in flame."

"Tamina, you then gift the first mortar to the fire. As I go into the Ab-Zohr, you will keep mixing the parahaoma, pouring between both bowls and the remaining mortar, until all three have the same liquid. Do you understand?"

Tamina nodded silently and looked over to Achaikos suddenly to see his head sunk into his chest.

"He has fallen asleep Mama," she whispered. Only to watch his head shoot up and stare at her with a smile that said to never underestimate an old man, thrice a young girl's age!

"And so now to the important part of the Ab-Zohr, Tamina, offering to the waters. Listen well," Kiana continued.

"I will praise the water, Ardvi Sura Anahita, the wide flowing and healing in its influence, efficacious against the Daevas, devoted to Ahura's lore, and to be worshipped with sacrifice within the corporeal world, furthering all living things and holy, helping on the increase and improvements of our herds and settlements, holy, and increasing our wealth, holy and helping on the progress of our Province, holy as she is. Ardvi Sura Anahita, who purifies the seed of all male beings, who sanctifies the wombs of all women to the birth, who makes all women fortunate in labour, who brings all women a regular and timely flow of milk. Ardvi Sura Anahita, with a volume sounding from afar, which is alone equal in its bulk to all the waters which flow upon the earth, which flows down with mighty volume from high Hukaiya to the sea Vouru-kasha. And all the gulfs in Vouru-kasha are stirred, all the middle doth well up when Ardvi Sura Anahita rushes in, when she plunges foaming into them, she, whose are a thousand tributaries, and a thousand outlets, and each as it flows in, and rushes out is a forty days' ride in length."

"And now we are nearly finished. We will take the sanctified and holy water to the Orontes and gift the waters."

Kiana released a huge breath, in relief and tiredness, which had suddenly overcome her. There was still so much to achieve, as she looked over to the dawn. A haze of glimmering light eased itself above the horizon, hinting at the sun who had awoken and was rising to make a new day for the Antiochians.

Achaikos eased his aching muscles into movement.

"We are very close now," he spoke to Kiana, "And thank you for the lesson. I am in your debt, as always. A wonderful teaching from a priestess of Zoroaster!"

"Ah, so now you know, priest to Abrasax," Kiana moved gently over to sit with her rescuer, "I believe we now reside on a level playing field, no?"

"Indeed, yes, and it is wonderful!" Achaikos' heart was full. He could say no more. Actions would speak much louder than any words, and he was not permitted yet, to express them.

… … … … … … … …

The sky laid washes of delicate pink and faint yellow to mingle with wispy clouds. An augury for a perfect day. Yet the ugly waters of the Orontes slapped a deep wound on the souls of those gathered on the foreshore that morning. Daevas forever choosing the evil, bad actions, were lurking around them, as the women prepared the parahaoma, on their knees, shoulders hunched in the business of pounding the leaves, twigs and water together to form the first pressing. Kiana was chanting in old Avestan, Tamina listening intently as she worked the pestle, picking up intent where she could. She began to hum, and Kiana smiled softly, gently nudging her in approval. Tamina felt at peace and at home in her skin for the first time since their tearful re-union.

And Achaikos' heart was fit to burst, as he watched his women reach the heights, in their awful surroundings, as they prepared to heal the waters for Zoroaster. Achaikos was not alone, for he had asked his old friend Amyntas Argyis to secure the ground on which they now stood. And he had done them proud. He stood now close to Achaikos, and the fire he had lit to keep healthy and strong for the priestess. Its flames flickered up into the still dark sky, casting dancing shadows around them as the wind picked up and became lively itself. The world was waking up and the women felt the energy building.

They were shaded and protected by a group of trees, whose whispering leaves sang their own song in the breeze, as they slanted towards the water's edge. The men standing, hands clasped before them, were silently protecting the women at their precious work. They were their guardians; Achaikos invoking the protection of Abrasax for them. The invocation was only just visible as his lips were continually moving in silent prayer. He knew full well the danger present. The evil ones still had dominion in this shattered land.

As the first pressing came to an end, the mortar was brought by Tamina, to dry by the fire. She looked up and gave Achaikos a beautiful smile. Amyntas watched as his old friend just simply expanded and beamed in return.

"Hey, my old timer," he whispered, as Achaikos shook himself back to the job in hand, "You are winning there. She actually likes you!"

"Hmmm, I know. 'Tis a miracle for sure. I must have done something right, but I'm truly vexed to know what it was!"

"Did anyone tell you; you have a glass face?" Amyntas replied, looking closely at his friend, "Maybe it is the love you hold for her mother that she sees."

"Hmph," muttered Achaikos, feeling a warm glow nonetheless, as he continued to keep guard.

Kiana was now entering the Yasna liturgy, keeping her breathing level and the intonation sound and strong. She never faltered. She was transported back to the Fire Temple, in her private space where she sang to Ahura Mazda. All those intervening years of horror evaporating as the Yasna took her spirit over and held it in awe. Tamina watched, herself transfixed at her mother's transformation. She knew now where her liberation was coming from. She could see clearly where freedom from the pain lay. Within the all-encompassing arms of Ahura Mazda.

Achaikos too, was being transported away from the pain of his Fall with his God Abraxas holding his heart.

Amyntas just stared, baffled. He did not have one spiritual genome in his entire body. Or so he would like to fool people with that statement. His good actions and huge heart spoke otherwise.

It was time for the second pressing. Both women now worked pounding the mixture. Then Tamina lay the parahaoma near the fire to dry.

The morning sun was cresting over the horizon, facing them across the river. Amyntas saw the light catch the bloated form of a cadaver, being gently pushed to shore by the tide, knocking it as if still alive, urging it to breathe again.

He shuddered and stepped closer to his friend who was oblivious of all in the temporal world. He wished he could join him.

The Ab-Zohr began with Kiana pitching the hymns to a higher level. Now it became intense, and emotions were being brought into actively empower the parahaoma. The first parahaoma was gifted to the Fire with libations in ancient Avestan that carried their own deep meanings.

Kiana was in trance.

Tamina was pouring the water between bowls until eventually all three contained equal amounts.

There came a pause, a silence heavy with emotion hanging still in dawn air. Kiana then signalled to Tamina to bring the bowl with the parahaoma to the water's edge.

Amyntas took a sharp intake of breath. They were walking straight to the cadaver, in all its gory detail.

He rushed forward to heave the thing away. Achaikos swung his arm out to hold him.

"No," he said plainly, "There is only one way to deal with the Dark Twin. That is to shine a brighter light. To bring the light to him. That is exactly what Kiana is doing. Leave her be!"

And so, it was, that early dawn on the shores of the Orontes, flowing through a shattered Antioch, that a Zoroastrian priestess gifted the Aban and invoked the power of Aredvi Sura Anahita to heal her. Then in a spontaneous action she asked Tamina to bring forth second parahaoma whereupon she invoked that same power to heal the soul of the person lying before them in the murky water. A blue haze glowed around the water. They had been heard. And it was done.

… … … … … … … … …

Chapter 22

Stultum enim senectute consilium quid absurdius augere viaticum iter propius accedimus destinatum
Advice in old age is foolish- for what can be more absurd than to increase provisions for the road, the nearer we approach our journey's end.
Marcus Tullius Cicero

No-one in the smallest caravan of three camels and a donkey-driven cart turned their heads for one final look at Antioch. Their tortured memories were leaving them with each thud of the camel's hooves on hardened sand. And each thud lightened their hearts.

Except for Andreas, who had no one to bid goodbye to, and Tamina and Kiana, who both had each other. It was left to Achaikos to hug his dear friend Amyntas and Agape his wife in fond farewells. Now it was done, he felt years being stripped away from him. They were indeed moving at a fair pace for Byzantium, overland and through desert.

They carried very little, so the camels were speeding, leaving the donkey cart, which held much more, to disappear behind them until it and Andreas were only a dot on the far horizon. They halted to wait and quench their thirst. The sun was fast sinking into the dunes on the far horizon. When Andreas did eventually catch up with them, his shadow was long and his patience thin.

"This is an unfair distribution of weight," he exploded, "and this damned donkey knows it!"

"Agreed," said Achaikos calmly, "You know what? We will ditch the donkey and the cart. I was wrong. We will purchase another camel and divide the weight evenly between us."

"Hah," Andreas continued, temper flaring, "Wrong thinking. Bad thinking old man! Thinking I am nothing but your slave, on a donkey with a cart! Absurd for the desert!"

"Agreed also," Achaikos replied, equally calmly, refusing to be baited into argument which would end in fists, he was sure. But he leant over to whisper in Andreas's ear, caked with sweat and sand, "Remember destitution! Look at it well, for you will relive it in the blinking of your one good eye, if you do not respect me, my women and the deal we agreed!"

The women looked on. Kiana had her head to one side, cheeks sucked in. That was a bad sign. When her nostrils started to flare, Andreas would need to duck, thought Achaikos. Andreas nodded silently bending down to take the water bag to relieve his thirst. He could feel the electricity in the air and the impending threat from Kiana, who had been vocal, mostly in Akkadian, at the very outset of their journey, and therefore untranslatable. But the intent was clear enough. She would, without compunction, dismember this vagabond and opportunist, and be very slow about it.

"There is an oasis of sorts just over there," Achaikos spoke up, pointing to the greenery half-hidden by sand dunes, and diverting the antagonism sparking in Kiana's face, stated clearly, "We will rest, sleep through the afternoon heat. I propose we move on and travel through the night, North-eastwards to reach Pessinus by morning. It is at least 80 *stadions* from here, so the camels must be rested to reach a good gallop."

"Agreed," said Kiana, looking over to Andreas to bend her camel's knee to dismount. He obliged with a wide smile and exaggerated bowing as he helped her down.

"And the others!" she retorted as she spun round to make her way to the small water hole. She knew she was acting like a spoilt royal princess, but every nerve in her body was tensed. She believed this Andreas to be a pure robber, and a Daevas. No good would come of the association.

Kiana settled down by a rock that supported her tired spine and opened the food bag, gratefully chewing olives stuffed with cheeses, flatbread and dried meat. Tamina joined her, as they talked between mouthfuls and relaxed in the heat. Achaikos was constructing a canvas shelter above their heads, pounding in stakes with rope that would withstand some wind, if it came. He then walked over to Andreas, settling himself down to talk to his companion, accepting full responsibility for the choice he had made.

"If we are going to be attacked," he turned to Andreas, looking straight at him, getting to the point of why he was there at all, "it will be here. Wandering Sassanids, or Nomads would view us as easy targets."

"Accepted and understood," muttered Andreas, "I will take the first watch. Go! Rest with your women, old man." He sat, arms resting on drawn-up knees, holding, with whitened knuckles, a lethal looking curved sabre, edges serrated along one side.

Achaikos knelt beside Kiana and Tamina, "He is useful Kiana, we need him."

"Go to sleep, you dear man," Kiana replied, brushing his cheek tenderly, "I will watch the Watcher!"

... ...

And so, she did, hardly withdrawing her gaze from him. He, on the other hand, held her intense stare for the shortest time, smiling only slightly, as he shifted his position to look outward to the far horizon. She searched for his soul, his spirit and found it hiding, tiny as an old walnut, encased in walls so thick, she knew his was a battered life from a very early age. And those walls had been cemented together with violence and supreme cunning. He was a younger Achaikos in every aspect. With sudden insight, Kiana knew just why her guardian and her lover had chosen Andreas. He wanted to save him. Perhaps that was the slimmest thread of honour that vibrated between them. And she was certain Andreas knew it also.

So, she gave up on him. It was a shared destiny between the young man and older master. She looked down on her daughter asleep, snuggled into the arm of Achaikos, who, with his head rammed into his ample chest was snoring in vibrato, his lower lip oscillating to the tenor while his nostrils quivered to the soprano.

"Oh, Hecate!" Kiana smiled whispering to her Goddess, "Help me find the herbs to make a decoction to stop this!"

She was being lulled to her own sleep by the symphony, when she became instantly alert. Andreas had suddenly shot up, sabre in hand, striding away from the safety of the tree and rock outcrop. Kiana shot her head round to see for herself the plumes of sand building rapidly on the horizon. The sun now a milky disc, trapped within the sand swirls.

Kiana felt icy spikes hit her spine and her heart stopped. She gasped in horror, as her past came to meet her again.

"*Sassanids*!" she hissed not able to find her voice. She had already reached inside her tunica for the curved sword she had acquired from the vagabond African boy. Holding it classically two-handed, legs bent, Andreas just stared open-mouthed at her.

"Why in the name of Hades does that old man hire me, when he already has a warrior?" Andreas questioned her.

"Oh, you know full well the answer to that lug head!" she scornfully replied, "He is after saving you from your tormented past. Honour him if you will. It is a wonderful gift he offers. If we survive *this*, that is."

Andreas squinted out to the oncoming sand cloud.

"I don't feel the thud of camel hooves, many hundreds of them that would shake up that kind of cloud. There is no glint of metal."

"*Sandstorm*!" They both shouted in unison, effectively waking up the sleeping pair behind, who wriggled in a hectic disentanglement of robes and blankets.

"Grab the camels and bring them here by the rocks," shouted Achaikos to Andreas, as he rushed to get the wagon and donkey to a safer place within the small oasis.

"We have but *seconda* to secure everything."

Kiana hastily untethered the canvas to haul it and the line of ropes over to the rocky outcrop. She and Tamina swung the heavy canvas over the rock and between them, secured it with ropes and hooks, into the ground.

"Tighter to the ground, Kiana," Achaikos shouted, "leave nothing for the wind to get underneath!"

"Help me bring the wagon up to shield us and the donkey against the storm, Andreas," he shouted as the wind began to pick up around them and the sand began its own dance. As tunica and robes began to swirl around them, so the elemental force of Nature took charge of the desert and reduced them, in its magnificence, to mere grains of sand, human, camel and donkey slithered into a huddled, communal mass, and waited.

When it hit them full force, it literally drew the very breath from their lungs. They hugged each other tighter under the canvas between the rock and the wagon. Eyes were screwed tightly shut, as a mere grain of sand hurtling in at that speed would blind them instantly. A grain of sand became the mightiest enemy. Yet they felt calm amidst this destruction. A binding part of Nature. Of Creation, itself. Anger at the destruction never found a place to rest in their hearts. Just acceptance.

Time became inconsequential. But the noise was not. It was deafening. And it was in its lessening that the taut muscles began to relax, and their frozen consciousness began to revive. Muscles twitched that had become fixed. And as the battering lessened, lungs drew in more air. Each one took on their individuality again.

"What about the camels?" croaked Andreas, to no one in particular.

"They knew what to do," replied Achaikos, who had survived more sandstorms than he would care to remember, "Look for yourself. I have witnessed it many times. Their action is built into their very souls. Passed from mother to young one."

Outside the protection of the canvas, a new sand hill had been created. Until it shook to reveal three humps so close together it looked like a trinity of little hills. And they had laid their heads to each other in a curve behind the humps, their long eyelashes protecting their sight. They each slowly, languidly got up, totally unperturbed and ambled over to the water hole to take their fill, knowing it might be days before they would drink again.

"We need to make haste," Achaikos commanded in some urgency, smacking the sand away from his tunica and woollen rug, "the storm is heading west, but the wind can change in a moment and come right back to overcome us!"

"We need to leave the wagon here!" Andreas said, "Surely there is nothing on that wagon worth dying for?"

"Kiana, Tamina, please take your most precious items, and leave the rest to the Nomads." Achaikos commanded, leaving them in no doubt. Yet, they had very little. It would be easy for them. Kiana took her Oud, a shawl in woven silk, honouring the Zoroastrian Eternal flame emblazoned in an intricate pattern to highlight her Sogdian name, Sumaya, Soul of Flowers. And her blue pottery vase, made by her relatives in Sogdiana, and whisked away that night of her flight to the Temple. Somehow, they all survived.

Tamina stood silently behind her mother, hands clasped behind her. She owned nothing but her willpower to survive and the clothes she stood up in. Kiana suddenly swirled around to face her daughter.

"Take them," she insisted, "All of them. They are yours by right. Especially the shawl. It has your name woven into it!" Tamina reached out and placed them on her heart. All except the Oud.

"That must stay with you, Mama, "I am no musician!"

"Come, you women!" Achaikos hustled them both back to their camels. Sorting through his possessions took much longer. A materialist by nature, it was hard to relinquish his goods. Eventually it was done, and the three camels loaded with goods, food and water, pounded onwards, with the donkey tethered, bouncing on his small legs in frantic fashion to keep up.

They sped through the night stopping only once to give the donkey needed rest.

As the dawn light spread across the sky, they saw, sitting proudly in the Syrian desert, the famed sanctuary of Cybele, Pessinus.

... ...

Chapter 23

Pessinus

Iterum redit iratum dum rationi repugnant
An angry man is again angry with himself when he returns to reason.

Achaikos watched both Tamina and Kiana kick their tired camels into a faster trot. Leaning forward as if to spur them on, they both stared at the growing spectacle before them. That famed city in the middle of the desert. Both those camels must be female, Achaikos mused, smiling, as they picked up speed, scenting the feminine that had ruled that sanctuary for millennia.

"What is their hurry?" Andreas spoke into Achaikos' left ear, sitting as he was, crushed between that portly Grecian priest and a camel's hump. It had been devastating on his spine, not to mention his other equipment he felt was crushed beyond repair.

"They are galloping to meet the mother of all the Gods, Andreas. A once-in-a-lifetime treasure to be savoured. To me Cybele is Gaia, the primal Earth Mother. To others she is Rhea, Hecate in Byzantium. I believe the Northern tribes call her Nerthus. And she is mighty indeed."

"Have you not heard of Her?" Achaikos twisted round to face his companion, who, at the movement winced and groaned audibly as his equipment was again twisted badly.

"No!" he hissed, vainly attempting to create some small space between him and Achaikos, "My whole life was the shady end of the palatium, the stadium and the circus, Priest! I was more interested in not starving to death than praying to some goddess, who had no interest in me."

"Hmm, well in that case, seeing as you are a materialist through and through" Achaikos conjectured, "Your time here, after you have washed that smell away, would be well served by visiting the other temple to King Midas. If you pray sincerely; you do know how to pray, I assume, he may gift much wealth. He is renowned for it and this is the only place where the God resides in the entire world, so I believe."

Achaikos prodded the camel into some speed, although it was languishing in inertia. He got the whip out and applied it to the poor beast's flank. The camel hissed and sprayed spit right into Achaikos' face. Andreas exploded with laughter until it hurt.

The women had disappeared into Pessinus. Achaikos became anxious to keep them in view.

"Dismount, Andreas," he commanded, "Now!"

Achaikos attacked his tunica ferociously, dislodging the *denarii* from its hiding place. He noticed Andreas' eyebrow shoot upwards.

"δο νοτ εϖεν τηινκ αβουτ ιτ! *Tu cumulus excrementum*" He growled in Greek, then Latin, "Here is enough *denarii* to see you clean, fed and housed for the night! We will meet at noon. Oh, and get what you can for the donkey. There will be enough to purchase your camel. It is yours."

With that, he raised the whip high and brought it down with force. The camel shot forward and galloped towards that hallowed white marbled city, shimmering in the early morning sun, with pink and turquoise hues reflecting off the columns and magnificent facias.

The white marble archway, glinting in the early sun, throwing into bas-relief the figures of Gods and Goddesses, with people in worship, all looking upward to the arch's apex, where the exquisite portrait of Cybele captivated all newcomers. As Achaikos sped towards the southern entrance, the archway grew rapidly forcing heads to arch upwards. He entered the fabled city of Pessinus.

He shook his grey locks, to clear the trance state that was overwhelming, half smiling, as he knew he was completely captivated by Her. He had travelled this route so many times, this archway should have remained what it was; an archway. The white marble was o.

hacked from the quarries at Istiklalbagi by a hundred ill-treated slaves. And it was to the residential quarters of Germakalonia 6 *stadions* from the *cardo maximus* that Achaikos would guide his women. It was important that he find them. As he galloped down the colonnaded street, head swinging to and fro, he caught sight of them as two disappearing figures, running up the steps to the *Peripteros*, the temple to Cybele.

He whipped the camel's flanks in a frenzy to get within earshot. He must halt them. It would be disastrous if they entered unannounced, dishevelled and odorous, smelling of camel and desert! He knew Kiana should have known better, but he also realised her need to enter this temple, and it absolutely overcame her reason. She was caught in the childlike naivety of her daughter and loving it. The freedom was intoxicating.

"*Prohibeo*," he yelled, a lone dishevelled vagrant on a camel who was spitting purulent venom into the air, catching anyone unfortunate enough to be passing down wind.

Kiana and Tamina both stopped and turned around, thankfully just before disappearing into the temple and lost from view.

"Do not enter the temple, I beg you!" shouted Achaikos, "Preparations and mediation are required." He knocked the camel's foreleg, who made no gentle bend for him. Instead it made a ferocious thumping down action to settle on the paved slabs, that hurtled Achaikos forwards, so his hair caught some of the camel's spittle hanging in mid-air and he was unceremoniously dumped on the ground.

"That damned creature is to be rugged, I say," he shouted, "He will be someone's dinner tomorrow. I would not taint my palate on his disgusting meat!"

Kiana and Tamina turned away and hunched together, arms around each other in quiet hysteria, shoulders gyrating with each intake of breath. After they calmed down and Achaikos swatted and flicked the desert dirt from his tunica and robes, they both looked to each other.

"Take my camel, dear man," Kiana said, "He is placid and kind as long as you do not beat him with the whip."

"We all need to refresh ourselves in the baths," Achaikos ordered, assuming charge of the situation, "Then we eat, while I give you the traditional teachings on Cybele and how this whole city is still run by the Priests." Achaikos then turned on his heel, his pride maliciously injured by a crazy camel. He was tired, even worn out and this had almost been the last straw to break this camel's back!

... ...

Sinking into the hot water, just laying against the edge of the marble, watching the ripples dance over the mosaics that spread in their beauty across the entire floor of the baths, stilled the mind into luxurious submission. Cybele lay in the centre of a huge medallion mosaic, her clear eyes piecing through the gentle water to fix on whoever dared look. Kiana issued a deep prayer of gratitude just to be alive at this moment, with her daughter beside her. She realised quite suddenly, and in peace, that this was the first moment of a peace she had not been allowed to own until now. She knew, soul deep, that her life was indeed being re-born at this moment, staring into the eyes of the Mother of all the Gods. And she submerged her whole body into the depths, staying there, hair flowing free to be cleansed of desert dirt, until her lungs screamed for air. She shot up with joy, facing upwards as if reaching for the heavens, and smiling in genuine happiness, she went to join her guardian and protector, to offer him her gratitude and her love.

They each emerged from that glorious cleansing, with a fragrant oiled massage reaching every tired muscle, springing them into tingling activity, jauntily striding out onto the *cardo maximus*. The noonday sun oscillated in white bright rays from a turquoise sky. The colonnade pillars of white marble rose in royal acclaim to meet that sun in shimmering reflections. And Achaikos' spine stretched, and he walked with a surer step.

Pessinus was fed by the seasonal tide river of Gallus. The Romans, true to their innate skill in capturing that element of water and bending it to their will, had created the miracle of the Pessinus canal stretching 500 *passus* in length and 13 *passus* wide. Ripples flowing casually out from the oars of passing boats, sent sparkles of intense sunlight so bright they left cyan and magenta after-shadows, so that *Cardo maximus* became, as was intended, a pure light show of colour.

The presence of water cooled the walkway to a pleasant amble and shade was provided by the tall fir trees of Cypress. They saw olive and orange groves to the edge of this city in the desert.

"My stomach is slicing itself up, for want of sustenance," remarked Andreas, who had joined them, clean and not foul smelling. Not from the luxurious baths, Achaikos thought silently, most likely from falling into the canal water, for free.

"There is a theatre over there," Achaikos pointed to the west, "it is surrounded with food stalls. We can eat there. You, Andreas, can enjoy an afternoon of gladiatorial butchery. If you so wish. We, of a priestly caste, must adjourn festivities to prepare for our homage to Cybele."

"Hmph!" exclaimed Andreas, his one good eye widening to stare at his benefactor, then reducing it to a slit, creating intentionally, a look of sheer malevolence.

It failed to have the intended impact. Achaikos exploded in loud guffaws, to look askance at his rescued waif and stray.

They walked on, arms linked together, Kiana chatting happily to Achaikos, and Tamina, listening and joining in when some comment had caught her attention. It was a relaxed and companionable walk. Andreas felt totally excluded, and for some reason he could not grasp, he felt angry and sad.

"What did these arrogant upstart religious idiots mean to *him*? he raged silently. Then, abruptly, he stopped for a second, watching the trio walk on. The crazy bastard is baiting me! he realised, quickening his step to catch up.

Achaikos spun round on his heel to hold Andreas firmly by the arms, leading him away from the women so they could speak alone.

"You are baiting me with your laughter. You think I am nothing!" Andreas spat out, thin daggers of hate reaching their target. Achaikos sighed deeply, shaking the barbs away.

"You remind me of myself," he said tilting his head, questioning this opponent, this vandal, ... this son!

"I knew you, the first moment you regained yourself, in my house. I recognised your antagonism, bitterness and sheer guts to fight the losing cards dealt to you in this shoddy life!

"And I trust you. Otherwise, why in the name of Abraxas do you think you are here, and not lying in some hole in Antioch where I would have put you, had I thought for one moment you held bad thoughts towards me and mine!"

"Hmph!" Andreas expelled exasperation through his nostrils, yet remained silent, looking intensely at this aging man.

"You are like the son I never had," Achaikos said simply, quietly looking at the ground. "We have but a few days before we reach Byzantium. I would like to share a good amphora of wine with you at the *popina*, we can share stories..."

Andreas remained silent, his one good eye intensely expressing all the astonishment he felt in duplicate. His other eye scarred and battered, exuded the frozen cynicism that had been his signature. Now something else, warm and strange was entering his mind. And his heart. Without any warning, his one good eye filled with tears. He bowed his head to hide the emotion that had suddenly overwhelmed him.

Achaikos took but a second to fold him in his ample arms, both silently rocking in an embrace that left Kiana open-mouthed in shock.

"By the horrors of Hecate," she muttered to Tamina, "This misfit family is growing by the moment. Have a care daughter, you might be finding a brother is being added to this one!"

"Oh, he's nay so bad," she replied, smiling indulgently, "and he will be gone in a few days. Off to make his own wealth on the money from Achaikos' fortune."

"Could these be the tears of a crocodile?" Kiana mused silently.

··· ··· ··· ··· ··· ··· ··· ··· ···

Chapter 24

Cybele

Μόνο όταν η καρδιά ενός έθνους, η μητέρα, είναι γονατιστή, αυτό το έθνος θα αποτύχει και θα περάσει από εμάς. Θυμηθείτε το Forst, γιατί εκεί θα με βρείτε πάντα: Babaru Babbanitu

It is only when the heart of a nation, the Mother is on her knees, will that nation fail and pass from us. Remember the forest, for there you will always find me.

Babaru Babbanitu

"My beautiful ladies," Achaikos had his hands pressed together before his ample chest, as if in earnest prayer. His head bent forward, looking at his "charges," like a benevolent patron giving them a course in spiritual protocol.

Both eyebrows of his "beautiful women" met in unison to project the deepest frown. And they simply stared at him. He was not to be side-tracked and blundered on regardless.

"Cybele is the mother of the gods, and so far-flung is her power and dominion, she is known by many names. In my homeland she is Rhea. Yet here is Pessinus, where her image fell from heaven, she is known as Agdistis. The priests here are possessive of her. They rule with a strict protocol that prohibits many. In Byzantium she is known as Hecate, who saved the city. So, Kianna you already feel a close affinity with Her."

"Achaikos, be careful!" Kiana, whose eyebrows had now risen to meet her hairline, took his aging hands in hers and squeezed, "you misunderstood my run to the temple, old man! I was pulling my enthusiastic daughter back from embarrassing us all. Now, let me explain.

"We have both saved our Ab-Zohr water, to gift to the Goddess. I understand this will be acceptable to the priests?"

"Indeed," Achaikos smiled, relaxing completely. "In that case, I will bid you my leave. Andreas and I have a meeting with Midas. A certain prayer and invocation for prosperity," he said looking pointedly at Andreas, who smiled slightly looking to the ground.

"Then a serious drinking session in the *popina*. The priests will give you hospitality and we will meet tomorrow for our on-ward journey."

They both strode away together, in unison, Achaikos animat-edly talking, explaining to Andreas the temple protocol. Unexpectedly, and quite intensely, Kiana experienced a deep thud to her soul. A realisation came home to her that literally had the air escape her lungs to chase after and capture that fleeting truth. She saw a memory, so long ago that she had buried. Her father the king of Sogdiana was walking in identical fashion, as those men, now before her, talking in the same way to her brother, the prince, and she Kiana was with her mother, the queen, watching. Her family united.

She had bent double with the impact.

"Mama!" Tamina bent over to support her mother, and lifted her back up, "What ails you?"

Kiana blinked several times, staring into space, and letting go a lungful of air she said quietly, pressing her daughter to her, "I believe, sweet daughter, my soul had just given me a glimpse of our future. And my heart is aching for it."

"How so?" Tamina asked.

"You will see your true homeland again, Tamina," she stated with conviction resting on every word, "Britannia is not for you. Besides it is cold and wet. My bones and yours will certainly com-plain.

"But the wheel will turn several revolutions before it settles for us to realise our destiny, together. For now, Tamina, we must live only in the now. Do you understand?"

"Oh, I am practised at living in the now, Mama" she replied, briefly living her own private memories of hell and the precise code she had learnt to ensure her survival.

Kiana also realised with growing sadness and some hostility, that the appearance and influence of Andreas over Achaikos had splintered their little family unit. Most likely forever. She decided to accept philosophically, that turn of the wheel. She had Tamina, and of that, there would be no casting asunder.

... ...

Mother and daughter stood silently for several *secunda,* gathering their spirits, and both staring in admiration at the temple before them. The gentle steps towards the five-pillared entrance graduated in width, the white marble subtly laced with pink inclusions, shone with a white aura hovering above the surface. It was akin to walking through mist. To each side lay steeper companion steps that held a numerology and symbols intended to initiate all who walked towards Cybele. The intention was to slow the incumbent pilgrim to a very careful approach.

The priests, all Eunuchs, maintained this perfection, and demanded the total dedication of all who visited. They also expected a very large recompense for their labours. They ruled Pessinus like an embedded army of spiritual caretakers.

"Count the steps as we ascend, Tamina," Kiana said softly, brushing town detritus from her *stola*, "and absorb all the symbols. You will be required to recite meanings as an initiatory task. "Now, "she continued, turning her daughter towards her, "close your eyes and take that white mist before us and circle it around yourself. When you are certain you are encased in it, we can proceed."

And so, it was, two slave women, slowly ascended the most unique Goddess temple in the known world. Kiana memorized the symbols, relating to the Mother of all the Gods, names and elements relating to them. Each an honouring. When Tamina halted to screw her young eyes to the unknown, Kiana whispered knowledge in her ears, and waited for her. It was imperative they approached the entrance, where the priest would emerge, together.

The sun, now a burning oscillating disc, sent heat in waves to shimmer onto them, the mist seeming to rise even more in the heat. The fire trees of cypress that twinned the pillars on both sides of the temple, cupped their branches to receive that heat in worship of the eternal life-giver.

It took some time to reach the shade of the entrance, Tamina released a long sigh, as the pillars granted them a welcome coolness. Kiana glanced in both directions, waiting. They stood there, immobile for several more *seconda*.

Two priests appeared from each side of the temple, with no apparent door, and so silently, Tamina jumped at the touch on her arm. They were not robed. Yet they were completely covered in tattooed symbols, in ochre and brown. Some reds highlighted a symbol. These were the same symbols they had seen on the steps behind them.

Kiana instantly realised that these priests, these Eunuchs were a walking manifestation of the Gods aligned to and birthed by, Cybele. And like her, they were wedded to Cybele, as she had been to Azura Mazda. Their stare was intense. Each reaching to the souls of the women waiting silently to enter. Kiana felt akin to them, and they knew it. A shadow of a smile crossed the face of one, who muttered the initiatory request for intention and gifts to the Goddess.

They both produced the phials carrying the Ab-Zohr water, carefully hidden in muslin. In offering to the priests, they chanted the symbols learnt and after an obligatory nodding of heads, the priests withdrew.

Suddenly there was a cranking of metal against metal, and very slowly the gargantuan doors of the temple to Cybele creaked open. Within was a haze of dust that floated effortlessly in the torpid air, as shafts of sunlight filtered down from circular windows placed impossibly high in a decorated ceiling that craned the neck to view it. Tamina felt her neck crack at the effort, and it sounded like a whiplash in the intense silence of the temple.

Kiana felt an unexpected sadness filter into her soul. She realised this temple was but a husk of its original magnificence. The image of Cybele had long been removed to Rome by the Caesar. They were so greedy and acquisitive; nothing was sacred to them. The temple was being maintained, but not honoured.

They walked slowly towards the circular altar that lay at the far end of the long approach, itself, almost bereft. The only image to the great Goddess that had been left, was a submerged mosaic, identical to one adorning the baths. It was said that the original Cybele had eyes that literally followed you as the circumference of the sacred water altar was paced out in prayer.

Now, fading flowers and submerged crystals were scattered above and below, leaving little of the Goddess showing at all. The light was intense. The sun was given full reign in the honouring of the Mother Goddess. It was the only part of the temple that Kiana felt was still whole.

They remained some time each caught in their own thought. Prayers of a kind left them in whispers. They reached the Goddess as a lament to Her loss, as much as theirs. Just as Kiana felt nothing would be celebrated here, no miracle, no revelation, a strong unequivocal voice entered her head. A strong feminine voice, deep and resonating.

"It is only when the heart of a nation, the Mother, is on her knees, will that nation fail and pass from us. Remember the forest, for there you will always find me. *Babaru Babbanítu!*"

Kiana sucked shocked air into her lungs. She had failed to realise she had stopped breathing. She looked to her daughter.

"Tamina, let us honour the Goddess with the sacred water, just as we did at the Orontes. The Gods were angry then, and the Goddess is angry now! Rome will fail. It will end. It is all clear to me now. We must make sure we are in our Goddess given land when Rome crashes to the ground."

They both raised themselves up from the marble floor and reached over the water altar, saying prayers to Cybele and to Zoroaster for the cleansing of the waters and the earth. The water bubbled as it hit the torpid pool. And Kiana knew the power of Ab-Zohr had reached Cybele.

"We require privacy," Kiana announced to the Eunuch, "and a rest for the night."

He nodded amiably and padded silently before them, head bowed, turning to head out of the temple and towards a long, low building that was the dormitory for visitors.

He stopped at the door, opening it, requesting they enter.

"We will recompense you after we have eaten. What time is the evening meal?"

He remained silent and pointed to the sundial in the garden outside the dormitory. Tamina realised he was mute. And took hold of his hand to lead him to the sundial. He pointed to the time, nodded and left them.

"Well," announced Tamina, as she sat on the only chair, "It seems they remove every usable part of a man's body to become a priest to Cybele. I'm very glad you chose Ahura Mazda and Zoroaster, Mama!"

"Hmph! This place has a sheen that hides a growing canker," Kiana replied, "I shall be glad for the morning and a timely exit.

They sat quietly, each within their own thoughts until a bell sounded for the evening meal. It turned out to be excellent. And they celebrated gifting their bodies decent nutrition with ample wine and sweet desserts.

Before they had met the priests, both Tamina and Kiana had attacked their hidden pockets of coin and gold. They felt much lighter and determined to fill the gap with food.

Denarii and a pouch of gold dust satisfied the priests. Kianna realised the priests led a charmed and affluent life. No taxes and a revenue of their own choosing meant opulence. But they were now servants to Rome, more than to Cybele and there would certainly be an end to it.

... ...

Chapter 25

Non tam pura voluptas sit anxietas perpetuo
There is no such thing as pure pleasure: some anxiety
always goes with it.
(Publius Ovidius Naso 43BC-17AD)

Andreas reluctantly followed Achaikos up the temple steps. He had never in his disreputable life ever entered a temple. He had no notion of what to do, how to behave. And he felt foolish. He thought of absconding. Going straight to the *popina* to get blinding drunk where all kinds of comforts were immediately accessible. There were no knee-bending invocations for comfort at the *popina*, no pleading prayers. Images of delicious sweaty comfort filled his mind. He smiled and decided he would hold those images to their glorious end. He felt himself go hard and placed the rug before him.

This god Midas would understand.

Achaikos stewarded his charge forward, meeting the priests at the door, which creaked open. *Denarii* changed hands as a token to the God of wealth. It was, thought Achaikos, a massive amount of coin. And to whom might it benefit? Certainly, these priests. But what of Andreas? He harboured an affection for the young man with a growing intensity that might border on foolish obsession.

There were, he had to admit, so many barriers and walls to demolish, dissolve, before Andreas had any hope of mastering the elaborate skills needed to survive the Silk Road, let alone prosper.

The temple to King Midas was eerily dark outside. And even more so inside. One single shaft of light full of misty dust mites descended from the oracular opening at the apex, to shed luminance to the towering God of Midas.

Andreas immediately realised that, knowing the legend of Midas, everything this God touched turned to gold, his effigy would exude power. Yet he was stunned to feel it overwhelming him with a strength that confounded him. All his instinctive street skills, his burgeoning logical mind failed him in this moment. He succumbed to it and all the erotic thoughts he had been revelling in, the glorious sweaty rhythmic pounding, simply vanished.

He would describe it later to Achaikos, as a white-hot bolt of blue white heat that surged through his whole body to every nerve ending, as he was first slammed to his knees, then collapsed to the cold marble floor. It was cold to the touch and soothed his burning cheek, as he watched, unable to do anything else, his benefactor mumble incantations on his behalf to this horrendous God Midas, whose dark face, immobile, stared down at him.

And so, it was, as Achaikos enthused later in the *popina*, and as his incantations reached the highest pitch, resonating around this musty dark mausoleum of a temple, that Andreas had miraculously received the highest blessing of Midas.

Achaikos and Andreas sat in companionable hazy drunkenness in the sepia and soft red earthy colours of the *popina*, as the second large Amphorae of wine was placed on their table by a seductive young woman, who leaned over to present her breasts to Andreas, whose one good eye glazed over as his grin expanded to a dimpled grin.

"*Brevi*," he whispered to her, leaning into her cleavage and gently licking her soft skin, "*Brevi quam primum.*"

Achaikos smiled indulgently. He had this inner glow, almost as powerful as the surge gifted to his adopted son, "adopted son" he repeated silently. He knew with some certainty that Andreas would achieve wealth and fame along the Silk Road. That his investment in this rebel and street vagrant was sound. They had shared many stories with each other this day. And it cemented a relationship that both had longed for, yet had never aspired to, until now.

"Hey, *Patruus*," Andreas could not quite bring himself to sound the word Pater, as he leaned back to gulp a final mouthful of wine, "you will be lonely this night, as your women are being celibate with Cybele and her eunuchs! Find a woman. Look. They are rare beauties here."

Achaikos smiled, leaning forward to grab a handful of stuffed dates, "This is all the stuffing I need, young man," as he filled his mouth with the delicious delicacies, "I will sleep easy, believe me. We have a long journey tomorrow. We could, with a fair wind behind us and happy camels beneath us, see Byzantium within days. And I am exultant and joyous at the thought I will see my city again."

Andreas nodded, and heaved himself up, unsteady on his feet, he swayed towards the woman, who took his hand and led him away.

... ...

Kiana and Tamina had been waiting in the near mid-day heat for some hours. They had paid the camel keeper his dues and led the animals to the appointed gate that was the designated exit from Pessinus. It was busy. Small groups of travellers were clustered around the vendors who offered all manner of supplies needed for travel. The subsequent bartering was noisy and had given Kiana a rare headache. Tamina was busy securing extra water bags and bread from an excitable Sogdian. Kiana watched her daughter bargain with a skill only a slave girl would know. She felt a wave of pride expand her heart. And so, they waited for the absent men to arrive. They had stripped the coin from their hidden linings and now had very little to bargain with. The Eunuchs had cost them dear.

Tamina skipped back to her mother with smile and an armful of supplies.

"Look," she declared, holding the bags forward, "That Sogdian was easy, Mama. I wound him round my little finger like a thread!" She moved over to the water hole fed from the canal and filled each leather bag to the brim. The straps were long and ideal to loop over each camel's head. This water would keep them for the long onward journey. The camels must have smelt the water coming for each one collapsed its long legs to the ground and waited in anticipation. It was pure nectar. Their long tongues noisily slurped the water up, their long-lashed eyes half closed in deep pleasure. The bags were re-filled until each animal felt satiated. Kiana had managed to buy two bags of grain which everyone would make use of. And with the dried dates and some goat cheese they would not travel hungry.

They now sat together, hunched in a mother and daughter embrace, chins resting on their knees, looking as dark as their hair, eyebrows knitted together in suppressed anger. Sweat was dripping from their brows and trickling down their backs, the light linen tunica clinging to their backbone, translucent with moisture. Neither moved a muscle as they saw the men amble towards them. No haste, no worry, an easy jaunt on a sunny Pessinus day. Achaikos and Andreas spied the dark energy coming from their women and hastened to a trot.

Achaikos held both his arms out to Kiana and Tamina as they neared the women, who responded by looking away.

"I do not wish to hear excuses!" Kiana shouted, "Just saddle up and let us be gone from this place." Andreas got thrown the empty water bags, with the words, "Fill them up" spat Tamina, who had a secret liking for the one-eyed villain, but would never dare show it.

Achaikos sighed, thankful this greeting was mild and not much worse. He would all too soon be bidding farewell to his adopted son and did not wish any ill-feeling to follow him down the Silk Road. Andreas made himself useful by re-filling the numerous water bags for human consumption, keeping his distance from both women, as he knew full well, he stank of wine and far too much sex.

They hoisted themselves up onto each camel, Andreas supremely grateful he had use of one that spared his overused equipment from further injury. There was never any doubt in his mind now about his future and he was both excited and fascinated by what lay ahead for him.

The small caravan pounded away westwards towards a now-dimming sun, and Achaikos had therefore decided to make a good space through the night, to rest up upon the dawn.

... ...

Chapter 26

Byzantium

Omne initium novum alio initio est ab aliquo fine est scriptor
Every new beginning comes from some other beginning's end
(Marcus Annæus Senaca
54BC-39Ad)

The blazing sun, with many ringed hues, burnt into their very bones as they galloped at a fast pace to Byzantium. Achaikos was leading and Andreas was getting more furious at having to share the old man's obsession with his precious gold. He looked back. The women were shrouded with only a slit for their vision. Their heads were bent down in thought or pain, probably both, he thought.

They were following the Roman road that led towards the great city. The camels' hooves were creating a din, but they had been spurred on by whip after whip on their hard flanks, and all were now in the same furious mind as Andreas. They had been galloping all night, now in the midday heat it was a rush to the finish like some god inspired gladiatorial race, with no winners and no laurels!

Achaikos was the only one who knew this city. The others had no expectations, and at this moment felt only intense frustration.

To add to this, hardly any food remained, and there were only a few *denarii* left hidden in the hem of Kiana's tunica. She thought about the gold dust swinging about Achaikos' aging balls and grinned. If he was still hanging onto those tight little bags, she thought, it must be sheer greed, or pain and pleasure combined, the rapacious old man!

The road now began an incline, slight at first but soon became an ascent of some degree. All the camels slowed considerably, and for the first time in hours, the women looked up to see in their amazement, large birds circling above them, cawing in a such a loud manner, it caught their breath. Achaikos came to a stop. He turned back to see Tamina and Kiana stare at these strange birds. He smiled and breathed a sigh of pure relief. He was home at last. His aching shoulders relaxed, and he felt a stabbing pain course down his aching body. He knew he had strained muscles in many places. Only now would they begin to scream and pulsate in pain.

Tamina caught up with him.

"*Avunculus*, those noisome crazy birds up there!" she pointed, waving her arm in the air imitating their swirling dance high in the oscillating heat before the hazy sun, "Are they a river bird? Are we near water?"

"They are our welcome, Tamina!" he enthused, smiling enough to show his mottled teeth. "They are the sea birds of Byzantium. They welcome all travellers from the Silk Road. To us merchants and travellers, they are pure joy. To the inhabitants, however, they are a blessed nuisance!"

"We are near!" shouted Tamina turning swiftly around to face her mother and Andreas, "Byzantium is just over that hill." And spinning back round to face forward, she kicked her heels into the camel and whipped his flank several times. He roared and spat in anger but galloped forward and upward. Achaikos followed suit. Kiana and Andreas shrugged at each other and silently decided a slower pace would suit them just fine!

When they reached the brow of the hill, tufted with rough couch grass and tall seeded grasses swaying gently in the humid wind, their breathing halted simultaneously to match the intense silence of Achaikos and Tamina. Theirs was a long communal prayer to their Gods and Goddesses for deliverance and pure joy.

Kiana's prayer was hushed and intense. For she had finally entered the hallowed energy of Hecate, the Goddess of Byzantium to whom all worshipped. Hers was a guardianship unequalled anywhere else. She had saved Byzantium from a massive attack. And the people loved her for it.

Looking down on the curving glistening snake of the *Sinus Ceratinus*, from their vantage point on the Asiatic side, meandering out to the largest expanse of water, three of the group had ever seen, Kiana immediately pointed to the flag erected above the colossal statue of Hecate.

"Look Tamina," she exclaimed, as she pointed first to the statue, then to the numerous flags dotted above the city walls.

"Look daughter, see the flags. It is the star and half-moon of our Goddess. They are honouring her everywhere. I have never witnessed such adoration!"

Achaikos leaned over to take Kiana by the hand, smiling he said, "On a very dark and dangerous night, so it is spoken down the ages, Philip of Macedon staged a sudden attack on the city. Then a bright starburst came forth in the darkened sky to illuminate the attackers and they, of course, failed. It was sent by the Goddess herself to save the people. She is called *Lampadephoros*, Light-bearer."

For her ears alone, Achaikos murmured softly. "This is your home from home, Kiana, should you ever wish to remain."

Had he realised already that she and Tamina would be returning to her homeland from Britannia as soon as possible? she wondered, looking down at her filthy nails and tattered shawl that she had unfurled to show her face to the sun. She squinted at the intensity of the sun as it shone off the sea, to meet in a brilliance of luminosity neither she nor anyone else were accustomed to. She longed for her true home in Sogdiana. Both the palace and the temple were preferable to this! She realised how excited Achaikos was. This was his true home.

Achaikos leant back on the hump of the now exhausted camel, stretching aching muscles in a bid to encourage movement. He folded his arms and quietly shared some history and memories of his home.

"To your left, you will see my childhood home, *Sycae Pera Galata*. I still hold the house there, dear to my heart. And we will rest there before venturing to the Nerorion Harbour, where my boats are moored for long sea travel. My wealth is stored in two quarters, holding banks within Byzantium, I am now ready and happy to share my wealth with each of you, my family. You will not want for anything ever again. You have my word."

A long deep breath expelled from Achaikos, as he realised those momentous words had just altered his life forever. Yet as the feeling of intense release and lightness overwhelmed him, he was silent, as he revelled in a sensation, he never believed he would feel again. The parallel world of spirit became his again. And fragments of his soul re-entered their home within his heart.

Kiana felt it and was pleased. "There is such an immensity of water here, of sea," she remarked looking over to her lover, "Yet the land is easy, comfortable with it. It has taken aeons for the land and sea to marry together in such harmony." The perspective was immeasurable, a huge vista. She pointed her head towards a temple that rose majestically above the milieus of humanity below.

"Hecate?" she asked.

"Yes," he replied, "of course, under another name, Athena. We will visit before we leave here." He personally felt less inclined to make the move to Britannia. He knew his soul was mending. Was it even needful to go?

They sat silently on their camels, deep in thought. Tamina watched the boat traffic, and the patterns in the sky those seabirds made in the trail of the boat's wake, heads switching, eyes intent on submerged fish that would mean a full stomach. Their dive into the sea was like a flash of lightning, wings pinned to their sides. When they surfaced with their catch, a chorus of cries accompanied the lucky bird. It was nature's theatre at its best.

The sun was losing her intensity and began to travel down to meet the rooftops of the immense city.

Achaikos kicked his camel into slow lumbering action, swinging his tired body in rhythmical action and meandered down the tufty hill veering a sharp left towards Galata and rest.

Tamina had her eyes everywhere, from the swirling sea birds above the high sails of long boats to the swish of oars from the Roman cargo boats. She became fascinated with the tiny circular-shaped boats, fit just for one and powered by one long oar that swung backwards and forwards. These tiny boats, and there were many of them, gyrated slowly across the meandering stretch of turquoise blue water that caressed the land as it moved out to sea. Oh, and that sea! She inhaled the fresh scented air and shouted at the top of her voice

"Achaikos! I can smell the sea!"

He turned around amidst the heavy swaying and felt his bones crack and muscles scream, "Tamina, my dear child, this air is almost the purest in the world. Bested only by the air you will breathe in Britannia. It is a small island surrounded by sea!" He winced in pain, not unnoticed by Kiana, who suddenly felt such sympathy for her lover and guardian. I hope he has maintained servants and slaves at this house of his, she thought. A deep warm bath is what this tired man needs.

Andreas had spent these last few minutes staring intently at Tamina. He saw a new vibrant young girl before him. The timid, angry shrouded slave girl was diminishing before his eyes and he was becoming attracted to her. And it had not gone unnoticed by Kiana either. She held her camel back and rode beside him.

Looking fearsome and intense she hissed at him, "Touch one single hair of her head, and I will kill you!" Without waiting for any reply, she kicked her camel's flanks, hard. It loped away in huge strides, catching up with Achaikos who was far ahead, intent on reaching home.

"You must lose that vagrant step-son of yours.... soon!" she declared.

"He will be leaving us soon," he assured her, knowing full well the scenario that was building between Tamina and Andreas.

Kiana doubled back to ride with her daughter. Andreas kept his distance to the rear.

This small caravan of weary travellers snaked down the slope leading to the Metaxas family estate. It stretched for two *centuria* on the gentle slope that held tributaries which fed the golden horn. Vertical mills captured the water to provide all the engineering needs for grinding corn, fuelling the hypocausts. Kiana noticed a waterbed irrigated to grow plants all year round. The tall cypress bordered the land, swaying in the late afternoon breeze. The Villam had a colonnaded entrance with gardens that boasted acacia, lily and even rose beds that flashed brilliant red and pink. Box trees lined the pathway to the entrance that had a dozen statued steps. It was luxurious. It exuded a power unknown to all the pilgrims, except the owner, who by now was grinning broadly and singing a Greek song, quietly, privately, to welcome his soul home.

... ...

Tamina and Kiana lay, luxuriating in their personal heated and mosaiced bath, the rose petals floating aimlessly on the steaming surface, wafting rose essence around them. Both in their own thoughts, their eyes shut, they gently moved their limbs as the grime and muck was lifted from them by the hot ripples that caressed their bodies. The contrast of the last few days to this luxury made speech irrelevant. Tamina had watched the hypnotic movement of the water wheel, its shadow playing on the green glass of large windows placed at regular intervals along the walls. It played with the sun, now throwing multicolours into the room as its last orchestra of light.

Slaves were waiting in the shadows to throw heated linen around them. They heard a gong being sounded and simultaneously opened their eyes.

"Time to leave this scented heaven, daughter," Kiana said, pushing a hand over her face to bring the reality back.

They padded over to the slaves who, with eyes discreetly lowered wrapped the hot linen around them so they were encased in a dry warmth that tingled their damp skin.

Achaikos had arranged for a range of attire to greet them as they entered their shared *cubiculum*. There were small shrieks of delight from them both, as they scanned the silks, cottons and the finest woollen garments.

Kiana picked up an *amictus,* gently rubbing her thumb and forefinger between the exquisite patterning sewn onto the silk in miniscule stitching. Feathered birds and pretty plants travelled around the toga in purple-red, indigo and saffron yellow. A border of woven shapes gave a flowing weight to the silk, that swayed rhythmically as she walked around the *cubiculum*. They had of course both chosen to wear the silk tunica, that rare feeling of silk next to the skin sent them both to a higher level of consciousness.

Grinning and dancing with each other in pure joy, Kiana's throat suddenly became tight, her heart opened as she realised all this was from Achaikos. This was Byzantium clothing, not Rome, it was Eastern and as close to Sogdiana as he could create for her.

Tamina stopped their swirling dance and took her mother's hands, holding them tightly.

She looked into her soul, "He knows Mama," she said softly, "He knows he is "borrowing" you for a while. His love for you is pure and I think I love him for that."

"I know Tamina," Kiana replied, looking to the swaying border hem at her feet.

"Go to him Mater," Tamina insisted quietly, "I know why he has put you with me, but I can look after myself. Andreas will not get near me! I'll post a slave, no, two big burly men to guard me this night. Besides, Andreas now realises he will be the second most wealthy man in Byzantium, Achaikos being the first!"

"He is hardly likely to jeopardise that, now is he?"

"Hmph!" Kiana blew out loudly, "Men's brains are between their legs daughter! Have you not realised *that* yet!"

Before they left their *cubiculum,* they gave what little coin they had left hidden in the hems of their tunica, which had been swiftly taken from them and burnt, to the slave girls.

"Forgive me, but our master Achaikos pays us all handsomely!" the diminutive girl said looking up at Kiana with long lashed brown eyes that held not an echo of any fear. "We are not slaves," she stated.

"Then let this be a gift to you both," Tamina smiled broadly as she handed the *denarii* to willing outstretched hands, "from two former slave girls!" she laughed as they turned down the corridor, their new leather sandals clacking on the marble floor and their fine-spun silk *amictus* and *stolæ* swaying delicately as they walked in unison. Shadows from the torches lining the frescoed walls, highlighted the delicate silk birds and flowers, seeming to come alive around mother and daughter, two survivors of the Antioch earthquake. Kiana thought her heart might burst at this moment. Tamina sensing her feeling, caught hold of her mother's hand, and grateful tears filled their eyes.

As they moved towards the *triclinium,* their spines straightened, and their heads both held aloft.

Two royal Sogdian princesses entered that room to a conversation suddenly hushed as admiring glances followed them to their seats beside Achaikos.

They were reborn.

... ...

Chapter 27

Degeneres animos timor argumentum
Fear is proof of degenerate minds
(Publius Verilius Maro 70BC-19BC)

"How do you like your new garments, my women?" Achaikos had leaned forward to admire them, chewing happily on stuffed olives, swallowed down with mellow wine from his own vineyards.

"They are exquisite, and I think rare, no?" Tamina ventured.

"Oh yes," Achaikos chimed with a proud delight, "they have been created using sea silk, *Pinna nobillis* a seashell that offers these long filaments that are spun. The golden sheen is exclusive to the *Pinna nobillis.*"

"And you own the rights," Andreas chipped in, listening intently to the conversation, picking up clues to the immense wealth of Achaikos.

"I do," he replied succinctly, not offering any more information. Achaikos shifted on the long settee, his back buttressed by several tasselled cushions. His back muscles and spine remained aggravatingly painful, even after the hot bath and vigorous oiled massage from his best masseuse.

"My women," he turned to Tamina and Kiana with a huge smile, "I have had news from Britannia. It seems my services are urgently required by an old scholar and dear friend, Vrittakos. He and his wife and family were sent to oversee the construction of a temple Villam on an island off the south coast of Britannia. In fact, there are seven villams in various stages of construction. The island is very special. It is sacred and has magical forces that abound over the landscape. It is also very fertile and temperate. Probably the easiest climate in the whole of Britannia and closest to the Celtica climate with warm sun and two harvests each year plus vineyards."

Achaikos sat back for a moment allowing this news to percolate around the gathering. He watched Kiana closely. Her face was inscrutable. Andreas, on the other hand, had a glow emanating from his one good eye that left no one in doubt. He was bursting with expectations. Wealth was getting very close to becoming real for him. And freedom too. Achaikos ignored his blatant display. Kiana was his concern.

"I have little choice on the matter, Kiana," he spoke softly to her and watched her long eyelashes flutter momentarily, as she stared downwards, fingering the delicate silk flower, sitting neatly on her knee, that had caught her eye.

"It is a matter of honour," he continued, "and I have always made clear that the hinterland is where we should go for soul retrieval. It is a spiritually advanced culture there, so he tells me. The Romans just use the island for agriculture and a staging post for the centurions. It is peaceful."

Kiana made no move to reply.

"We will talk later," he murmured.

"Andreas," he turned to face his newly adopted son, and glared at him, "Kiana, myself and Tamina will be leaving Byzantium within the next few days: By boat."

"Boat!" exclaimed Tamina incredulously, "*Avunculus,* how wonderful." For a moment, Tamina became a little excited girl who had just been gifted the most exquisite present, and Andreas inexplicably felt his battered heart break a little more. He loved her, and he was about to lose her forever. It did not go unnoticed by either her mother or Achaikos.

Their lives were about to separate irrevocably.

… … … … … … … … …

"You must stay this night with your daughter, Kiana," Achaikos muttered, head almost submerged into the linen pillow, "And the next and next until we leave for Britannia. Why, you ask? Because that fool Andreas thinks he is head over heels in love with your daughter and he will take her!"

"He *is* in love with her, you dear fool" she replied, slapping him hard on his aching shoulder bone. She was sitting astride him, nestling on his buttocks, oil of cedar beside her, as she massaged his back away from the crippling pain that had prevented the lovemaking she needed and he, unable to give.

"And yes! I will do as you command. But as soon as your pain eases expect my return to your bed and sexual contortions you have not even thought of!" Kiana grinned.

"Oh, for love of Hecate, spare me this vixen!" Achaikos exclaimed.

She lent down and bit his neck, hard. And then hugged him, for tenderness overcame her. "This Hecate loves you, dear Achaikos. Have no fear on that."

She continued rubbing the oil in those painful areas, as she studied the large ornate *cubiculum* with vibrant frescoes adorning the walls. He loved forests and wild animals. It felt as though she was back in their *Babaru* and saw the plants almost dance before her eyes. The tall window, paned in green glass brought the night light into the room, for the moon was full and shone a subtle radiance onto the bed where they lay. She felt sorrow for his aching body. And with this feeling came another, unwarranted vision, lucid and strong. A scene flashed before her.

A boy, her boy, suddenly broke out of the dark moon night, shouting to her in a language she seemed to understand, though it was not her native tongue,

"*Mōdor, Mōdor!*" he shrieked at her, "*Híe are hèr! Gebrengan þæt wund oferfaran und manig beadorinca. Wè sculan flèon und gesecgan þæt Wihtwara.*

Ic willan begietan þæt hors."

"*Tamina,*" she shrieked.

"*Hèo hèr, Lōcian!*"

She turned to see her.

They were suddenly on horseback, high on the tip edge of a hill, overlooking the vast acreage of a Roman villam, built in luxurious style. The land edged out to the sea, and the river inlet meandered out to those tidal waters that were bringing in the Roman ships full to the gunnels with soldiers.

She could hear so clearly the thumping of their hardened leather studded boots, and the clank of metal on their taut muscles and bones. How many? It was a ludicrous atrocity! She saw the white-robbed priests before the centurions. They carried a huge ornate cross held high above them as if their mandate was already sanctioned to kill and mutate innocent people.

They moved forward, these soldiers. With four lines deep, they even performed a testudo, an insulting arrogance of almost comic proportions. To protect their Christian emissaries from two invalided and crippled old men.

They both came limping out, holding up each other, into the moonless night. No stars for them to look to, in their last moments. No moon to hear their last prayers. The Villam stood as testament to their dedication. They had created a temple for many religions, many pilgrims had felt honoured to worship there. It was now a backdrop to their murder, by a jealous god who craved exclusivity.

She wanted to laugh.

Instead she cried.

And then she screamed. A hand suddenly shot forward and rammed a cloth in her mouth.

"They have chosen to die a noble death," a voice spoke quietly in her ear, "They are defending your Gods and Goddesses. Never let their heroism be forgotten. That is all they ask of you."

And she screamed until her throat became bloodied as she watched the swords impale her beloved Achaikos and the Greek old man beside him.

Kiana's eyes shot open, wide, staring at a void, as she inhaled a deep breath to fill her empty lungs. She had tears streaked down her face as she pushed her hair aside, Achaikos took hold of her and held her tightly, waiting for the shuddering to ease.

"We must not travel to this hinterland, Achaikos!" she blurted out to him when she eventually found her voice.

"I'm afraid that is something I cannot, nor, will not alter, Kiana," he replied, gently stroking her hair, "I am pledged by an honour of years ago, to help my companion and oath-sworn friend, "What have you been shown, priestess?"

"If you will not alter your course, then there is absolutely nothing I can tell you!" she shouted, leaping off the bed and striding out of the *cubiculum*, the swish of the hangings blowing the candle flame wildly, sending distorted shadows flitting chaotically amongst the frescoed birds and flowers.

She spent a sleepless night, tossing and turning, images refusing to leave her tortured mind. So many unknowns and questions entered then left her conscious mind. And her unconscious mind that held all those answers remained closed.

Tamina lay and watched her mother suffer, knowing she must not interfere. Exhaustion eventually overcame them both and in the small dark hours they fell asleep.

… … … … … … … … …

Chapter 28

Si deus est, unde mala? Si quis bonus non est Deus unde veniet?

If there is a God whence proceed so many evils? If there is no God, whence cometh any good?

Anicius Manilius Severinus Boœthius (480AD-525AD)

A brilliant morning sun, as ever, graced the city that blessed in every grey marble cornice, pillar and column, the Mother of the Gods. From the island offshore, that was Her gift to humanity, the marble was eased out in monumental chunks, intact and carved, pillared and squared, grooved and embellished with sacred images and historical events. If just one crack appeared, it was abandoned. But those chunks were broken up, secretly by gangs of merchant slaves, to grace the bazaar stalls. Those slave lives were counted as cheap. If they were caught, it was surely followed by their death, in public and painfully slowly.

This, then, was their first day in the city that held the heartbeat of all humanity on Earth. The eastern Silk Road co-joined with the west in a jostling dance of cultures and religions. Pagan Gods and Goddesses were worshipped alongside this new male God whose exclusivity was constantly mouthed by the men who spoke on behalf of him.

Tamina, Kiana, Andreas and Achaikos had been almost ceremoniously oared over to the Western side, in a long elegant boat that accommodated six oarsmen and a raised platform that could seat eight at least. It was Achaikos' personal ferry and the occupants felt like royalty.

Tamina had fidgeted wildly, pointing at everything that caught her eye, talking all the while. She simply adored being on the sea.

Why, Kianna had asked herself, does a daughter of the desert become so enamoured of water?

Achaikos, whose entire mind had been filled with their lovemaking the previous night, and which still excited him this sunny morning had held his lover close and whispered to her

"We are made of water my love. She is only communing with the feminine part of her soul. As shall I this very night!"

Kiana lovingly lent into him and kissed his knarled hand. She was at peace. And she was in love.

Andreas, on the other hand, was sitting apart from the women, as far away as he possibly could, without falling into the *Aureus Cornu*, and he was anything but at peace. His heart was breaking and his soul in torment. All that was left for him, was to look out from the ferry, to the distant horizon, and wish himself on the lonely Silk Road this very moment.

And now they all stood on the scorching slabs of Prosphorion harbour, hopping slightly to save their feet from burning, through the leather of their sandals. They parted company again, this becoming a familiar pattern while Andreas was present. With bowed head, he followed his benefactor. Achaikos had realised by now, that he did in fact own this young man's soul. A nod of consent would send the young man's heart to the heavens. But he had absolutely no intention of doing such a thing. Why? Because his new daughter was beholden to him, as he was to her. He was hardly going to give her away!

Let this young rapscallion prove himself first, he thought.

He had loaded his women with pockets of coin to spend in the markets that lined the main thoroughfare in the city. The men were to other business, as he guided Andreas towards the banking quarter where several tall buildings exuding wealth, boasting colonnaded and intricately decorated cornice facias, held the money, promissory scrolls and the debt of half of Byzantium.

Achaikos was about to relinquish nearly half his wealth to an unknown vagrant. And yet he felt absurdly calm. He straightened his spine, squared his shoulders and shot a half look over to that one-eyed "vagrant" that had opened his heart. A shard of sheer

panic nearly pierced that old beating organ that insisted on keeping him alive, as Andreas held a look so inscrutable, so cold, it
might have occurred to Achaikos that he was about to make a
monumental blunder.

Except he really did not care. He knew his true motives well
enough. He had searched his soul and found true peace in the love
of a family he believed he would never experience. The important
and immense wealth he kept in the secret vaults deep in the hidden quarter, his family home, the vineyards and water meadows,
olive groves and silk production would be solely for Kiana and
Tamina. And the most precious family asset, the holding his *Avus*
had secured from Septimius Severus, when the Cæsar was re-
building Byzantium after the terrible destruction and carnage. A
large area of the Marmara island, with its exquisite grey-veined
marble was owned and held in trust by and for the Metaxas family. He was the very last Metaxas. He felt deeply grateful to the
Gods that he now had a family, albeit adopted, who would inherit
it all.

For Andreas, it was the wealth of the Silk Road. Every part of
it. Achaikos was in no doubt. He would gladly be shot of it.

They stood together, both still, saying nothing to each other.
As silent as the huge grooved columns that towered above them.
Yet those marble columns held the laughter, misery, ambitions
and ruin of thousands of souls, sent up to the Gods and Goddess
that dwelt within the sculptured marble cornice and facias high
above. The air thrummed with high-velocity emotions. Yet it was
the very silence, the counterpoint, which held the largest money
hall in place.

The grand doors creaked open. They were admitted and
walked silently through to initiate the greatest money exchange
Achaikos had undertaken in his whole life.

The doors slowly closed behind them.

... ...

Tamina peered through the silk hanging of the rattan carriage held by four runners. She re-adjusted the pile of cushions and knelt forward, so she could see clearly and miss nothing, as they bobbed along, swerving to avoid those on foot. Byzantium in all its tumultuous glory flashed before her. They turned into the main thoroughfare. Tamina pulled her head through to stare quite openly at the sights before her. The walkway glittered in white stone and the marble columns holding elegant archways stretched into the distance. Market stalls occupied every colonnaded space. People were constantly milling around them, haggling, changing coins and carrying goods away. Deep into the archways the stalls stretched back into the shadows. The whole area was simply heaving with colourful noisy humanity.

"Mama!" Tamina twirled her head around to face her mother, "When can we stop and explore?"

Kiana's eyes shot open wide, staring into space as a shard of reality shattered her deep meditation. She had, on seeing the immensity of Byzantium elected to be elsewhere. She was, in fact, at her home in Sogdiana, the King's palace. Since her elevation from slavery, so many memories were colliding over each other for recognition. She decided the only way was to honour each one. It would take some time.

"We are meeting Achaikos' family friends who will be our escorts. Patience Tamina, we have much of the day to enjoy." She wished she could join her daughter in the joy of this new life. But the experience of this new wealth and privilege left her bereft with old memories scorching her soul. Not least her frequent escapes to the markets of Samarkand, as the rebellious young princess, now sepia tinged with the soft golden glow of selective imagery.

But here now, the present overtook her. They had slowed to stop. Before them stood the family that had a daughter, Tamina's age and the women, mature and rather tall to accompany Kiana.

The two male slaves jumped forward to assist the women to the still steaming hot stone path. The sun assaulted them, and Kiana winced.

"*Salutatio!*" the mature woman stepped forward to hold Kiana gently by her arm, "*Ego sum Helena Palsiologina et hic is meus fillia Nikolina Palaiologina.*

Id is feridus hodie. Concedo mihi ambulation vos propter the opacus forum."

Welcome, I am Helena Palsiologina, and this is my daughter, Nikolina Palsiologina. It is f far too hot, allow me to walk you through the shaded area."

"Greetings to you," Kiana replied, "I am Kiana, and this is my daughter, Tamina. We are very happy to accompany you out of this heat!"

"Oh, Tamina!" exclaimed the mother, "What a beautiful name. It suits you, my dear," As she turned to take Tamina by the hand and give her, her daughter's hand, Kiana sighed inwardly, wishing the day to be over.

The close group of women wove into the darkened recesses of the closed quarter, followed diligently by the slave guardians who would lose their very heads if, but a single hair was taken from any of the women in their care. It became a very mixed blessing for Kiana, for they had exchanged the searing heat of the sun for an airless, stifling and dark warren of bazaar stalls and heckling merchants. Droplets of sweat soon became rivulets down her back and she found an almost constant shifting of her *stola* necessary to hide the wet silk sticking to her back and bottom. This was one of those times when she wished dearly to be back in a homespun tunica.

Tamina strolled in front of her, chatting amiably with Nikolina and totally oblivious to the heat and what it was showing to the world!

Kiana, whose mind lay elsewhere, allowed Helena to babble on in fast Latin that Kiana barely understood, as they both handled thick rolls of cloth whose sheen had caught their eye. They were of high quality and the designs brought Kiana back to reality as an ice shard punctured her heart. They were indisputably Sogdian. Helena failed to notice the clenched fist on the fabric as she babbled on. Kiana began to pay attention to her with the mention of Antioch.

"The edict of the Emperor has reached these lands," Helena said with the rushed breath that was her personal signature. The woman could not, it seemed, stop talking.

"What edict?" Kiana interrupted, "And what has it to do with Antioch?"

"Oh! of course my dear!" Helena exclaimed, "Your home territory I believe."

"No! my home is in Sogdiana," Kiana interjected quite loudly. She was beginning to feel frustrated with this woman. "What has happened in Antioch?" she continued, looking straight into the eyes of Helena, hoping for some straight talking.

"Well," she took a deep breath at the same time as heaving the cloth off the roll and holding it to her, "Don't you think this colour might suit me?"

"*Antioch*!" Kiana shouted.

"Oh yes! Antioch. The Christians are being persecuted terribly because of the edict by Emperor Decius. The Christian Pope Fabian, Babylas "something" of Antioch and Alexander of Jerusalem have both been put to death. In a most terrible fashion so I have heard."

"But Antioch has just suffered an earthquake of momentous proportions," Kiana replied, "I saw the young Christians gather together with their elders to physically and courageously pull the city from ruin!"

"I doubt they were Christians my dear," Helena stated, as she decided on the fabric and was about to haggle for a reasonable price with the scarred and rugged merchant, who eyed her lasciviously.

"They were most probably apostatised Christians to the Jews, their elders, who have all been exempt from the demands of the Emperor."

Kiana's expression froze, for both the disturbing news and the surprising depth of knowledge from Helena, made an impact.

"Why!" she demanded to know.

"Well because the Christians are being forced to give sacrifice to the Roman gods, publicly, I might add. And all against the laws of their new-found faith. Personally, I feel some pity for them."

"I will give you three *denarii* and not a coin more!" Helena insisted to the merchant whose nose twitched and mouth curled in disgust at the offer. But three *denarii* were better than none and shrugging at the fate of his day so far, pushed the luscious fabric into Helena's hands, who immediately passed it over to her slave.

Kiana suddenly felt a palpable threat wash over her. Her heart thumped wildly, so loudly she felt all could hear. Fear became present and she could not push it away. It was so rare in one so very courageous, but the edict could and might come to meet her, Tamina and of course dear Achaikos. She could say nothing here in this sweltering cauldron of shifty commerce. She must not say anything to this woman either. She looked around to find Tamina and searched in her mind for a good excuse to leave. Yet both young girls were having a delightful time, excitedly parting company with their coin, oblivious to the airless dark fecund and smell-ridden market.

So, she pinched in her nose, bringing the fragrant oiled cloth to her face and carried on. She bought the beautiful Sogdian cloth, refusing to haggle and paying much more than Helena, much to the delight of the aged merchant who gave her a yellow-toothed grin that printed lust on his face.

She held the cloth to her heart, for it had the Zoroastrian eternal flame embellished on the border, and it immediately calmed her heart, gave her solace.

The day wore on, sweat now claiming much of her body and the silk clinging tightly to every crevice. She gave up caring, the priestess in her retreated further away. And Helena continued talking aimlessly, threads of spittle gathering at the corners of her mouth with its overuse. She wondered how Achaikos had fared with the huge release of his wealth to a vagrant. She wished the day over and prayed to her Goddess to speed the sun's setting, if possible.

They eventually reached a much broader horizon, the sun gracefully dipping behind the elegant grooved pillars that lined the broad walkway, a perfect perspective shrinking in geometric accuracy into the distance, where, sounds of revelry, or debauched shrieks could be heard from the hippodrome.

As the cooler sun lent longer shadows to the pavements and a breeze filled her lungs with clean air, Kiana thought, "Someone has just been slaughtered for entertainment. That is the heartbeat of Rome!"

... ...

Chapter 29

Spes autem super gradum tenet in mundum. Spes est vigilantis somnium ab hominibus.

Hope is the pillar that holds up the world. Hope is the dream of the waking man.

(Pliny the Elder. 23AD-79AD.)

"We cannot assume, however much we may wish it," Kiana pressed her hand onto the table's cool surface for emphasis, looking deep into Achaikos eyes, "We cannot assume that we will be passed by, overlooked by the Roman officials. They are meticulous to their very souls!"

"Agreed," Achaikos admitted, "I have placed an urgent message with all my workers to speed up our departure. Our sea-going vessel is being made ready now. Provisions are being amassed in readiness for a hurried departure, though I hope to gods not!"

Kiana banged the table in frustration, "This is unjust! The Romans have made it their business to steal from all other cultures' religions, taken the peoples' Gods and Goddesses and changed their names to suit. Take the robbery of Cybele! Her gift to humanity was sent from the heavens to land in Pessina, her earthly home. The Romans stole the jewel and left a lifeless mosaic in its place. That temple had died, Achaikos."

They were sitting together, close, on two winged chairs ornately embellished in gilt and cerise, one accenting the other along the arm rests in grooved patterns twisting into knots as the design cascaded down the legs to finish in swirl of exquisite form. Plump cushions in shot silk were luxuriously comfortable, but Achaikos and Kiana were troubled and tense, neither noticing nor appreciating any of it. Indeed Achaikos' *tablinum* was a feast for any designer's eyes. The brazier in the centre to warm the chilly evening coupled with the torches bracketed against the walls created a moving dance of shadows upon beautifully painted frescoes adorning all the walls.

Those shadows played on Achaikos's lined face, deepening every line and accenting the tired shadows under his eyes.

He heaved the deepest sigh.

"Rumours have reached my workmen. They are saying the persecution of the Christians has begun here in Byzantium. It is a travesty of the intent of Decius to enforce an extreme version of his declaration. He wants all to bow to Rome, that's all. He desires a return to the Golden Age of Rome"

"The Jews are exempt, Achaikos!" Kiana interjected with each word clipped with suppressed anger. "I fail to understand. If this Christ is their messiah and he was also a king of the Jews, why are the Jews exempt and the Christians singled out for this persecution of their faith?"

Achaikos reached over to caress her bare arm. He felt her frustration deeply. It was an offence. Sectarian madness had been allowed to enter the high sophistication of ancient Byzantium.

"The authorities have always respected traditional religious practices and the Jews are following the ways of their ancestors. This gives Judaism high status, *Religio Licita* throughout the Empire." Achaikos leaned forward to catch her glance, making sure she knew the unpalatable truth that lay before her.

"The Roman authorities have never viewed the Christians in the same light at all. They see Christianity as *superstitio* as excessive religiosity that is socially disruptive."

"And I must agree with Tacitus," Achaikos added, "For there lies the rub!"

"So, all Christians are zealots!" Kiana shot back, removing his hand and sitting bolt upright in her chair, staring forward in steely anger Achaikos knew could find expression in many ways.

"Yes, apparently so," he continued, trying to find the right words to pacify rather than inflame, "It is a new religion. Many of the followers are young and passionate. This unerringly gets translated into rhetoric and dogma which viewed from the outside will get translated as zealotry."

"I am a true believer in Interfaith, Achaikos," Kiana spoke clearly, still with eyes fixed on a point within a mural on the facing wall, "As are you, old man!"

"Indeed," Achaikos nodded.

"But I will no more kill a bull, black, white or pink to honour their Roman Gods, their Mithras, than I would sacrifice a goat or sheep to my Gods, who do not ask it of me!"

"We are priest and priestess to the very oldest religions!" Kiana continued, still looking straight ahead, but with a softer tone to her words, "Abrasax and Azura Mazda are before Time itself. Older than Rome. Yet we find ourselves standing shoulder to shoulder with the very youngest. This Christianity."

She held her face in both her hands, head suddenly bowed down. All was silent within the *tablinum*, Achaikos held a look of deep profound compassion for her, unaware completely that Kiana was now fixed in the future, watching again, his death at the hands of these young "passionate" Christians. She slowly lifted her head.

"Yes, it will become their hallmark," she intoned, deep and darkly resonating to Achaikos, who sat back in his chair, his spine tingling, "their legacy to an unsuspecting world. Zealotry will abide with them like a sticky stain of blood of which their Christ became enveloped."

... ...

It was pre-dawn when the three travellers emerged from the villam. No servants stood to fare them well. No moon to guide their way. Kiana and Achaikos had both elected to spare Tamina details of possible Christian persecution, which they hoped to avoid.

They were intent on giving the proper libations in the respective temples to their Gods and Goddesses before their arduous and final, dangerous part of their journey

All that could be seen of them was a wandering snake of tallow lights down the hillside to a murky black water's edge. Waiting for them was Andreas. His task was to oar them across, then bid farewell to go his own way. Achaikos had relented. He was fond of the man. And it was a final chance for Andreas to see his beloved Tamina. And love her he did!

The light shone from his one good eye, leaving no doubt, and Tamina, at first shading her eyes, looked up to respond with equal intensity. Achaikos sighed deeply and shrugged knowing that forbidden fruit is more alluring. Yet some inner voice quietly told him to release his old cynicism and embrace what was strikingly evident. They loved each other, and it was real.

As the water gently lapped against the oars in a serenade of slow rhythm, and barely a seabird hawked a call, they made their way to the city. Tamina, as always, when on water, leant sharply over, to put her hand in to feel the cold caress of *Sinus Ceratinus*, as the interplay of currents between the sea of Marmara and the Bosphorus danced around her hand. Sea nymphs were at play and she knew and delighted in their dance.

Andreas was transfixed, barely taking his eyes from her, and he was in no hurry to reach the other side.

Achaikos gave out a rumbling cough. Andreas released himself from his vision and begrudgingly fixed his attention to the oaring. Dawn was beginning to break. A light golden glow subtly highlighted darkened objects of birds and people to reveal that Byzantium was waking up. Movement on the quayside they were now approaching, confirmed it with golden shadows moving to and fro.

Achaikos had laid the responsibility on Andreas to organise and furnish a carrier for them all to weave their way, with slaves running at top speed, to the temple of Hecate, for the women, and to the monastery where he would give his libation to Abrasax. They were situated wide apart, and the meeting point for them to reach the harbour where the large boat had been made ready, was indeed close to the Forum of The Ox. This meeting point was dedicated to Mithras, the bull-slayer. If there were to be enforced sacrifices ordered by the magistrates, it would be carried out here, in full public view.

Achaikos smiled as he saw the large carrier waiting for them with six slaves posted on the handles each side to adequately pull their combined weight easily.

"For a vagrant with no education, you are learning fast, Andreas," he whispered as they leapt off the ferry to sit comfortably within the heavy curtained carrier.

"I watch," was the only reply Andreas gave.

"Humph!" Achaikos gave a deep-chested rumble, making sure he sat in-between Tamina and Andreas. The balance was uneven, and the carrier gave a lop-sided lurch as the slaves tried to achieve the impossible.

"Kiana, please sit with your daughter," Achaikos commanded, and as they switched sides, the carrier levelled, and the journey speeded up. This pleased both the young lovers as they could stare at each other sending an entire conversation in wordless signs and expressions.

"Andreas," Achaikos leaned forward to grab his attention fully, "we are nearing the temple. I ask you to guard with your life, my women. Keep the carrier to take them to the Forum of Arcadius after their libation.

"We will meet there, midday."

And with that he briefly kissed Kiana on her head, and as she looked up, she returned a full passionate kiss of her own. Somehow, she needed all the courage within and the help of Hecate to make this journey she neither wanted nor asked for and which she dreaded to her very soul.

… … … … … … … … …

Kiana found the temple to her Goddess vibrant and alive. The pillars shone in that beautiful pink sheen of Mons Claudianus marble. They formed the tall elegant walkway to the altar. And as she looked to see the height of them, the breath left her as she soaked in the power of Her, Hecate, at her most divine. The half-moon and star shone out everywhere in this temple. No Roman inclusions of false and inferior icons. For the first time since Kiana had offered her soul to the Goddess and pleaded for her guardianship within those terrible slavery years, she felt Hecate enter her and fill her up.

Tamina felt the power. She stood agape as her mother sank to the marble floor and submitted spread-eagled to the presence of the Goddess. No sophisticated offerings, no ritualistic incense burning. Not yet. She followed suit but felt immediately inadequate. Tamina made a pact of honesty with the Goddess. Her only prayer, which she repeated many times, silently, was to be reunited with her other soul, her Andreas and to protect him while they remained apart.

Kiana was not in her physical body. She felt herself elevated upwards and was looking down on her supine form, frozen on the floor before the Altar. Love and the feeling surrounding a perfect love entered her spirit. Hecate was gifting her power. She knew she must always relive this moment in times to come, be they bloody or otherwise. Pure white light swirling with iridescent colours flooded her vision. She did not wish to leave or change this moment. She had no idea of Time.

Tamina grew cold. She quietly made an exit. She had an urgent need to be with Andreas. Her mother was not present at all. As she padded in bare feet to the exit, she looked back furtively to see her mother almost unconscious, and a wave of guilt washed over her. Should she go back? A silent voice entered her head with a resounding no!

She opened the door and saw Andreas waiting. She ran to him and hugged him passionately, kissing his hair, his eye, and then his mouth. He pulled her tighter to him, as if to meld her to him. They sought each other stroking and then grasping, flesh and hair, bound in a breathless kiss, exploring each other. Andreas broke away and took her hand, leading her to the carrier.

The slaves looked away and wandered off.

Andreas pulled the heavy curtains down and very gently, with extreme care, took his beloved Tamina into his arms and possessed her, as she possessed him in a union of love and of thunderous energy and white light that equalled her mother's union with Hecate. They lay breathing heavily entwined around each other.

"Our union is now made, Tamina," Andreas whispered, "And I am yours forever. And I will come to find you. Believe this. I will find you and we will go to your true homeland together."

"My stepfather will kill you if he finds out we have done this, Andreas," Tamina replied, reality suddenly overwhelming her, "I must go."

"Send word of where you are. This is all I ask. I will in return, learn the skills of the Silk Road. I will come back a rich man and impress your stepfather to fully claim you for my wife!"

Tamina wrapped her arms around him, as if to hold him, tightly, impressing his spirit to her forever. She was shaking, her soul already in crisis at the parting. And he cried. She joined him, their tears mingling as they kissed. Then she pulled away and almost threw herself out of the carriage. She stood away from his sight, her head against the cool pillar that hid her, and in deep breaths pulled her spirit back to her, as she straightened her spine, held her head high and crept back into the temple.

Her mother was still outstretched on the floor, arms held out as if already on a crucifixion cross the Romans used to kill their prisoners slowly. Tamina felt estranged from her for the first time since they were re-united. She looked around for some offering to Hecate and found a selection of resins in small bowls already burning and offering up sweet incense to the Goddess. She picked one, smelt it and knew it to be frankincense. She crept forward holding the bowl before her.

As she knelt at the altar, gifting the Goddess in silent prayer, her mother shifted. Maybe it was the incense that brought her back to consciousness.

Kiana blew a long breath outward, emptying her lungs of the deep breath she had just inhaled to bring her body back to life. She stayed kneeling for several minutes, head hanging down in deep contemplation. Tamina had her back to her, so close to the altar was she. She turned to watch as her mother slowly got to her feet.

"Tamina, my daughter," she whispered, still staring at the floor, "Please can you fetch myrrh for me?"

Tamina walked past her to fetch the bowl. Kiana's head shot up and she looked intently at her daughter's retreating form. A dark shadow crossed her serene face, and her cheek twitched involuntarily. She knew what had just happened with her daughter and Andreas. She had just smelt him on her beloved Tamina. She fought for control and won. She prayed silently to her Goddess for protection for her daughter even before herself. She prayed his impregnated seed within Tamina would not live. She also prayed for the courage to keep silent. This secret would remain between the two lovers. Tamina would need her love.

She gifted the myrrh to Hecate in trembling intensity. First in gratitude, then supplication.

"Hecate Girru ed-de-su-u nur ilāni kajãnu
Eddesu babbanítu"

Hecate Ever brilliant fire Goddess. Steady light of the gods. Constantly renewing, ever brilliant, beautiful woman.

It was all over, completed. Kiana hugged her daughter, wordlessly and they left the temple. All was the same, yet absolutely everything had changed, irrevocably. One act, at the crossroads of life had altered the course of their lives.

She looked around for Andreas and found him gone. He had left them. Tamina let out a low moan and crumpled to the floor. Kiana brought her arms around her daughter and cried with her pain, stroking her hair and whispering words of compassion and yet a still small hope.

She lifted her up and they both slipped into the carriage, the slaves miraculously re-appearing to carry them to the Forum.

... ...

Achaikos wandered through the early dawn in a relatively deserted city. He had left his beloved women in the hands of six trustworthy slaves and Andreas, keen to prove himself. He should not be worried, he chided himself. But he was. He could feel the sharp residue of tension lingering in the city and here, as he neared the forum. If persecution had happened, it would be here, in the Forum of the Ox.

If layers of screams and howls of anger had rent the air, their echoes would be heard here in the darkness before the new dawn.

And hear them he did. So, it was happening now, he thought. The decision to leave this day had been made for him by their anguish. The forum was the largest in Byzantium. Achaikos halted to stand for a moment in the deep shadows of the colonnade. His heart missed a beat as the white stone reflected the light of an emerging sun. It highlighted the massive plinth and seating area that had recently been constructed. The enforced sacrifices and apostatizes : the infamous *libellous* had been made a public spectacle.

Achaikos felt bile reach his throat and gave a voluminous amount of spit as his gift to the Roman magistrates. It landed and spattered on the pristine white pavement stone.

He moved on, keeping to the shadows of the colonnade, working his way out to the Lycus river, whose underground course through the city, was visible and marked by filigree wrought iron showing its meandering through the paved streets. Its path would take him close to Lips Monastery, enclosed by tall cypress trees and completely hidden from view.

He was expected. A knock on the entry door, and a crooked smile from the aged monk who recognised Achaikos. He was admitted as the giant oak door creaked open. He stood for a few moments allowing the monastery's sanctified energy to be absorbed into his aching muscles and tired heart. The sun was rising. He gazed with a heart beginning to pound, as its gentle rays shone through the Cypress "fire" trees, their near-vertical branches like flames swaying in a wind that spoke of a warm day to come.

Achaikos hurried on, swiftly relinquishing his sandals to walk barefoot into the hallowed sanctuary of Abrasax. He had to prepare the libation with all its intricacies by the third hour of the sun. He found the door leading to the ancient and small spiral stone staircase that led upwards to the sanctuary above the main hall. Each step worn to a waxy brown by many barefooted pilgrims.

He entered the sanctuary, suddenly realising his lungs ached from the exertion and that any breath had left him in sheer anticipation. He had brought white candles, frankincense incense, pure water with sea salt. Achaikos fumbled with the candles. Each one to be placed in the small gold holders. This was the most important invocation of his life. Imploring protection for his adored women to the most ancient One. He had decided to honour the feminine. He was to alter the ritual to bring in the moon first. He hoped it would suffice particularly as the form of this rite honoured the famed Alexandria. It had been many months since he had performed honouring the Seven planets or indeed empowerment of the Abrasax stones he had quietly procured for Tamina and Kiana. It needed to be done well.

He picked up the white candles one at time and laid them in the seven-pointed configuration already laid out in engraved gold. He stood away; his head bent low. Nothing should be inferior.

He disrobed all his outer clothing until only his tunica remained. He felt the sweat trickle in droplets down his back. The sanctuary was airless in a calm way. He looked up at the spherical dome above him and hoped some breeze would find its way through the opening. As if this prayer was instantly answered, a wave of air percolated down with the rising of the sun to its appointed position, the flame of all seven candles flickered. Achaikos took this as the formal entry and beginning of the libation to his God.

He bathed briefly, sponging his body with the sanctified water held in a silver bowl suspended on the plinth of fluted silver. Achaikos slowly turned to face the altar, the candles were burning well, all with even flames. This heartened him as the call for equilibrium was in place on the ethereal level at least. He went through the cleansing motions expelling any turgid air from his lungs for several minutes. He focused on the planets, their order and the invocation to them in preparation for calling in Abrasax.

Breathing slowing in expanding his lungs to a near painful level, on breathing out he visualized the white ethereal mist snaking outwards to envelop not just the heptagon but the whole sanctuary. He did not intend any gaps to be present before him. He replaced the washing water with the bowl of sanctified water on the plinth and carrying it with care placed it and himself within the heptagon. The Abrasax stones lay deep within the pouch, waiting for their empowerment.

Facing south-east, stretching his spine and fixing his feet to the earth, Achaikos began. Intoning the "A" to open the portal of the moon, his deep reverberation echoed around the small temple. The flame in that candle grew and danced as he went into trance. After the seventh round, he turned to intone the "B" to open the portal of Jupiter. He then turned to the next fixed point on the heptagon, his voice becoming deeper, more resonant. Intoning "R" to open the portal of Mars, he suddenly felt an energy swirl into him, into the heptagon. The flame on this candle holding the Mars energy swirled and dipped, smoke escaping as the flame hit the wax. His voice faltered for a split second as fear entered him. This was a warring male energy. "Why?" he pleaded within. No answer came. He renewed the intonation with vigour. He moved to invoke the power of the Sun. He intoned "A" again with more force of will than he knew. It worked.

Suddenly the whole temple became aglow in intense light. Achaikos opened his eyes and looked skyward. Indeed, the power of Abrasax became evident as warmth entered the sanctuary. The sun was beating down to him, through the opening in the spherical roof.

As he intoned "S" to open the portal of Venus, he heard the unmistakable echo. He was not alone! The Ancestors, most probably both Greek and Persian, notably female had come to gift equilibrium.

Achaikos felt emotion nearly overcoming his trance state. Then deep peace entered his heart and he continued with devotion unabated until the conclusion. The portals of Mercury and lastly Saturn were opened.

The last act of this rite was the longest and so deeply connecting with the most ancient God of all.

Achaikos looked up to face the sun fully. He had to close his eyes, so brilliant the light. The warmth soaked into his body. He meant to fully engage with his Creator.

ΑΒΡΑΞΑΣ Ψου τηε γρεατεστ γοδ , τηε ηιγηεσρ γοδ. Ψου αρ ε Λορδ τηε Χρεατορ! Ψου αρε τηε Χαυσε ανδ φιρστ αρχηετψπε. Ψου αρε τηε 365 ηεαϖενσ ανδ γαυρδιαν το τηε πλανετσ ανδ τηε σταρσ.

Ωε ηαϖε βεεν χρεατεδ ιν ψουρ ιμαγε. 365 παρτσ ηολδ υσ.

Ι πλεαδ ωιτη ψου το βεστοω ψουρ λοϖε ανδ προτεχτιον ον μ ψ ωομεν, Ταμινα ανδ Κιανα φορ τηε χομινγ 365 δαψσ οφ ουρ τρ αϖελ το ανεω ηομε.

"*Abrasax*. You are the greatest god, the highest god. You are Lord the Creator! You are the Cause and first Archetype. You are the 365 heavens and you are the guardian of the planets and the stars.

We have been created in your image. 365 parts hold us.

I implore you to love and protect my women, Tamina and Kiana in the coming 365 days of our journey to a new home."

Achaikos fell to his knees, strength failing him as he fumbled in his tunica to pull the rope of 365 seeds. He began to call his God to him for 365 repetitions.

ΑΒΡΑΞΑΣ

He focused on the beneficent energy of the planets, particularly the Moon and of Venus. The Goddess of Love. This in part to bring their protection to his women.

He had never known a love such as this. So starved of it in his Silk Road days and as Magi, the tenderness now was breaking his heart, as tears flowed down his cheeks.

It took longer than he knew. In the trance state, Achaikos did not notice the sun waning past the portal opening and the sky filling with the rich colours of that sun setting.

He came to with a jolt, as if one of his Ancestors had kicked him in the back, as he sprang upright, eyes popping wide open.

Οη! Ηο Σαξ, Αμυν, Σαξ, Αβρασαξ: Φορ τηου αρτ τηε Μοον, Τηε χηιεφ οφ τηε σταρσ, ηε τηατ διδ φορμ τηεμ, λιστεν το τηινγσ τηατ Ι ηαϖε σαυδ, ανδ φολλοω τηε ωορδσ οφ μψ μουτη. Ρεϖεαλ τηψσελφ το με, Τηαν, Τηανα, Τηανατηα, οτηερωισε Τηει. Τηισ ισ μψ χορρεχτ ναμε!

"Oh! Ho Sax, Amun, Sax, Abrasax: For thou art the Moon, the chief of the stars, he that did form them, listen to things that I have said, and follow the words of my mouth. Reveal thyself to me, Than, Thana, Thanatha, otherwise, Thei, this is my correct name."

Achaikos shook his head, trying to remember where he had learnt that. It was an old invocation. From the Greek papyrus, he thought. He stood, faltering in mid-rise, to realise how numb and stiff his joints were. He eased up, bringing the precious Abrasax gemstones out of their pouch. These were Basililidian originals and the carved symbols were obverse and reverse giving an elegant sculptural effect both in viewing them and feeling them. They felt the most alive amulets he had ever seen. He felt lucky to have purchased them. On the obverse side he had asked for the goddess Venus to be inscribed for Tamina. And for Kiana, it was so obviously Hecate. On the reverse side, the magical code was written, of which Achaikos was about to invoke in the empowerment of the deep veined jade gemstones. All was nearly complete. The light was holding. Could it be early afternoon? Achaikos wondered.

He gently laid the gemstones into the bowl before him and raised his hands palms upwards, arms stretched forward. And he cried out in his mother tongue-

ΑΒΡΑΣΑΞ Οη Λορδ οφ Χρεατιον, ψου μαδε βεαυτιφυλ ωιτη λ αυγητερ τηε υνιϖερσε.

Ψουρ φιρστ λαυγητερ χρεατεδ Λιγητ.

Ψουρ σεχονδ λαυγητερ διϖιδεδ τηε ωατερσ.

Ψουτ τηιρδ χρεατεδ τηε μινδ.

Ψουρ φουρτη λαυγητερ χρεατεδ φερτιλιτψ ανδ προχρεατιον.

Ψουρ φιφτη χρεατεδ Φατε.

Ψουρ σιστηε λαυγητερ χρεατεδ τιμε, ασ ιν τηε Συν ανδ τηε Moον.

Ανδ ψου σεϖεντη ανδ φιναλ λαυγητερ χρεατεδ τηε Σουλ!

"Abrasax, Oh Lord of Creation, you made beautiful with laughter the universe. Your first laughter created light. Your second laughter divided the waters, your third created the mind. Your fourth laughter created fertility and procreation. Your fifth created Fate. Your sixth laughter created time, as in the Sun and the Moon. And your seventh and final laugher created the Soul."

Achaikos then lowered his arms to put his hands gently around the bowl holding the Abrasax amulets. Now was the moment. He emptied his mind of all thoughts. He began to tremble with energy. With a voice so clearly not his own the magical codex was sent to each of the stones.

Αβλανατηαναλβα

Αβλανατηαναλβα

Silence remained. The candles' flame still danced in the gentle breeze. Achaikos' head lowered until it was almost touching the water. His shoulders were deeply hunched. He had no energy left to him. It had escaped with the sounding of the codex. Slowly, inch by inch, his hand reached in to reclaim the amulets and in putting them back in the pouch, declared the rite's completion. He carefully replaced all in their original positions, pinched each flame in silent thanks to the planets, looked upwards one last time and cried in thanks to his God.

... ...

Chapter 30

Roma crevit ex tenui principio se habet cum sua magnitudine est oppressae.

Rome has grown since its humble beginnings that it is now overwhelmed by its own greatness

(Titus Livius 59BC-17AD.)

Kiana held her daughter tightly. There was no anger in her. Achaikos will have enough for both of us, she thought, as she stroked Tamina's hair rhythmically trying to send the pain away from her. She whispered in her ear soothing words in Sogdian, childhood phrases of love and comfort. Words she would dearly loved to have said to her child, and never did. Her heart suddenly broke for those missing years. She knew Tamina would not understand the words, but that her soul would know every feeling passed through the tears which soaked her tunica and streaked her young face.

Kiana let go and her tears joined her daughter's. It became a moment of soul-wrenching anguish, a bottomless void of terror, humiliation, pain and torture. The world outside meant nothing; their salvation halted as they both relived their worst moments that had been locked away.

Andreas and his love had opened that lock. In this moment, Kiana united with her daughter. They both felt bereft of love. Kiana knew her daughter had been raped and violated as a mere child. She knew she had been impregnated in those tortuous years. All the compassion she could find, all the empathy she held for Tamina, would never be enough and her guilt rippled into her very soul and stayed there.

"You deserve so much more than this, my beautiful child," she managed to utter in-between the gasps of emotion. They were both trapped in this void of despair. "I pray he will return to you."

"He *will come and find me!*" Tamina shot up and looked directly into her mother's eyes, as if her Will could make it happen.

"Yes, I believe he will," she replied, deciding to be open with Tamina about what she discovered in the temple to Hecate, who she felt sure, would not condemn the act. Neither should she. Morality, when love was the principle, entered the very rhythm of nature and the Goddess herself.

Kiana turned to look Tamina straight in the eye.

"I know the act of love took place between you and Andreas, whilst I was in the Temple."

Tamina gulped her tears away, the shock silenced her.

"I smelt him on you my love," Kiana stated simply enough, "And I am not angry. Achaikos will have enough fury for both of us if he ever finds out. These slaves know for sure. I will offer them an outcome, should they think of talking, that will ensure their silence.

"My prayers daily, and yours Tamina, will be to Hecate, who saw it all since we called her in, and will be to make his seed die."

Tamina's hand went to her womb. She sighed and looked out of the carriage, whose drapes had been tied back. She saw one of the slaves slant his eyes towards her as he bobbed along, the sinews of his arms in relief, straining against the enormous load.

"Pay them, mama," she announced, "Threaten them, but pay them handsomely."

"Yes, I will certainly do that." Kiana nodded knowing from bitter experience, so recent and still taunting, that life for slaves revolved around begetting *denarii* and dreaming of gaining their *libertus*, their freedom.

They had come from the temple and had now reached the intersection that joined with the great *mesa,* the broad and elegantly columned road that was the thoroughfare for many Byzantium citizens. It travelled all the way through the city to the Golden gate. And it connected nearly all the forums, the meeting places and gathering points for all citizens. There was no detour. They had just passed the forum of *Theodosius* and had entered the *Amastriana,* that opulent and royal walkway, that displayed rare and distinctive foliage amidst the fluted marble columns. This was Rome's glory, its nadir in the scheme of the Cæsars to own Byzantium. To squeeze its native heart to a mere pulse, and then replace it with its own.

It was nearing the high point of a blazing sun, which beat down on the *Amastriana* to almost create the mirage of undulating white pavements and waving marble, if it were not for the intrusion of a rushing body of humanity that suddenly burst around the carriage, careering forward in a blaze of togas and byzantine robes of many colours.

The slaves began shouting at each other. The carriage veered to left, crushing and grazing a foliage with bright magenta flowers.

" *Σταμάτα να μας βάλει κάτω. Nolite posuit in nobis,* Stop! Put us down!" Kiana shouted through the drapes in two languages and was just about to speak in Sogdian when the carriage hit the ground with an almighty thump that jarred their teeth and impacted on the coccyx. They tumbled out to view the human traffic heading in a singular direction and taking up the whole avenue. Kiana jumped forward to grab a passing woman who was holding of all things, a moderately sized gilded eagle of Rome, wings outstretched and talons gripping the painted pole she clung onto with both hands, the white of her knuckles showing. She carried a look of intensity that chilled Kiana's spine.

"*Ubi is. Et ea quae hic aguntur nota?* Where are you going and what is happening here?"

"*Christiani magistratus ductus est ad Romanam studium ostendit libellus immolate. Caesar laudanda.*"

"It is the Christians being brought before the magistrate to say the Libellus and sacrifice to show devotion to Rome. Caesar be praised," the woman pointed to the end of the *Amastriana.* "There at the Forum of the Ox," she waved her hand and clutching the eagle surged forward, leaving Kiana and Tamina to stand immobile, staring at the transformation of the majestic Byzantium people to become a rabble with blood-lust overtaking their sensibilities and their compassion.

"Dah! We both know this feeling well, Tamina," Kiana wove her arm around her daughter's waist and gripped tightly. She will never let go, never abandon her again. She turned to the slaves.

"I give you leave to abandon the carriage. But I will not pay you if you do not protect me and my daughter until we are reunited with Achaikos. Is that understood?"

"Ναι, ναι, θα σας προστατέψουμε και με τις ζωές μας. Yes, we will protect you both with our lives." The eldest slave spoke up clearly, "What do you plan to do?"

"Walk of course!" replied Kiana, "To the Forum. Circle around us and do not stray."

The crowd thinned out as they neared the Forum. The noise became louder, as Kiana looked up to feel shame at the very view Achaikos had seen that dawn and had replied with all the spittle he could muster. The Forum boasted a massive fountain in its centre, fed by the Lycus river, its underground course stretching under the Forum and beyond as it snaked its way to the warm waters of the Marmara Sea. But it was dwarfed by the coliseum style erected plinth that was now seating hundreds. All to see the degradation, apostatizing or brutal murder of Christians.

Kiana held her hand to her heart as she realised the slaves at work with water and rushes were sweeping someone's blood away, their soul and aspirations hanging over the forum, trapped in shock at the brutal ending of their lives. The persecution had begun.

The agitation in the crowd was growing with calls from all directions. This almost drowned out by the baying and cries of the sacrificial animals tethered and straining to run. They had watched their kind axed to death. Their blood mixing with the Christians'. The sun beat down relentlessly, steam rising from the scorched stone as the slaves worked.

Kiana twisted her head around to find an escape route. Centurions in full military uniform encircled the forum, making escape impossible. They were both standing directly in front of the main dais which had been draped in luxurious blue cloth with gold tassels. On it were seated the magistrate, a bulbous overweight official whose Roman short fringe was plastered to his brow by his own sweat that ran down his face. Beside him sat the senatorial legate who handed him linens to wipe the sweat from the creases. He was not enjoying the day. Neither spoke.

Suddenly a gong sounded, and the forum was reduced to a hush, save for those poor animals. Reluctantly the magistrate rose from his throne, to announce the following Christians to bow to Rome in full public view.

"Byzantiorum civitas tu testimonium duarum familiarum christianarum libellus honorare virtutem Romanam ab Deci eventus recusatio acclamat sacrifica diis Romanorum imperatore. Qui nunc nobis operam sine sanguinis effusione offerant. Ave Caesare!

Citizens of Byzantium, you have witnessed the libellus of two Christian families honouring the might of Rome and the dire consequences of a refusal to acclaim Emperor Decius by sacrifice to the gods of Rome. Let those who now come before us offer their commitment without the shedding of blood. Hail Caesar!"

Hail Caesar! came the uproarious cries of the crowd whose collective consciousness had plummeted to a deep new low. They were baying for more blood. The creaking of the doors of the senatorial building to the left of the dais brought the wicked sun to the faces of the emerging family, whose eyes squinted at the glare. They had been in enforced darkness hitherto and met the crowd with confusion written on their faces. They had believed it would just be a matter of signing the libellus, making a token sacrifice and going home. They were as lambs to the slaughter, no more than the captive creatures tethered and bleating wildly to the strokes of the whip from their handler.

Kiana stood bunched with tension, almost quivering with repressed rage, her knuckles white and her eyes blacker than her hair.

Tamina wore an expression of deadness, of frozen feelings. Her trauma was ever present, and she had shut down. Kiana turned to see her daughter and expelled a huge breath, taking with it her pent-up anger. She relaxed to put her arm protectively around her daughter.

"I wish I could take you from this spectacle, Tamina my love, but we are, for the moment trapped in this crowd. But know this dear one, we will be gone from this place in a few hours at most. On your beloved water, listening to the seabirds and watching them swoop and swirl in the skies."

She watched as Tamina shut her eyes and relaxed.

"Stay there, Tamina, just stay *there!*"

Kiana focused back onto the hapless family whom it seemed would comply.

A young official of the magistrate strode forward wearing the official toga with stripes. He carried the certificates in a bunched hand. Facing the family, who were clearly Greek and pagan to a man, the official spoke in a clear voice,

"*Tu, et universa domus Kyrgiakos Alexius, Puer, ut debita Loulia Demetrius et sacrificium et libamen deorum maiestas?*

Will you, Alexios Kyrgiakos and your entire family, Despina, Dimitrios and Loulia make the required sacrifice and libation to the glory of the Roman gods?"

The father, Alexios, straightened his bent spine, squared his shoulders. His face bore the twisted expression of repressed anger, his swarthy olive-toned skin rippled with tension as he sought to protect his entire family from slaughter. He held his wife and his daughter, while his son stood behind him. He was much taller than his father and his was a face full of defiance. His eyes bore into the back of his father's head, willing him to reject this abomination.

"*Quod sic. Nos faciet sacrificium et libatio. Ave Caesar.*

Yes. We will make the libation and the sacrifice. Hail Caesar," Alexios looked up to the sun as he spoke, praying to his god for forgiveness.

"*OXI*," his son grabbed Alexios by the shoulders and tried to twist him around, shouting in his mother tongue, "Έχετε προδώσει τον πατέρα μας Ιησού Χριστό. Πέθανε για σένα

Πατέρα. Η αγάπη του περιβάλλει αυτούς τους κακούς βαρβάρους. Σταματήστε αυτό τώρα!

NO, you have betrayed our father Jesus Christ. He died for you Father. His love outshines these evil barbarians. Stop this now!"

"Βούλωσέ το!" The father hissed back at his son, twisting to yank his shoulders away from the iron grip of his distraught son, "Θέλετε η μητέρα σου να εκτελεστεί και η Λουλιά να βιάζεται και να σκοτώνεται,

Shut your mouth! Do you want your mother executed and Loulia raped and killed?"

"Clearly your son will not comply," the official stated, with a twisted smile. He looked up to the magistrate, who nodded callously as the two centurions pulled open the giant double doors, allowing entry to the executioners. They came carrying their tools in full view. They were both masked for anonymity, the stiffened and polished leather reflecting brightly in the afternoon sun. As their sandals flapped on the white stone, soon to be dyed blood red, the mother let out a piercing scream and collapsed. The daughter shook with fear.

They grabbed the son roughly by the shoulders, forcing him to kneel.

"*Manere!*" the Magistrate shouted down from dais, his veins standing out in his podgy neck to make himself heard above the baying of the crowd which had reached fever pitch, "***Ad suos conversus vigilantes videre. Ultima occasio est in conspectu Dei vos occursum vestri Miserator, filius Kyrgiakos. Numquid gratiam Graecorum Christiana, quod parcens vobis mulieribus.***

Wait! Make him look and watch his family convert. one last opportunity before you go to meet your compassionate god, son of Kyrgiakos. Be grateful Greek Christian that we spare your women."

He flopped back on his throne, waving the linen in front of his face, and watched dispassionately, wanting this done with so he could retire to sleep off the heat. He had never even chosen this elaborate sweat box as a home, and reminisced of his true domicile, Rome, as the persecution continued.

The sacrificial goat was brought forward, bleating, head straining sideways to escape as panic swept over the creature. It had watched his mate sliced open. The gladius was handed to the father. He took the goat's head and pulling it high, the eyes staring wildly, he swept the sword deeply across the throat, watching in horrid fascination as the blood flowed into the waiting bowl. The creature went limp. Alexios let go as it flopped to the ground, still twitching in muscular spasms. He lifted the bowl and offered the blood to the fountain as his libation to the gods and reluctantly, steeling his stomach, drank a small amount as part of the ritual. Rather that, he decided, than pulling the still warm heart out and sinking his teeth into that!

"Χαλάστε τη δύναμη των θεών και τη δύναμη της Ρώμης

Hail to the power of the gods and the might of Rome." Alexios uttered in a stricken croaky voice knowing what would follow this. His son's execution. Suddenly a voice rang out,

"**Θα αποσταθώ. Θα μετατρέψω**. I will apostatise. I will convert." Dimitrios suddenly blurted out to everyone's amazement, not least his father. A wave of relief washed over the family. The official handed over the libellus for Alexios to read to a hushed crowd, who had been denied the bloodletting and were in a mood, heavy with anti-climax.

"Read in Latin," the official ordered.

"*Commission elegit ut instarent super eos ad sacrificia sua*," Alexios read to no one. His head down in shame, he spoke without conviction or any feeling, "*A Federico, et de cognatione Kyrgiakos nos autem sacrificaverunt diis Romae ex edicto, et coram te: et sacrificium tibi feci, et libaverit et participes forerun in sacris victimas. Indicans infra detulisse.*

To the Commission chosen to superintend the sacrifices. From Alexios and the family of Kyrgiakos, we have now sacrificed to the gods of Rome in accordance with the decree and in your presence, I have made sacrifice, and poured a libation, and partaken of the sacred victims. I request you to certify this below."

The official stepped forward brusquely taking the scroll back. With just the formality of the wax seal, legalising the document, all was finished for this family, still intact but with souls torn apart and bleeding. The might of Rome was crushing the people underfoot like so many ants. They did not even register what they were doing to the Empire.

Kiana knew. She had been given the vision of the future showing clearly terrible torture at the hands of these Christians against Pagan people. "This is the beginning of their downfall," she thought, as she watched the courageous Greek Christian family return to their home. More followed. A Roman family, the Albinus Flavinius family, just husband and wife, who both took part and made the libellus look easy.

Kiana looked up to the dwindling sun, and silently implored Achaikos to appear before his stepdaughter would be forced to witness horrific torture that might split her mind for a long time. She turned to the slave behind her.

"Please find some water for us," she whispered, and turning back saw the next victims enter the forum, turned arena. She could see immediately that these people were devout Christians. They dressed differently and had been given new names. They entered with a proud walk; hands linked in a line that faced away from the magistrate. That incensed the official, who strode forward to manhandle the family to face forward.

"*Familiae Christoforou Ionas Helias vivit et tu et sacrificate diis convertere*? The family, Christoforou, Jonah, Elias and Eva, do you convert and make sacrifice to the Roman Gods?" the magistrate barked the order with a flick of his hand knowing this family were devouts and he had washed his hands of them.

The father yelled out in Hebrew, head held high, turning as he spoke to the crowd now with the horrifying cadence of a bloodthirsty horde.

"אנחנו מסרבים. ישו נצלב בידיך הרצחניות. אז אנחנו חייבים במסירות שלנו אל אדוננו לעשות כמוה

ללא שם: אתה ארור פעמים רבות!

We refuse. Christ was crucified at your murderous hands. So must we in our devotion to our lord do likewise. You are damned many times over!"

Kiana gasped. "Shield my daughter!" she ordered to the slaves, who quickly surrounded Tamina. She still had her eyes shut, but nothing would deafen her to the cries of this family. But the slaves were Namibian and very tall. They closed in as a glistening muscled blanket that muffled the sound. Kiana was ever grateful and determined she would, as a last act in Byzantium, offer them their *libertus,* their freedom. She would insist.

The executioners were hurried in. The family huddled together praying fervently for any divine help to reach them in their last moments. The sun was sinking behind the senatorial building creating long dark shadows. The air, still stifling, had a stale sweat smell clinging to everything and was empty of oxygen.

The boy was tragically young. His mother held him to her whispering ardently in his ear. For some comfort, spiritual strength. He was shaking, and he was wetting himself, as it settled in a yellow puddle at his feet. He broke and cried useless tears, shaking and holding his small hands in white-knuckled fists, banging his sides relentlessly.

"*Sit primum rogo. Et testimonium nostrum non esse occidendum, dicent ei pater ejus et mater. Quaeso!*" The mother shouted to the official, falling to her knees, her hands together imploring some mercy within the horrific moment

"Let him be first I beg you. He need not be witness to our murder, his father and his mother. Please!"

Someone shouted from the front of the crowd who were the standing spectators, very close to Kiana and Tamina. Kiana saw plainly a pouch being thrown into the forum. The woman had thrown her arm back so far to achieve a long throw.

"Take it quickly," she shouted, as it landed with dull thud at the feet of the father. "give it to your boy. He will feel nothing I promise you."

He hesitated. But not the mother. She seized the poison and lifted it to her boy's lips, tears now flowing freely as she told him she will meet him so very soon at the gates of Heaven. Almost instantly, young Elias crumpled as his eyes went up into his head and he became unconscious. There was no pain. Just eternal sleep.

"Thank you!" the mother cried. But it was said to an empty space. Kiana turned to see the woman had already fled. Then she saw the raised Gladius glinting in the last rays of the sun, firmly held in the hand of the executioner, and ready to open the throat of Eva.

Kiana let out a deepest throat-wrenching scream. But it was drowned by the baying shouts of the crowd, now stamping and waving their arms in the shrieking of insults and abuse at the Greek Christians.

Before she could draw another breath, she was swirled around to meet the chest and open arms of her guardian and lover. Achaikos had come at last. He held her tightly, whispering in Greek to calm her. She would have preferred Sogdian or Akkadian. But she was intensely relieved to be led away with her daughter, still guarded by the faithful slaves out of the horror which was the Forum to the Ox.

"We will talk later, "he assured her, "For right at this present moment we must make haste to the harbour where my vessel awaits us, ready to haul up anchor."

"The *palanquin* is left along the *Amastriana,*" Kiana replied, "how can we retrieve it now?"

"Leave it. I have taken another one. It is right here." Achaikos pointed to the larger more opulent one. It seated four admirably and another slave to bear the extra weight.

"These slaves," Kiana began, when they were comfortable seated within the safety of the *palanquin*, "They are deserving of their freedom, Achaikos. As my last gift to Byzantium, will you grant their *libertus*?"

"Hmm, we do not have the time, my love. Ask them if they are prepared to travel with us to the first port of call, where I can arrange the scrolls of freedom."

Achaikos sat back against the hugely padded cushions, sighing with relief that his family was safe. Andreas was now caretaker of his silk road routes and he was on the cusp of a great adventure. He held Kiana's hand and brought it to his lips, kissing tenderly the sweat ridden but beautiful hands of his lover, his friend and his guardian also. He turned to face her looking deeply into her raven eyes.

"Will you do me the honour of becoming my wife?" he asked simply, without preamble. He had never uttered those words before. He did not know how to phrase the most important words any man can say in his lifetime. Nor how to beguile.

Kiana smiled. She knew all the defects of this man. She also knew his pure heart and burgeoning soul. She knew his intense integrity and his honesty.

"Yes," she replied as simply as the request had been offered.

Achaikos blew out a huge lungful of air, unaware he had been holding it. He was ecstatic. He embraced her long and ardently, silently thanking Abrasax, Hecate and all the Gods and Goddesses.

The vessel was built to take the roughest seas. A virulent plague had reared its ugly head so Achaikos had decided to hug the coast all the way to *Bonensis,* close to Celtica, to present all the wonders to his family, for theirs was a journey to be savoured. He knew it would take a month or even two months longer, but an overland journey would be hazardous and take much longer again. The river *Saonne* would take them to the borders of Belgica, near to Britannia where, at the coast of Gaul, they would take ship one last time to reach the island of Wihtland, as Vrittakos named it. The Romans called it Vectis instead of its name Wectis, after Wecta, grandson of Wōden. Vespasian saw to that.

On board the homely quarters for the women had been refurbished, standing high on the stern, double lagged for warmth and boasting a window looking out to sea. "This is for Tamina," Achaikos had said simply. The storage, which for them was so very little, was aft, and no doubt would be occupied by goods gathered on the way. There were many ports of call. The decking became the roof for the oarsmen. Eight each side to see the boat surge against the calmest of waters. The sail, when hoisted made Kiana's heart suddenly burst open. For there in all the glory of a craftsman's skill sat the crescent moon and star of Hecate in beautiful colours set against the purest blue. It would always remind her of the first moment she saw Byzantium.

She hugged Achaikos. She shed tears for the beauty of his care, for the symbol of Hecate that would be with her this journey. But most of all, for his rescue. He had saved her life and that of her daughter.

"Thank you for all that you are" she said quietly.

... ...

BOOK THREE

Chapter 31

Wihtland
Berandinzium Villam

Aelius stood, legs apart, his hands resting on hips that were now relatively pain free, eyes squinting into the sharp mid-day sun. His Roman fringe was growing out. He pushed his locks back deciding it urgently required plaiting and greasing. He would soon be a *Libertus* and he was going native at long last. His wife, Aife stood silently beside him, looking over at the preparations for his travel. He reached to her and gently put his arms around her shoulder, squeezing her shoulder blade affectionately, reverting easily to Durotrige he whispered quietly,

"Fy ngwraig fach, mae gennyf y cyfle hwn i iacháu, i ddod o hyd i fy hunan wir unwaith eto. Byddaf yn dod o hyd i fy heddwch allan yn fy Wihtland annwyl. Rwyf wrth fy modd i chi mor ddrwg.

My sweet wife, I have this chance to heal, to find my true self once more. I will find my peace out there in my beloved Wihtland. I love you so dearly."

Aife closed her eyes against the sun, feeling its warmth on her skin and smiled broadly to match its warmth.

"Rwyf wrth fy modd i chi y tu hwnt i unrhyw eiriau fy ngŵr cariadus. Teithio'n dda.

I love you beyond any words my loving husband. Travel well."

Aelius bent over to kiss her crown and nuzzled into her beautiful dark raven hair, breathing in the scents of camomile and jasmine she loved. Committing the aroma to memory, he knew he would not be gone for long. Yet he would miss her as the wounded and fractured part of him knew full well, she had made him whole again. Perhaps that would change. Re-uniting with his tribe, the Warinni as a freed man would bring his spirit home. His eldest son, on seeing his father about to leave, loped over to his parents in few strides. He was an exceptionally tall boy. A Warinni giant, pure and true. He stood another hand above his father, with a straight back and with tousled wavy copper brown hair he could be a *Cyng* of the Wihtwara! But he was yet a slave boy to the Romans and his defiance outmatched his father. He had the welts to prove it, much to Aelius and Aife's agony.

"Fæder, forhwōn dōn þu ne, lǽtan mè æt midsiþian þu? Humeta cunnan ic geleornian æt Geweorðan a hearra cræftmon." Cahal spoke loudly to his *Fæder* in the Ancestor tongue whenever the Romans were absent or out of earshot.

"Father, why do you not allow me to accompany you? How can I learn to become a master Craftsman?"

"Simply because, son, I have not yet the authority," Aelius replied slapping his son on his back, weary of the question often asked, "We will all be Libertus soon enough. Help your mother." Cahal drooped, his head nodding slowly against his chest.

"When I return," Aelius shot back, pulling his son's face up to stare directly in his ice blue eyes, "I will be Eyvindr and only Eyvindr, my Goddess given name."

There came a sudden bellowing, hooves thudding on the hard-baked earth. They all turned to watch, mouths agape, at the discharge from the Roman *navigium* as it swayed and listed on the water, from the huge weight moving through its bows, of the largest herd of long-horned heifers, with accompanying bulls taking up the rear, that anyone had witnessed at Berandinzium Villam. The heifers were rolling, heavily pregnant, as they came to a near stampede, showing their calves would be born here on the new pastureland. There were too few men with long whips and poles trying to push the herd forward.

Aelius took a sharp intake of breath as in amongst the heaving flesh he glimpsed the unmistakable glint of pure white flashing against the sun. The Warinni in him broke through in sheer joy. The young white heifer was a symbol of the sacred, as was the white horse guardians of the Wihtwara. This then was the sacred herd brought for the Mithraism and the Roman elite.

A small group of young bulls broke free, hollering in panic, eyes wide and rolling. They were making for the pride and joy of Venitouta's creation, her precious garden newly completed.

Shrieks from the slaves exacerbated the fright of the cows, whose hollering went up an octave. Some brave slaves banded together to form a human barrier, waving their arms to protect the young box trees and lilies from being trampled on.

The sharpest scream then emitted from a woman standing at the entrance to the Villa. That stopped all in their tracks. Venitouta had spoken. And in that second's pause, the heifers turned away and were driven back along the path to the main herd being ushered into the lush pasture adjacent to the pinto bean crop.

"Eyvindr! my dear man," she exclaimed, striding forward to bid him farewell, "Vrittakos sends his deepest apologies. Events have overtaken us, Eyvindr," she placed her hands on both shoulders and looked deep into his questioning eyes, "The elite are not coming here so quickly. But they are still giving out their orders to us, as you can plainly see. Their religious belief takes on an urgency when their temporal power is about to be snatched away! Hence the sacred heifer must now take predominance and we will all stink of cow muck!"

"Oh, my lady!" Aife exclaimed, "I'm sure we will manage."

"We have not been given enough notice!" Venitouta replied sharply, heaving an inward breath for patience, "Now Vrittakos must oversee the building of a strong enclosure and over-wintering buildings. He cannot accompany you Eyvindr. What he did wish you to know, is you must take as much time as you wish to visit your people as you inspect the Villams around Wihtland."

Eyvindr smiled and planted a loving kiss on her cheek. "Aife will assist you." He caught hold of his piebald by the mane and leaped up, shouting to his two slave assistants gifted by Vrittakos to steer the wagon full of equipment and materials. Just as he turned to leave, his son's gaze caught his eye. A longing so profound, hit him square in the chest. His son was pure Warinni, yet he had never met his true family. Until now.

"Begietan þin hors mín bearn!" Eyvindr shouted, with a huge smile creasing his face as he waved at his son, *"Þu are becuman wiþ mè æt gemètan þín ðèodscipe, Þæt Wihtwara!*

Get your horse, my son. You are coming with me to meet your people, the Wihtwara!"

... ...

Chapter 32

Re-union

Eyvindr's heart began to flutter wildly in contrast to the plodding slow progress of the oxen pulling the loaded wagon. They had stated what their progress would be from the outset, heads sunk low, their hooves rarely meeting even ground on sunbaked earth. The Villam was receding to just a white speck in the valley, as Wihtland opened to him and his aching soul opened to meet it.

In the eighteen full summers since his return, he had rarely ventured to his home. Several seasons were spent with the Durotrige at *Frescewætr Èalond* learning his *drýcræft* skills with forging metal, then meeting and falling in love with his *wíf*, Aife who bore him the son now riding at his side. A wonderful thought passed through him. Would it be possible or even permissible to have a re-naming rite for his son, gifting him a Warinni name? Cahal was his son's Briton name. Would Aife accept this? He wondered. Cahal had Warinni blood coursing through his veins. It was plain to see.

On the few occasions his *sweostor* Dagrun had reached out to meet him at the Villam, her eyes sparkled when she first cast her penetrating gaze on his son. Her old soul had connected with an even more ancient one and her eyes were tinged with tears when she first embraced him.

Eyvindr's "Romanesque" title he had adopted for his very survival in a strict Roman culture had prevented him from feeling his way back to Nerthus and Wōden. All the Gods and Goddesses of his youth had stood aside, looking on, silent and watching, as he attempted to win over Mithras and become an adept.

Just as Dagrun's eyes had sparkled when she first saw Cahal, so Nerthus came to greet Eyvindr again, as the sea sparkled Her welcome to him, nearly blinding him, and from the depths of his soul, came absolute love, sweeping over his body like the wave that swept onto the beach below. It took all the air from his lungs and he reined in his stallion to a trot, then stopped. He breathed in the clean sea air, his head bowed to his chest, and began the release, tears flowing, and body wracked with freed emotions.

Cahal had stopped some spear lengths away and in stopping, twisted his mount around to see his father bent over the piebald. He galloped back.

"*Hwæt ãdlian þu Fæder?*" Cahal reached over to hold his arm. "What ails you father?"

"*Ic am becuman æt seledrèam bearn. Willan þu geðèodan mè?* I am coming "home" son. Will you join me?"

Eyvindr looked up and saw what he had always dreamed he might see in his son.

"*Giese!*" Cahal responded, gently shaking his father's arm to press the point home, "I have wanted this since the very first time I saw Dagrun and she pierced my soul with her love!"

"Go back and tell the men with our wagon, and the soldiers to be keen-eyed and follow the old trackway. We will meet them at the mead hall at *Lãfadūn* this twilight," Eyvindr spoke through a wide-beamed smile, nodding in acceptance of the huge gift he had just been given.

"We need to travel in the footfalls of our Goddess Nerthus, our Earth Mother along the *Niðdraca foldweg,*" Eyvindr added as he shouted back spurring his piebald to a gallop. He stopped on the ridge of *Ceofodūn Scyte* allowing his stallion a brief pause to munch on the tall grass that grew in clumps on the rich dark soil. As he waited for Cahal to join him, hands clasped in the horse's mane, he stroked it gently, he received childhood memories that had been locked away. *Eorþ-ceafer,* earth beetle, he remembered. That one day in the hottest of *Sumors* they came!

"Cahal, my son," Eyvindr turned to him, as he caught up and joined his father, as they trotted together along the ridge, "This *dūn* is very special. When I was maybe two *sumors* younger than you, Dagrun and Eystein coaxed me to run away and escape the second planting time in the fields. We just bolted up the *dūn* to here! Just where we are now. We hid in the gorse and drank in the smell of those heady yellow flowers" He pointed to the line of bushes that still festooned the *Ceofodūn Scyte*. "It was then, suddenly the air became thick and noisy. The *Eorþ-ceafer* had arrived! In their multitudes. The air was so thick with their numbers, if we opened our mouths, they would simply have flown in. They were black and had hard bodies and they made this clicking sound as they gathered together in groups. We did not belong there at all! They outnumbered us by many countless bodies, all arriving at this moment in time, at this one place. And they came just to mate, lad. And we were in the middle of the biggest swivving dance ever!"

Cahal let out a guffaw, laughing at the thought.

"They were mating in our hair, on our bodies, they had no shame those swivving *ceafer*, I tell you Cahal! We hit the Earth Mother, breathing in the smell of her dark soil. And then we decided to bolt for it. We found out when we got back, after being soundly chastened by *Fæder*, that we had chosen the one day in the year when those earth beetles arrive from across the big water. "*Ceofodūn* is their mating ground," my *Fæder* said," We should be honoured to have been present!"

"So, this *dūn* is named after them?" Cahal questioned.

"We name our lands after the animals and people that live on that land son," Eyvindr smiled and nodded quietly, "*Lãfadūn* is named after your first cousin, Lãfa. You will be impressed with the Mead Hall where she lives now. It was Eileifer's honour gift and creation to Dagrun, his love. But first I want to take you to *Sudmōr* to meet your family. They are not expecting us. They will be overjoyed!"

Cahal shifted his gaze to the horizon, seeing the different hues of blue dance on the water, the sun truly sparkling on the surface of each ripple and wave. He was much more cautious than his father. He suspected joy would surface after the first shock. He felt quite certain their initial response would be that they had suddenly become accomplices to an escape from the Villam. And surely what else could they think, as he had not met his *Ealdmōdor* or *Ealdfæder*. Suddenly appearing before them, the long-lost *Nefa*.

The seabirds had caught a wind, the breeze had picked up and they were dancing circular swirls and swooping low to catch the up-current. Cahal felt their freedom and decided to relax and enjoy the feeling so rarely experienced at the Villam. His *Fæder* was caught in his memories returning to him and was describing with ever more alacrity his best moments as a *scōp*.

"I never got to act out the last moments of our *Thing*," he recalled, glancing at Cahal, who nodded and stroked his mount, reflecting silently how sad that his *Fæder's* talent had been lost to him. Eyvindr kept pulling his growing hair back out of his eyes. Cahal tried to imagine him with long waving locks tied tight in a swabian knot intertwined with beaded plaits. And failed completely, so used to seeing him with short, straight-cut fringe and sides like a Roman centurion.

"I was acting out the swooping down of Huginn, Wōden's familiar, when the Roman's invaded our celebrations," Eyvindr continued, lost in his memory now re-claimed, "I so dearly wished to offer the *drýcræft* of that birthing of our name, gifted directly from our Ancestors in song, for those who were not present that twilight. That will remain in the mists of Wryd, floating on the currents for those with ears to hear."

Eyvindr suddenly stopped, temporarily shocked, as those words never used, were uttered again. And he felt the closing of an yawning gap in his soul like a physical thing. His body reacted to that return with a definite lessening of tension. His shoulders eased, and his back flexed pushing out the remaining painful memories of his flogging.

They were now dipping downwards along the *Scyte,* both mounts swaying with each footfall, changing gravity as each man following the rhythm of their horse, moved as one with them. In easy companionable silence, father and son arrived at *Slācum,* close by was *Plaish Bearu* and good watering ground. They dismounted and led the horses to the clean bubbling water of

Luclèah broc and as the horses dipped their heads into the chilly water, both men fell to their knees and did likewise. Cahal felt the life-giving water course through his body jolting it alive like no other fluid could. His was a life born into Roman captivity. His young body knew wine. The Roman distrusted water, they had to be in control of nature and change it. So, wine was the preferred drink. Eyvindr picked up his son's thoughts. How does he always do that? Cahal muttered silently.

"Our first visit will be to *Gãrdūn*, Cahal," Eyvindr nudged him, "Many spear lengths of grapes as far as the eye can see! The vineyards have won recognition as far as Rome. Well, as far as the Villam Regis Cogidvbni in Britannia which counts for much these days, son."

Cahal nodded, wiping the water away from his face and hair. He was no judge of Wihtwara countryside but his instinct for nature's pulse, inherited, he always thought, felt a momentous change to the heartbeat.

"*Plaish Bearu* looks diminished *Fæder*," he muttered looking around to witness a clutch of bodies, some with backs bent, others straining, carrying heavy loads, all in the deep labour of birthing this latest Villam, seen clearly in limestone washed white against the disappearing backdrop of the once substantial wood. Large areas of pastureland had been levelled for crops like the wheat the Romans preferred and all along the *Broc* they had harnessed that once free-flowing gushing stream, to grow the dark leafed cress. The sheep had been relegated to forage on the *dūn* side.

"*Giese*," Eyvindr said, "And we will be visiting the cause of all this damage in a few twilights' time, Cahal. And we will enter the Villam with a Roman smile of fixed teeth and a surveyor's eye!"

"You don't look Romanesque anymore, *Fæder*, you look like a Warinni rebel!"

"Hmph!" he growled, "I will ask Lãfa to wax down my unruly locks!

"Come, let's go." He hauled his aching body to standing, realising that his thighs were lamentably out of condition to horse riding any distance at all. In fact, substantial time had elapsed since he had travelled Wihtland. He felt the conflict of emotions suddenly rise to jostle with each other. The trapped loss of Time in whole seasons, hurt him deeply along with the surfacing joy of freedom and release.

They mounted and kicked their horses to a gallop eager to find the ridge of highland along *Rãnadūn* and *Lãfadūn*. Eyvindr saw the Mead Hall appear before him. It was by any reckoning an impressive oaken presence of the Ancestors and of the Wihtwara. Energy seemed to thrum around the carved symbols of guardian animals, painted and polished to come alive in the mounting heat and light of Sunni, whose dappled rays played upon their faces and bodies in a dance of hues and shadows.

Eyvindr looked up to calculate the time and made an instant decision. He reigned in his piebald suddenly, who bucked and reared up, causing clods of earth to spray upwards.

"We have the day, Cahal. We are paying a visit to my *nefene,* Lãfa your *modrigensunu!*" Eyvindr kicked the horse into action and galloped forward, urgency overtaking reason, as if the whole mead hall might suddenly evaporate in a *drýcræft* spell working.

The immense height of the Mead hall towered above them as they cantered towards the large oaken doors, and it cast them in shadow. A swarthy looking lad ran towards them, offering to take their horses to be fed and cared for. Yet another youth walked towards them, head on one side, not recognising either of them. He stared at Cahal with an intensity that offered both hostility and confusion. He was immensely tall and lithe, and his gaze met Cahal's head on.

"*Ic hãlettan þu gíest. Hwæt is þín gemynd hèr? Þes is þæt Cwèn's Heall.* I greet you strangers. What is your purpose here? This is the Queen's Hall!" the youth stated, lifting his head to glare at them, his eyes half closing in hostility.

Eyvindr took an involuntary step backwards in some shock. The lad did not even recognise him. He arched his back and squared his shoulders, replying in a as loud a voice as he could muster,

"*Mín bearn ond Ic ãgan cuman æt biscoprice mín steopdohtor Lãfa. Ic am Eyvindr*! My son and I have come to see my niece, Lãfa. I am Eyvindr!"

"My *sweostor* is not seeing anyone. She is ...."

"Eyvindr!" came the cry from an opening high above their heads, the wooden shutters springing open to show the tousled head of his niece peering down, mouth open in amazement, her hands reaching up to her mouth in shock.

"Oh, beloved Nerthus, Wōden *Eall Fæder* you have answered our prayers!" came the excited voice of Lãfa as she disappeared, and with a clattering of hard sandals on the worn oak floor, appeared at the yawning gap of doors being forced open. She squeezed through and ran to engulf Eyvindr in a Warinni bear hug, long free flowing wafts of her chestnut hair covering his face.

The boy stood away, head down to the earth, hands clasped before him, sneaking sideways looks at Cahal, who ignored him.

Lãfa stood away holding Eyvindr by his arms and kept laughing and smiling unable to find the right words.

"Lãfa sweet child," Eyvindr smiled, "you are breaking my arms and mending my heart both together!"

"It is almost unbelievable to see you here!" she replied, letting him go and moving over to Cahal, offering him a Warinni greeting.

"And this is your son?" she said smiling, inspecting him with an admiringly fond look that made Cahal blush. "He is a Warinni, Eyvindr, through and through. Your name young sir if you please?"

"Cahal," he answered, feeling his cheeks begin to blaze.

Lãfa put her head to one side questioning the name silently.

"It is from his mother's tribe, the Durotrige," Eyvindr offered, "It means powerful in battle. Ready for war! Their past is full of conflict and brave boys grow to be warriors early."

"The blood of Wōden flows through him Eyvindr. You know this." Lãfa moved over to hold this tall lad, looking deeply into his soul as only a *spakōna* can and nodded.

The boy who was looking on, shifted uncomfortably from foot to foot, a fixed expression on his young face that spoke of anger even hatred.

"He is of the Wihtwara now, Eyvindr. Let it be said, known and honoured!

"Cæna, come forward and greet your *fæderansunu*. You have much in common, not only your ages!

"Cahal, this is my *brōðor*, Cæna, the rightful heir to the *Cyngship* of Wihtland, son of Dagrun and Eileifer."

Cahal extended his arm in greeting, leaning forward to clasp Cæna's forearm in the Warinni way. The boy eyed him with shaded lashes that hid the hostility. He brought his arm forward, reluctantly. Eyvindr frowned, shaking his head but saying nothing. An awkward silence followed, broken by Lãfa's loud voice offering hospitality.

"Come, let us eat and drink. Let me know all your news".

And with that, they were led into the great Hall. It was the first time since that terrible night that Eyvindr had walked down that aisle. Echoes of laughter came to him and he saw himself swooping and dancing in the shifting of the raven, jumping onto the tables and shouting his joy. The echo faded, and he came back. It had all changed. There was sadness and melancholy here. An absence of any joy because the *Cyng* had gone. He had passed to *Neorxenawang* and the magnificent hall he had created and built for the love of his life, Dagrun Wahl, would never be the same again. For a moment, Eyvindr's head sunk into his chest, as he passed a deep prayer to his brother that twisted his heart and stopped his breath. He remembered the sword he had lovingly created for their handfasting and how he had risked everything to bring it into life. So soon his *Cyng* had gone and the sword with him.

Lãfa saw his grief and instantly waved to a girl to fetch food, led him gently upwards on the oaken stairs leading to the Solar, said gently,

"This is the open and sun-filled part of our hall. You have never seen this. Eileifer created it for my *Mōdor*. It has his love woven and beaten and fixed into every part, every corner. There was so much light from Sunni cascading into the Solar, the dust mites could be seen dancing in the rays. She highlighted the flowers and herbs picked and displayed around the room. An almost permanent ray highlighted the beautiful fur-covered bed with red tassel hangings swaying in the gentle breeze.

"It is where I live now with Arkyn, my beloved, who has Wōden's blood running through him, so my *Mōdor* says."

"How is my *sweostor*?" asked Eyvindr, coming straight to the point as the serving girls placed bread, cheese and ale before them.

Lãfa put down her warmed bread and sighed, deeply.

"She is white angry, Eyvindr, whiter than the centre flame. At your treatment, your lashings. And it is, I believe the only thing that is keeping her here. Keeping her breathing. Her grief is beyond any words I can give you. It was so very sudden." She put her hand to her belly, caressing it gently as if to pacify.

"You are with child!" Eyvindr exclaimed, smiling briefly and nodding with gratitude.

"*Giese!*" Lãfa replied, ploughing into her food once more, "My appetite, once the sickness went, is huge!"

"I so wish *Mōdor* to stay with us long enough to see her *Nefene*, but life is seeping away from her, Eyvindr. She does not wish to be here anymore," Lãfa choked briefly, yet again, after all the tears, yet still more were waiting to escape her broken heart.

"Maybe you can bring her back, *Fædera*. Her love for you is as deep and profound as is her love for Eileifer. You know this. Maybe seeing you, really being with you, will turn her soul away from the *Neorxenawang*."

"*Giese*," he replied, "I will make my move very soon. I have my wagon with supplies arriving here at twilight. I was hoping to make fast over to Sudmōr to see Dagrun and all the family. They have yet to meet my son Cahal. Well the *Ealdmōdor* and *Ealdfæder* have not. Dagrun found the Warinni running strong through him. He feels it too," Eyvindr said looking over to his son, who was busy slating his hunger with ale and cheese, in that order. "As you can see, he is a young giant, with an appetite to prove it!"

"Can I ask you," he continued, looking directly into Lãfa's eyes, "What ails the son of Eileifer?"

She looked around briefly to see Cæna sitting hunched in the only shade available in the solar, scowling and refusing to join them in eating.

"Well there you have it. He is every inch the son of Eileifer, yet he is living in the most profound bitterness. He has not forgiven his *Fæder* for dying. And he has not forgiven his *Mõdor* for abandoning him to a ghost. I cannot understand this myself, in truth."

"Oh, I do," Eyvindr replied, "I will see what I can do. Vrittakos has given me my *Libertus* in all but signature on papyrus and leave to re-unite with my family, before the work on the Villams begins."

"Dah!" Lãfa exploded, "Speak not to me of their damn Villams. These Romans have no respect for our Mother, no understanding of Nerthus. We have witnessed them boring into our Mother with no ceremony, no offerings. Her white skin is being ripped from her like a flaying. This they say is for the whiting of their villas, to make them look pure, so they shine in the light of Sunni. It is for making their *opus cæmenticium* to build all these villas. What are they all for Eyvindr?"

"I will tell you, all in appropriate time. We must away to see Dagrun."

Eyvindr rose and beckoned Cahal to finish up gorging and made for the door.

"Eyvindr, are you still a *Romanesque*?" Lãfa spoke, head to one side questioning.

Eyvindr remained silent.

"Until today, I would have replied yes to that," he turned to take Lãfa in his arms to hug her gently, "but now", he whispered, "I can no longer say that. Nerthus has flooded me with her love and I am walking in two worlds. It is not a comfortable place to be!"

"Tell Dagrun, Eyvindr, be sure to tell her!"

... ...

As they approached *Sudmōr*, Eyvindr experienced heady memories cascading over each other for prominence. So much of his early life had been hidden away in the darkest part of his mind, for sheer survival. Now they were free. And he spent precious minutes viewing and feeling them live once more.

Cahal was experiencing the nervousness of facing the unknown. He glanced at his father; whose beatific smile spoke of a life Cahal would never know. He felt suddenly estranged from him. He kept up with Eyvindr, who had suddenly broken into a canter, when, Cahal would have simply turned and sped away.

The *cæsterwic* of the Warinni came into view, the low-lying *hūs* of a growing number of families clustered around the mead hall and meeting *hūs*, the tanning, weaving and forge buildings extending away to the paddock where the white augury horses lived in peace. Plumes of smoke rose from the working buildings, almost vertical in their path to the sky, so calm was the day and hot now that Sunni had reached her zenith.

Eyvindr slowed to a trot, Cahal tight at his side so the horses almost rubbed flanks.

"Be calm, son," Eyvindr commented, feeling the tension rise in his son, "Dagrun will have certainly spoken of you to *Fæder* and *Mōdor*, they will warm to you with ease. But please allow Dagrun her space, she is in mourning still and will not be her normal self at all. I believe she has just returned from deep *seiðr drýcræft* and may not even be present."

They eased past the acrid-smelling weaving *hūs*, where vats of dye were outside in the sun offering up acrid waves of urine, lemon, and limestone to taint the air. Within the shade of the *hūs,* a woman with a long pole was gently stirring the mix which held skeins of wool. She was singing a chant softly. It was their *drýcræft* working into the wool.

Eyvindr felt her magic join the wafting smoke trail upwards towards Thunor. Again, his soul's fractures swam to join on the powerful river of Wryd. He suddenly felt he had truly come home.

He came to a grateful halt outside the much-altered family home. It had been substantially enlarged. The *Cyng* Eileifer had brought his influence to bear on the Warinni *hūs,* now rising to gift a higher floor. And he saw the depth had grown also. Was that a bread oven? He wondered, as he jumped to the dusty hard packed earth. There was movement within. A shriek came from inside the *hūs* as the thick hide covering the opening shot sideways and Eyvindr caught the unmistakable face of his *Mōdor*.

A flurry of skirts as the hide opened and out stepped Gudrun. She stood stock still, her over-kirtle crunched to her mouth, as she stared completely dumbstruck at the sight of her youngest and most bitterly missed son of the Wahl family. She shook her head and began to cry, tears of loss falling and soaking into her stained work kirtle.

Cahal stared, and shifted awkwardly from one foot to the other, then stared at the dusty ground as his *Fæder* strode forward to wrap his *Mōdor* in his arms, burying his head in her still ample hair.

"*Mín Bearn, Mín bearn,*" she whispered, then pulled back, "You've escaped that awful villam!"

Cahal nodded slowly to himself, awarding points, for accuracy.

"*Nah, nah,*" Eyvindr repeated, smiling, grabbing her arms, "I am, we are," he turned to his son, "Libertus in all but the mark on the papyrus. We are freedmen *Mōdor*!"

Gudrun gasped, and her eyes travelled to meet the tall swarthy-looking youth who met her gaze with almost equal astonishment. He recognised so much of himself in her, for she was of the giant race, a Wahl. Some ancient memory, a song sprang up in his young soul and he made the first move. He extended his arms for the Warinni greeting. She met him, eyes level and shining, her tears wiped away and replaced with pure joy. They bonded in the traditional way.

Then she stepped forward to embrace her *Nefa*.

"Your name *mín Bearn*," she whispered.

"Cahal, *Ealdmōdor*," he replied.

She stood back.

"This is Durotrige. I believe its meaning is strong. You are courageous in battle. Strong." Gudrun starred into his soul, "You will be needing that Wōden gifting, *Nefa*, in your lifetime. You will be needing that and more." She nodded slowly at some far-reaching picture and patted him affectionately.

Gudrun turned about and led them into her *hūs*.

She strode over to the far end of a spacious living area. She flipped over some flat breads that were browning on top of a *Romanesque* looking oven. And then stirred the ubiquitous cauldron of vegetable porridge hanging over the open grate piled with logs hissing and sparking away. This was her domain. It was her sanctuary and forever a peaceful place. Gudrun made it so.

Yet another energy floated and slithered through this, like a weed on the River Wryd's surface. It was unable to free itself. It was snared on a rock that moved slightly with the current but was itself trapped and stuck.

And that rock suddenly embedded itself in Eyvindr's soul, leaden and deadly. He felt his spirit struggle and sink under the miasma. This then is how Dagrun was feeling, he realised, and empathy for his *sweostor* engulfed him.

"Dagrun," he said simply to his *Mōdor*, and as she turned to face him, and knew he too was sinking into the darkest pit, she said simply,

"If there is anyone who can reach her, it is you. I thank the Goddess you have come at last for I don't believe she will be with us for much longer."

"Her son grieves for both his *Fæder* and his absent *Mōdor*," Eyvindr replied, bluntly, feeling frustration rise in him for the pain Dagrun was causing Cæna.

"She is blinded, my son," Gudrun answered, "Give her that breadth, allow her to mourn in the way she can and no more!"

"Have you seen Cæna," she continued, looking deep into his eyes, "What do you see?"

"Eileifer," he countered back without a second's pause.

"Exactly," Gudrun muttered, pulling on a pile of earthenware plates and placing them on the oak table that sat square in the room, a place for talking, arguing and eating. It was the centrepiece piece around which hung all the drying herbs and vegetables in strings hung from the rafters above. Flavours and scents wafted around each other for supremacy, but the subtle aromas came from the pot and won. Mouth-watering additions of spices that Gudrun had learnt to use from the *Romanesque* himself. His was a favour in thanks to Gudrun, for uplifting his damaged son, bringing him into the light and giving him a vocation and a life, he loved.

Eastmund's devotion to his adopted *fæder* was so deep.

The loss of Eileifer almost killed him, yet the devotion to the white horse auguries clung to him like that rock trapping Dagrun but which for him, was pure and never allowed his spirit to waver. It healed him. Dagrun's rock was of the blackest night.

Gudrun broke into his thoughts, "I will talk with her, Eyvindr. She has kept to herself and is completely alone since returning from the *Seiðr drýcræft* with Aslaug. She travelled to see the Nornia on your behalf. On behalf of the Wihtwara. That is all I know. Perhaps you should visit Aslaug before you see Dagrun. That is my advice. And you should be meeting with your *Fæder* and Eystein, who are both with Eastmund and the auguries. Perhaps your son would enjoy that more."

Gudrun wrapped her arms around her youngest *bearn* gifting him a kiss on the cheek and gentle slap on his back, muttering and smiling, "*Geðoncian þu mín Nerthus, geðoncian þu,*" as she returned to her cooking and her peaceful haven.

… … … … … … … … …

Chapter 33

The white Auguries revisited
Wisdom shared and wisdom given

Sunni was sinking in a cloudless sky, the afternoon progressing to early twilight. The season of the second planting had been gifted with hot days and torpid nights. Now they needed Thunor to grace them with life-giving rain. As Eyvindr and Cahal walked towards the horse's pastureland, Eyvindr caught sight of Aslaug. She too was making her way there. Now that is fortuitous, he thought.

She was carrying her head low. She was deep in thought or prayer. Her back always ramrod straight, gave away little of her inner turmoil. But Eyvindr guessed at her stricken heart and urgent prayers. He also guessed her purpose. She needed to commune with the white auguries to find out. To reach a peace, a conclusion and a way forward for the Wihtwara. Their *Cwèn* was not present in mind or body and most definitely not her soul. He sensed an urgency, so he veered towards her, hoping she may feel his presence without the need to introduce himself. Cahal, with consummate delicacy, kept several paces behind his father. Eyvindr felt a surge of pride for his son.

Aslaug sensed him indeed. She turned and bowed slightly towards him and nodded imperceptibly.

"*Gewadan wiþ mè. Þin ontimber are mín ontimber.*

Walk with me. Your concerns are my concerns."

"*Mín ferhð is wíþ þu, Aslaug,*" Eyvindr gently welcomed her with the Wihtwara arm clasp. "Please tell me of Dagrun. How fares she?

"She is almost lost to us, sweet *brōðor,*" Aslaug stared deep into Eyvindr's eyes, searching for a rescue in him for his *sweostor.*

"Eileifer left us so suddenly," she continued in a low barely perceptible voice, as she nervously pulled her linen over-dress straight with nervous hands. It was so unlike the indomitable, strict to letter *Spakōna*.

"He complained of subtle agues; things we could not pinpoint as urgent. Dagrun prepared any number of herb potions. Then she went to *Seiðr* to seek the answer. But *Wyrd* held a curtain of fog around her every time she tried. I believe it was at this point her soul fractured and departed from her in shards of dissolution. It was not pride that defeated her, Eyvindr. She knew she could not save her beloved. It was sheer desolation. Her helplessness overwhelmed her soul and froze the courageous spirit that had defeated all odds and could overcome any obstacle. That is what we know of Dagrun Wahl. An inherent fighter for peace.

"Now a shell remains. Eileifer died suddenly in great pain. The poison had dominion over his once virile body. And even the Glory wands held no power, for they were indeed used, many times, by desperate hands seeking a cure for their *Cyng*.

I used them also and from the enquiry I received there lay before me, a damning lack of healing for Eileifer. Put plainly, Eyvindr, it was his time to travel to *Neorxenawang*. Acceptance now was the only path to travel."

"And Dagrun refuses to take that journey," Eyvindr stated, holding Aslaug's veined and calloused hand, stroking, caressing as if this was the hand of Dagrun. "I am sore afraid she will not receive me, Aslaug," he said softly, not looking up, but staring intently at Aslaug's bony hand.

"*Besèon æt mè!* Look at me!" Aslaug commanded.

"Why are you here? Why have you come?

"Is it not to try heal your *Sweostor*, who lays near dead to us whilst she still breathes!

"And trying is the important energy here, Eyvindr. What will your son think of you if you slink away without trying? Everything you do now, here on Wihtland, is a marker for him to live by. Is that not why you brought him with you!"

"To learn the true ways of the Wihtwara, *Giese!*" Eyvindr responded, "He has been isolated from that for too long. He has had only Roman ways set before him and they are deficit at best and downright brutal at worst. Cahal has a Durotrige name but little or no cultural gifting to go with his name. I want him to embrace the Wihtwara. I believe in my heart he wants this too, as he has too much of Wōden's blood coursing through his young body!"

"Dah, these damn *Rōmwèalas*," Aslaug spat out the word, "I have little but condemnation for these invaders of our land. Has Lãfa spoken to you of the rape of our mother near the Grand Hall? They dig and scrape her white skin like a flaying, to horde the white stone for their villas. I shall never set my foot in one, as long as my heart beats!"

"*Giese!*" Eyvindr countered, "I have seen worse whilst I was in Cantium and heard from Vrittakos of the gaping holes in our Earth at Mons Claudianus where the pink marble is wrenched from the ground in gigantic pieces for the columns that front most buildings in Rome and Byzantium."

"Eyvindr, you are living in two worlds. They will collide and damage you and yours if you do not choose one over the other, soon."

"Hmm, you are right, Aslaug, as ever," Eyvindr nodded, and suddenly broke into a wide smile as Eystein noticed him and punched his *Fæder* to look over yonder at the return of the son sorely missed.

Eastmund, the adored stepson of Eileifer was bending over, inspecting the hoof of the eldest Augury to gauge lameness, and stood up erect hearing Eyvindr's name shouted loud by both *Fæder* and *Brōðor*. Eastmund had grown into a very handsome young man, straight backed and elegant in his walk. Eyvindr had seen more of his *step-Nefa* as the love of his life was Aia, daughter of Vrittakos. He visited Berandinzium Villam often when weather permitted and sometimes when it was atrocious, to show his pure love and devotion to Aia, who was herself very beautiful. Vrittakos had permitted the romance to flourish as he held the Warinni in high esteem.

Eyvindr opened his arms wide to meet Eastmund, shaking his head and laughing. They collided and spun each other around in mutual comradeship, both of equal height and weight to counterbalance the other.

"It is purely a wonder to see you here, *Fædera,* and Cahal, *Hālig Nerthus*, what brings you to our Warinni land?"

"Ah, a race across the Sudmōr sands with your finest stallions' springs to mind!" Cahal countered, spitting on his palm to outstretch it to Eastmund, to firm an accord.

"*Giese!*" he replied, slapping his hand into Cahal's with firm intentions to win any race. They wandered off together, heads down, talking over one another in a flurry to exchange news. Eyvindr's attention became fully focused as he silently watched Aslaug make straight for the elder white guardian who had outlived all others and was the connection to Dagrun who had cared for him most.

His coat was not the white sheen of the younger stallions. It was yellowed and grey with many seasons, his shaggy mane twisted in knots, almost touching the long lush grass kept pure for them all. Aslaug gently grabbed the handful of his mane and pressed her head into his neck, whispering a welcome. His hoof beat on the ground, he neighed and blew out from his nostril steaming warm air and he shook his mane. He took steps backwards. Pulled his head up high and neighed loudly, swinging his large head from side to side. Aslaug heaved her old body up onto his back, lent down to touch his head and stayed there. They were now in communion.

The two men, father and son, waved with outstretched arms to greet Eyvindr from afar. They were at the extreme end of the paddock, fixing broken fencing with young willow rods woven and fixed in the ground. They beckoned Eyvindr to join them. Aware that the paddock was now charged with spiritual energy, they quietly leapt over the new fencing and walked to an adjacent field of pinto beans, the second planting field.

"*Mín Bearn hwæt gebrengan þu hèr?*" Folkvarthr called out, "My son what brings you here?

"Have you escaped the Villam? Your son is here, how wonderful. Call him over so we may greet him as family!"

Eyvindr waved both boys to come. They bounded over like unfettered puppies, leaving a swath of crumpled meadow grass behind them.

Cahal lumbered to a stop and faced his family standing to his full height, and grinned.

"Wōden be blessed!" Eystein said stepping forward to give his *Nefa* a Warinni bear hug that left the youngster heaving to put air back into his lungs.

"Eyvindr *brōðor*, your son has Warinni giant's blood! We are doubly honoured," Eystein beamed, his rugged features now creased to almost eclipse his eyes completely and with his once thick hair, now greying and thinner, the furrows on his brow were deep enough to envelop seeds.

Folkvarthr extended his swarthy arm, now covered in grey hairs. His age was telling on him. He seemed shrunken, his spine bending out of shape. And his face showed worry. Eyvindr's heart clamped tight. Sorrow was eating away at his *fæder*.

"*Wilcume!*" Folkvarthr intoned in his deep gravelly voice, "*Bearn fram Eyvindr. Ic am þín Ealdfæder ond Ic am blíðe æt gemètan þu.* Welcome! Son of Eyvindr. I am your grandfather and I am overjoyed to meet you."

Cahal, still holding his Grandfather's arm, replied in native tongue, which made Folkvarthr beam even more. His eyes too, were now totally eclipsed under heavy creases, yet his smile showing still perfect teeth, radiated his feelings across to the lad.

"*Ealdfæder*," Cahal said holding his gaze towards this grizzled elder of the Warinni, "*Hít is Ic hwã ãre welðungen ond blíðe æt wesan þín Nefa.*

Grandfather. It is I who are honoured and blessed to be your grandson."

Eyvindr knew now for certain that his son would accept a Warinni name. And he felt emotions rise to choke his throat. He coughed to bring them back down. Aife would be outvoted two to one. And yet another shard of his broken soul made its way back to settle within and give Eyvindr a quiet joy.

The men quietly left the planting field to wander easily around the *cæsterwic*, Folkvarthr talking quietly to his grandson about the village, its industry and seasonal gatherings at the mead hall. The ceremonies under twilight and the honouring of the Gods and Goddesses. It was as if he had been starved of the opportunity for so very long, the elder of the Warinni was imparting wisdom to the youngster at breakneck speed.

Cahal held his nose tightly as they passed the weaving *hūs*. Folkvarthr tossed his head back, laughing, "If the women can stand the *fulstincan* so can we!" He pushed the youth into the weaving hall. Shrieks greeted them as the women stopped their work at the looms to berate the entrance of two Warinni men in their midst.

"*Ut Ut, Folkvarthr, þu cunnan betera ðone þes! Ylde are forbèodan!*

"Out Out, Folkvarthr, you know better than this! Men are forbidden!"

"Ahhh, please ladies forgive us," Folkvarthr pleaded, though smiling in a way that he knew he was already forgiven.

"Please let me introduce my grandson, newly arrived to our *Cæsterwic*, son of Eyvindr, who arrived today!"

At this, the women stopped their weaving, their dying of cloth and their songs to cluster around the youth who was surrounded by women. And he loved it. After much acclamation at the swarthiness and the handsomeness of Cahal, the men bade their farewells to the weaving women and continued to meet with Eystein and Eyvindr, who were deep in conversation. And there was only one subject that dominated all their minds.

Dagrun.

... ...

Chapter 34

Dagrun Wahl

She shifted uneasily, painfully, pulling her body up on the weight of scrawny, muscle-wasted arms, to receive her *Kornmjölsgot* which her *Mōdor* knew full well would remain largely untouched. So, a wooden cup of pure spring water accompanied it.

Eyvindr had quietly brought food to his *Sweostor*, treading lightly on the oaken stairs that led to her separate room, curtained off and holding the one opening to allow sunlight to fill the space that had become her home, her prison, her sanctuary from life.

Her head hung down, her once lustrous hair keeping her face private from her long-lost *brōðor*. She looked up at him through the tangled mess. And what greeted him made Eyvindr catch his breath.

Dagrun's eyes held no spirit, no soul reached out to him. They were lifeless. Those once sparkling eyes were now encased in bruised shadows, deep lines and wrinkles held dominion over that once porcelain face.

But he caught the shadow of a smile, a lightening of those tormented eyes that made him take heart. Otherwise he may simply have turned and walked away.

Dagrun heaved herself up some more, displacing the fur hides, pushing her tangled hair away from her face and licking dry and cracked lips, spoke in a husky under-used voice,

"Eyvindr, *mín brōðor*, oh dear Nerthus only knows how much I have longed to see you!"

Eyvindr, swallowing wracking tears, swivelled round to place the food on a table nearby and turned to simply wrap his arms around his soul sister. He wept.

And so, they both cried, shoulders heaving together, tears soaking each other's clothes. Eyvindr felt Dagrun's heart pound, her life blood coming back. She was gasping in air to fill dried out lungs. Eyvindr also felt the soul of Eileifer finally come, he even looked up to see the air oscillate with spirit presence. And Dagrun saw him too.

She gasped and held her arms out,

"Oh, *mín Cyng*, Eileifer, *mín ceorl. Mín ferð is bebrecan. Ic ne mæg æþm. Ic me mæg biscoþríce!* Oh, my King, my Eileifer, my heart is breaking. I cannot breathe, I cannot see you!"

Dagrun spoke these last words in sheer disbelief, gasping for breath in each utterance. Her visioning, all her *Spakōna* gifts eluded her completely. And she could not countenance that the vision of her own dear husband, kin to Wōden, had been denied her.

Eyvindr held her tightly, stroking her hair, her forehead, her bruised eyes, hoping to soothe and placate her battered spirit. This was a woman willing herself to die.

Then suddenly on the last outtake of her breath which wafted past his eyes, he saw the expression on her face almost explode with hitherto supressed emotion. Dagrun was coming alive as she was clearly listening intently and staring wide-eyed at the oscillating energy in the room.

Eyvindr willed himself to remain still, not to turn and see his oath-sworn companion. Not to break into the *drýcræft* that was not his to own.

Dagrun clung to each word. Nodding and sighing in compliance. A quiet ecstasy settled around her as she and her soul joined together once more in acceptance.

"*Hit is forðǽm þu āre bebrecan þín āgan ferð þu ne mæg biscoþríce mè.*

Biscoþríce mè in urè bearn!

Wè willan ongeador in Neorxenawang eftsōna genōg fǽle."

Dagrun turned to her brother, searching his eyes for a few seconds to marshal her own thoughts.

"I will be returning to Nerthus' meadow soon," she uttered as a statement of irrefutable fact. And with it came an acceptance of the present that she must live within it to reach the moment of reunion with Eileifer. That it had entered her heart to settle there was a miracle.

"My husband sees this broken heart of mine and insists I must mend it if I am to see him at all. If I am to see him, I must look to our son."

"Oh, ðoncian þu, Eileifer," Eyvindr muttered, *"Bletsunga Beorhte!"*

Dagrun shuddered to shake away the past, lifting herself higher on the bed, straightening shoulders and peering around as if her world held at least some interest and fascination.

She beckoned for the porridge, smiling at the utter basic simplicity of the meal, and took the water first, draining every drop, as it filled her stomach and revived her muscles and bones almost immediately.

"Eileifer always said that pure water from the stream was a life-giver, pure and simple." She uttered and smiled for the first time since returning from the *seiðr drýcræft* and that meeting with the Norn sisters.

"He could never see the *Romanesque* fascination for wine. "It dulls the senses," he said," she took the wooden ladle and spooned the first solid food for many days into her mouth and nodded quietly. "Just beautiful."

Eyvindr watched her, in silence, as a sense of elation came over him. He quelled the sudden desire to rush from the room to share the good news with Dagrun's troubled family. They would thank him of course, but he had done very little. It was Eileifer who had worked the miracle, and Eyvindr experienced, for a split second, the incredibly hard energy needed by Eileifer's spirit to manifest in the physical world. Only the deepest love can accomplish such a feat, he thought.

"And how is your back?" Dagrun asked swivelling round to face her *broðor*. Will you allow me to inspect the damage and the healing?"

Eyvindr came to, shook himself and obeyed. There remained a few sore areas. He eased his tunic over his head and turned to sit carefully on the edge of the bed.

He could feel her fingers moving gently over the scars and some prodding made him wince.

"Hmm," she muttered, still prodding and pulling the skin to inspect closely, "Lífa has performed some healing *drycræft* here. Yet there are some stubborn areas still with poison beneath the surface. I will consult with her shortly. We need to make up a few poultices with yarrow to pull this poison up and heal the skin around it."

"*Giese,*" Eyvindr said twisting round to smile broadly at Dagrun, who responded with a heart-opening grin of her own, "*Ðocian þu.*"

"Oh, and you must know," he continued, beginning to enjoy this re-union with his *sweostor*, "That the harbour at Breredingas is bringing in new cargo from the East, the Silk Road. Unusual spices with great healing powers, so I am told. Turmeric is regarded as an All-heal."

Dagrun gave him a piercing look that made him falter.

"*Brōðor.* Do you still have a Roman heart?" She never quite forgave him for his leaning towards Mithras and the whole Roman culture.

"They are the most revengeful, greedy, lascivious and cruel peoples that ever conquered the breadth of Mother Earth!" she retorted, "And their days are numbered, Eyvindr!" she stated thumping her fist on the sheep hide that nestled against her legs. She relaxed and smiled at him, "Look at your hair, a signature of Rome now growing into a swabian knot if I'm not mistaken!"

"*Giese,*" Eyvindr replied, "Nerthus had commanded me Dagrun, she has wrapped her love around me. I am re-born! I have brought my son with me on this visit because he demanded it! He is more Warinni than he is Durotrige. There will be a renaming ceremony for him before I return."

"Wōden's eye be praised!" she replied, "I am greatly relieved to hear it. Both for you and your son. Does Aife know and agree?"

"Not yet," he looked down at his feet, "But she will!"

"*Giese*, she will do, to please both men in her life, but that is to acquiesce. It is not permission and you know it! The Gods and Goddesses will not bless this at all. Go get her permission Eyvindr!

"And please ask *Mōdor* for more food. And then I will tell you about what the Fates and the power of Wryd will bestow on our Roman invaders!"

Eyvindr simply sprang into action, now released to share the news with *Fæder* and *Mōdor*. Clambering down the heavy and uneven steps, he nearly tripped and caught himself on the bottom step. All eyes were on him.

"Dagrun is back! She is asking for more food, if you please *Mōdor*" he said smiling broadly.

Gudrun held her tunic to her weary face and cried silently into it. Folkvarthr turned to Eystein and they too hugged tightly and cried into each other's shoulder.

Dagrun had come home.

... ...

Chapter 35

Þæt Nornír
Rúna, Rãdha, Rèff, Rãdh!
The Three Fates

"It was white hot fury pulled me forwards, Eyvindr, dear *brōðor*," Dagrun gave a half smile, still showing a dimple that crushed men's hearts when she decided to flash those eyes with that famous smile, "and it was the only energy that sustained me. I thought that I would see this one last pledge through, then I could leave happily to join Eileifer."

"These Romans bear a long grudge in their twisted hearts, *sweostor*," Eyvindr replied, as images and pain flashed across his mind as memories of that day took prominence.

"I try to rise above the deep hatred. I succeed most of the time. But it owns me Dagrun, as much as the slave owner captures the spirit of his slave!"

"They are the most acquisitive grasping race that has dominated our Mother Earth," Dagrun flared up, a deep intensity flooding her eyes, "They jerk their knee and flash their gladius, scream and holler. But it is always in their temporal world. They expect the Gods and Goddesses to join them there, as if it is their right to call them whenever they so choose. They are arrogantly stupid on that score!

"The river of Wyrd is open to them. They do not realise they must travel upon it to gain wisdom. And it is this that separates us from them. And it is this one weakness that will destroy their misbegotten culture, Eyvindr."

Her brother sat up as this statement filtered into his consciousness. He leaned forward staring intently at his sister, who smiled back at him, knowingly.

"*Giese*," she said softly, "we have confirmation from the three Fates, our Sisters. All has been set in motion. We deal with our difficulties in an entirely unique way. More ancient, more knowing and wiser. We learn patience and we learn compassion while travelling on the river of Wyrd.

"Aslaug guarded me, Eyvindr. She protected me in this delicate state I am in and she strengthened me. She took my anger, swallowed it and spat it out. All for my sake and yours. I love her most deeply. She saved me and in doing so has secured a high place with the Nornia, when her time arrives."

They were sitting by the opening looking out onto the burgeoning *ceasterwic* and *tunstede* of the Warinni. It was another supremely balmy day. Heat waves oscillated in the distance and joined the man-made waves of heat from the salt workings down by the water's edge. This labour had grown from just a small venture of a few salt ponds to many fired briquetage salt pans, whose white treasure had become solid currency with the Romans.

Eyvindr and Dagrun grew silent, watching their world thrum with work and activity. Dagrun was growing strong, her heart was at a plateau of acceptance and some peace. She was smiling now looking out on her son and Cahal who had at last formed a friendship with his cousin. Wounds had healed. Dagrun's first act after her re-birth was to call for Cæna and hug him with tears flowing and words spoken until he knew for sure his mother loved him as much as she had loved his *fæder*.

Bodies were hunched over in the planting fields, making the second sowing of pinto beans, a reality. She had been watching Aslaug as she gave prayers and offerings to Nerthus and Thunor for a rich harvest. Aslaug's body was aching with the effort but Dagrun also knew nothing would prevent this old *spakōna* from performing her duties.

She watched her leave, tracing her steps towards their *hūs*.

"Aslaug is coming," she spoke softly to Eyvindr, not wishing to break the calm, "it is Aslaug who will give the Telling. Miss nothing, Eyvindr, and remember well. It will sustain your wounded soul for years to come."

Soft footfalls and the slightest tap on the oaken door saw Aslaug enter the peaceful room that had become Dagrun's sanctuary. She wafted forward as if suspended on air, her back ramrod straight as ever.

"Dagrun, my dear, you look radiant!" she whispered softly as she brushed Dagrun's head with her hand and leant forward to kiss her lightly on the cheek.

"And Eyvindr, you look more Warinni than you do *Romanesque*! However, how will you perform your duties in that area, may I ask?"

"Ah, Nerthus has re-claimed me, Aslaug. And I am *libertus* now. My son is wishing to join the Warinni and be given a new name in honour. As to my wayward hair. I will not be cutting it. I am hoping Dagrun will see fit to grease it into shape just for my last dealing with the Romans and their villams."

"Tush!" Dagrun laughed, "See my daughter. She is adept at that."

"Aslaug, please sit," Dagrun pointed to a chair laden with furs, "and refresh yourself before you give the Telling to Eyvindr." Aslaug drank with dedicated silence as the cool water reached her parched body.

She took a deep breath inward and turned to face Eyvindr.

"Allow me to say firstly that it took consummate preparation before Dagrun had the strength to travel on the river of Wyrd. The sisters would not have forgiven me had this been piecemeal. And she is difficult! I'm sure you are aware. As it was, we faced a crisis."

"And it is all due to your courage," Dagrun said.

"It was agreed we would place our physical bodies within the Ancestor circle," Aslaug began, placing her hands firmly before her, staring into the world beyond *"I was so concerned for the wellbeing of Dagrun I lay fur upon fur over her and under her, leaving only her mouth and nose visible. I made sure she was well nourished.*

She held my hand. I had never travelled so deeply into the spiritual world, never experienced the full tide of Wyrd hurtling us away from the temporal and into spirit. It is without expression: words are insufficient, so I will not try. Suffice it to say I was not prepared. As you may know Eyvindr, if Dagrun has described to you any of her travels with Wōden, it takes consummate skill and determination to not falter, to keep vision and mind in tune with the ephemeral and not bring human feeling into play. This old mind had to learn very fast.

We decided to reach Yggdrasil and that is where we found ourselves. Yet again, nothing had prepared me for the enormity and breath-taking power of the Life Tree. It shimmered with a life force I had never experienced before in our temporal world. And it reached up beyond our sight. I felt humbled and magnificent both equally intense. For all manner of experience is intense there. And it took some moments to adjust and feel a part of the miracle.

I was concerned for Dagrun. Her spirit having left her bereaved physical body was not at peace. She was not with me and I saw her fade and retrieve herself several times. I knew her will to remain was powered by anger and fury. And this would not sustain her in this spiritual world.

This world oscillates and thrives on love. So, I entered her troubled mind and simply said, "Wōden." I saw most distinctly the colours weaving around her alter from deep and dark orange to a sustaining purple. The fractals of peace wove around her and entered her until she too joined us.

"Wilcume, dèore sweostor," I wrapped my arms around her and felt her spirit heart take a leap and a warmth surrounded her.

"Geðoncian þu, dèor Aslaug. Þu āhreddan mè!" Dagrun whispered and smiled.

"Now let us call Ratatoskr."

She intoned the sounds as only an accomplished Nigt-gala would do and almost instantly we saw a rustle and vibration of nearby leaves and the messenger squirrel appeared before us, his head on one side, enquiring as to why we were here in his realm. Humans were not known to make this journey often, if at all.

"Ratatoskr, surely you remember me?" Dagrun asked.

"Of course!" he replied, "How could I possibly forget our "Wōden Watcher." You are well remembered, Dagrun Wahl of the Warinni. And who is your companion?"

"This is Aslaug, my teacher and Spakōna who has come to talk with our three sweostors, the Fates. We are on a mission for our people, the Wihtwara. It is important."

"Greetings to you Aslaug, guardian to my Wōden Watcher. You are welcome here. I will summon Wyrm Niðhöggr to lead you to our Nornia."

He disappeared into a black hole near the very base of the Yggdrasil. Time is no consequence here and before we could even blink or catch our imaginary breath, the rounded, slimy head of Niðhöggr appeared and commanded us to follow him. He slivered back into the black hole and I must admit my whole spirit energy faltered and faded as my rational mind objected to the very idea of squeezing into that small orifice!

"Do NOT think Aslaug!" Dagrun commanded, "Follow me please"

And I saw her whole spirit-self shrink and disappear into the hole. And I found it similarly easy once the intention was set. The experience of expansion and contraction, that shrinking and growing of fractals created a wisdom in me. All wisdom is maintained in the smallest blade of grass, the tiniest spider or insect. I will not view our material world in the same light as I have done. It made me humble and it made me mighty.

And it is this element of universal understanding, the Romans lack. To their cost.

We emerged from the dark worm hole in a flop of spirit bodies. It was not elegant, and it was how the mighty Nornia, the Three Fates found us.

Urðr, Verðandi and Skuld stood, legs akimbo, hands on their ample hips, staring down on us from their great height. I am not *of the giant's race and their size caught my breath. They just looked at us, silently, with slight grins and furrowed brows.*

"Ic biscoprīce þu are swā forðgeorn swā æfre Wōden Watcher.

"I see you are as impetuous as ever, Wōden Watcher!" Skuld announced wiping her hand over her face and gently shaking her head.

"Und hwā āgan þu acænned wiþ þu nūðā?

"And who have you brought with you?" Verðandi enquired, smiling indulgently as I wriggled myself free and stood to my full ramrod straight height. I am no giant, but I was not going to feel intimidated by any one of them.

Urðr *added with her twisted smile, looking straight at* Dagrun, "Gif þu āgan hopian fram biscoprīce Wōden þu willan wesan gefrucod!

Hwæt brengan þu hèr sweostor?

If you have hopes of seeing Wōden you will be disappointed! What brings you here sister?"

"We come to you on behalf of all the Wihtwara and indeed Cantwara and Meonwara also," I announced.

"And who are you!" said Skuld impatiently, irritated at the obvious lack of protocol.

"I am deeply sorry," I replied quickly, not daring to look up, "I am Aslaug, guardian, teacher and spakōna to my Cwèn, Dagrun."

"Well you fall short on manners!" chided Verðandi.

"Please forgive my elder guardian," Dagrun interceded, "She is unaccustomed to such deep and extensive travel, and she is maybe somewhat set in her ways!"

All three Nornia exploded in raucous laughter, their combined noise made Yggdrasil shake. Dagrun supposed the ancient tree was laughing too.

"Welcome dear old One," Skuld reached out to take me by her bony hand, "Come sit with us."

"Having come this far under unaccustomed duress, you must give us your Telling. Leave nothing out!" Verðandi said, as she

resumed her seat on a log, piled with furs. The stick she had been holding lay limp in her hand. The intricate map of Fate drawn before the three sisters was unfinished. Gaps yawed at them. It was a work in progress and I suddenly became aware of the ultimate importance of this map. They were present at this very moment to finish it, to fill in the gaps.

"Your telling Old one, please," Urðr leaned forward to offer both women a seat. I felt the fur beneath me, only it seemed suspended. Of course, I thought, the wood beneath was just pure energy. I looked over to Dagrun. She was relaxed now and seemed happy for me to take on the Telling for her.

"I was present in the Mead hall when the Romans came," I began, bringing forward all the terrible detail that altered the lives of the Warinni forever. Certainly, it changed the life of beautiful Eyvindr.

He was a talented scōp, a future storyteller for the entire Wihtwara. And he was taken simply because, at that moment he was like a Cyng, standing tall on the mead table capturing everyone's imagination with a most important Telling, the birth of our true name.

The Romans, led by a cruel and quite ignorant man, knew nothing of this. His purpose was to belittle, insult and bring fear to the people. They took Eyvindr as a royal prisoner. A hostage taking that was meant to bring us to heel under Roman rule. It worked.

We lost all contact with Eyvindr after that terrible night. Then sometime later we heard rumours and then reports from Cantium, that he had fled.

"Remember Gandolfi," Dagrun whispered.

"Ah Giese," I uttered, "such poison came from that dwarf! The worst kind of evil found its place in his twisted heart. And there is much of it in Cantium. The Romans had built squalid hūs for the slaves and prosperous dwellings for the legionnaires. Because of Gandolfi and his twisted ways, the Royal messenger to Eileifer was brutally murdered."

I looked over momentarily to see Dagrun with her head down, And I knew she was hurting at the mention of Eileifer. She began to fade and shimmer. Verðandi reached over to hold her hand and whisper words that brought her back.

"The truth of it is that these Romans are a cruel race of people, bent on ambition to rule, both the natives and their homes and land. We are always able to mix and integrate with others, like our Durotrige neighbours in Wihtland. The Romans deign to give us their pretence of harmony, but it is as thin as a spider's gossamer threads. Their true face shows, their mask slips and we see the ugly poisonous intent in their furious and hateful indictments and edicts. It is as arbitrary as it is cruel."

I watched Verðandi nod her head slowly, pensively. She was in deep thought listening to my description. Hers was the realm of the present, verðr, that which is happening. And as I continued, she picked up and held her pointed twig at the blank sand before her and began to create symbols.

She was creating galdor-drycræft using the twin runes of Ísaz and Nauðiz, a combined destructive force that was relentless as it was all-encompassing.

"This will mark the beginning of the end for the Roman Empire," Verðandi declared softly, deeply, and with all intention driven into the galdor-drycræft. "Nothing is left to chance. The river bends back on itself, the wheel turns, albeit slowly for you, my human sweostors. Patience and your lack of it will always be your inherent weakness."

Dagrun looked up and smiled. I knew she was famous for her impatience.

Skuld turned to her. She had yet to create on the map. Hers was the place of the future, Skulu, what needs to be, what ought to be and what shall be. This place was intricately balanced with many facets, multi-layered and therefore interchangeable.

"Dagrun, we need your Telling of your dear bróðor Eyvindr," Skuld was apologetic, but firm, "The deepest feelings must accompany this part of the map, the Skulu, for it is these that form

the "cement" as the Romans call their limestone "cow-glue" for the galdor dry-cræft to *work*."

What a hard test! I thought, watching my dear Dagrun sit up, square her shoulders, and perform the difficult task of allowing feelings to flow out of her whilst keeping her spirit detached enough not to falter and fade from this magical world.

"Eyvindr shared his life with me, under the rule of the Romans," she began, clasping her hands together, steeling herself to remain calm, above all to remain calm, "He was treated well at Berandinzium Villam, because the owner is Greek and not a Roman lover at all. It was he who organised his training at the luxurious Villam in Cantium, where all the top generals and legionnaires go to recuperate from their warring campaigns with the Britons. Eyvindr was to learn skills, tiling, wood crafting and most important for him, making tesserae and learning the art of mosaics. He was never allowed near the foundry as seax and most weapons are forbidden to the natives.

"The intention was to raise him above the slaves, creating an opening for him to gain his Libertus.

"They cut his hair away and losing his suevian knot crippled his soul deeply. Their motive always is to crush the spirit out of men and abuse women. The Romans' own training bleeds sensitivity away like an open wound. So, they reciprocate with cruelty whenever they can. And of course, their own souls diminish to nought.

"Eyvindr witnessed depredations of all kinds, daily, and there was fear embedded in witnessing daily beatings and whippings meted out to slaves in all areas of the Villam.

"One particular morning will remain with him all his life, apart from his own whipping, that is," Dagrun clenched her teeth, the muscle in her cheek spasmed briefly before she took control and carried on, "Eyvindr was dovetailing wooden joints together, making ready for the second-floor construction of the east wing of the Villam. It was to complete the latest opulence in bath houses.

"One young boy who had already received two whippings for refusing to crawl into the hypocaust pipes to locate a leak was left screaming in agony from the third beating from the overseer. This brute just picked up his bleeding body and physically threw him into the tunnel, pushing his backside in with each boot, each mangled scream became less and less. Then nothing, silence.

"Eyvindr risked his own back by running forward and squeezing into the pipe. He managed to pull the poor boy out. His Mōdor saw the whole thing and broke free, running to him, screaming. The overseer slapped her hard to the ground. He walked off leaving the centurions to pull both bodies away.

"Eyvindr has said repeatedly, to survive this you become Roman. You begin by acting out the role to please them. Then by degree Rōmānisc seeps into your soul and claims you. This happened to him, until the day when all changed for him.

"It had been a tempestuous few days at the Villam, strong winds and rain had battered the coastline and gone inland to make most people's days difficult. At last Thunor changed the course of those thunder clouds and Sunni broke through to bring warmth and a lightening of spirits.

Eyvindr was kneeling in the Atrium, sorting the coloured tesserae. The design sparked his interest as some of the tiles had come from Wihtland. They gave a precious link to the Isle. In the middle of his reveries, the sun was suddenly blotted out, a chill entered with the shadow that was cast over him. The tightening of his stomach was a warning of a threat. His spirit felt it.

"As suddenly as Sunni was blocked from him, he felt the insidious, sharp intrusion into his backside. He yelped and turned whilst still kneeling to view the legs of a præfect, a soldier young in years. Scars were laid bare on both legs. Eyvindr screwed his neck upwards to see an aquiline face, a perfect Roman, very tall, with the straight nose and deep-set eyes. His hair was immaculately cut straight to the sides and clipped to contour his strong cheek bones. His fringe was ruler straight. Yet it was his eyes that transfixed Eyvindr. They were the same colour blue as Eileifer. But they held a sadistic intensity that made Eyvindr's stomach clench. This præfect's eyes held a void, whereas Eileifer's held love. He did not give his name, he just smiled. A very charming smile that dimpled both cheeks.

"Eyvindr will always remember his first words, "You shall serve me just like that, arse in the air, servus!" Eyvindr clattered the isle tesserae to the floor. It was the initial shock before anger filtered in to claim his disgust, knowing he would have to defend himself to survive.

"He could not escape, though every bone and muscle twitched to just get up and run. He had to assume concentration for his work. He lay and fixed the tesserae until Sunni was dipping below the skyline. With head bent low to his chest Eyvindr walked briskly back to his small cubiculum, taut as one of Ingvar's cnearr ropes."

"Why do you think he chose Eyvindr?" Urðr broke in with a sideways glance at Dagrun.

"I believe with all my heart that my brōðor never lost his gentle Warinni spirit. It shone, even behind his Roman mask. This high-end præfect had decades of brutal soldiering to build his black spirit, with each turn, his own soul shrinking to a wrinkled walnut. Black souls always reach out for that which they cannot obtain. So, they steal it, break it to own it. And if it is a person who holds that light, why then they will break them into pieces to continue their own destruction!"

Skuld was sitting hunched over the map drawn into the Yggdrasill earth. She had been creating very slowly, carefully, muttering under her breath, her hair hiding her face. She looked up straight into Dagrun's eyes.

"The balance is being restored dear heart. Multiply Eyvindr's pain thousands of times across all the seas and all the countries these Romans occupy. Genōg is genōg," she said as she bent over to concentrate again on the powerful Galdor dry-cræft.

"Continue Sweostor," Skuld said, smiling gently, nodding, to let Dagrun know she was on target and doing well.

"Eyvindr could not escape immediately," Dagrun continued, her spirit eyes looking into the past, pulling up images created by Eyvindr's telling.

"In fact, he had time to learn something about this "perfect" præfect who left him alone. Although he quietly followed him, Eyvindr would look up from his work to see the præfect staring, unblinking, at him. This unnerved him more than the direct threats. He felt he was nothing more than a goat being stalked by a clever lynx.

"Eyvindr found out all he could with careful questioning of his superior craftsmen. He leant his name. Gallus Flavius Aquilinus, the last name meaning eagle, giving him a high-status family lineage. He came from Rome to Gaul, as a centurion, rising meteorically up the ranks to præfect. It was said his methods were brutal. Gaulish men captured in his unit were subjected to terrible and slow torture, before they were beaten down enough to bolster his growing army. Away from the battlefield, he was exceptionally pleasant and charming bringing with him a new wife to Britannia.

"They moved to the Villam in Cantium from Noviomagvs Regnorvm, and there were rumours that followed him too. It was said he was forced to leave in some haste from the palatial life at Villam Regis Cogidvbni. Eyvindr realised this charmer led a double life. To hide his crimes, he worked relentlessly to appear charming, intelligent and cultured. The perfect Roman.

"And his crimes were dark shadows, where lay the shattered remnants of some wretched slave. He searched for victims to slake his thirst for violence and Rome presented many to him by its partisan slave culture and dis-empowered women.

"When Eyvindr tried to save the poor slave boy from his horrendous beatings at that hypocaust tunnel, where several child slaves had died from earth collapse and were suffocated, he heard the name of the præfect on the dying lips of that boy, for the first time. When he heard it again from his friend working the tesserae with him, his blood ran cold. Real fear set in. And *that was exactly what Gallus Flavius Aquilinus needed. He could smell fear.*

"My brōðor *looked around him for support in his plan to escape. He soon realised there was no-one he could ultimately trust. He was on his own. He had one secret weapon, however, brought from Berandinzium Villam, secreted in many layers of clothing and hidden in an innocuous looking box. A* seax. *It was forbidden for any hostage slave to carry any weapon. It meant instant crucifixion. Vrittakos had not a single hostile bone his Greek body and allowed Eyvindr, while he was domiciled there to learn metal cræft skills. He made our hand-fasting sword."*

Dagrun stopped. I saw her fade as the memory took her to her wedding day and consummate sorrow overtook her.

"I plead with you," I interjected to the Nornia, "a break please, in the Telling."

The three sweostors *looked up in unison, staring at a fading Dagrun who was shimmering away. Verðandi spun and twisted her hand and a rune of courage hurtled towards Dagrun before she faded from us altogether.*

"I am sorry, but there can be no break in this telling. It has to flow, just as the river of Wyrd flows without a break."

"Continue brave Dagrun, please." Skuld smiled at a fast returning sweostor.

"Eyvindr knew he had to lure this devil to a place of his choosing. He knew he could not wear the seax *but hide it somewhere. If he could draw this præfect to that hiding place, he stood a chance of defending himself and to escape. Yet he knew he needed all the assistance he might muster after he had fled, to reach home. And that assistance suddenly arrived. A friend of Ingvar appeared one morning from a mist that had hung around the villam for days. It was autumnal, heralding in the colder days. Sounds were muted, and sight reduced to a mere spear length. The friend was Bjartr, the seaman who aided my older* brōðor *find justice to free me from the clutches of Gandãlfr. He had arrived with precious tesserae from Antioch, and as he walked into the Atrium, he looked dishevelled and travel weary.*

"Eyvindr told me his heart simply stopped when he saw his brother's friend. And equally, Bjartr nearly dropped his precious cargo on the marbled floor. He simply gaped at his Warinni friend, now a Roman in every way. But he collected himself swiftly before the overseer caught the exchange between them. He placed the beautiful tesserae before the overseer whose attention was immediately focused on the tiles from Antioch itself. Bjartr tilted his head over to Eyvindr, wordlessly asking him to follow.

"They made plans instantly after Eyvindr shared his plight to Ingvar's oath-sworn companion. Bjartr would find a messenger. And if the feared attack took place before they could finalise his escape, Eyvindr must flee and run to the tunstede of the Èoþings where a man named Æðelræd would hide him."

Dagrun's voice petered out. The silence became loaded and heavy. I knew she was reaching details Eyvindr had shared with her, that she wished he had not.

"Sweostor, shall I speak for you?" I asked, dipping my gaze to meet her eyes, which were shrouded in deep pain.

"Giese," she replied in a voice I barely heard, so I pulled my back straight and looking straight into Skuld's penetrating eyes. She held the power in her hands of what shall be, and I began to tell her of the horrifying attack on gentle Eyvindr.

"Eyvindr feared he had asked too many questions to the slave boys the præfect favoured and word had got back. With one, he had held tightly, while the boy wept. He had just returned and was bleeding and could not sit down. This Gallus Flavius Aquilinus had begun to appear before Eyvindr more often. His stare was penetrating and filled Eyvindr with dread.

Autumn passed quickly into freezing winter mornings. No-one was dressed adequately. The thin linen tunica was all that covered their freezing bodies. Blankets of all kinds swaddled their bent bodies as they all hissed steamy utterances into the chilly air, muttering and swearing quietly. They worked with frozen fingers on the interminably long and intricate mosaics. They were in the Exedra which was open to the elements.

It was the worst possible time for Eyvindr. But there he was, this præfect, standing behind him. Saying nothing, just exuding a dark shadowy malevolence, almost peaking with malice at the sheer vulnerability of his quarry. Cocking his head to one side, he decided to speak.

"Aelius, that is not your real name," he spoke softly, almost beguiling his quarry into submission, "I know. I have made it my business to find out about you. You are our barbarian royal hostage." He laughed. "you will tell me your genuine tribal name." Eyvindr blew steamy air out in exasperation and some fear.

"I am not permitted to use that name," he replied, turning to see the persecutor behind those false words.

"Oh, but you will, barbarian, you will. You are to come with me NOW." The force with which the præfect shot his command out to Eyvindr, made him almost jump to attention. It was on that freezing morning that Gallus Flavius Aquilinus pushed and shoved the Royal hostage away from people who might defend him. Away from view in the main villa, through the peristylium, the frozen earth crunching under their hard leather boots. His head down, Eyvindr noticed minute details, as if to pin his mind in simple reality. Early shoots had risen then withered with the snap frost. The præfect seemed to get into his mind instantly, knocking him forward towards only he knew where. Eyvindr realised Gallus had planned this attack on him. The freezing morning would not see the Villam guests rise any time soon. This was not a legionnaires barracks where the centurions would be roused even before the cockerel. Then he saw where they were heading, and his heart failed him, stopping him dead. The præfect raised his golden head and laughed, billows of vapoured breath reaching Eyvindr's nostrils, making him recoil even more. They were making for the most sacred place in the entire complex of Saxum Demulceo Villam, the temple, built and raised in honour of pagan deities, his nature spirits, Nerthus herself.

"Hah, I see you realise the importance to you of this building," Gallus sneered, pulling Eyvindr's arm, twisting it sharply behind his back to a bone crunching level, "We Romans are adepts at

stealing, acquiring what is not ours to own. We are a race of thieves. And we revel in it. Your Nerthus is now mine! Just as you are about to become just a body I can use and abuse. She will be watching, Aelius, yet she will do nothing. I am in control."

Eyvindr fought back, wrestled and twisted, getting punched and beaten as they made their way across the immaculate lawns, edged with box that hid them from sight. No-one would be visiting the temple this early because it was also a mausoleum, containing the earthly remains of Emperor Pertinax, an early governor of Britannia.

Gallus pushed the heavy door open, carvings in the oak panels of nymphs and foliage made Eyvindr's heart break. The temple was square in structure, frescoes adorned the walls of trees and brightly coloured birds. All manner of natural adornment to pacify the spirit and which was about to be splintered by the most sadistic act of abuse.

"It could not have been worse," I stated, looking over to Dagrun who was holding herself in absolute stillness, frozen in dedicated effort to remain and not dwindle away from us.

"Gallus tied him up stretched over the mausoleum tomb, so he had no way to fight back. Eyvindr was a bloodied broken man after the præfect had finished with him that morning. I do not believe that part of his soul will ever come back to him. It is gone.

"What happened next was the poisoned fruit of that abuse come back in revenge, pure revenge. It was after all the only outcome. Justice prevailed.

"Eyvindr brought all his skills as a scōp, to the fore. He acted out a dangerous ploy to lure the præfect to his location, not far from the temple, but out in the open. He chose a balmy evening, the light fading, and his escape planned with the help of the boy messenger from Bjartr, who was waiting in shadows of the wood beyond the Villam. Should anything go awry, Eyvindr was to call the owl hoot and Bjartr would come. Gallus was a very clever scheming man, who spent more hours plotting and playing out possible conclusions than is normal. He was a deviant in *every sense. But his compulsion to hurt and maim overcame his common sense and he fell for it.*

"Eyvindr had hidden his seax and placed himself near. He saw Gallus approach, Sunni had sunk below the Villam's roof, and cast darkening shadows. Eyvindr was past fear, his whole being thrummed with revenge. He was taut and knowing this, he played the frightened dormouse to fool Gallus.

"Just as the præfect grabbed Eyvindr to pull him down, Eyvindr whipped the seax from its hiding place and hit Gallus hard in the groin. Blood spread onto his toga. Eyvindr was overtaken with fury and kneeling low lunged the knife upwards again to pierce the præfect's testicle.

"I think he would have killed him outright if Bjartr had not suddenly appeared from the wood, having watched the whole thing and pulled Eyvindr off the prone man, his blood soaking the earth.

"Had he killed him, it would have been a summary crucifixion, if he had been captured. Bjartr sped him away to Èorþing, where relatives of the Wihtwara protected and cared for him whilst waiting for his brōðor, Eystein to bring him back to Wihtland."

"And of course," I continued to finally complete the Telling, "the Romans bear a long grudge. They do not forgive. Gallus was injured and lost some of his manhood. He swore vengeance and sent the Overseer to whip and scar Eyvindr at Berandinzium Villam!"

"Genōg!" Skuld announced, "Wè āgan geāscian genōg. Enough! We have heard enough."

"The map of the Fates is almost complete," Verðandi looked up from her deep contemplations, her expression kindly, "Yet we must seek a balance, for there is always two-sides to the coin. What have these Romans done for the good of all?"

Dagrun suddenly came alive after many moments of almost frozen stillness. She looked around and smiled slightly as if in a faint apology.

"They have created the written word," she stated, "And my people are beginning to recognise this as a gift. They are learning to write for themselves."

"And they have built roads from ceasterwic to tunstede," I interjected, remembering the journey I had undertaken from Clausentum to Venta Bulgarum, "the cobbled road made travel so much cleaner, although it was hard on the hooves, we appreciated the lack of mud."

"They reward initiative and honour high climbers, free slaves", I added.

"For all their building accomplishments," Dagrun spat out with deep feeling, "Their defamation and ruin of our Earth Mother will be their undoing! They rape her daily, it is no different from the rape of my dear sweet Eyvindr. Yet she does not wield a seax. We are Her guardians and it is why we are here, sweostors."

"Giese," replied Skuld, "We know. We know everything. But we could not act without your testimony. Yet, as I am in Skulu, I see beyond even this, my dear sweostors. Dagrun, has Nerthus not already spoken to you? She, who has said these Romans, for all their destructive violent ways, will not bring the end of Her, our Earth Mother. She will recover. She is ultimately strong and indestructible. No, it is as Eyvindr experienced, the quintessential evil gift from the Romans to the world of Humanity. It is the crushing of their soul, your souls, in a tidal wave of corrupted religious dogma. A group of men changes the faith of one man, to fit their own twisted ideas and make it orthodox. Which means everyone must succumb to them. One man, one Roman Emperor changes the spiritual course of all humanity. And your precious gentle faith way will be lost to us for many seasons. His name is Constantine.

"You were told to leave the wisdom in the stones, Dagrun. Make sure you teach your children to pass this gift on. It is the only means with which your people will survive to be remembered and honoured again in the Skulu!"

"Now the time has come," Verðandi announced. She brought the three Fates to standing. They held arms in a triangle of power. The ground beneath them began to shift. Ripples appeared in the map and all the runes created there, began to gently oscillate in a rhythm of a deep earth beat. Then so suddenly, within a heartbeat the whole map was swallowed. I turned to see where it had gone, and only saw the world tree, Yggdrasill, shudder momentarily.

"It is done," the Three Fates echoed together. "So, may it be!"

"The tide of Wryd will turn now against these Romans. Their days are numbered. But it will be so very long before humanity grows beyond their influence. They will never again, ever truly succeed. This day has been written into Yggdrasil and cannot be changed. Well done my sweostors. Now return to your time. Bletsunga Beorhte."

I came alive again in the Ancestor circle to see the huddled form of Dagrun shaking in tremors that halted my breath. She was in deep trauma and I rushed for our horses and I had to tie her to her stallion as we sped home.

"And now our Telling has been given, may we move on," I said heaving an enormous sigh of relief.

... ...

Chapter 36

CULTUS LENAEUS
HONOURING BACCHUS
"Prandeo, poto, cano, undo, laro, cæno, quiesco"
I dine, drink, sing, play, bathe, sup, rest!
(Avienus. Latin Author 250AD)

Mercury's raven villam

Eyvindr and Cahal were rhythmically bouncing gently on their stallions, as they cantered at a healthy pace towards the coast, on the ridge leading down to the Mercuri vilpes corvum villam. The villam came into view. It was dwarfed by the rolling land filled with vines, both red and white grapes swayed gently in the torpid breeze. This part of Wihtland seemed to hold Sunni and all the gentle weather to its heart. The God Bacchus was indeed honouring them. And it was here that the initiates to Mithras held their first level of ceremony. And then celebrated with a feast of wine and decent food and submissive slave women.

Eyvindr felt free, the *libertus* had taken full root in his soul. The Telling had gifted him back shards of lost spirit. His actions vindicated, his injury was at last honoured and in some way healed. He knew it would open and bleed again in the future, and he would contain it as best he could. What he did not expect, honestly surprising him, was the difficulty he felt towards pretence. He was a *scōp*, a storyteller and an actor. Yet now in this present moment, his one task was to live a lie, pretend to be the Roman and surveyor of villams under his scrutiny. He could not care less about the villams, and even less about Mithras and his attainment of initiation that placed him close to the fourth level.

He had lengthy discussions with Dagrun, who was now with her world and her beloved son again. She had attained more knowledge of Eastern religions, the veneration of the planets and of very ancient gods, than any of her Wihtwara relatives. Her deep friendship with Venitouta had gifted her this rare knowledge. Eyvindr always turned to his older *sweostor* on most things esoteric and now thanks to her, he felt the jarred edges of two ancient spiritual ways were conjunct. He had to feel confident enough to persuade his fellow initiates in the Mithræum of the similarities and not the differences.

"It is a pure matter of reflection, *brōðor*," she had said, smiling and taking hold of his hand, "the Wihtwara have always held a deep and wise understanding of our Earth Mother and all the workings here upon Her. And, her relations with Sunni, Mōnã, Thunōr, Wōden and Yggdrasil and the Nornir. Our eyes seek out the infinitesimal, the Wights and Sprites, for we are bound to Nerthus in this realm. Yet, if we spent more time looking above, we too would get to understand we are reflected in the stars.

"Abrasax holds the 365 realms in his wide vision. And I have been told by Venitouta that we humans hold an abiding relation with this ancient God of Gods, as we have 365 parts to our body. More importantly for you *brōðor*, Abrasax is aligned with Mithras. The heavens and those stars in the heavens are but a reflection of us in this world as we reflect them. Separation is a human invention against all-natural laws.

"Test that with your Mithraic initiates."

Dagrun had oiled his hair down tight to his skull. It almost creaked against his skin when he moved his head. The only concession she gave was to trim his hair to the Roman fringe. He had tied his hair at the nape of his neck and forced his growing locks underneath a high-necked tunica.

Eyvindr sighed. He felt uncomfortable and ill-at-ease.

Dagrun had asked him which initiate level he was bound to attend. It was to be the fourth level, the Leo grade, where it starts to get serious. He would be bound to the oath of secrecy and perform both a dedication and a catechism. To make matters worse, his accompanying initiate, who would be moving to the next, fifth level was Brutus, in both name and stature, a difficult man. All this would take place at Iuppiter igne villam, where they would be inspecting the Mithræum the following day.

"Thoughts, *Fæder*," Cahal, who had grown in stature and confidence since his departure from Berandinzium Villa, turned to look intently at the rather strange visage of his Roman/ Warinni father. He looked not just odd, but uncomfortable.

"Dah!" Eyvindr exploded in frustration, "I am living in two worlds, *Bearn* and it just will not do! It is fine for Dagrun to try and teach me in one afternoon the mightiest and ancient of wisdoms, but she has had precious time to accumulate this knowledge.

"I have been nothing but a slave and workhorse."

"*Fæder,* how do you feel? Think not of the Romans. They have diminished you in so many ways. They are not worth your consideration.

"Does your soul sit easily with this expanded view of our human and celestial existence?"

Eyvindr pulled back suddenly, leaning back on his steed, who faltered completely in his step and just stopped, with a loud explosion through steamy nostrils.

"Son!" he exclaimed, reaching out to grab his arm, "Have you been talking with Aia by chance?"

"I would be a fool not to *Fæder*," he looked straight ahead with an enigmatic smile that spoke a thousand words and none.

"Best keep your feelings to yourself. She is betrothed to Eastmund, and that is it!" Eyvindr closed the subject with a menacing glare at his son, of whom, he suddenly decided, he knew very little.

They reached the villam in silence. It nestled within the acreage of vines. The air was steamy, and the heady fragrance of the grapes settled in Eyvindr's nostrils tantalizing his head to swim in thoughts of amphoræ of rich red wine. He glanced over to his son and caught a similar expression. They had arrived well into *weodmōnaþ* and Eyvindr counted *ðrítig* Wihtwara, in hemp hats against the glare of Sunni at her fiercest. Some were from his *ceasterwic* and *tunstede*. So, they were being summoned at the will of the Romans to be taken from their fields, which also needed harvesting. He determined to have a word with the overseer.

The large woven baskets at their feet were becoming full. He watched as a giant Warinni woman placed a bag on her head, that flopped over the top, and eased down to place the hemp rope squarely in the middle and raised herself and the basket up, walking evenly along the track to the vat placed at the side of the field.

It made him aware of his own head and what was happening to it. Sunni was melting the thickened grease Dagrun had lovingly layered all over his hair. It was coagulating at the base where he had tied his thick locks and was steadily dripping down his back. He wriggled and swore in old Norse.

"*Forstoppian*," he called to Cahal, who immediately reigned his horse in. Eyvindr swerved round to pull his leather sack from its hook and rummaged within to pull out a squashed leather hat. He pulled and punched it into shape, muttering more ancient Norse under his breath. It was a gift from Vrittakos. And it was a precious and thoughtful gift. Eyvindr felt ashamed, quite suddenly, at his terse acceptance of it back at the villam. It had been a tense departure. His friend had gifted him the Pileus, an awarded hat for a recent freedman, the *libertus*.

"And the old Greek *knew* it would be needed!" Eyvindr muttered.

"Of course, he did *fæder,*" Cahal commented, leaning over to begin wiping the grease away from Eyvindr's sticky hair and neck, with a cloth, "Hold still *gecwèman*. The Wihtwara do not wear hats any more than the Romans do, who obsess about hair. But our kin hold their hair as sacred to Nerthus do they not, *Fæder*?"

"*Giese*," Eyvindr smiled at the "our kin" response from his son. A warm glow entered his heart. And an almost instant clutch strangled it, as the Roman duty he was bound to endure became ever closer. As the grease left his body, he rammed the hat on his head, and became a *Rōmãnisc*.

He made a quick mental survey of the villam building as they trotted down the incline, swaying with their mounts, as the horses searched out easy footings for their hooves. He realised the villam would never be an expansive site. The winemaking took precedence, as it should. Wine was water to the Romans. The villam housed the slaves in a wing set to the west. A hypocaust was evidently under construction and looking woefully unfinished for this stage of development. The elite would not stand for it. And it was Vrittakos who would suffer their wrath.

Eyvindr began to feel a tension that was born of anger.

He dismounted and strode forward without a break in his step. Cahal hurried behind him, curious to see his *fæder* angry. He couldn't remember the last occasion. Eyvindr kept a supreme hold on his emotions.

There were shouts and calls within, obviously the master was totally unaware and came hurrying out of the vestibulum scraping his sandals on the loose stone entrance. These loose stones appeared to have been recently dumped there without levelling. The master of the villam was obese, unshaven and looked as if he had just risen from his bed at high noon. He wiped his chubby hand over his face to wake himself up.

Eyvindr's temper erupted.

"*Hoc est a villam ignominiam. Quanto tu propediem huc venit et legati Caesaris! Hic eris felix vita excedere.*"

"This villam is a disgrace. Do you realise the Caesar and the legate will be arriving here very soon! You will be lucky to leave here with your life." Eyvindr roared stepping ever closer to the master with each sentence sending waves of anger to hit his crumpled face. His had been a life of indolence and constant wine tasting, drinking a permanent toast to Bacchus. And it had just come to an end.

"Your name!" Eyvindr spat, inches away from the master's face, who was now sweating profusely, "So I can pass it onto my master, Vrittakos Eluskonios."

"Martialis Dannotali," he rasped, unable to look at the face of his accuser.

"Well, Martialis Dannotali," Eyvindr replied, "Within the next two lunar phases, you will be facing Titus Desticius Juba, the governor of Britannia Superior himself, along with a party of Elites from Rome. They will be arriving here straight from the Villam Regis Cogidvbni, which, as you may know, has been constructed to be identical to Caesar's palace on the Palatine Hill. I have heard it described as magnificent and luxurious. And they come to this...." he waved his arm around to take in the dilapidated state of the exterior walls.

"You have a thriving vineyard, to your credit," he continued, "Your *denarii* reserves must be large. Put those stubby fingers of yours into that pot and use it quickly to finish this villam to the standard the Governor of Britannia will accept."

"And find me a scroll," he added, walking into the *atrium*, "I need to make a full list of repairs, frescoes and possible tesserae requirements."

Martialis pattered away, his back hunched, and his head lowered. Cahal just stood and stared at his *fæder* who had walked over to the bare walls of the Atrium, heaving a deep sigh. They had not even been well tempered with lime and would require more coating before any frescoes could adorn the walls.

"Cahal, my son," Eyvindr spoke carefully, fully aware of his son's expression, "Looks like I must become Aelius for the time being. But know I am a Warinni in my heart and my soul belongs to Nerthus."

"*Giese*," Cahal replied, "*Ic gecnãwan*. I understand."

"I need you to travel back to Vrittakos. Describe to him what you have seen here. Ask him to send messages to as many craftsmen and artists, builders he deems fit to come and repair this sorry excuse of a villam." He clapped his son on the back and hugged him for good measure. As he watched him canter away, Eyvindr noticed a pall of steam rise from the cliff edge. Salt working was apparent. More *denarii* being kept and hidden. He made a note to visit it while his stay here had been lengthened.

... ...

Aelius was making copious notes on the scroll which was extending very nearly to the floor. First on this list was a strong comment on the visitor's cubiculum he was given. It was akin to a monk's cell. Adornments that were rushed in did not repair the bare state of the walls, only made them more acutely visible. With no hypocaust or warmth under the stone floor, it was, even in this *Weodmōnaþ*, chilly at night, so close and exposed to the sea breezes.

The one completed area, and the showpiece of the whole villam, was of course the temple room dedicated to Bacchus. Stunningly beautiful frescoes adorned these walls, with statues of the God and Goddesses spaced in between, and one large central mosaic of exquisite tesserae was a portrait of the God Bacchus. An altar at the far end was equipped and had a beautiful silk drape, fringed almost to the floor. The atmosphere was peaceful yet fecund, undertows of latent ecstasy rippled through the room. The frescoes were undoubtedly created with seduction in mind.

Aelius met the creator of the Bacchus room, an overseer named Gallus. His heart immediately made a flip when Gallus introduced himself, but he was an absolute antithesis of Aelius's persecutor over in Cantium. He relaxed as they walked the villam in its entirety, chatting and exchanging comments. Gallus was a master craftsman, learning his skills in Gaul and Antioch. He was of middle years; his whole demeanour was hunched in frustration and near resignation at the tight-fisted labile life of Martialis Dannotali.

"You will be getting assistance very soon," Aelius remarked, as they walked from the Atrium into a shabby garden with tired looking box trees, a few stunted looking olive trees and interspaced with rocks and rubble carelessly thrown about.

He suddenly stopped in his tracks.

"Where is the Mithræum?" he turned to stare at Gallus.

Gallus hunched his back even more, turning his head sideways to look ashamedly at Aelius before replying softly, "There is no Mithræum here, Aelius."

"*Adhuc Mithrae sacrum est et confusa. Dannotali et poenas ob hodiernam hanc contumeliam!*

"Mithras is disgraced. Dannotali will pay dearly for this insult." Aelius spat out each word quietly and slowly impacting each syllable with deep anger. Where is this coming from? He thought silently. I am Warinni. This is but a show, an act. Yet he knew he was not acting at all. What he felt was a desperation to belong.

He wiped his hand across his face. He was in silent turmoil. Gallus took it as intense frustration.

"Allow me to take you down to the salt workings, now," he said, now staring at Aelius with honest intent. He did not want to be paired with the indolent and mostly drunken Martialis or his wanton wife Banona. He knew he was in deep trouble and wanted desperately to be part of the solution and not the problem.

"I know of a cave that might meet the needs of your initiates."

Gallus led the way, in silence. Aelius noticed his rolling gait, legs bent in a twisted way that spoke of bone illness. He felt the pain and grew ever more sympathetic for the overseer who had been dealt a sorrowful lot in his life.

They eased down the cliff, traversing along a well-trodden pathway until they reached the immense and expansive yellow sand which stretched for many spear lengths in each direction. Sunni was again oscillating a growing heat that sent wafts of intense aroma from the yellow gorse flowers that lined the pathway. The small vibrant coloured vetch flowers poked their heads in-between to create a tapestry of summer colour.

The sea was in indolent mood, the tide receding in softly whispered rushes of water. The salt ponds were laid out just above the sea line, glistening in the sun. They were tended by the Warinni who were scooping up the salt from the sun-baked water. Aelius was intrigued to see a dish of beaten copper angled to Sunni to intensify her rays on the water. This was bubbling with the heat and producing salt crystals more rapidly. He made his way over to greet them.

"*Hãlettan þu,*" pointing to the dish, "*þes is wunderíc. Èacen geweorc.* Greetings to you. This is wonderful. Great workmanship."

A Warinni man looked up, questioning, staring and muttered something in reply before returning to his scooping.

Eyvindr was stunned, he had become Roman: he was a Roman and they did not recognise him at all. He was caught in a turmoil of never belonging to either tribe now. He shook his head and walked away.

Gallus was talking away describing the boiling of the saltwater in briquetage pans, preferred by the Romans as it was a quicker method. Salt was valuable currency and Wihtland produced a huge amount for the Romans to trade with. They were stealing yet another gift from Nerthus to gain wealth. So, at the heart of the matter, Eyvindr, now Aelius was a traitor to his own people and they were showing it to him.

His day was reduced to a mere echo.

They walked on, the sand burning through their leather sandals. Aelius was glad of his pileus. Sunni had reached her zenith by the time they arrived at the cave. Settled neatly behind a gathering of trees, up a small incline, the cave held a mystique, a peaceful energy. Aelius knew instinctively that it would be adequate for the seven initiates and master. They sat for a while resting from the walk and grateful for the shade.

Aelius elicited as much information about the state of the villam from Gallus, who was more than happy to relieve himself of woes he had hung onto for too long. Aelius now knew where the huge stock of amphorae lay hidden. And how Gallus had not been paid for several seasons. Aelius did not have the authority to sack these wanton owners and wished his son had impressed upon Vrittakos the urgency of the situation. He was more than gratified when Gallus produced food from his bag. Excellent cheese, wine and stuffed dates proved so satisfying. The wine was aromatic and strong.

"If you could improve the look of the situation, the rest is above standard and will meet with the elite's approval," Aelius turned to look straight at Gallus, who responded with a slow smile, sincere and widening to show what teeth remained. The tense atmosphere became relaxed, and Gallus slapped his knees in a sudden display of enthusiasm.

"It will be done!" he replied.

"Look," Aelius came back holding his hands as if in prayer to make the point, "I have sent my son Cahal to report to Vrittakos all we have seen. You will not be made responsible. I am hoping Vrittakos will make his way here to see for himself. He has the authority to remove Martialis and Banona Flatucias and introduce a better master for the sake of all!

"Do you know of someone here on Wihtland who may be qualified?"

Gallus leaned forward to stare at the ground before him before answering.

"Yes, I believe there may be. It may be opportune for you and your master to visit Heliodromus Villam. I have heard it said that too many overseers are spoiling the energy there. Both are vying for supremacy and neither are any good at backing down. They may not be suitable, but I think either of them might flourish away from the other, if you see my point."

"Oh, I do indeed," Aelius agreed, feeling more hopeful.

They both stood and shook themselves down, releasing sand and dried seaweed from their tunicas. Sunni was sinking in a cloudless sky, the sand was less hot, and the way back seemed quicker. They chatted amiably.

Aelius decided he needed to talk with the slaves. They have eyes and ears and were not bound to secrecy. He found them in the *culina*, heads bent over preparations for the evening meal. A circular open fire in the centre of a large rectangular table, held an iron grate upon which lay several joints of different meats. Delicious aromas were wafting towards him making his stomach churn.

Two ovens held baking breads and a top hotplate had unleavened bread frying. Amidst all of this were clay pots steaming over a hearth fire as vegetables were softened. It was as hot as the fires of Hades itself and he felt supremely sorry for the women locked within its clutches. He left them alone. Outside he saw two women bending over, picking herbs from the *exedra*. As he came close, he heard the familiar dialect of the Durotrige. His heart leapt. He hurried over to them.

"*Helo merched, fy enw i yw Eyvindr ac rwy'n edrych ar y lle hwn. Beth yw eich teimladau o'r villam hwn ac sydd â gofal?*

"Hello ladies, my name is Eyvindr and I am inspecting this place. What are your feelings of this villam and who is in charge?"

Their two faces were a picture and Aelius knew he would remember this moment all his life. Both women's eyes became as rounded as duck eggs, and they took a few moments to collect themselves. This strange looking Roman in the odd hat was speaking in their own native language to them, mere slave women!

"*Mae'r villam hwn wedi bod yn lle anodd ac anghyffredin i fyw a gweithio ynddi. Ac mae wedi sydyn yn dod yn hynod od. Pwy ydych chi'n syr?*

"This villam has been a difficult and odd place to live and work in. And it is has suddenly become extremely odd. Who are you sir?" questioned the tall dark-haired girl, whose pretty face held a cheeky smile and whose eyes twinkled with mischief.

"Umm your name first, I think," Aelius checked, trying to be stern and failing, he was so glad to meet these two young women, he was fighting back a roar of grateful laughter.

"My name: my born name is Blãthnat. It means little flower," she said with meaning, jutting her chin out in defiance, expecting a rebuff.

Aelius simply smiled, "That is a beautiful name for a very pretty girl."

"And yours?" he turned to the older woman.

"Angharad. And you know full well what it means as you know our language so well for a Roman!"

"Oh, sweet Nerthus!" he exclaimed, sitting down on the stone nearby, "I am a complete mixture. I'm not at all sure who I am!" he patted the seat for them to join him.

"All I ask is that you describe the life here. Both for yourselves and others. Be honest. Leave nothing unsaid you wish you had shared. Trust me. Nothing bad will come of this. Rather I am hoping for a speedy improvement of your lives here."

By the end the sharing, Aelius knew beyond any doubt that he had enough evidence to shed the villam of two wasters. They gave each other a Durotrige farewell and he spent the remainder of the day missing his wife to his very soul, aching with each breath to kiss her and feel her close.

... ...

The following morning brought a loud banging on the wall outside his *cubiculum* and a loud muttering of Greek swear words strung together without a pause. Aelius yawned and smiled in similar fashion. Vrittakos had come. And he was not happy.

"Eyvindr, shake yourself man. We have no time to waste," he commanded, though refrained from entering the tiny room. "If this sorry place boasted even the smallest hypocaust and bathing, we could talk there. As it is, the nearest water is down an impossible cliff and the tide is halfway to Gaul!"

"It is Aelius, Vrittakos," Eyvindr shouted back, as he pulled his tunica over a tousled head and grabbed an *amictus*, deftly swinging around the linen to secure it with a rounded clasp at the shoulder. With that last gesture, he became Roman. He quickly bound up his hair under the *pileus* and strode out into the corridor.

Vrittakos eyed him sharply, nodding peremptorily and clapped his arm around his shoulders.

"It is sensible for you to maintain the role of Roman overseer for now," he said quietly.

"Did my son return?" Aelius asked.

"*Certe*," Vrittakos replied reverting to Latin with a sardonic grin, "he is flirting with the Durotrige *culina* slaves and breaking his fast, in that order." Ah, like father like son, Aelius thought.

"Come, food is waiting for us in the *triclinium*. No talking about this shameful villam, please, it will give me indigestion!"

That discussion took place amidst the grape vines, as Sunni was rapidly rising in another cloudless sky. Aelius was towering above Vrittakos and he had to bend forward to catch his words angrily spat out in directives. He was too tall for a Roman. He was given stares from the Warinni in the fields. One young woman recognised him and suddenly ran forward, skipping in between the vines to reach him and demand a Wihtwara greeting and then a bear hug. He gave her an awkward look. She nodded slowly, returned a half smile to him and muttered, "*Bletsunga Beorhte Eyvindr.*"

He felt diminished.

Vrittakos sighed sadly, stopping suddenly as he reached a decision. Flies were buzzing incessantly around overripe vines. He swatted them and turned to Aelius.

"Gallus has implored me to remain and I have agreed, Ey... Aelius. He is a dedicated and sincere man. I would wish better workmen and craftspeople at his disposal and keener leadership. You have described the shortcomings of this villam, and he has augmented your observations.

"I also think it would be good for Cahal to remain with me and learn from his own observations. He is quick thinking and astute. I would want to see him in a position of some skill before too long.

"And there is another matter that needs addressing regards your son. He is growing up swiftly, too swiftly. He has developed a yearning for my Aia, Aelius. And that must be stamped on, forgotten. I'm sure you appreciate that. She is a beautiful young woman, but she is betrothed to Eastmund with our blessings.

"Absolutely agreed Vrittakos," Aelius interjected, "This has come to my attention also. He is as obdurately fixated as those damn flies!"

"Well he is fortunately young," Vrittakos replied smiling, "and his attention has just been drawn to a pretty young Durotrige woman in the culina.

"Hmm, I know," Aelius grinned back, "I've had the pleasure of talking with her in some depth about this villam. She is spirited and very outspoken. A true native woman of Wihtland."

"Good" Vrittakos clapped his hand on Aelius' shoulder, "Now to business. Cahal, Gallus and I will be travelling to Heliodromus Villam, to recruit a new overseer. Gallus has been promoted. Then onto Point Ægypti to get building materials and hopefully more crafts people at Sol Rex Villam.

"I wish you continue on your journey to inspect Iuppiter igne Villam and Persici Luna Villam. These represent your onward initiations to Mithras, do they not?"

"As you wish," Aelius said quietly, feeling the jagged edge of spiritual confusion sideswipe him yet again.

"And in between those visits," Vrittakos continued looking at him deeply, "You must visit your sister and niece at *Lãfadũn*. I order it!"

Aelius remained silent, but nodded his ascent, for inwardly his heart opened at the thought.

Cahal was eagerly waiting for them to return, his stallion jittery and stamping the hard-impacted earth. He sensed a journey. Also waiting a mere spear length away was Blãthnat with head demurely lowered on seeing the master appear with Aelius. The thralls had groomed and fed all the mounts who were lined and waiting to travel. They snorted and tossed their manes in anticipation.

Aelius had had little to pack. He jumped up to his stallion and patted him enthusiastically, relieved to be going.

In fact, all the visitors seemed relieved. Gallus could be described as ecstatic. Even his bent posture had straightened somewhat over the last days. His new life had truly begun, and he had fairly sprung up onto his gelding to the amusement of Vrittakos. He had formed a bond with the ageing overseer and looked forward to their long association.

The drink-sodden life of the villam's owners had just ended. They were absent from the gathering exodus. They had been given just two days to leave.

Just as they were about to leave, Blãthnat ran forward and grabbed hold of Cahal's hand, placing it over her heart. His eyes widened, and a broad smile lit up his face. He leant down to kiss her fully and she closed her eyes to return the love that was springing up in both their hearts. Aelius looked on and felt another piece of his broken soul find its way home.

… … … … … … … … …

Chapter 37

Dèowen und Dèowen

Þu are halig

Bondsman and Bondswoman, you are blessed

Eyvindr was surprisingly ahead of his *nefa*, Cæna, as they hurtled down the steep incline, laced with gorse bushes, towards the rippling lake at the *botms*. He laughed lightly as skimming the bright yellow flowers sent that heady perfume to his starving senses. Sunni sent shards of white light to dazzle his eyes and the hot breeze rippled past his aching muscles. He had shed his tunica and sandals. He grabbed his pileus and threw it high in the torpid air. That symbolic gesture freed him. He was no longer *Romanesque*. He was Warinni.

"*Ic willan betst þu, Fædera*" I will best you, Uncle," shouted Cæna, as a tousled and grubby shirt flew past Eyvindr, followed by a muscled young body, arms outstretched, feet tight together, as his *nefa* dived like a kingfisher slicing into the water clean. Eyvindr followed suit, diving deep, remaining submerged for a lengthy time, his head bobbing up, shaking the water from his eyes.

Dagrun watched from high above, from her solar window which she refused to have glassed, overlooking the lake. She had returned to her home, now with Lãfa, Arkyn and Cæna to watch over her. Eyvindr present, even temporarily, eased her broken soul. But she knew, and she could hear the *sweostors* calling her. The river of Wyrd was relentless on the one hand and welcoming on the other. She would abide by her promise to Eileifer, to live well for her remaining time here.

Yet still she whispered the prayer,

Ðèowen und ðèowen
Ōð geswerian und Hearð kin
Heofon cwícian æt þu
Hu gif þu willan hit
Gesècan Valhalla und Neorxenawang
Follow Þín Lufian
Þu are halig
Þu are welðligen
Restan
Bliðnes, Bliðnes, Bliðnes
Lufian und Bletsunga Beorhte

Bondsman and bondswoman
Oath sworn and hearth kin
Heaven comes to you if you wish this
Go to Valhalla and Nerthus meadow
Follow your loved one
You are blessed
You are honoured
Be at rest
Bliss, bliss, bliss
Love and bright blessings.

Eyvindr swung round in the water, treading hard, to see Dagrun turn and walk away from the window, her head down and hunched into her shoulders. He determined to give Cæna as much love as he could, while he remained at Lāfadūn.

My soul has been in drought, through lack of this, he thought, realising quickly that his skill in water was weak. He watched Cæna, who had so obviously seen too much of it, had become like a water sprite, dipping and swirling in the gentle current of a still lake, and Eyvindr knew his *nefa* had made this rain and underground water lake his sanctuary.

They both turned to see Lāfa calling from the solar and dragged their sodden bodies from the lake. Arms clasped around each other's shoulders, they took the steep incline route, the aroma of cooked meat reaching them before they entered the door of the hall.

Arkyn greeted them, throwing two rough hemp cloths at them to stop puddles of lake water from soaking into the newly laid rushes and lavender-seed floor.

"*Wætr screwas bã*! Water shrews both," he boomed, "I've got dry clothes waiting for you in your rooms. Food is piping hot and ready."

"*Đoncian þu*," they both echoed and walked away rubbing legs and arms vigorously, smiling and laughing at each other's jibes.

Arkyn stood watching them, smiling broadly, displaying those Nuithone dimples in both cheeks, that was pure Wōden. He was very tall, of the giant race like the Warinni. He was blessed with a full head of dark brown hair with the same red chestnut streaks as Wōden. Yet his eyes were very different and exclusive to him. They were of the most opalescent hazel colour. Sometimes going to dark brown when his temper was challenged. But in the strong Sunni light, they became almost translucent and very penetrating. Dagrun was said to exclaim that it was the only feature that separated Arkyn from her beloved Eileifer.

"They have bonded well," Arkyn murmured to Lāfa who came and put her arm through his and leant against him, leaning up to kiss his dimpled cheek. He leant down to nuzzle her tousled hair, breathing in the heady scent of lavender, bergamot and ...something unknown, vague yet quite pungent.

"You have put something new in the cooking pot, *wíf*?" he turned to ask.

"Hah, I will tell you at the table, *ceorl*," Lāfa replied, letting go and walking off to join the others in the mead hall.

The "something" turned out to be spices, curcumin and masala from a merchant just arrived at Berandinzium Villam all the way from the Silk Road. Lāfa had been very liberal with it, "shutting my eyes" as she put it when unsure of quantity. They needed many jugs of mead to waylay the heat. And it predisposed them to a jaunty and merry end to their meal.

Arkyn and Eyvindr met and quietly talked together in the *gangern,* set back amongst the trees, the broadleaf pile having been lessened considerably since the meal.

"That meal shot through me like a spearhead tipped with molten iron!" Eyvindr complained, head hanging to his knees, speaking to the earth.

"Dah," Arkyn replied, "I would have thought your stomach would have been accustomed to these Eastern spices, living with the Romans."

"I lived as a slave for the most part," Eyvindr retorted, "Our diet consisted of leftovers of the basic kind. Spelt and pinto beans mostly with the rare treat of artichokes from Jerusalem."

They drifted into companionable silence watching through the silhouetted, darkened trees as Sunni sank languidly into the hills, leaving a splatter of crimson and pink behind fluffy clouds that drifted slowly past. The mead hall stood erect, huge against the horizon, a bastion in the landscape, still theirs, still Wihtwara, but both men felt the encroachment of Romans into their sacred land. They could see clearly the roof of Iuppiter Igne Villam, the swathe of scraped earth and whitened chalk that left its trail from the quarry.

Eyvindr let a deep sigh escape.

"I do not have the least desire to attain this next level of Mithras, Arkyn. This Fourth level of Leo will see me as an adept. It will be a lie. My soul sits with Nerthus."

There came a moment's silence between the two friends. Eyvindr completed his ablutions, tying his breeches vigorously as he dipped down beyond the low branches of the sycamore to stand alone silhouetted as an amber shadow against the sinking of Sunni.

"This current you find yourself in has many tributaries swirling around you," Arkyn spoke loudly from his leafy throne, "and you must take account of how your decision will change the direction of each life you touch, Eyvindr!

"We live on an island, but *we* are not an island, *dèore frèond.*"

He joined Eyvindr, looking out onto the horizon, twinned in the joint wonder of Nerthus' beauty shimmering on their sacred Isle.

"She will never desert you," was the statement Arkyn whispered as Eyvindr shuffled his foot into the loose earth before him.

"I know," Eyvindr replied, then after a moment's thought came to a decision of sorts.

"It will be Vrittakos and his family that would suffer most if I walked from my Roman life completely," he stated quietly, mulling over the implications for others, more at this moment than for himself.

"The Roman hierarchy are making their way here, to Britannia and then to Wihtland. I am the famous, or infamous, royal slave in their perceptions and to see me rebel would impoverish Vrittakos in a permanent way.

"Let us not forget Aia and Eastmund," Arkyn joined in, "for their relationship would be affected too."

"Dagrun would lose the companionship of Venitouta," Eyvindr echoed, "Impossible at this time!"

He straightened his back to the decision just made. He was living in two worlds. Outwardly, for the time being at least, he must become Roman again. His heart and mind would jostle around each other and that he must live with. More deeply, his soul and his desire would dance around his responsibilities until such time as they could part amicably. To signature that decision, he pulled the *pileus* from his belt and slammed it on his thick Warinni mane knowing full well it would be cut within a few hours.

As Lāfa sheared his hair, later that evening, she sighed, repeatedly, almost with each lock that fluttered to the rush floor, to mingle with the lavender seeds. No words were spoken. Dagrun remained in the shadows, watching. For her, it must have seemed like she was losing her beloved brother once again. When he was fully shorn, the Roman fringe straight as an arrow and neckline cropped close, he walked over to his *sweostor*.

"I am with Nerthus still and for always, Dagrun," he whispered as he wrapped his arms close around her, willing her soul to meet his.

"I have to free myself this way. Be patient. There will a homecoming, I promise you." Yet within his loving embrace, he felt her collapse slightly, and silently her soul drifted away somewhere he could not follow.

... ...

Chapter 38

Iuppiter Igne Villam
Fire of Jupiter Villam

Aelius strode through the deep encrusted chalky ruts in the pathway that led to Iuppiter Igne Villam. He looked and was imposing, due to the temper that was rising swiftly as he scanned the chaos before him. A mixture of chalk and mud were spattered up his legs, grating his skin against the leather thongs and muddying his toga.

He was in the approach to the villam that the Roman elites, equerries and even Caesars would be taking in a few moons' time. The fourth initiation level of Mithras, Leo, was being insulted. Aelius stopped, standing almost ankle deep in the pile of mud and roared,

"*Affer mihi, inquit vilicus! Nunc. Hic situs est omnis ignominiam. Capi volvent!*

Bring me the overseer! Now. This whole site is a disgrace. Heads will roll!"

Several backs of the *servus* straightened in unison and turned to gape at the originator of this tirade. One slave ran inside. Aelius' face was blotched red with anger. He had not felt such fury in a long time. Perhaps, he thought to himself, he was releasing anger from his entrapment in a life he despised.

He drew breath to calm himself as the overseer appeared, papers flapping in his bony hands, as he hurried forward. He made a low bow, muttering "your Excellency" as he pushed the papers out at arm's length for Aelius, who only noticed quite arbitrarily the thick scabby growths on this overseer's scalp.

He kept him bending low, hands supporting his bent back holding onto his knees. Aelius studied the villam plans. Architecturally they seemed quite adequate and as he scanned the building, he began to feel slightly hopeful. The villam itself looked impressive, moderate in size but housing all the necessary bene-fits needed to complement the Mithras initiation and following celebration. The grounds were an absolute mess.

"Why are these grounds in such a lamentable state?" Aelius demanded, "Stand for Juno's sake will you!"

The overseer, stood and looked Aelius in the eye, his face con-torted with his own anger,

"We have only one gardener and no slaves to create the garden approach. And we were given orders out of the blue to construct immediately, the largest cattle and bull pens I have ever encoun-tered. All building has stopped to build these pens and outhouses to contain this huge herd arriving any day now. Why this num-ber?"

Aelius did not reply, his mind reeling, remembering the white calves and bulls arriving at Berandinzium villam.

"I need papyrus and quill, now," he barked at the overseer, "And the very best rider. And do your baths and hypocaust work? I need refreshment and a hot bath to soak away this mud".

Aelius strode through the *vestibulum* taking swift mental notes of the décor, the finish and the flooring. Leaving muddy tracks on the tiled floor, he briefly washed his muddy hands in the small fountain situated in centre of the *Atrium*, scanning the mo-saic dedicated to Bacchus rippling by concentric circles of water. He relaxed slightly, realising the true situation was not at all des-perate, just an organisational nightmare that would be solved with skilled men and equipment. He walked into the small *ta-blinum*, seeing the hunched figure of a man busy scraping a quill on papyrus, writing a list in somewhat of a hurry, while focusing on the clay tablet that had scored notes upon it.

He looked up as Aelius hmphed and dragged his leather san-dals across the floor.

"Ohh," came the exclamation from the office worker, "*Paenitet me sume sedem. C. Suetonii Tranquilli me. Quomodo te adiuvare possum*? My apologies, please take a seat. I am Gallus Suetonius. How can I help you?"

Aelius blanched at the name Gallus, his face whitened, and he took a deep breath. When will I ever be free of this! he thought bitterly!

"I have need of a quill and parchment?" he said as a command. The man shuffled the pile of tablets to extract a quill and a clean piece of vellum. The man then leaning down to pull a portable table from under his desk, handed it to Aelius to lean on. He proceeded to write the urgent message to Vrittakos for men and equipment to complete the colossal stock yard in time.

There must be more bulls arriving, he thought as he wrote and mentioned as such to Vrittakos, offering up the opinion that Wihtland was about to become the sacred isle to Mithras for many years to come. The favoured Isle to Romans, as Mōnã had been to the Druids. A shudder went through him, icing his belly. He sent a prayer up to Nerthus. What else could he do? "I will have a very hot bath," he said aloud.

"The baths are just to the side of the *exedra*, a small door on the east wall opens up to the baths. We have an attendant waiting." The man replied, smiling slightly and offering a small nod. Aelius bowed equally very slightly and walked out. The chalk residue was making his skin red and he decided it may well have limestone mixed in.

The garden room was delightful, some feminine hand had worked here. And the door to the baths was part of a wall mural of leafy trees and spring flowers, dancing nymphs and water features beautifully frescoed. On Aelius opening the door, steam immediately escaped. The bath itself was covered with petals and flowerheads. Aelius shed his toga, tunica and *indutus* which was immediately whisked away by the two male slaves in attendance, and he sank languidly into the warmth and shut his eyes from his present world. He went back to Lãfadūn, reliving his visit, and languished in the water until he felt his fingers become prune-like. The slaves stepped forward offering large, warmed linen sheets and led him to the long table where they massaged warming oils into his tired limbs putting marigold and comfrey oil into the red sores on his legs.

Food was waiting for him in the larger *triclinium* along with most of the villam's residents and slaves. He was ravenous and decided to eat before explaining the forthcoming situation. Flatulence would surely follow otherwise.

As the talk became more focused and the food digested, Aelius presented the uncomfortable truth.

He cleared his throat and banged the goblet on the table to silence the chatter.

"In case you are unaware, my name is Aelius and I've been tasked with overseeing the progress of all the Roman villams on Wecta," people looked askance at him and he realised the mispronunciation. "I mean Vecta," he continued.

"Vrittakos Eluskonios, owner of Berandinzium Villam has been promoted to Governor of Vecta in preparation for the upgrading of our island home to that of Sacred Isle for the celebration and ceremonies to Mithras and Bacchus etc!"

The hush that ensued within the *triclinium* was swiftly followed by gasps and ebullient chatter from owners to overseers and slaves. This bombshell affected everyone.

Aelius slammed the table once more, shattering the goblet.

"Listen!" He shouted, throwing his arms in the air, "We have very little time, maybe just two or three full moons, I mean three months to make our villas fit for Caesars, Equerries, Governors of Britannia and elites of the academic world in Rome! They will be travelling here from Villam Regis Cogidvbni, in Noviomagus Reginorum. And they will be bringing in full intent, Initiates and Fathers alike to commit to the process of devotion to Mithras. That is the reason for the massive stock yard, which will house untold number of bulls and heifers for the sacrifice to Mithras!"

Aelius paused for this information to sink in. The silence was deafening.

"What level is this villam dedicated to?" asked a man seated at the far end of the room, leaning on the velvet couch, swinging a bunch of black grapes in his mouth.

"The Fourth level, Leo," Aelius replied, watching closely this man's reaction.

"Hmmm," came the reply, a smirk crossing the face of this man which remained as he stared rudely at Aelius. "Well that is *magnifico!* If you will pardon my absence, *Prandeo, poto, cana, ludo, laro, cæno, quiesco, Libero glorioso Bacchus"*

I will dine, drink, sing, play, bathe, sup, and rest with the glorious Bacchus!"

"Pontius!" roared the owner, "Remove yourself from this gathering. NOW!" The man lurched up from his couch and sauntered unsteadily out of the *triclinium.*

Aelius stood up and faced the owner, pulling the sealed vellum from his tunica, and waving it at the man whose care for this villam was solely his responsibility. He was steadily losing his patience.

"This message needs to reach Vrittakos at whichever villam he may be residing. He may be back at Berandinzium Villam. But he must have this in his hand within two days and an answer within four. Your fastest rider if you please."

Aelius handed the message over and left for his *cubiculum,* a bed and rest, preferably unconscious and with no dreams to trouble him.

... ...

Aelius left Iuppiter Igne Villam at dawn the next day, making the short journey to Lāfadūn where he could see the arrival of men and equipment from the comfort of the solar and in relaxed company. He could shed his *Romanesque* mask for a short while.

Yet there was an atmosphere weaving inexorably around the hall that Aelius knew entwined at his feet. It was born on the invisible wind from Dagrun. She had taken to her private quarters. She would not even mingle with her family. Cæna had become morose.

"Your decision to become *Romanesque* again has pained your *sweostor*, Eyvindr!" Lāfa exclaimed refusing to utter his Roman name and holding him by the shoulders looked him square in the face, "You need to explain to her, *nūðã Fædera!*"

He climbed the oaken stairs slowly that led to her solar. He knocked in deference and heard her muted reply. The solar was darkened with all the shutters closed. A single candle burned, and he saw Dagrun hunched over the sacred memorabilia of Eileifer's that she had kept back from the funeral pyre.

He shed his working boots and came to her barefoot, kneeling before her.

"My *sweostor*, beloved, please allow me to explain this change you see." Dagrun, still with head bent fixed him with a dark impenetrable stare. Yet she nodded and held his hand. Hers were bony and very cold.

"I came to my decision, not because of a pull to Rome. Absolutely never will that be, Dagrun. It is because of Vrittakos and his family, their care for me and their loyalty. They hate Rome as much as we do. You know this!

"So, I must tell you that their lives need to be protected. I have just discovered that Rome looks to this sacred Isle. Wihtland has been chosen, Dagrun. It is to become the Isle of Mithras!"

Dagrun's expression of sheer disbelief followed by a string of Norse blasphemies brought colour to her cheeks.

"This was not foreseen by the Nornir!" she exclaimed.

"Well it is an intricate web the Romans weave," Eyvindr replied, blowing heat into her frozen hands, "We must be patient, for I have heard rumours that the Caesars, both past and future are travelling here to regroup, to plot and subvert. Rome is becoming unstable. They have chosen to leave and reach out to the hinterland. And they cannot go anywhere without Mithras."

"So, all eyes of Rome will be on Vrittakos," she uttered with a smile, "and my beloved rebel of a brother!"

"That is so," Eyvindr replied, "for now until they depart, I must become Aelius, the pretender.

"And now dear *sweostor* will you accompany me down to the hall. Your son needs you and Lãfa needs your assistance."

Dagrun nodded and made to rise. She stopped.

"I know my daughter is with child," she said looking deep into her brother's eyes, as his mouth gaped open.

"It is a skill no mother is without. We know. Yet I also know I will not be present at the birth of my granddaughter. And I cannot say a word."

It was Eyvindr's turn to bow his head, as he held Dagrun's hands tightly in his and prayed she was wrong.

··· ··· ··· ··· ··· ··· ··· ··· ···

Chapter 39

Η συνάντηση των μεγάλων μυαλών
The Meeting of Great minds

Aelius shot bolt upright, Sunni sending shards of intense light into his eyes, as he squeezed his lids shut against the glare and brought his hands to his ears, shutting out the sounds of the giant cockerel that seemed to be inside his *cubiculum*. His feet rustled the bedlinen to the floor as he stood and tweaked one-eye open, and promptly shut it again with a groan. The last evening had been celebratory with endless horns of the best mead passing through eager hands and much good-natured banter. Dagrun had succumbed to her family's insistence that she join the festivities. The Warinni were in fine form. What were we celebrating? Aelius asked himself.

Just being together. Was that not enough?

The sound of that damned cockerel was reverberating inside his head. And suddenly reality for Aelius took a shift sideways. The world expanded. He felt his own consciousness grow to admit a higher energy. He invited the incoming to show him the immense connection to the cosmos, a fleeting but nonetheless intense knowledge of worlds beyond this one.

Abrasax had come.

Aelius sped out of his room to reach Dagrun, who had just opened her door to him. He knew just by her expression that she had experienced this moment in all its glory too.

She had spent many hours with Venitouta exploring the cosmos. It was her joy. Now Aelius was to join them.

They both reached the shutters of the solar and flung them open to allow Sunni and all else to burst in.

Coming up from the Roman road below and galloping apace up the steep incline to the hall, came familiar figures astride two stallions, their tails flaring, and ears pricked. Vrittakos and Cahal were speeding their way to Aelius. They were bringing news.

Aelius gave his son, who wore a look of total shock, a Warinni greeting, pulling him close and whispering the reason for the about-face in appearance. "I am Aelius until I say otherwise, and not a word to Vrittakos."

Cahal nodded and bent his ear to the exuberant discourse of the Greek, who was leaning just a little too much into his native tongue, so excitable and joyous.

"Μπορείτε να φανταστείτε τη χαρά, τους φίλους μου, τη συνολική χαρά στην ανάγνωση των ειδήσεων!

"Can you imagine the joy, my friends, the total joy on reading the news!" Vrittakos flew his arms to the heavens in gratitude and danced around in a circle clapping as if he were indeed back in his homeland.

He stopped and encircling his great arms around Aelius, puffed up and exploded, "And what in the name of Juno have you done to yourself Eyvindr. Did I not make it clear enough that you are, in all essence, a Libertus!"

"Yes, indeed you did," Aelius responded, extricating himself from the bear hug, "Yet I have a Mithraic initiation to attend and in which I must play and indeed *be* the adept of the Leo fourth level. No mean thing Vrittakos. No mean thing."

"Hmph," Vrittakos mumbled and opened the missive instead, that told all on Wihtland that Achaikos would be arriving in two twilights on the high tide and bringing his family with him.

"Η οικογένειά του, σας λέω. Τι οικογένεια?!!

His family, I tell you. What family?!!"

"And not only that, my friends, but Apollo himself must have conjured up some magick, for waiting for the ferry at Gaul, were two more elders and wise men, my dearest Venitouta invited to keep us company while the Romans jaunt about and boast incessantly. These men are, in my humble opinion, the most elevated and erudite thinkers in all Rome. I must tell Dagrun."

With that he flapped away to the great hall, pulling the great door open as if it was mere matchwood, leaving everyone none the wiser as to who these visitors from Rome were, or indeed why they had made the difficult journey to this speck on the hinterland of the Empire!

They stood for a while outside as Sunni was warming their bones and the fragrances from the flowers and herbs settled their spirits. Cahal gave his *fæder* a full discourse on the remaining villams that Vrittakos and himself had taken in turns to visit. He had learnt a great deal very quickly, overseeing, in some cases, the increased workforce brought in and directing some of the improvements. Heliodromus Villam was now near completion. The overseer sent to Mercuri Vulpes Corvum Videt Villam, had determined a fast pace in improvements, and Cahal had determined an even greater improvement in his burgeoning courtship with Blāthnat. Aelius congratulated his son, now a young man. He felt his heart steadily open like a lotus flower. This new heady emotion brought a lump to his throat which he hid by bending down to tie his leather thongs.

After a while they made their way inside, Gudrun smiling unbelievably seeing Dagrun sitting opposite Vrittakos at the big hall table, laughing loudly at some witticism which she reposted swiftly, Vrittakos bellowing in response.

The rare scene before them collapsed as swiftly as it had arrived. Dagrun was now convulsed in a coughing fit which left her breathless and in pain. Folkvarthr sped forward to wrap her in his arms as Gudrun bowed her head to hide her pain. Time with her daughter had become so very precious.

... ...

Chapter 40

Ο τερματικός σταθμός του δρόμου του μεταξιού
Η Ανατολή συναντά τη Δύση.

The Silk road Terminus
East meets West

Tamina and Kiana sat huddled together aft on the *Cnearr* with just the crown of hair visible over their *birrus Brittannicus*, knots of hair whipping wildly about in the ferocious wind. The wind had cursed the sailing from the outset, and they were now tacking miserably about hoping to gain a few spear lengths between them and the Gaul coast. The owner was just on the verge of turning about, back to the harbour, which was still in plain sight, when the sail caught a new wind and hurtled forward. Achaikos could hear the timbers groan, move, then grudgingly it seemed to him, surrender to the speed. It was an ancient *Cnearr*, almost as old as the crew.

Achaikos was simmering with frustration and anger. It had been the only voyage available, the *Cnearr* being designed to tackle the rough channel waters. He simply hated seeing his women suffer, after the spasmodic, idyllic, honeymoon voyage. And as he watched his compatriots from sunnier climes, both of huge spiritual stature, being reduced to a puking, trembling mess of sick humanity, he despaired of Britannia and wished he had remained in Antioch.

He looked over briefly to study his aging companions, who had mentored him as a young student and whose tutorship had grown into a deep and abiding friendship. Their spiritual knowledge and understanding of the mysteries, both mundane and cosmological imparted to him as a young man, had been the bedrock from which he grew in stature and wisdom to accomplish all he had. He owed them his life.

He kept his treasured copy, perhaps the only copy here in the western Gallic empire, of Antoninus' Metamorphoseon Syngoge, wrapped in oiled leather, tightly bound, and in a leather chest.

And here they were, huddled on this ancient *cnearr,* their heads bowed, parchment features protected from the icy blast of a salt-laden wind by the large and generous cowl of the *birrus Brittannicus*.

Vrittakos' beloved Venitouta had spun her magick to bring them here, but now Achaikos had learnt of the true nature of their journey in the brief conversation on the quayside in *Gesoriacum*. The Roman Empire was teetering on collapse. And it was within the Gallic empire that revolt and plotting against Rome was being nurtured and fed. Achaikos had heard and seen the near-invisible dark shadow of usurpation ripple against the sun of Rome, the further west they moved. It was unimaginable that the conquering might of Rome was being challenged.

Antoninus Liberalis and Censorinus, Magis both, were travelling into the storm, bringing their magick with them. Yet their intentions were guarded. Achaikos was excluded, and he decided silently, he really did not wish to *be* included.

The passengers remained in silence, the buffeting and lurching of the boat as the wind hurtled them towards the Britannia coastline sent them all inwards to wrap their souls in prayer and reflection. The crew gave the briefest call to action to each other in guttural *Plattdeutch,* the language of the Ingavonii. It was not long before the sight of the sacred diamond isle of Wihtland hove into view and the sea calmed in response. Landfall was so close Kiana nearly let loose her emotions and cried. She hugged Tamina and whispered in her salt-knotted hair,

"Voyage end, my brave daughter."

"Mama, we are both completely crazy! You do know that." Tamina held a sideways grin that could not grow to a smile. Her cheeks were frozen to her teeth.

The *Cnearr*, now bereft of wind was being rowed into Berandinzium harbour, creaking loudly and showing her age. As the oars were lifted skyward Achaikos took first glimpse of the villam, their new home. Silhouetted against it by the sinking sun, stood his dear old friend Vrittakos and a whole tribe of other islanders he had yet to know.

"Αχαϊκός, αγαπητός μου φίλος. Καλως ΗΡΘΑΤΕ. Και καλωσορίζουμε στον Αντώνη και τον Κένσορνο. Θερμαίνετε αυτή την παλιά καρδιά, στην αλήθεια.

"Achaikos, my dear friend. Welcome. And welcome to Antoninus and Censorinus. you are warming this old heart, in truth."

Vrittakos extended his arms to encase his dear friend. Achaikos felt the years melt away and they were back once more in their beloved homeland. Vrittakos pulled away and reached out to take the hands of the two esteemed elders and magicians, and bowing low he whispered,

"Ο αρχαιότερος και σεβαστός Θεός Αμπράσαξ περιμένει τις προσευχές και την αφοσίωσή μας. Ο μυστικός μας ναός είναι δικός σας για να δημιουργήσετε μια μεγάλη μαγεία.

"Our most ancient and revered God Abrasax awaits our prayers and dedication. Our secret temple is yours to create great magick."

Kiana and Tamina had placed themselves at the outer edge of the circle, watching. Neither was at all sure of the etiquette on this strange island. Kiana felt its power before they had set foot on land, it radiated out to sea in a mixture of energies that were odd and very powerful. There was an element that held dominion over this island, its power extraordinary and quite daunting to meet head on.

Kiana felt this was expressed in the women and looked over to them to reach their spirit. She connected immediately with the young woman, holding an elder in a caring embrace. This elder was ill. Mother and daughter, she thought instinctively.

"Oh, but this is so remiss of me," Vrittakos bellowed, "You must think us entirely rude. We have not introduced you to the

Royal family of the Wihtwara in whose guardianship this beautiful island, their sacred home, remains, by all that is holy!'"

Kiana was brought back to the present. Tamina went immediately to Aia and Eastmund, Cahal and Cæna. Joining the youth of
the Wihtwara seemed only natural.

The men were clustering around in a huddle, most unseemly,
Kiana thought and went to the mother and daughter for introduc-
tions.

"My *Mōdor* is the *Cwèn* of this island, she is our queen," the
young woman said. She spoke in a mixture of Roman and her native tongue. "My name is Lãfa, it means love. And my mother is
called Dagrun which means day rune. We are the Warinni."

Kiana gave her first wide sincere smile since leaving the Gaulish coast.

"My name is Kiana; its meaning is of the Earth. I am the Royal
blood of the Sogdians. My daughter is named Tamina, meaning
worshipper of Ahura Mazda and she is a princess. We were both
freed from slavery and rescued by Achaikos during the earthquake in Antioch. We are both Zoroastrian priestesses."

Kiana held the gaze of Dagrun the queen, who smiled, then
coughed mightily, concern washing over the face of Lãfa.

"I would wish to find a quiet place to sit and share with you,
Kiana," Dagrun nodded and took her hand, "We have much to
learn from each other, I do believe."

"*Giese!*" replied Lãfa, "It is obvious the men have worldly aspects to talk over. We need to hold the balance with Nerthus do
we not?"

"Nerthus?" Kiana asked.

"Our Earth Goddess," Dagrun replied.

"Ahh, Cybele, Hecate, Diana," Kiana answered with a smile.

"*Giese*, our Goddess."

They walked along the path towards the villam, mirrored on
each side with immaculately pruned box trees, interspaced with
roses. Venitouta lovingly brushed her hand lightly against the
blooms, bending down to breathe in their perfume.

The women settled in the *exedra*, the central fountain's water tinkling delicately into a pool layered with lily leaves and pink blooms peeping above to shine their light on the women, now settling themselves on the cushioned seats to discuss and share wisdoms of the earth and the heavens.

... ...

Chapter 41

Si est praevaricator legis, non-ad occupandam virtus: in omnibus ceteris casibus servare nequeat!

If you must break the law, do it to seize power: in all other cases observe it

(Julius Cæsar 100BC-40BC)

The men had adjourned to the *tablinum*, after the rapturous greetings by Vrittakos and Venitouta, not to mention the gravitational pull of both Cæna and Cahal to Tamina, who pulsated with gorgeous energy no man could resist. Kiana gave her a gimlet look and an arched eyebrow. The youngsters had retreated to admire the villam, the grounds and most importantly each other.

Meanwhile, the immobile but powerful statues of Juno and Apollo stared down on the men as they settled into the couches and cushioned seats that had been placed in a semi-circle around the table now filled with food. Slaves stood in attendance in the shadows of these statues, as the sun poured in through the tall glassed windows.

This was the men's sanctuary room and it oozed politics.

Censorinus spoke first after an appreciable silence as they tasted the medjool dates filled with honeyed nuts and creamed cheese.

"Many thanks Vrittakos for providing such a taste of home."

Mumbles of appreciation echoed from filled mouths and came with the nodding of heads.

"We give thanks to your beloved wife, Venitouta for inviting us all those months ago. It was for us affirmation that we are required to make this long journey to the hinterland of the Empire."

Censorinus paused as he wriggled his vast undercarriage further into the silk cushion and adjusted his spine, which creaked audibly. He winced with pain. He was of middle years like his companion Vrittakos, but his insatiable appetite had led to a blotched skin housing jowl and two double chins. Yet his eyes sparkled with passion and wisdom.

Achaikos nodded silently to his servant to bring extra cushions.

"It has always amazed me that this hinterland, this Britannia holds a hidden jewel, *Villam Regis Cogidvbni* at *Noviomagus Reginorum* the shining replica of the Caesar's palace on the Palatine hill in Rome!", Censorinus opined through a full mouthful of dates, "Why you may ask?

"The Caesars' have made this arduous journey from all over the empire, over many decades to gather, plot and scheme. Yet their over-riding need after all the politics has ended, is to cleanse their souls.", he continued.

"After the destruction of the Druid enclave at Mōnā, that island, spiritually powerful though it undoubtedly was, became a pyre, a dead island to the Romans. I believe it was Vespasian who first spoke of Vecta as being a sacred island. It is why, we believe, he was careful with it and its inhabitants.

"It is called Wihtland, I believe, by the native people here?"

"Yes," responded Vrittakos, smiling, "they are a spiritual caste of people called the Wihtwara. The meaning is "People of the Spirit" and the island is called Isle of Spirits. They first migrated here for just such a reason. To be with Spirit."

Achaikos, who had been studiously watching and listening to this, suddenly exploded into action in true Greek style.

"Ahhh! so now it is making wonderful sense my friends," he exclaimed, "As an atonement to Abrasax, I am experiencing the Fall. I came here to re-discover my fragmented soul. Yet I find Abrasax in all his immaculate wonder had a bigger plan all along. My new family, my beloved women are both priestesses of Ahura Mazda. And here they are too!"

"It is to Mithra we are looking," replied Antoninus, "the Cæsars and Equites, governors and legates are making their way here as we speak. They call our god Mithras the bull slayer. We do not. It is a Roman aberration of our peaceful and wonderful God from the East; Mithra."

Censorinus interrupted, kindly leaning over to lay his hand on Antonius's arm, slender and veined with arthritic knuckles.

"We must educate our hosts and friends on the hidden nature of the empire, needs must my dear friend.

"The Empire is crumbling from within. And it is being expressed in its extremities. The Gallic empire, the Western reaches are bloating with usurpation. The days of purity of bloodline are behind us, almost," he countered, drawing breath to reach the crux of it, "Gallienus will be made Emperor of the whole empire, if reports just handed to me are true. His father has made a huge error of judgement, in our humble opinion, in persecuting the Christians.

"We have witnessed their growth and eagerness to climb up the greasy pole of power. They are ambitious and wealthy. You witnessed this yourself, Achaikos?"

"Yes," he nodded, scratching the beard he longed to shave away, "They were saving Antioch after the earthquake. And doing a fine job. But we witnessed horrifying deaths and torture of Christian families and nobility in Byzantium just before we fled by boat to journey here."

"A huge mistake," Censorinus countered, "we will pay dearly. And to let you know that plague has slaughtered much of the Roman army and the Sassanids are victorious. Valerian is captured and remains a prisoner of war.

"Anyone who can lead an army can now take a shot at being made Emperor. If the men vote you in, you are elevated next morning, and coins are minted by evening!"

"Gallienus will be seen galloping with his equites," Censorinus continued almost without taking breath, "from one end of the Empire to the other, vainly, in my opinion, keeping a tenuous control on a sprawling, over-weighted and corrupt empire!"

Achaikos drew a long intake of breath as if to assimilate this far-reaching description of Rome's end days.

"And who are the usurpers?" he asked, looking at both elders.

"Shall I rub the genie bottle for him to raise up and tell us the answer?" Censorinus countered with a sarcastic grin.

"One thing we do know for certain," Antoninus interjected, slapping his palm for emphasis, "they will be travelling here, or I should say, to the *Villam Regis Cogidvbni,* as it is and always has been, a place for usurpers to gather and plot assassinations. Why? Because it has been stewarded by a Briton usurper family for generations!"

"It is why we are here," Censorinus continued, "a meeting of great minds needed in guardianship."

"And a meeting of Magi to effect the change." Antoninus added, linking his arm with Censorinus.

Achaikos looked on, feeling a clamp suddenly knot his belly and icy fingers reach his heart.

… … … … … … … … …

Kiana's gaze travelled the breadth of the *exedra*, as the women talked amongst themselves. She kept her silence. There were layers of energy to this mysterious villam, as many as the murals that covered the walls. The goddess Coventina lauded amongst an array of *lares* and *penates*, faerie in character. Reds and yellow adorned her garments that flared delicately out to mingle with roses and peony.

Statues of Dianna and Venus sat on tall plinths gazing down at the central pool. Absolutely every feature was feminine. Kiana settled into the beauty and the calm. She felt the rigours of that sea journey finally waft away from her. She let out a deep audible sigh.

"I am so very grateful to be here at last," she said turning to give a welcoming smile to the three women.

"You are welcome indeed," Venitouta replied as she rose elegantly, sweeping her silk toga aside with one hand, to reach for wine with the other and hand it to Kiana, "your journey along the silk trade route is arduous and impossibly long, so I have heard from the traders who reach this far-flung hinterland!"

"Oh, it was not hard at all," Kiana gave her rare full smile that reached her eyes, "it has been deeply informative and enjoyable for both me and my daughter, compared to the life we endured before the earthquake that destroyed much of Antioch." She then gazed at the women and knew her story would be safe with them. They held her trust as a fledgling bird released from its cage.

So, Kiana, princess of Sogdia and Zoroastrian priestess told her story.

There were gasps of wonderment and sighs of pure sorrow as she retold moments of ecstasy and pain. She left nothing out, knowing their interest was held. Yet it was the descriptions of mother and daughter honouring the god Zoroaster and Ahura Mazda that kept Dagrun and Lāfa in intense concentration.

Dagrun reached forward to take Kiana's hand in hers. Kiana felt the bones creak and the parchment skin fold under the warmth of her own. The effort made the queen's breath escape her battered lungs and Kiana felt the effort for Dagrun to bring that air back.

"Would it be considered an imposition for my daughter and myself to join you and Tamina in an honouring to this ancient and wonderful god?" Dagrun asked.

"It would be an honour," Kiana replied, "For Zoroaster is a supreme caretaker of our Earth and our precious water. Good Thoughts, Good words, Good Deeds. Nerthus would be pleased to welcome him."

"Shall we plan then for *Dona Dea* day," Venitouta interjected, "Calling in Coventina, our goddess of the water is essential and Cerunnos, our god of the forests would be welcomed also."

"Oh excellent," Lāfa pronounced eagerly, "With our gods, Wōden, Thunōr, Freya, with Sunni and Mōnā we will be honouring Nerthus completely.

Swã mōtan hít bèon!"

"And what of our men?" Venitouta asked.

Kiana sat bolt upright at this, staring at Vrittakos' wife with questioning on her lips.

"How well do you know your husband's companions?"

"Not well at all," came the hesitant reply.

Kiana herself hesitated, took a breath in and stated clearly, without taking her eyes from Venitouta,

"They are not what they seem. We must take great care. Be watchful."

... ...

Chapter 42

Villam Regis Cogidvbni
Fishbourne Villam

"Please be so kind as to look forward and act as if this is a fairly normal vista before you," Vrittakos snapped, looking askance at Aelius, whose expression mimicked a stranded fish out of water.

"Was not the Saxum Demulceo Villam of similar grandiosity?"

Aelius straightened, replying in hushed tones, "Nowhere near!" Grandiosity was left standing in the wings as a descriptive of Saxum Villam compared to this vast palace. It was unique this far north of Rome. And it could host most of the Cæsars and Elites in opulent comfort in many rooms built around the approach garden and box tree avenue leading to the giant pillared entrance. Much would be made of it when company arrived, and sociability, artifice and downright smiling hypocrisy laid the ground rules. For now, Vrittakos remained tight-lipped, proud owner of Berandinzium Villam in all its secret glory and which was his prize and his alone. They had arrived without announcement, quietly, planning to meet a colleague and friend, who would bid them enter secretly. It was more than four days before the arrival of the Rome hierarchy. Vrittakos had elected to do some spying and Aelius was eager to join him. Cahal walked silently behind them as a third pair of eyes.

Both Magis had elected not to join them, but to be announced in regal manner with the legates and Cæsars. Disquiet had flashed across Vrittakos' eyes, his face being a total mirror to his soul. Aelius knew something was very amiss. Vrittakos was rarely as tight-lipped as this.

A tall man in a purple-trimmed toga appeared from the nearby *exedra*. His squared fringe and classic Roman nose gave Aelius a missed heartbeat as his tormentor Gallus flashed across his mind.

His muscles instinctively tensed then relaxed as the man lost all appearance of that tormentor long gone and became a smiling warm-eyed friend who met Vrittakos with a bonded arm grip.

"Welcome dear Friend," he exuded joviality and looking over to Aelius and his son, commented, "And this must be Aelius and Cahal is it?"

"Indeed, it is," Vrittakos beamed back," My friends this is Octavious Sabinus who has had my back more than once. Loyalty personified! He is on secondment from Eboracum."

"And if it is possible," Vrittakos continued earnestly, looking about him, eyes darting from one corner to the next, "can we go forthwith to our *cubiculum's* without too much notice being made?"

"Yes of course," Octavious replied, "there are work clothes waiting for you and you will be part of a team repairing the mosaic floor. Vrittakos, you are appointed supervisor, more fitting for your age, I think. These youngsters can bend their backs with ease I'm sure! Listen well! The talk amongst the tesserae is boundlessly interesting, so I'm told. If you want to learn some truth, always ask the lowest workers!"

"What can you tell us?" Vrittakos smiled over to Octavious whose face bore the scars of military engagement. The wheal ran from eyebrow, missing his right eye by millimetres to end at the corner of his mouth, twisting his expressions to caricature level. But the gleam and spark in his eyes eclipsed the scar and made the man. Aelius warmed to him.

They skirted around the colonnaded walk; whose columns boasted the rare shining pink marble from Mons Claudius itself. This had been hoisted bodily from the quarry and shipped intact all the way along the Silk Road, for thousands of dusty miles and choppy seas to arrive in pristine condition, here at the hinterland of the Empire.

Aelius suddenly felt his anger rise, "Eyvindr" railed at the stupendous harm to Nerthus, his mother. And decided silently that the Roman mind was cruelly obsessive and sick. He looked over the scarred face of Vrittakos' companion and knew violence would always inherently be on the Roman breath.

Octavious suddenly darted sideways, almost at a run, beckoning the interlopers to follow, dashing quietly through the main walkway, sconces alight with dancing flames to shadow their path. He pulled aside a thick drape and they followed him inside. They were in the servants' quarters, and the partitions to give some privacy were almost paper thin.

"You would be well advised to speak only in hushed voices here," Octavious motioned them over to the single window, muffling his voice, "All the slaves must speak in Latin or face the whip. You must do likewise," looking over to Cahal whose features shouted loudly "Durotrige".

"Get changed, food will be served in 20 minutes in the slaves' *culina*. I will take my leave. And we will share information later, at nightfall. I will seek you out." Octavious, erstwhile governor of Britannia Inferior, swished the drape aside and disappeared, a grim look furrowing his brow, tension bending his shoulders.

The mention of food brought a chorus of stomach gurgling. They had not eaten since before dawn. They simply followed the aromas to seek out the *culina*, situated at the farthest end of the slaves' accommodation. It was a long walk and when they entered the *culina*, they all stared in astonishment, at the number of slaves imprisoned to work at this Villam Regis. Scores of both male and female workers were sitting at benches, on the floor, or perched on grain sacks, anywhere to eat the slops laid out in the wooden bowls. The queue was long, and they shuffled along silently, looking down and avoiding all eye contact. The slop was not too bad, nutritious with meat and vegetables, and hunks of unleavened bread to scoop up the juice. But there was lamentably short time to eat or digest the stew before an officious Roman appeared to bark names and orders. In an ascending trickle of bodies, the *culina* was evacuated.

"You must play deaf," Aelius whispered into his son's ear. Cahal had as much knowledge of Roman as his mother, and that was precious little.

"Be my shadow and say nothing, leave all talking to me, and do not under any circumstances react to what you may hear. Stow it all until later. Your mother will never forgive me if you return with wheals on your back. Truly she won't!"

And so, the spies were set to work on a mosaic situated in a *dormitoria* suite within the guest quarters, its tesserae in poor condition, cracked and uneven. With just four days remaining until the formal gathering of Cæsars, the work was frenetic, whips hanging in readiness by the overseers, should there be unwarranted talk, and the crack of that whip, followed by a scream was heard intermittently as tensions grew.

Aelius looked over to Vrittakos standing alone looking on and he smiled slightly, winking. An acknowledgement to his "master's" humanity and compassion. Heads now down Aelius and Cahal bent their backs into the work, Cahal looking on and copying everything his father did. There was no opportunity to find out anything in this tortured atmosphere, but on a swift glimpse up, Aelius saw Vrittakos in deep conversation with an overseer, who seemed to have plenty to say.

... ...

The tesserae design was completed quickly, so Aelius and Cahal were bundled away to begin repairs on a much larger impressive mosaic medallion, centred on the floor around which other mosaic medallions encompassed the centre. This was an important floor in one of the several *oeci* and Aelius caught the hushed whisper of the slave to his left saying: -

"This is where they will be treading," this emaciated youth whispered without looking up, "I have heard Postumus no less will be setting foot here. With his acolytes. All the way from Gaul. Shall I embed these nails, sharp end upwards?"

"Shush, you fool," came the reply from his neighbour, "You will be whipped then crucified! We all will!"

"I am hearing he murdered the son of Gallienus, our Emperor! He is a murderer."

Silence prevailed as the overseer sensing the whispers sidled over and threatened both with a whipping. Aelius and Cahal froze both in dreadful anticipation of being pulled over and the weight of the news, froze their breath for a moment. On the wave of this news, Aelius realised just how pure the island energy was and how naïve he had become. A sense of iced dread hit his stomach and he recoiled. Postumus was a usurper. And he would be taking the island pilgrimage to honour Mithras along with others, expecting, *nah*, demanding exultation, a sign from the Sun god himself. What if it was not forthcoming? Aelius sagged. Cahal felt the emotion from his *fæder*.

"*Fæder*," he whispered, "What ails you?"

"Later," came the muffled reply, "There is absolutely nothing we can do. It is in the lap of the gods, *Sunu*." He reached forward for a decent piece of tesserae, scraping his already reddened knee, placing the white mosaic carefully, with minor adjustments into the *opus cæmenticium*. It had been copiously limed for a pure halo of white, yet the mix was gritty, pieces of sharp sea grit to scrape the knees badly. Coupled with the lime additive it was a scourge on the flesh. The *oeci* was truly expansive, the workers there trained and requiring fewer overseers. Aelius took time to look about him, always making sure the overseer was looking the other way. He did not need any more wheals to add to his damaged back.

The full mosaic disappeared in a sharp perspective to the far end of the *oeci*, and he imagined each medallion was in honour of the Gods and Goddesses. A full array, nothing was left to chance here. The weather had suddenly deteriorated, into an early snap-winter. There were braziers being positioned at regular intervals in-between the *lectus,* the couches festooned with silk cushions, their tassels in gold-intertwining threads. The Mons Claudianus marble columns, adorning the entrance, shimmered in their pink glory, shadows forming on the intricate artwork as the sconces were lit up.

It was bone-achingly cold. Their slave garments were thin and the tunicas barely covered their sore legs. The hypocaust had not been fired up; the empty braziers stood as a leering epithet to their slave status.

They worked until the encroaching darkness made accuracy impossible and their day came to a grateful end.

They sat huddled on the straw mattress in their *cubiculum* saying little, for even after the shutters were pulled across the window, thin blasts of winter-winds whistled through the gaps to bend the flame of the single tallow lamp. Vrittakos was nowhere to be seen. And Octavious had not appeared.

"*Hwæt in þæt genemanan fram Nerthus are wè dōn hèr Fæder.*

What in the name of Nerthus are we doing here Father?" Cahal swung his lowered head around to stare accusingly at Aelius. "You are Eyvindr, and this is you pretending to be a *Romanesque* in a *unfæger* farce!"

The curtain swished open, and they both stared open-mouthed half expecting an overseer to stride in with his whip.

"Keep your Wihtwarian voices DOWN!" hissed Vrittakos, swinging a knotted linen bundle onto the bed, "Food" he said simply, "Shut up, eat and listen!"

Aelius and Cahal pounced on the bundle, spreading out before them an array of cold meats, cheeses, both hard and soft, and stuffed Medjool dates. And in amongst it was a salve in a clay pot, smelling atrocious.

"For your knees," Vrittakos muttered, leaving them for a moment to slake their hunger. As they ate in silence with Vrittakos, his head bent in deep thought, Aelius watched his benefactor, his furrowed brow moving and creasing with each threatening thought. There was a swish of the drapes, and Octavius marched in. Standing to his full senatorial height, he cut a noble stance. Yet his face was puce with supressed fury. Aelius choked on his food. Vrittakos jumped up, beckoning the governor to sit.

"Please, Governor, sit, I have been slouching all day as a pretend supervisor to these fools here!" as he strode over to plump his ample weight on the bed, the food crumpling into a heap.

Octavious, with his hands clasped to his knees, leaning forward, spoke in hushed tones,

"We are facing a grave threat here at Villam Regis. People are in great danger.

"So, are we....?" Aelius whispered.

"Yes, I believe we are" Octavious hissed.

"And most certainly any supporter of our Emperor Gallienus, and to Gallienus himself! Will he make the journey here to our Villam Regis Cogidvbni? As he has said to me personally in a sealed vellum. If he does, he may be assassinated, here in Britannia, along with many others. A bloodbath!"

"Postumus," Aelius interjected.

Octavious' mouth moved energetically to expel a huge globule of spit, which landed neatly on the compressed dirt floor, and sank leaving a dark stain.

"I've been drinking amphorae of wine since I have been in receipt of news that frightens me more than the battlefield ever did!" Octavious muttered, "Listen please, I will tell you all I know from the beginning.

"In the message from Gallienus came the knowledge that the Roman Empire could crumble now! In this time. I did not doubt him. And it is this salacious development...any "grunt" on the battlefield can now wriggle their way up the greasy pole and become the centurion, then a Centurio Primus Pilus, a part of the Prætorian Guard, ultimately, ever closer to the ear of the Cæsar, a Prætorian Præfect."

"Postumus is nothing but a grunt!"

"But an insidiously clever grunt" Vrittakos replied, "I have been sitting next to the most talkative overseer imaginable. Granted these are rumours, but they have a terrible ring of truth about them nonetheless."

"It is said that our true Emperor Valerian, Gallienus' pater, has been overcome, the Roman army crushed by the Sassanids led by King Shapur in the bloody battle of Edessa. It is the first time an Emperor has been made a prisoner of war. And the true shame of it is that Valerian, and his family are probably the last noble-blooded Romans to rule this crumbling Empire!"

Vrittakos looked over to Octavious with great sympathy pouring from him towards his compatriot, who was every inch a pure-blooded royal of Rome.

"And so, "he continued, "Gallienus will not be attending here, leaving the way for Postumus to rally his usurpers and make claim to the title."

"This web of treachery is now well established," Octavious replied, "looking back for a moment, it was the rebellion by Aemilianus against Gallus in 253, I believe, that made Gallus turn to Valerian for assistance in crushing the usurpation. But it was too late. Gallus was killed by his own troops, who had joined Aemilianus, before Valerian had even arrived. But usurpation tends to swing about on a *denarius* and the Rætian soldiers declared Valerian emperor and marched to Rome. Aemilianus was killed, obviously, and in Rome the Senate quickly acknowledged Valerian, not only because of fear of reprisals but because he was one of their own. Royal blood is strong in Rome!"

"Was strong!" Aelius interjected, winning a cursed look from Vrittakos and glare from Octavious.

"And now, in this present moment my friends," Vrittakos said more loudly than was safe, and had several shushes directed at him, " according to my source, and he has heard this from several angles , these usurpers now have a name, and some of them, The Thirty bloody Tyrants, are all heading this way, to this Villam where a rebellion is being brewed in the *atrium, tablinum and peristylium* and Apollo knows where ever else!"

"And what are their names? Do you know?" Aelius demanded, "Who should we look out for, avoid?"

"I know some names," Octavious replied, his expression hardened, "Along with Postumus will come his "shadow" Honoratianus. He is the power behind this Usurper. Beware of him. He is very dangerous. Then in close ranks behind them and jostling for supremacy will come Lælianus and Victorinus. There are more but my source does not know their names!"

Octavious Sabinus, Governor of Britannia Inferior, took a huge intake of breath, and rubbing his hands over his eyes in a moment of sheer frustration and uncertainty, looked over at the three visitors and said,

"There is a certain other matter I must share with you. It seems you live a very sheltered, protected life on your sacred island. None of you have talked to me of the plague." He let it rest there for a moment, gauging their reaction. All three held an expression of silent shock.

"Yes," he continued, "I thought so. It is raging across parts of the Empire, more to the East but because of the Silk Road traffic, this plague has managed to rear an ugly face here in Britannia. In the north I hasten to add. My home in *Eboracum* has had a few deaths. But here in the south, we seem safe enough. So, Roman elites have taken to braving the voyage to foster out their children to protect them from the plague. It is customary to foster, it leads to an expansiveness of mind in young souls, but this is expedient to safeguarding their young bodies as well.

And," he continued, "there are two such young elites here, at Villam Regis, now. One Constantius, a promising if rather sickly child, who is of royal blood, so I am told, and I have hopes for him.... indeed, I do. Then there is a young girl by the name of Helena. She arrived but recently, very fatigued I may say, as she braved the arduous journey away from the East and is resting. Her health is good. She does not hold the plague in her blood, I have been reliably informed."

Vrittakos suddenly slapped his hands on his knees, "You two Wihtwarians are going home. I release you both forthwith. You will not be dragged into this. I want you safe. Eyvindr, your devoted wife awaits you and Cahal, Blāthnat is pining for you. That is what is important."

"But what of you?" Aelius demanded.

"Ohh I am old and ugly enough and Greek enough...to sit on the fence and watch!"

... ...

Chapter 43

Despicable Clique et tyrannos solus
The Despicable Clique: The 30 Tyrants

Vrittakos stood, his jaws clenched rigid, and not just from the freezing rain that had now turned to sleet. It was snapping at exposed skin like a myriad attack of bees and had soaked his toga, creating a small waterfall onto his leather sandals. They had been ordered by the king no less, to wear togas, with no *Birrus Britannicus* to shield them. Albanus Antonius Cogidubnus, 3rd generation client King of Britannia, the most arrogant and manipulative of all "client" kings since Tacitus first penned the title, stood, head erect, waiting at the harbour's edge for the arrival of Postumus, with his acolytes, elites and newly appointed Prætorian guard.

Vrittakos was not just freezing, he was horror-struck, mouth slack in disbelief. He was not just staring at the over large *Trireme* war ship creaking and banging in an unsteady approach to the harbour, but the smaller single sail *naca* negotiating the larger boat's slipstream. On board were not only his wife, but Achaikos, Kiana and Tamina with his friends, Censorinus and Antoninus Liberalis.

He had sent an urgent message with Aelius to relay the absolute prohibition of what he was now witnessing. Octavious, standing beside his friend, looked over to him, questioning, raising an eyebrow and shaking his head.

"This is not good, my friend," he whispered, "but at least now you will have family guest quarters to lay your aging head and a daily visit to the baths!"

The *Trireme* had managed to secure its bulkheads to the quay, both fore and aft. The three lines of oarsmen, had lowered their oars in practised unison, elegantly closing them like an enormous eagle wing coming to rest. The boat itself was magnificent, with an all-seeing eye painted at the bow, and the stern raised like a fan of eagle tail feathers, under which a canopy stretched protecting the passengers from the hail. The seamen were rolling the red and blue twin sails up as the drawbridge was lowered onto the quay. Postumus and his party began to emerge, the usurper Emperor leading the way with his shadow henchman, followed by a slave holding the golden eagle high above them. It was swaying precariously in the wind as they walked down the gangway. There followed behind the Emperor a myriad collection of friend and foe. Who amongst them were the future usurpers, the potential assassins?

Octavious expelled a misty bellow of cold breath and hissed *"In inferno defuit oculi sunt serpentes ante nos*! On Hades' missing eyeballs, there are venomous snakes before us!"

"Who do you recognise?" Vrittakos turned to see Octavious shaking his head and looking to the sodden ground, now being eclipsed with snowflakes at a fast rate.

"Co-conspirators, Lælianus and Victorinus who would kill and eat their own mothers!" he spat their names, his spittle nearly freezing in mid-air as the temperature rocketed downwards. Vrittakos would have asked him to expand but his sole attention lay with his family, now shivering in a close huddle, waiting for protocol to allow them to advance, at the very rear. Achaikos was fuming, stamping his feet, and not just to keep the blood flowing. His family were of the Royal Sogdian hierarchy, older and more venerable than any who had disembarked from the *Trireme*.

No-one knew the truth behind this extravagant arrival of supposed Cæsars and elites. The dark circumstances seemed an almost daily occurrence in the teetering Empire, a jostling for power by opportunist soldiers. One undeniable fact hit Vrittakos in the stomach, knotting his bowels: they were embroiled in a very dangerous drama, and his family had walked straight into it!

All the visitors had been encased in the thickest of *Birrus Britannicus* so no detail of them had been gleaned. And it left both hosts and visitors scurrying for the heat of lung-searing saunas where amidst the billows of steam, dark gossip was hurled about in hushed whispers. As soon as the weather had worsened, slaves had been sent to stoke up the hypocaust to blistering levels. Theirs was a subterranean hell. Hades did not hold a candle to it!

In the steam bath, Octavious had led his friend away from dissolute members of the "Royal" entourage, yet still within earshot of dependable gossip. Amidst the bulging sweaty stomachs and dripping jowls, with stale male sweat competing with astringent cleansing aromas, they learnt the enormity of the rebellion.

"I have heard this part from the slave girl to Agrippa Aquila as her eldest son, Aurelius Cæsar boasted of his kinship with Postumus" Octavious began, wiping rivulets of sweat from his brow, stinging his eyes, "How favoured he is and how he will become the next King here. Well this is what reliably occurred in Gaul only just recently.

"Last year, 259 I believe, mid-season, Valerian was campaigning in the East against the Persians, the dreaded Sassanids, while his son Gallienus was up to his royal neck in holding the Suevian horde at bay. Gallienus gave his son, Saloninus, and the top military commander, Postumus, responsibility to protect the Rhine. Amidst all of this, Valerian, Gallienus' dear father was captured by the Persians and made a prisoner of war. And to add to this, the chaos of invasion by the Alamanni and Franks, Gallienus' army went into revolt, spurred on by a very clever move by Postumus.

Under the command of Postumus, the Roman army crushed the Juthungi and proceeded to distribute the spoils, including many slaves amongst his army. Saloninus, on the advice of his Prætorian prefect, Silvanus, demanded the transfer of said booty back to his offices at *Colonia Claudia Ara Agrippinensium*.

Postumus made the required half-hearted response to comply. His army instantly revolted and declared him Emperor of Gaul!"

"Hade's dead eyes!" swore Vrittakos, "but he is a clever bastard!" They both fell silent, absorbing not just the heat of the baths opening all the pores on their skin, but the depth of pure nastiness that lay at the heart of Postumus. A shadow sidled up close to them, smaller in stature and recognisable to Octavious as the youngest son of Albanus Antonius, Balbus Decimus. He reached out to put his arm about him.

"How fairs you, young man?" he asked gently, showing a level of compassion and fondness for the odd boy out in the burgeoning Cogidubnus family.

"G-G-Greetings, sssir," the boy stuttered, "I-I-I have grave news for y-y-ou. I-I over h-h-h-eard a terrible desc-c-c-ittion of m-m-m-m-urder!" The dark-haired boy gulped down the last word, murder, stopping to look wide-eyed and baleful at Octavious who tightened his grip around Balbus.

"You can cease the stutter, Balbus," he whispered, "you are safe around these loyal friends here." He turned to Vrittakos. "My loyal watcher here is the outcast son of Albanus Antonius. Treated cruelly I may add. So, we have a clever arrangement, do we not young sir?", Balbus nodded grinning widely to show an eagerness and charm that entered his eyes, bringing warmth.

"I taught him to cease his stuttering if he would become a watcher for me in this nest of vipers, we call Villam Regis! So, tell us Balbus please."

"I was sitting, hiding in my favourite spot in the *exedra*, in between the bust of Juno and the aspidistra." He began, leaning into Octavious as he would to his pater. Octavious had become a father-figure to the vulnerable boy, "when Honoratianus, the "shadow" as I call him, sidled in with a man I do not know but think he is a conspirator. Ah! I remember," he blurted out, "Lælianus!"

"Shh," came the reply from both men, "Keep your voice down Bulbus!"

"The "shadow" spoke in venomous terms of the fate meted out to Gallienus' son Saloninus", Balbus whispered, "And it was he, I am sure, who was responsible. He enjoyed watching, Sir, he is an evil wicked man!"

"What did he do to them? Quickly, if you please," Octavious said insistently, "We simply do not have all day, we are needed to present our honouring to this imposter of a Cæsar!"

Balbus took a huge intake of breath, building courage to speak, "He, they, put both Saloninus and Silvanus to the cross, Governor. They crucified them!"

An expression of pure horror came to Octavius as he relieved his intense emotions by diving under water, the eruption of bubbles, a soundless symphony to his silent cries. Vrittakos wiped his hand over his face, as he too was acquainted with the men, as boys coming to their first initiation into Mithras, the bull slayer.

"They were both tortured first," Bulbus continued, needing to relief his own trauma, "They were dragged out of the cellars, where they had been chained for two days, by Honoratianus, who grinned horribly in the telling to Lælianus, as he detailed what he had done to them in the night previously. They could not walk; their legs had been broken so no one could come to their aid on the cross by pulling them and their tongues cut so they could not swallow any draft of poison to speed their way to peace.

"So, there they hung, nailed both hands and feet, their agonising cries echoed beyond the hill where they were taken. The army of soldiers they had both commandeered stood by, jeering and throwing detritus and faeces at them as their heads hung in the slow agony of dying in humiliation and shame.

"Saloninus cried for his pater to forgive him, sir!" Balbus was crying, "but Silvanus screamed at the soldiers who had betrayed them both, he prayed the plague would claim them all.

"I heard The Shadow laugh after he described how many days it took for them both to die."

Within the misty silence that followed, each encapsulated in their bubble of warm steam, there came a booming voice; -

"*Nihil nisi quod tyranni est, redundat Postumus, barbara, phasianae Germanica paganus. Et factum est gravis error est. Mox rursus erit in gregem sicariorum contuli cum to bear cultro.*

"The usurper Postumus is nothing but a barbarian, a pagan German peasant. He has made a grave mistake. Soon it will be his turn to feel the assassin's knife."

All three froze in the steamy water, as a figure loomed out of the torpid haze, a face, aged and wrinkled, the steam settling in rivulets within the deepest grooves in his face. He was smiling slowly in recognition of the voices who had spoken treason in the now very public baths. Yet his was the most outspoken. He dared because he could.

Titus Desticuis Juba, septarian and senatorial elder waded in to grasp his junior by all of two decades, in the Roman greeting.

He had retired from office as governor of Britannia Superior. And he was immune from censure and alarmingly forthright as a newly converted and very strict adherent to the new religion, Christianity.

"Titus!" Octavious exclaimed, a grin breaking out on his face, relaxing for the first time in days, "You are a welcome sight for these sore eyes; indeed, you are!"

"Salute" came the reply, "I've made good speed from *Lundinuim* to make my presence felt here and vex these impostors and conspirators. I am disgusted and will make these feelings felt, that they have been stupid enough to make martyrs of two young souls, now embraced I'm sure by Christ himself. There will be retaliation!"

The aged senator looked at the youngest recruit. Balbus shone with pride, for he knew the grand reputation of this elder.

"Your name if you please?" Titus asked gently, looking down at the young man with such tenderness, it melted the heart of Balbus, instantly.

"Balbus..." he began

"No! your true name, the one your own mother gave you. It surely cannot be *that*!" Titus shot back.

"Claudius," Balbus replied shyly, having almost forgotten he had a true name.

"Then, Claudius, my brave young soldier of Truth, I am rescinding any and all demands made upon you in this spying exercise," Titus said solemnly, looking over to Octavious, who nodded in total agreement, "You shall retire quietly and keep out of the way. Leave this drama to an old septarians' like myself who enjoys nothing more than a good spat with imbeciles and liars. This game has become too dangerous." He turned, patting Claudius on the back, "and never let me hear that insulting name ever spoken in my presence...ever!"

Titus began to wade from the steaming bath saying abruptly, over his shoulder to Octavious, "Come old warrior, we need to share our thoughts over a long massage. Yes?"

Octavious immediately turned to Vrittakos and mouthed silently, Venitouta! At which Vrittakos had all the appearance of being stung by a manta ray and leapt from the bath, grabbing a linen from one of the rows of slaves holding hot towels, and ran to meet his wife.

... ...

Chapter 44

Constantius and Helena

Kiana stood watching Achaikos, who stood uncharacteristically erect, as if a gladius had been placed up his spine, his hands clasped behind his back. He had still not reconciled, nor made any peace with Vrittakos, who also uncharacteristically, had exploded upon meeting with them, steam still exuding from his skin. He looked like Vesuvius about to erupt, and Kiana was compelled to suck her cheeks in. It was an exclusively male debacle. Privately, she had decided to talk with Vrittakos, alone, to reach the true heart of the sad discord. The reunion had turned sour. But for now, she did not intrude.

Instead, she and Tamina watched the two young children playing *tali* in a protected part of the *Exedra*, seated on plush *cathedra supinas* with the children's guardian and foster mother, Agrippa Aquilla. Like her name, wild eagle, she was utterly imposing, over tall for a Roman woman, but with the classical aquiline nose and piercing eyes. And those eyes rarely left the sight of the children, most accurately the girl, even when Agrippa was talking, her eyes fixed on the child.

"Helena has settled in well," Agrippa intoned in the deep voice that carried authority. She was definitively of noble birth, totally Roman. Kiana decided quietly, that the marriage to Albanus Antonius must have been arranged. He was an arrogant, rebellious client king that would not have naturally attracted her to his bullish ways. But like all Roman women, she remained silent in company, and left the throwing of porcelain to the privacy of the *cubiculum*.

"*Vide, ut vincat.*" The girl shouted, clapping, then throwing her arm up in the air, her hand in a fist, "*Ad vulturem ego Venus! Tu es amissis Constantio celeberrimus fuit. Tu pauperum et aleo.*

"Look, I win. I am Venus to your Vulture! You are losing Constantius. You are a poor gambler."

"Ελενα, ξέρεις Αγρίππα παρακολουθεί!" Constantius replied reverting to Greek knowing that Agrippa did not understand, "Πρόσεχε. Είμαστε απαγορευμένα τυχερά παιχνίδια και εδώ είστε, καλώντας σκληρή γλώσσα της!"

"Helena, you know Agrippa is watching! Be careful. We are forbidden gambling and here you are, inviting her harsh tongue!" Constantuis stretched out a pale arm to grab the *tali* throwing them heavenwards to catch all five on his long-fingered elegant hand. At knucklebones, he was expert.

"We have saved them from the ravages of the Cyprian plague," Agrippa settled back into the cushions of the *cathedra supina,* "Neither would be here today, playing, if their mater and pater had not had the foresight and courage to transport them here to Britannia, which has been quite saved from the scourge. And I give thanks every single day to the Jesus Christ, our Saviour for this act of mercy, this miracle!"

Kiana had already noticed the large crucifix in gold hanging on a golden chain around Agrippa's neck. It hung on her heart and moved with every gesture as if alive. She had also just noticed a smaller identical cross sitting over Helena's little heart, competing with her obligatory *Lunula* talisman she would not be allowed to jettison until her wedding day.

Agrippa settled into her dialogue.

"Our good God is wreaking justice, so he is! For all the atrocities to Christians, the killings and torture. Because we believe in the One God, that should never be a crime. But my people have been made martyrs. So, the plague is the vengeance of God. Jesus Christ is looking down and seeing those who believe in Him in their souls, against those who worship craven images and statues of pagan idolatry. And they will suffer. The plague visits those unbelievers with terrible wracking pain, so I've been told. The humours within burst and they drown in their poisoned blood.

"Both Constantius and Helena have seen plague deaths before they were whisked away. Helena was particularly marked, poor child, and she is taking much solace in the love of Christ."

Kiana's mind had suddenly turned to revisiting that terrible vision of the future, given to her in Byzantium. Watching again from that hilltop above Berandinzium Villam, which she had already begun to love, the imminent death of her loved one at the hands of Christians in killing ferociousness at their pagan ways. The worm turns, she thought as her stomach had turned to ice. She deflected Agrippa's questioning look by asking her about the children, now taken to racing about the water-lilied pond flicking water at each other from the fountain.

"Where do Helena and Constantius come from?" she asked, looking over to Tamina, who was being silent and contemplative. "Tamina, why don't you go and ask Helena to show you the Villam?"

Tamina shot her mother a look that said, I would rather extract a rusty nail from my foot, mama, but obediently rose to take Helena's hand, who began chatting eagerly to Tamina, relieved at the opportunity to be with another young woman. Constantius, on the other hand stood quite forlorn, looking after the receding figures.

"Constantius was born in Dardania, son of Eutropius, a high-ranking nobleman and Claudia, niece to Emperor Claudius 11. The province of Moesia Superior has been heavily afflicted with the plague. Constantius was fostered out for his protection. He is destined for great things," Agrippa's voice took a tone laden with pride. Her role as guardian and protector of a potential future Emperor sat with her like a crucible.

"Helena," she continued in a brighter tone, "Now her birthplace is a mystery. She is of Greek blood, most certainly. I don't know the Greek tongue so well, but Constantius has taken to learning it very well. They often converse in that language and he is learning the written word also."

Kiana suddenly turned around to see Achaikos, her beloved Greek, had left, quietly, a worried figure of a man.

Umm," she turned to Agrippa, "I must apologise but I really must beg your indulgence. I need to leave and talk with Vrittakos on an urgent matter, but I do hope we will meet this evening for the grand celebration for Postumus elect as Emperor."

Kiana stood and kissed Agrippa lightly on the cheek, turning quickly with a swirl of her silken toga to vanish within the corridors of Villam Regis.

... ...

Kiana worked her way along the frescoed corridors of Villam Regis, her eyes cast downwards, following the intricate tesserae that patterned the marble floors. The grandeur and sheer size of the Villam brought back shaded memories of her childhood in the Sogdian palace in Samarkand, where the intricate blue and gold patterned walls stretched up to neck-breaking height. And she suddenly had to choke back the tears from falling on these haloed Roman floors. "Damned if they will see *my* tears," she thought. The villam was busy, so she kept to the side, almost hugging the walls, and if she possibly could, she would have disappeared into the frescoes and become a nymph, dancing with her silks floating around her in a dance of sheer joy.

"And that is the great lie," she thought, "the mirage to cloak the ugly sinister truth of this palace." Her palace home held tranquillity and peace within its walls. The bustle in Villam Regis was building to frenetic levels, as the afternoon drew on. The grand entrance of Postumus and his Elítes was set for the evening, yet the winter had closed in, the snow had continued to fall through the night and uncharacteristically laid nearly a *gradus* of hard large-flaked snow. And this kind of Britannia cold cut into the eastern bones of Kiana, as she hurried to find Vrittakos and the warm heated rooms.

She had been working her way from the *exedra* that over-looked the fountained garden favoured by Aquilla. She was forced to navigate through, then around, the majestic imposing front entrance. Its Mons Claudianus marble columns had collected ridges of pure snow, and the formal garden was now an undistinguished landscape of white. The wind had picked up and flurries of snow had collected in the corridors. Kiana slid on the wet surface and hit the marble with a crunching thud, followed by a string of Sogdian swearwords. No one came to help her, as she pulled herself up, using the pillar as support. Everyone seemed to be carrying a leaded weight about with them. They were preoccupied about something. Social courtesy had been buried with the snow, along with the white silhouetted box trees. Only a tall gangly-looking youth that was Constantius, came to her aid. He helped her up, asked after her welfare and offered his *Birrus Brittannicus* as he swung it about her shoulders.

She smiled gratefully, speaking in the Greek she knew he favoured

" Σας ευχαριστώ πολύ Κωνστάντιος. Μπορείτε να δείτε πού μπορώ να βρω τις αναζητήσεις, πού μπορεί να είναι?"

"Well thank you kind Constantius. Can you tell me where the guests may be?"

"Μαζεύονται σε αριθμούς στο βόρειο vestibulum."

"They are gathering in numbers in the north vestibulum," Constantius replied.

"Tell me," he continued, "I heard you speak in a strange language. Who are you and where do you come from?"

"I am Kiana from Sogdiana, I was a princess in my land and priestess to Ahura Mazda," she answered simply, staring straight at him, discerning his reaction.

"What in Juno's name are you doing in this piss-hole hell?" Constantius replied in a cynical sneer, his head on one side, questioning.

"I fell in love," Kiana said truthfully, not wishing to elaborate.

"Ahh," came the youthful reply from the young man, "I understand completely. I wish you well." Constantius, in a flair of manly virtue, took hold of her hand and brushed a kiss elegantly on her knuckles and strode away, disappearing quickly into the adjacent room.

Kiana stared intently about her, with strong feelings about Achaikos jabbing her heart centre. She knew he was in some turmoil. She stepped carefully along the remaining snow-covered walkway, darting right to navigate the long corridor of guest *cubiculums,* almost tiptoeing past the state rooms with Prætorian guards by the solid doors, immobile and menacing. Kiana inwardly froze. She had never witnessed or felt such concentrated warrior-power in a man. She was an accomplished fighter and knew full well self-control was the necessary personal armour to get through the day.

But these Pretorian guards bristled with a menace she had not encountered. And behind the door was the usurper Emperor Postumus himself. Or so she imagined.

 She followed the buzz of conversation, exclusively male and onerous. As a single female, Kiana knew full well she was breaking protocol. At the entrance of the largest *atrium* she had ever seen, colonnaded in pink marble with exquisite mosaics around the expansive floor, she quickly scanned the men, who were all standing informally in several groups, talking heatedly about topics she was totally unaware of. It was intense. And in the middle stood her lover, Achaikos, doing what Greeks do best, gesticulating in a flurry of Greek expletives, interspersed with Latin, for good measure.

Kiana took a huge intake of breath, and strode forward, like a spear thrumming through dense air, she broke through the cluster of togas, the men clearing a space for her, the babble reducing swiftly to a tense silence. There were expressions of openmouthed shock on straight-fringed Roman visages, to knitted brows and sharp hatred emanating from many men, looking at this single female interloper.

Achaikos, on seeing his beloved stride towards him, was a picture of frozen horror. He went puce-coloured and began to tremble. He had been taking up more airtime in speaking against many of the surprise edicts and postulations, than was wise. This was a humiliation.

"Αχαίκος, πρέπει να μιλήσουμε!" Achaikos we need to talk to each other!" She spoke loudly, from nerves and anxiety combined. Apart from her concern and pain over their private matter, she also sensed Achaikos was treading on very dangerous ground criticizing these hypocritical power-crazed Romans. What did they care if another Greek foreigner suddenly disappeared!

Achaikos spluttered, momentarily lost for words.

Euge Domina, bene quidem. tu autem adsecutus hanc conclusionem bellicosa Graeca!" A loud voice thundered to Kiana's left. She spun round to see a very tall stocky man of swarthy complexion, with copper-red curly hair and beard looking as un-Roman-like as anyone could be. He was Suevii.

"Well done, Madam. Well done indeed! you have succeeded in shutting up this bellicose Greek!" he said, with a wide grin showing yellowing teeth hidden within the masses of curly tenacious hair growth. He looked her up and down in a predatory male stance. Kiana bristled.

"You are forbidden to enter this Atrium, madam," he continued, head to one side, judging her, "So the very least you can do is present me with your name, if you please."

Kiana hesitated, then produced her winning smile, which she hoped would work on Achaikos later, "My name is Queen Sumaya, my home birthplace Esfahan, Sogdiana, Naqsh-e-Johan in Avestan, meaning Half the World, and I am a Zoroastrian high priestess of Ahura Mazda." Kiana felt the air leave her lungs as her heart raced ahead of the words she had never uttered until now.

She was diminutive against this tall German. He bent down to study her, his expression alert.

"Well," he said, after a lengthy pause, "I am inclined to give you my name before I expel you from this Atrium.

I am Marcus Cassianus Latinius Postumus. Soon to become Imperator Cæsar Marcus Cassianus Latinius Postumus Pius Felix Augustus Germanicus Maximus…. your new Emperor of Gaul." A spattering of applause followed and cries of "Hail Cæsar" at this announcement. And deep silence elsewhere. The most exuberant applause came from the client king himself, Albanus Antonius Cogidubnus, who had raised his hands looking for followers to join him in this premature celebration. It became mildly embarrassing, and he dropped his hands, silent. Kiana, with Achaikos were both ushered from the Atrium by Prætorian guards who were permanently posted within a gladius reach of the Emperor.

"*MANERE!* WAIT!" came Postumus' booming guttural voice, "Queen Sumaya, what brings you to this hellhole, this Brittonic freezing hinterland? You are far from home!"

Kiana turned, and brazenly took the opportunity to eye up Postumus, who halted and looked embarrassed. His bulbous feet poked out from a purple-edged silken toga, and they looked dirty and scraped. He was a soldier, a "grunt" Kiana decided. He boasted an over-large stomach, typical of the Germans and what you could see of his face amidst the thick curly copper-coloured beard, held red and broken veins. "He will not make old bones," she thought.

"I am happily now residence, with my husband," she intoned, feeling a wave of surprise and warmth reach her from Achaikos, "on the sacred Isle of Wihtland, you call Vecta, I believe, after the ancestor Wecta of Woden's bloodline. We are staying at Berandinzium Villam."

"Excellent, Queen Sumaya, our paths shall meet again. We are taking ship again for Vecta to perform our rites and service under the ever-watchful eye of Mithras. After my inauguration tomorrow evening." Postumus positively postured and preened on this announcement. Kiana felt Achaikos stiffen.

Standing behind the erstwhile Emperor, and who had not shifted at all, was a tall figure, dressed plainly, but who held an air of latent authority. He leant over to whisper in Postumus' ear, and he nodded silently in understanding. Kiana saw this man's face emanate a kind of evil intent that screwed up his face into tight balls of resentment.

"Who is that man, standing guard behind Postumus," she whispered to Achaikos, as they were finally released and led out.

"Honoratianus," came the clipped reply, "the power behind the throne and to be truly feared, I might add!"

… … … … … … … … …

Chapter 45

Veni, Vidi, Vici

I came, I saw, I conquered

Julius Caesar
47BC

The Inauguration

Achaikos and Kiana walked swiftly and silently back to their guest quarters. Heads bowed; they did not want to attract attention from the milieu of visitors now filling the corridors of the palace. The rustle of silk togas, the finest *stolas* in beautiful colours competed, as did the women who wore them. The atmosphere bubbled with expectancy. Questioning and debate took place behind closed doors.

Vrittakos and Venitouta were waiting for them in a sumptuous apartment, secure and private. As was Octavious who had taken to pacing the floor.

"That evil villainous shit has executed, nay crucified, my ward, Saloninus, whom I tutored and cared for, while Gallienus was occupied on the battlefield," Octavious thumped the table in anger, sending all on it upwards to crash down a second later. Venitouta jumped and physically withdrew into herself. Aia stroked her Mater's arm, saying quietly, "Mater, let us go and find a women's room."

"No!" came the reply, "I need to know what is going on here beneath this feathered surface. But, please, you men, hold your anger in check if you please."

"I apologise madam," Octavious said, "Crucifixion is particularly barbaric, and for a young man not even past his thirtieth year, it is evil!"

"I believe they crucified an innocent man," Vrittakos said, shaking his head in sorrow, "The real criminal was Silvanus, silver-tongued and of evil heart. It was he who began the revolt of soldiers by advising the spoils of war to be returned to the Consul offices of Saloninus. Had he not become part of the conspiracy to overthrow, Postumus would never have been awarded the chance to become Emperor at all!"

"And there are more traitors championing the usurper cause here at Villam Regis," Octavious remarked, "A clutch of them in fact. Victorinus is busy arse-licking, excuse the language," he looked over to the women in apology, "and is in private, plotting with Lælianus all the while. I have several hounds to the ground, but I have no reports coming back to me of an assassination attempt. But I would most certainly not rule it out."

Venitouta gasped at this outburst.

"If I had known this, I would never have invited you here," she pointed around her, "This is beyond my wildest nightmares. I believed we would unite in spiritual accord, honouring our ancient Gods and Goddesses. A chance to offer great minds and souls up to our Ancestors. Not this!"

Vrittakos' expression, as he looked over to his wife, was sending a wave of love and sorrow over to her.

"And yet my friends," he said quietly, "I fear there may be a spiritual conspiracy taking place behind this twisted physical reality we find ourselves within."

Achaikos suddenly straightened, leaning over to give his hand to Vrittakos, and nodding in agreement. Kiana suddenly realised the heart of Achaikos' pain did not come from a personal agony at all, but this, a spiritual plot, and it had nothing to do with her at all.

Vrittakos, leaning forward, his elbows planted firmly on his thighs, outstretched both hands, almost in supplication as he engaged in the difficult exposure of exalted and honoured Magi.

"My dear family, Achaikos, Kiana, how can I begin to explain these feelings, these suspicions I hold towards both Censorinus and Antoninus, without seeming to betray my brothers and mentors?"

"They are changed," Achaikos interjected, rubbing his brow to release some wisdom locked in his mind, "Censorinus and Antoninus have great power, together they have incredible energy to affect a rip in the veil." He paused, trying to form the thought.

"I believe they are intent on creating a void. Within that space, using the universal Law of alchemical replacement, they intend to create a change in spiritual devotion for all humanity...I mean everyone!"

Vrittakos fairly jumped in his chair, "Yes, I concur. I know they are disillusioned and angry beyond measure at the turgid immorality of Rome, and have watched, first-hand, the persecution of the Christians. Attacks on plain common sense. Violence around every corner."

"I believe they are adopting the Christian focus," Achaikos joined in, "and with that in mind, they are planning to ask the Ancient Ones, Abrasax and Ahura Mazda, Mithra and Zoroaster to assist human effort, in stamping out the plurality of Gods and Goddesses in all cultures and turn their eyes to Christ, the One God! They want to save Rome, from itself!"

"Αυτό είναι παράλογο! Είναι αδύνατο! Ο Θεός μου δεν θα το υποστηρίξει! That is insane," Kiana shouted, bunching her hand to slam it on her open palm, "My God would not allow this!"

There came a heavy silence. Octavious put his hand out pleading for calm, for he sensed ears might be listening in to this extraordinary discussion.

Vrittakos whose personal pain was plain to see, spoke, almost in a whisper

"My dear friends, it is not only possible, it is almost inevitable. The empire is teetering on collapse, power-hungry usurpers at every turn. Nobility and blood lines are forgotten. Romans are suffering the agonies of plague, earthquakes and famine. They will turn away from their gods, blaming them with the high shrill voice of hysteria.

"Of course, they will turn to a new god. Any god is better than the old ones.

"Do you not think our Ancient Ones, benign, benevolent, compassionate and loving of the human family, will not look down and feel pain? Abrasax who brought our world to us with laughter. Ahura Mazda who knows dualism will always be present, yet the eternal flame always shines against the dark, and always the stronger. Zoroaster knows full well humanity is weak and is constant in his prayer to prevent destruction."

"Do you think for one second, they will stop? And if this one-God religion will end the torture and the killing, believe me, they will stand to one side and give consent."

Kiana released a painful cry, from the depths of her soul, which fractured in this moment. She raced out of the *cubiculum,* to be followed swiftly by Achaikos. She swallowed the overwhelming urge to tell him of his future, how it will all end for him and Vrittakos, at the hands of demonic Christians thirsty for blood. As he held her, her silence was made permanent on this, she told him her heart was broken for Zoroaster. And he believed her words. It was true. Also, true without doubt, was that nothing, absolutely nothing could be done to alter this future.

When she had calmed down, Kiana told another truth lying in wait for the future to unfold.

"There is no real need for all this alchemical posturing with over-inflated egotistical men performing their tricks," she stated, flatly, devoid of all emotion, "One woman has already planted the seed. Just one woman," she reiterated, "Agrippa Aquilla, the wife of Albanus has converted the young girl Helena to Christianity. And Constantius, who will no doubt become Emperor, is completely in love with the girl. She will give the waiting world, Christianity. There is no need of any men. They will only ruin it." She hooked her arm in his and led them both back to their guest *cubiculu*m. Some serious lovemaking lay in wait.

"And you are not amongst that multitudinous army of men, my love. You are far above."

… … … … … … … … …

The weather was becalmed, and brilliantly eye-achingly white. The morning sun reflected off the blanket of snow in the courtyard. All the guests were now in elegant togas, *stolas* of every hue and intricate embroidery. Hair was piled up as high as the snow drifts, with gold dripping from elaborate curls and twists.

Everyone moved with extreme care. Even though the snow had been summarily swept away, the marble was infamously slippery. And hands were held to eyes as shields against the shimmering snow. The day of the inauguration had arrived. Gaul had enthusiastically declared Postumus the new Emperor, followed swiftly, not to be left out, by Germania, his home territory and Raetia. Britannia had hesitated, so the decision to visit Villam Regis was politically motivated from the start.

Governor Juba of Britannia Superior had settled in, and more dignitaries had lurched their way through blizzard and snow to reach Villam Regis, hoping to catch the eye of Postumus. Yet the weather had prevented many from appearing to honour the usurper, whether by design, or accident, Villam Regis was severely under populated. The inner circle, who always hovered within a few feet of Postumus, remained aloof. The one character, who remained within inches of the Emperor, Honoratianus, acted like a "shade." The nickname adhered to him like cow-glue. Octavious on giving explicit instructions to one of his most trusted and experienced "hounds," needed some real information.

"You are sure?" he asked, grabbing the slave by the arm, hoping he would not need to twist it behind the lad's scrawny back. He would break an arm if needs be and the slave "hound" knew it. They were out in the freezing cold, away from the Villam. It was past the courtyard, and close to the river's edge. Octavious wrapped the Birrus Britannicus closer about him and waited for the youth to gather his thoughts.

"Sir," he replied, looking Octavious straight in the eye, "as sure as I will ever be. I followed the "shade" from a safer distance and slipped through two corridors. He was in a hurry to meet with someone, that was for sure. The Roman was waiting for him. I heard his name. Lælianus, a tall thin man. He wore a soldier's uniform, scraped and worn too. The "shade" hissed at him to change immediately.

"Yes, good," Octavious interrupted, not accustomed to this depth of cold, stamping his feet on the crushed snow "but what did they discuss? Hurry lad, I'm getting frostbitten here!"

"There will be a killing sir!" the boy replied, "Someone is coming, a killer paid to see off Postumus for crucifying Saloninus, the son to the real Emperor, Gallienus!"

"No!" cried Octavious, "Honoratianus is conspiring to commit murder!"

"I don't know," the slave blurted back, "I didn't catch any more. Only that someone is here. Can I go now please sir?"

"Yes and thank you for all your efforts. Here take these *denarii*, you may have prevented an assassination." Octavious reached inside a voluminous purse and handed a huge treasure to the lad. A shriek emitted from frozen pursed lips as he skipped off.

The hunched figure of the governor to Britannia Inferior strode back, not caring who might see him. His footprints marked a clear path in virgin snow through the gardens to the main eastern entrance. And in those footprints, he incised his anger.

He felt nothing but revulsion for the usurper Postumus. And he fought the base desire of pleasure on the possible assassination. Octavious had known the son, Saloninus. He inwardly wept again at the waste of a young and promising life. He knew and respected Gallienus, who despite all his weaknesses, was a just Emperor who held a moral high ground. He hated dishonourable killing. Gallienus had rescinded the Decian persecutions on the Christians carried on by his father Valerian.

"*Ita magna pars meī esset laetus.* Yes, a large part of me would be glad," he thought, as he stamped the snow from his *carbatinæ.*

… … … … … … … … …

Octavious strode down the corridor leading to the private quarters of the client king, Albanus. His *Britannicus* flowing behind him, his head bunched into his shoulders. He was deep in thought and noticed no-one, including Victorinus, who, on seeing the governor, instinctively and furtively stepped back into the shadows created by the wall-sconce issuing dancing flames from an overfull copper dish of wax. His intense stare followed Octavious as he reached the door of the king's apartments.

Octavious gave a growled request to the Prætorian guard positioned in front of the door, for permission to enter, realising in doing so, that Albanus was not alone. The guard, in turn, pulled the door ajar and hissed to a slave standing inside the anteroom. Octavious stiffened on hearing the voice within. He had not anticipated having this audience with the Emperor himself.

He walked in, clicked his heels and bowed low to Postumus, who was seated so close to the brazier, his exposed hairy legs were near to singeing. Albanus, seated a little further away from the fire, immediately clasped both his hands on the arms of a voluminous *lectus* and glared at the governor of Britannia Inferior, curling his upper lip.

Octavious straightened his spine, ignoring the slur from nothing more than a Romanesque Briton, who defeated honour with every breath. He looked to Postumus, who was studying him, silently, a sardonic grin fixed, beneath his unruly facial hair.

"*Salvete Octavious præsidi. Et quid hac voluptate non debere. Quoniam in torpore tenebrosam noctem calidis locis esse. Hoc magni momenti esse necesse est. Nec?*

"Greetings Governor Octavious. And to what do we owe this pleasure. A dark and freezing night should be seeing you in your warm quarters. It must be important. No?"

Postumus held up a large golden goblet of wine in acknowledgment, while toying with a pure golden Diadem in the other hand. Deep shock entered Octavious. To his knowledge, and that was extensive, no Emperor, Cæsar, Augustus had ever elected to don a crown. The laurels alone signified status.

Octavious decided, there and forever, that this usurper was a posturing egotistical upstart. He smiled and nodded, infinitesimally raising his eyebrow in comment. What struck him immediately, above all the Germanic physiognomy of this usurper, were his eyes. They were the most startling ice-blue colour, peering out from bulbous eyelids and a reddened complexion. Postumus showed sharp intelligence, belying the "grunt" soldier's body. This man was no fool.

Octavious paused, taking in a calming breath, knowing instinctively that half-truths and even lies would be perceived as traitorous. And in the shadows, lurking, was the "shade," ever watchful.

"I have", he began, clearing his throat, suddenly feeling choked, "at my disposal, a small group of "watchers," my eyes and ears. Mine are in deficit now with age. They are above all loyal."

"You mean they are paid well," came the velvety voice from the shadows. Honoratianus was following every word, like a spider waiting to pounce. Octavious suddenly felt like a fly trapped in a monumental web. He squashed the feeling of panic that suddenly gripped his bowels.

Postumus rumbled a low laughter, remaining silent. He was watching Octavious with an ice-blue penetrating stare, his eyes never leaving the governor.

"Firstly, a grave matter has come to my attention. Is it true that the son of Gallienus has been put to death.?"

A pause.

"It is," came the reply from Postumus. The silence that followed, stunned Octavious, who expected a denial, an excuse, or even an apology.

Octavious summoned all his will power to resist screaming "you piss-pot of a barbarian" in the face of the new Emperor.

"Saloninus was my foster son for a brief while. Was he afforded *Justa Facere*? At least was his body laid to rest along the Appian Way?"

"It was the army who put both Saloninus and Silvanus to death," Honoratianus stepped forward, leaning protectively over

Postumus, staring all the while at Octavious, "And it was a disease-ridden city in which they both came to their end. Their bodies were cremated for health reasons."

"They were treated as riffraff then! Just three handfuls of dirt!" Octavious shouted, staggering backwards, disbelieving. He gathered himself together. "We must give them *Justa Facere*, here at Villam Regis!"

Honoratianus leapt forward, booming at Octavious no more than inches from his face, "*Imperare ausus Caesari Tu, qui nihil nisi de tergo ad finem dominatur sniffling Britannos. Vade et iungere barbaros. GO!*"

"You dare to command the Emperor! You, who are nothing but a sniffling governor to the backend of Britannia. Go back and join the barbarians. GO!"

Octavious, who could stand no more, turned to leave. Then abruptly swung around to face Postumus.

"Augustus, my "watchers" have told me of a plot to assassinate you, here at your inauguration. I came to warn you."

Postumus relieved himself of the elaborately designed Diadem with pointed gold triangles, studded with jewels. He got up to face Octavious. A kindly, almost generous look came over him, transforming his rugged face into a benign man.

"Do you not think we have spies too, governor? We are aware and are preparing to resist. Our Prætorian guard are on high alert. I would advise your immediate family, especially the women to be removed for their safety. Do not under any circumstances repeat this conversation. We do not want the assassin to be scared off. Where there is one, there will be more. And we must catch all of them. Do you understand?"

Octavious nodded.

"And furthermore," Postumus came forward to place his hand kindly on Octavious, "We are taking ship to Vecta, straight after the inauguration. We would wish you to join us, as I know you are Pater in the Mithraic levels. I am taking the level of Leo and would be honoured to have you guide me through the rite to become an adept. We will give full honour to Saloninus then. Do we have an accord?"

"*Sic erit et decoremque perveni*"

"Yes, it will be my honour." Octavious bowed and turned to go. As he did, he noticed in the far end of the large *cubicula diurna,* Agrippa and the young Helena were sitting heads bowed in deep conversation. Agrippa was holding a scroll open and pointing to texts within it. Helena, nodding and smiling in agreement, was caressing her cross, devotion enveloping her yet leaving her crescent *Lunula* to hang lifelessly from her neck. But it was Constantius sitting on the *arca*, with his hand resting on Helena's shoulder, that caught Octavius's attention.

Constantius was staring with pure venom in his eyes. A hatred of the men before him. The usurpers. It was intense and overpowered the obvious love he held for Helena. Indeed, Octavious noticed the identical bracelets they both wore, glinting in the light of the flames from the brazier near them. They had named their love. Soon to be parted as they would be sped back home. Would the love endure that separation? Of course, it would, Octavious decided.

Then a realisation hit him like a *pattilum* on the back of the head. Constantius might well know of the plot and even who the assassin might be!

Constantuis suddenly shifted his gaze to meet Octavious head-on. A sudden look of alarm swept over the youth. Octavious returned that look with compliance, a smile and a nod of support given. "No-one will ever know", was silently given and Constantius relaxed and nodded in return. But nothing escaped the gaze of the "shade".

… … … … … … … … …

Achaikos pulled the delicate and exquisite diadems from his trunk, wrapped in blue cotton. Kiana and Tamina stood silently watching with a fixed expression on their faces. Achaikos marvelled at their identical look. He had witnessed twinned looks flash across them both in miniscule seconds. As Tamina matured, she was becoming her mother. So, it was fitting indeed, he thought, that identical crowns be worn by them both, on this day of all days. This flouted convention, as Tamina was not of age, but in her soul, she was as mature as her mother.

Their dress was similarly rebellious. Achaikos cared not, and neither did they. They wore identical pure white *toga prætexta* in a pure cotton silk mix. Added to that was the *stolæ* and *pila* that was decorated in a trimming of the red and blue ribbons symbolising the Zoroaster eternal flame rather than the flame the Vestal Virgins wore. The *stolæ* were both held together by two identical *fibulas*.

They would enter and be presented, *capite velato,* head covered as the priestesses they undoubtedly were. Not as Vestal Virgins, but Zoroastrian priestesses. And it would bring an uproar, no doubt.

Then, after the shock had died down, both mother and daughter would bring down their veils to reveal their undisputed royalty. Queen and princess of Sogdia. Tamina revelled in the jewellery Achaikos had bought on their various landings en route to Britannia. They were all Eastern designs and intrinsically Persian. Kiana became quite tearful as she slipped her feet into the Sogdian slippers, upturned at the toe. The silk embroidery of the Zoroastrian flame shone as she moved her foot about. Memories of home flooded her mind.

Achaikos had spared no expense to show his love. Kiana spun round and wrapped her arms around her guardian and lover. She nestled into his hairy chest, as he had not even dressed himself, so intent on presenting his family properly. Neither of them had experienced any ceremony quite like this one. And with the presumption of arrogance and elitism as the hallmark, he needed to educate them both quickly.

"Οι όμορφες γυναίκες μου" Achaikos said gently, leaning over to fix the gold and carnelian necklace for Kiana.

"Ceremony will be held in the *Oeci*, and it is important for you to know where to stand, for you will not be with me. Men and women gather separately for official ceremonies. In fact, it is usually just the male members who attend. But Postumus has announced a relaxing of the traditions. A new broom sweeps away much that is good."

Both women arched their eyebrows simultaneously. Achaikos burst out laughing, "Oh it is so very easy to inflame you ladies. And you are so alike. It is a veritable joy to behold. I am teasing you!"

"Your rank and Royalty will allow you to be near the front of the audience. So, expect some outrage to be wafting your way from women with lesser status than you. And you are both so deeply foreign looking, and diminutive next to taller Roman women."

"But uncommonly feisty and powerful," he added quickly, before either woman could respond. In fact, both had yet to respond to anything, and it piqued his interest.

Both women were beautifully adorned with matching earrings in gold filigree, serpent bracelets, one on the forearm and yet another up high near the shoulder. The twin *fibulae* that held their *Pila* in place was a semicircle in gold plate embossed with the Zoroastrian symbols. Pearl-drops hung delicately from gold chains.

"What is troubling you, my dears?" he asked

Kiana took a deep breath and just as she was about to share her worry, there came a heavy knock on the door.

"May I enter?" came the muffled voice of Vrittakos.

He entered with the customary salutation, large flakes of snow dissolving to water from the heat of the brazier. The blizzard did not bode well for the numbers of dignitaries that would fill the magnificent *Oeci*. Vrittakos stood still to eye Kiana and Tamina with shock rather than admiration. The expected flattery on their beautiful appearance was not forthcoming.

" Για την αγάπη της Τζούνο, γιατί οι γυναίκες σου είναι ακόμα εδώ, Αχαίκου; Θα πρέπει να είναι με τη Βέντας στο δρόμο για την επιστροφή τους στο Wihtland και την ασφάλεια!"

"For the love of Juno, why are your women still here, Achaikos? They should be with Venitouta on their way back to Wihtland

and safety." He bellowed at his old friend, almost unbelieving at Achaikos' apparent gross callousness.

"Venitouta came to us with the news of an actual assassination threat, real and frightening, here at Villam Regis. She begged us to join her ", Kiana stood straight and gave her lover a direct and commanding stare. Mirrored of course by her daughter.

"We refused," they spoke in unison, "we will not leave you undefended," Kiana stated, placing her hand over the heart of Achaikos.

"ΑΝΥΠΕΡΆΣΠΙΣΤΗ!" Vrittakos shrieked with a piercing staccato shout. "Undefended. What nonsense is this, your women speak. Have they lost all their senses?"

Achaikos' face changed with every emotion as he silently battled the verbal onslaught from all present. From disbelief, that Kiana had not told him, to anger at her silence and deep resentment at Vrittakos for the insult on them. Then an understanding came. A gentler emotion settled on his haggard features, transforming him, sending a wave of love to his women.

"Vrittakos, old friend," he said, smiling wryly, "In insulting my women, you insult me. You have no notion of what hazards and battles these women have endured. Even I do not know the full extent. One fact I do know, however, as well as being High Priestesses and Sogdian Royalty, they are trained in the ancient art of self-defence. It is the Persian way in some quarters apparently."

Vrittakos gave a truly deep Greek growl, an ancient swear word no doubt, Achaikos opined silently.

"The usurper emperor had increased the Prætorian guard to maximum levels, each hand gripped to their Gladius", Vrittakos hit back, "If this assassin is successful and the emperor murdered, blood will be split, with no chance of escape!"

Vrittakos spun round, pulling at the door, "You are all mad!" he growled, making to exit the cubiculum.

"And so are you it seems," Achaikos called after the vanishing snow spattered cloak.

… … … … … … … … …

The *Oeci* was filling slowly with Roman Elite. They had trudged their way from the guest quarters, wearing *birrus Britannicus* cloaks over their silk togas and thick *carbatinae* as protection from the thick carpet of fresh snow. The storm had not abated. A hasty cloak area had been erected with slots for their *carbatinas*. The governors and tribunes, elites, Præfectus, dux and consularis, with their wives, donned the felt *soccus* slippers. The slaves had excelled. The floor was exuding such a pleasant heat, it felt like summer had visited the *Oeci*.

The emperor would be taking a lengthy time to appear. The Prætorian guard had been ordered to search incoming guests. It had created a queue. As the moral custom dictated, the women were left unmolested. And it was a shock for Achaikos to feel, most sharply, the distinct cold of metal against Kiana, a curved blade won from the African vagabond, her favourite weapon, concealed completely under her priestess's toga.

"You are infamous, madam," he whispered, brushing against her hair with his lips.

"Hmm," she replied, "I pray it will not be used. But I am ready as ever."

Aquilla, who had overseen all arrangements personally inspected by her husband, Albanus, equipped the largest area in Villam Regis to sumptuous proportions. All the couches and chairs had been re-arranged to skirt the *Oeci*, leaving a wide mosaiced walkway for the Emperor and his elites to process. The statues of the Gods had also been pulled from their resting places, and gathered around the far end, as a silent audience to Postumus. A vacant throne marked his place. Their gaze rested on said throne.

"Oh, this is just too much!" Achaikos whispered in a hiss to Vrittakos.

"Octavious informs me he plans to don the golden crown, as God!" Vrittakos replied, "New times, old friend, new times a cometh!"

"Oh Abrasax, defend us," Achaikos said. His further reply was drowned out by the sudden onset of music, enthusiastic and loud.

Two groups of ensemble musicians were placed at both sides of the *Oeci* and together they created something of a cacophony.

Several of the musicians wore *scabella*, their feet tapping the beat in tinny accord. Achaikos realised they were tuning up, not playing at all, and he let his gaze wander over the incoming guests. "Who are those ancients in purple-stripe togas, over there, standing by Octavious?" he whispered to Vrittakos.

"Nonius Philippus and Egnatius Lucillianus, both old and retired, now to be consularis for Eboracum," Vrittakos replied, "look how Octavius is bending their ears, prodding, I suspect for reliable information on the attackers."

"*Do you believe it will happen!*" Achaikos whispered in a hiss, so close to Vrittakos, he bent his head away.

"Yes, I do!" he almost spat in his face, anger gripping him yet again, "You stupid fool! Endangering the lives of your loved ones. How could you do that, I ask?"

Achaikos remained hunched, silent, for he was in truth stricken with worry for his loved ones. Kiana could tackle four men twice her size, at once. He had witnessed it. But Tamina, poor young Tamina. He sighed audibly, and felt a warming hand grip his shoulder.

"We will get out of this, my friend," Vrittakos, said, lowering his voice still further, whispering so it was barely audible, "I have a small *Naca* waiting with crew in the shadows of the wharf. Single sail and eight oars. They have been ordered to wait until we appear, be it in the next hour, or next day. They will wait."

The musicians had completed the warmup and the dulcet melody of the single *hydraulis* could clearly be heard, hissing the soft notes out, like an ancient one clearing his lungs. As the wind chest built up pressure from the displaced water in the tank beneath, so the *hydraulis* became a living and breathing testament to Greek ingenuity. It was hauntingly beautiful and Achaikos, for a few brief moments, forgot his fear, and was swept away by the music. Back to his homeland. Then two musicians both playing the *Tibia* joined in to add staccato notes. Conversation eased and dimmed as people turned their hearts to the music and the Roman mind stilled the strictures of its' logic.

They were being lulled into a peaceful state of mind. Agrippa had planned it well. Postumus was waiting in Albanus' *tablinum* preparing for his grand entrance. The "shade" was by his side, a constant murmur of advice in his ear. And Prætorian guards gathered around him, nervous, almost in *testudo* formation, like a worried turtle protecting her offspring.

Suddenly, at a show of Aquilla's upraised arm, four musicians, two with *Cornu*, and two with *tuba*, suddenly raised their long instruments, to sound a fanfare into the *Oeci,* the signal for the procession to begin.

At the same time, high-pitched screams ricocheted around the room, adding a truly discordant note to the fanfare. Two more screams followed, and all spectators swung their heads to see the cause. Four women clustered together were in a tangle of togas and blood, most of which had collected at their feet. And they did not seem capable of getting up, although they did not seem fatally hurt.

Achaikos searched for Kiana and Tamina. His young stepdaughter stood, alone, staring wildly at him, frozen and fixed to the mosaic floor.

"Μην κουνηθείς, don't move!" he shouted across to her. He turned to Vrittakos and barked an order, "Get Venitouta, NOW, we must escape." He lunged forward, shoving a gaping elder statesman in front of him and made it across the floor to grab Tamina by the arm. "Where is Kiana?" he demanded, as they ran from the *Oeci*.

"She just disappeared, Pater!" she had bunched her fist around his toga, and was shaking in fear, "She told me to stay still, not move an *uncia,* then she sped away, just as the screaming began."

"Don't worry μικρή," Achaikos spoke gently, turning his head to whisper in her ear, "your dear Mama is quite capable of taking care of herself...and everyone else, I do believe."

"Vrittakos," he shouted back to his friend, "We have no time to lose. Take them to your *Naca*. Take Tamina. I will catch you up."

The heave of elite bodies scrabbling to exit, togas disengaging from their owners and tangling up in the chaotic, frenzied milieu, coupled with the instant appearance of Prætorian guards waving their gladii in alarming fashion at everyone who entered their space, led to a hysterical crush. Women screamed in a cacophony of fear. It became quite apparent to Achaikos, that a single nod from the Dux Novomagnus Reginorum, who stood silently watching, gauging the response of his soldiers, could result in a massacre, if it were not for the fact, that many entangled in the human mass were consularis, governors and Præfectus from several provinces.

He saw from the corner of his eye, Vrittakos, Tamina and Venitouta had managed to dive under, and around, to seek full standing postures at the edge of the chaos. And not only that, they had somehow managed to grab some *birrus Britannia* cloaks and *carbatinas,* hastily wrapping the cloaks for anonymity as much as warmth, as he watched them disappear. He let some of his tension and anxiety waft away with them, only to be replaced by white-hot fear hitting his intestines! Kiana!

He knew she would have run to tackle the assassin. Or maybe more than one. As he spun round to double back along the colonnade leading to the atrium, where Postumus would have arrived before the procession took place, he had a realisation that made him falter.

He remembered the slave workers on that part of mosaic floor. The morning they became spies for Octavious. He'd heard them whisper, loud enough for him catch their plotting. They really had laid poisoned up-ended nails in the floor. They knew people would be wearing flimsy felt slippers. And those poor women, unknowingly, had become decoys for the main act. "That's why Kiana reacted so quickly" he said to the dark night and the swirling snowflakes, brushing them aside as they settled on his eyes. He hurried on. He almost slipped, as he sped to a halt, seeing the discarded toga, *pila* and *stola,* now gathering their own mantle of snow. Tucked underneath and showing just an edge, was the glittering jewel in a gold diadem.

"She shed this load," Achaikos opined silently, "too much care shown here." He picked up the diadem in a rash moment, tucking it in his tunica, and followed that with the *stola* which held the Zoroastrian ribbons. This went the same way, as he had bolstered his chest quite significantly.

"Τρελέ γερο-ανόητε." He swore in Greek.

As he turned the corner, his heart stopped, and he had a fight to bring air back into his lungs. Before him stood a Prætorian soldier, immensely tall and muscular, growling something in guttural Latin, his gladius, bloodied and sticking into the neck of Kiana, who he had rammed up against a wall, frescoed with pretty nymphs in scanty tunicas dancing around a fountain. Absurdly he thought how beautifully detailed it was. It stuck in his memory. He could barely face what was clearly a hideous reality.

Then fury took its hold. *"Dimittet eam de te bastardis. Haec femina uxor mea. Ea innocentes. Iam"!*

"Let go of her, you bastard. This woman is my wife. She is innocent. NOW!"

And with the fury came madness hot on its heels. Achaikos bent his arm back, fist clenched and swung at the Prætorian, knocking him back enough to dislodge the gladius.

Kiana gave a small cry and held her hand to her neck. She went to tackle the hulk, but she had been injured, blood trickling from her leg. She was too slow, and the Pretorian grabbed her again, spinning her around to smash her face against the wall, ripping her tunica from her.

"Well, you are a stupid husband," he growled, "You can watch while I kill your wife, slowly, after I have taken her, that is."

Achaikos lunged again and was rewarded with a blow to his head so acute, his vision darkened and thought he might lose consciousness altogether. White light swirled in front of him and he noticed, as he lay on the marble, her sabre lay, dripping with blood. The assassin, he thought.

"She is innocent, you thick as shit fool!" he shouted. The cool of the marble covered in a thin layer of snow, brought his senses back to him.

"I concur!" came the loud resonant voice of Titus Desticius Juba, Consular of Britannia Superior. "Let go of the Queen of Sogdia, you malformed imbecile. You will be punished. I will see to it personally! Now fetch the Dux."

Achaikos heaved himself up and caressed Kiana, gently, hugged her fully, feeling the tears rise, he let them flow, and she took them.

"Many thanks to you, Titus," he gave the consul the Roman greeting.

"Your wife saved the life of our Emperor, whatever we may think of him now. He may surprise us. Now you both need to escape from here. There are accusations flying faster than a plague of locusts. Reprisals will surely follow. The poor innocent women poisoned, are in a critical state.

And you, I believe, Achaikos were unlucky enough to be present, as acting supervisor when this poisoning plot was hatched, even though you were spying for us. Yes, Octavious has explained everything to me."

"Where is Postumus and did the assassin work alone?" Kiana asked.

"He is safe, dear lady, locked up in Albanus' private quarters. As for the assassin, he is very dead. So, we will be vigorous in questioning everyone. I will tell him you asked after him. You intrigue him, you know. I think you intrigue us all!"

The noble presence of Titus, saw them safe to the wharf. And it was a joyous moment to see the Vrittakos family safe, waiting for them. Kiana was limping badly, and she allowed Achaikos to carry her the remaining *stade*.

As they embarked on the *Naca*, she turned to Titus.

"Please can you get a message to Octavious. Tell him the Young Constantius *must* leave Villam Regis now. And the girl, also." Titus' expression deepened and he studied Kiana for a long moment. He gave the slightest nod.

"It is already in hand. He will be leaving for *Eboracum* on the dawn tide." He bowed low, "I bid you farewell. You are the most extraordinary women I have had the pleasure to meet."

… … … … … … … … …

Chapter 46

Deaō-gerihte
Dearth rite

The *Naca* was an old boat, named appropriately *eald ãc,* and like all aging oaken hulls, it talked. Kiana was almost lulled into a fitful sleep by its soft murmurings, able to dull the pain for precious moments, until a windward lurching or noisy flapping of the single sail, sprang her mind into consciousness. Achaikos had applied a tourniquet, ripping his fine woollen toga to obtain strips strong enough to halt the bleeding. She settled into his ample, soft form, her breath, white and steamy, billowed out into the dark night, as words were spoken to release mental pain, if not the physical.

"You brave old fool," she said, looking up at Achaikos, who returned her words with a wry smile, "you tackled a brute monster of a Prætorian, with no regard to yourself. You saved my life dear heart."

"Hmm, I think it was Titus who saved us. I was not up for much more Kiana. That soldier wasn't human." He gently brushed her raven hair, brushing away the snowflakes, forever falling it seemed. It was so freezing now they were at sea and past the warmer waters of the inlet, her blood, had long since stopped oozing. It had almost frozen.

"Yet he came at the right moment," Kiana murmured, "led, I would venture to say, by the Ancient Ones."

"Zoroaster."

"Abrasax." They both intoned in unison. And laughter burst out from them, for the first time in many days. It was a grand release of tension.

"Well, it must be Abrasax my dear one," Achaikos chuckled. "He was the god who brought laughter to our world, did he not?"

"Yes, that he did," Kiana concurred, and fell into a more restful sleep until they were nearing the coast of sacred Wihtland. Tamina quietly hugged Achaikos and followed her mother into dreamtime.

Eald Āc creaked up the river to Berandinzium Villam. The wharf hove into view just as dawn was breaking, a weak, hazy, lemon-yellow Sunni broke through ochre-tinged clouds pregnant with snow. They were home. Ever thankful, there would be much talk around the braziers for days to come. But now, Kiana desperately needed healing hands. And only one angel would do. Dagrun Wahl.

Vrittakos literally jumped from the *Naca*, the second it had been tied, swirling his *birrus Britannicus* about him, he stepped into a *cubitum* of untouched virgin snow. He turned to shout at a young crew member.

"Move! Quickly and find Eyvindr...I mean Aelius. We need four good horses here. We must get Kiana to Lãfa Dūn.

As Vrittakos' hunched form trudged off into the snow, Venitouta suddenly came alive. She had been eloquent in her silence during the voyage. She had not spoken a word. So Vrittakos had remained quiet also.

Now she jumped off the *Naca* and strode towards him, knees riding high to negotiate the deep drifts. Her arms swinging in rhythm, she soon joined him. Greek expletives could be heard wafting back to the *Naca*. Whatever had held their silence, they had thrown it off.

The Sogdian royal family and the priest remained, silent, huddled against each other for human warmth. They remained in the *Naca*. The crew had dispersed, trudging to their homes through the night. This was the aftermath, the vacuum created by those terrible events over which they had had no control. They felt helpless and diminished. Kiana felt it most keenly for she, who prided herself as the fearless warrior, was found wanting. She was awake and trembling. Now more than ever, she needed to face her weakness, that vulnerability she believed she had extinguished a long time ago.

Her tormentor, Raptis, had meted out enough blows and cracks of the whip to teach the young Kiana how to withstand torture and ultimately to fight back. But this latest attack, and the monster who delivered it to her, took violence to a new level. In the spiritual dimension, she was unassailable, she knew that, but now, here in the mundane world, she was nothing but a weak and feeble woman. And it hurt more than the deep laceration to her thigh.

"Did you really kill that assassin, Mama?" Tamina's voice burst through her silent agony.

Taking a full intake of freezing air, "Yes my lovely daughter. I did," she replied, "But he was a stooge. A scrawny half-bit of a man. I have no doubt he was bribed to do this deed. And he lost his life for it. Whoever was really behind this attack, they will not stop.

"Young Constantius knew the identity of those involved. And Octavious also. It goes into the very heart of old Rome. Postumus is a usurper. He will need to be on constant guard. I do not envy him."

The freezing cold had deepened, the chill entering their bones. It was hard to talk without teeth chattering. Their breath intermingled against the grey dawn sky.

"That Prætorian soldier was a specimen," Kiana spoke into the cold air, "every single nerve, every muscle was honed, twitching almost, to wreak really evil violence. He has had half of his humanness expelled from him. What is left is a husk, a vacuum to be filled with hatred so pure, he could only lust for more."

Achaikos' face had gone dark, his pupils black as pitch. It was not only the fury he felt over the attack, but his own memories of that cave with the dark Goddess, come back to haunt him. He was, at an earlier time, not much better than that hulk.

Kiana watched him carefully and hugged him closer to her.

He looked down to see her gaze fix on his own.

"You can be Hecate in spirit form," he said quietly, almost in a whisper. She smiled and nodded. "Yes," she replied in his ear, "I brought the young Achaikos to his knees, snivelling into my incense!"

"You are a goddess and please do not forget it!" he said kissing her fully holding her to him.

… … … … … … … … …

With Sunni rising came hope. They heard the shouts of Eyvindr before the shapes came into view. No less than four horses tethered together, carrying Vrittakos and Venitouta and with hooves rising to each footfall, they danced their way in quickstep to rescue the stranded humans.

"Grata domum, amicis meis epularer. Berandinzium Villam est prorsus Snowbound. His commota sunt durior habemus ephippium autem ens. nix autem amo!"

"Welcome home, my friends. Berandinzium Villam is totally snowbound. These stallions are the toughest we have, but they are being skittish. They love the snow."

"Kiana can ride with me," Achaikos insisted, "We go straight to Lāfa Dūn."

"I think it may be better on my stallion, dear friend," Eyvindr said, "He is a white augury, and he already knows the urgency. He knows the land and will get us there much quicker. Follow us please, if you will."

"Loosen my tourniquet!" Kiana implored, "I can no longer feel my leg." Eyvindr pulled the binding loose, and blood began to ooze from her wound. "Tell me when you feel pain again, I will tighten it before we begin the journey."

It took several precious minutes before Kiana felt the pulsing of blood reach her feet and the throbbing pain accompanying the surge. Wads of cotton were pushed into the wound to stem the flow. She began to feel faint. Oblivion became a welcome escape.

She felt Eyvindr hoist her limp body onto the huge stallion. And felt his strong arms wrap around her, as she lay her head against his chest. The white augury bucked for a second, releasing pent-up energy, then cantered forward, high stepping, his hooves hitting the snow cleanly.

He knew the way. He also sensed the urgency, so he sped along, especially when they reached the new Roman road leading from the small harbour inlet to Iuppiter Igne Villam, and close to Lāfa Dūn.

Hooves hitting solid stone made a welcome noise. The dancing stallion jolted Kiana most painfully. Her head was bobbing about, her raven hair swinging with each stride.

"*Nigt-gala, Èðnes þín hefig strídan gecwèman. Bèon bilewit wiþ þæt daru cwèn.*" Eyvindr cajoled his mount with clicks and the high expelling of breath.

"Horse language," Kiana thought.

"What language is that you speak?" she asked, turning her head, trying very hard to keep it attached to her neck.

"It is our ancestor Mother tongue, Cwèn Kiana," he replied, his voice softening, "It is more ancient than this island."

"It is very beautiful. And my name is Sumaya, Queen Sumaya," she replied, "Μιλάτε Ελληνικά?" Do you speak Greek?"

"Μόνο αν χρειαστεί. Only when I have to" came the quick reply. "*Latine deinde?*"

"*Quando solum habent! Romani non placet.* Only when I must. I don't like the Romans," Kiana shot back, chuckling softly. Then her head fell forward, and she blissfully fell into oblivion.

... ...

She came around with a howl of pain. Eyvindr and Achaikos were manhandling her up thick oak stairs, only just wide enough for the two of them, going sideways. She was hunched in between them. Pain surges of extreme intensity coursed up and down her leg. The blood was flowing again. They placed her in an l-shaped room, with a high-timbered ceiling. Two large shuttered windows faced each other. The bed was soft, layered with many sheep pelts. She gratefully sank into them. Tallow-filled sconces and a brazier gave a warm glow to this bedroom. The bedroom of the Queen, so she had been told.

Dagrun Wahl, using what little strength remained in her fragile body, made her way over to Kiana.

"*Mōtan Nerthus bindan þu und hǽlan þu, Cwèn Sumaya. Ic am Dagrun Wahl, cwèn fram þæt Wihtwara. Und Ic am a Wíscwèn hālian.* May Nerthus bind you and heal you, Queen Sumaya. You know who I am, Dagrun Wahl Queen of the Wihtwara, and I am a wise woman and healer."

Dagrun studied Kiana and felt an affinity with her spirit. And she was so fragile, small, yet undoubtedly courageous. A great warrior. Her tangled black raven hair fell in a mess around the bleached white of the sheep rugs. Her black eyes pinpoints of pain. A young warrior woman from the East.

"We have mighty things to discuss, you and I, before I part company," Dagrun thought, as she gently washed around the deep sword wound that threatened this woman's life. "But first, we must save this life!"

She gave swift instructions to Lāfa to gather herbs, powder, and her sacred bundle. The boar's tooth talisman. And the dagger. She hoped she would not need the latter. She tightened the tourniquet again, washing the wound with her own potion of Lukely spring water and golden seal. It stung, badly. A good sign, she thought, the nerves were still working. She saw immediately that the blade had sheared a big blood vessel. If the bloodstone did not staunch the flow, she would need to resort to the burning it down to seal it.

Kiana had lost too much blood. She had now lost consciousness. Dagrun could feel a presence behind her, the constant movement of the oak floor, talking and groaning, mirroring a mind in agony, as Achaikos paced the floor.

"*Gecwèman ālǽtan ūs. Wè willan hãtan þu*" Lāfa ordered Achaikos to leave. His head turned in puzzlement.

"*Placere relinquere nunc! Habemus ad salvum facere opus uxor tua. Et beatos vos faciemus*" Dagrun wheezed loudly in

Latin, as she unfurled the bundle containing herbs, potion and her boar's tooth.

"Please leave now. We have work to do to save your wife. We will call you."

Achaikos made to protest, but Lãfa gave him her warrior look. He made a shuffled exit muttering Greek under his breath.

"Now," Dagrun commanded, "Lãfa, wash the wound with this," she handed her the water thickly sedimented with crushed bloodstone. "And wait," she ordered. "We must watch to see if the crystal will work." She went into prayer, placing the talisman over the wound. It was instant. Kiana moaned and shifted her body in response.

"Give her poppy, if she wakes up," Dagrun muttered as she continued,

"*Erce, Erce, Erce,*

Sãwol fram Blōdstãn. Gehlýstan ús-Bringan þín hãlwende drycræft æt þin mæg wif. Drèogan hiè blōd swã neah æt þín blōd. Swelgan hiès æt elnian þín swæs.

Erce, Erce, Erce."

"Spirit of bloodstone Hear us. Bring your healing medicine to your kinswoman. Feel her lifeblood so close to your blood. Swallow hers to strengthen your own!"

Mother and daughter waited and watched closely. Lãfa carefully picked up a bloodstone crystal that lay in the bundle. The inclusions were clear, blood red weaved its way around the beautiful dark green stone, spotted in places and flowing in others.

"I traded these with a merchant from the Silk Road," Dagrun whispered, in a supreme effort to avoid the endless coughing spasms that always now ended with blood-soaked linen. "They come from her country, *dohtor*. Oh, she is a true treasure in our midst. A rare one. She is what they call, an "adept." Listen to her. She knows so much more than I!"

The prayers spoken took effect, and Lãfa stared open-mouthed as the blood pulsing from the deep wound became a trickle and then stopped.

"*Giese, giese!*" Dagrun almost chuckled, "Now we must work quickly. Hand me the strongest horsehair, and needle. We are going to sew her up!"

Lãfa was shocked. She had never witnessed this work of sheer wonder. Her *Mōdor* worked without a hint of her own pain, carefully joining the broken vein, which could now be seen clearly. It was an horrendous slash of young flesh. But age was on Kiana's side.

The excruciating pain had, however, worked up to bring Kiana to the edge of consciousness.

"Poppy!" Dagrun shouted, "Now. Else this work be wasted." Lãfa held Kiana's head back, supporting her, as Dagrun skilfully opened her mouth for the potion to slip down her throat.

"*Gōd!*" she wheezed as a deep coughing fit convulsed her completely and left her limp and shaken.

"*Mōdor!*" Lãfa cried, "let me finish this. Stay where you are. Just tell me what to do." She fetched the horsehair and Dagrun told her to twine into thicker thread.

"You must close the skin, Lãfa, tight. Each thread tied and cut. It was the way I was shown in the Wyrd. Then you must put a poultice of bread soaked in this potion, herbs to stop the wound going bad."

Dagrun's head sunk in exhaustion. She so badly needed her bed. Her days were now so few. She knew this Queen from a distant land had been brought to her from Wyrd. And wisdom needed to be shared for the safety of her land, her island.

Lãfa sensed the bond between these two, so she called for the servants to build a good bed for their guest, close to her *Mōdor*, who now fell to her layers of soft sheepskin and immediately fell asleep.

... ...

"Your Queen will live," Lãfa announced to Achaikos, who dropped all reserve, and became the ebullient Greek peasant boy, rushing forward to sweep the giantess off her feet, and literally swing her around amidst his cheers of Greek salutations.

On landing Lãfa pulled herself and her dress together, "We must leave both Queens to recover. It may take several days. I would request, therefore, Achaikos, that you might take this time to discover our island. The storm has passed. Sunni shines down on us."

"Uncle, perhaps you could take some clean air into your lungs and show Achaikos around?"

Eystein resisted the urge to roll his eyes heavenwards and gave his niece the intense Warinni stare that spoke volumes.

"*Giese*," he smiled at the Greek, "My pleasure. May we speak in Latin, of which I know some words. Your mother tongue just defies me!"

... ...

Kiana opened her eyes, like slits, her eyelashes glued together. She had cried and sweated in her unconscious state, briefly seeing her reality and not gruesome dreams. She glimpsed the elderly woman lying close to her, for brief moments. Once, they stared at each other, a knowing, an age-old wisdom passed between them. Kiana knew her to be of another world yet unknown, but in some way, so like her own.

Once, she saw her sitting up and taking food, before she, herself, lapsed into those chaotic images. She felt burdened by them. The little man she had killed, became a slow-motion event, gross and bloody. She could feel her sabre drawing against bone, and in place of the clean thrust to his heart, a macabre recurrence of many hits, as she looked up into his face. He had morphed into Postumus himself, except he was laughing hysterically. She screamed for it to stop. It was answered and she came back to reality, gulping for air and crying out, with Dagrun's daughter Lãfa bending over her and holding her closely.

"Tamina," she gasped, "My daughter. Where is she!"

"Cared for!" answered Lãfa, stroking her face as gently as she could, passing love to her, "She is at Berandinzium Villam, with Vrittakos and Venitouta. Being spoilt as only a Sogdian princess should," she added with a smile.

"And your anxious husband is taking the air with my *brōðor* Eystein," Dagrun said, "He was driving everyone quite mad, so I'm told. He adores you!"

"We are so very happy to have you back with us," Dagrun said.

Lãfa handed her a wooden cup filled with water from the *Dūn* pond. Kiana felt it coursing down her throat, life-giving and revitalizing. "I will leave you two *Cwèns* to talk," Lãfa said, "I believe there is much to share."

Dagrun shifted on her sheep furs, to gain more comfort, to ease her aching bones. Facing Kiana, she asked her most immediate question, "Are you able to talk with me, Kiana," she asked.

Kiana nodded, although she was unaware of the depth they would both be engulfed in by sundown.

"Why did you save the life of Postumus?" Dagrun was keen to know. "Was it possibly because he was a Suevii? From my homeland. A German if you like."

"No!" came the reply, "He will be murdered by his own people soon enough! It is the poison of Rome growing into every vein, Unstoppable."

"Ahh, yes," replied Dagrun, with a sardonic smile spreading across her aging face. Kiana thought her skin was parchment, "I visited the Nornia, our sisters of Fate, to weave their *drycræft* to "speed the process." Justice for my *brōðor*."

Kiana became very alert on hearing this. She eyed Dagrun, her intense black eyes piercing into her soul. "You are an Adept, then?"

"Our spiritual faith, our path, is as ancient as yours, I believe," Dagrun replied, sending a Warinni focus as powerful as the one she had just been gifted from Kiana.

"Our pathway to the Ancients is on the river of Wyrd, past, present and our futures weave in a tapestry we can access. My doorway is through the *Godcund stãn*. What is yours, may I ask?"

Kiana smiled in remembrance of the precious ceremony with Tamina in the Agora.

"It is through the Eternal Flame of Zoroaster," she replied, "He is the Avatar to the most Ancient god Ahura Mazda, and he believed we humans would poison the waters of our world. He gave us instructions to save it. It is called the ritual of Ab-Zohr. And that is what we do. Ahura Mazda knows our world is divided. And we are forever working to deny the evil named *Druj*."

"Zoroaster walked the Earth at the time of the Roman expansion. He knew what the Romans would create. A monstrous bulbous empire."

"Ahh, our Avatar, as you call him, for us, is Wōden, and our Ancient one is the goddess Nerthus, mother Earth." Dagrun sipped some water to release the awful dryness in her throat. "We prefer to live very close to the earth. I don't believe we will adopt or live at ease in Roman villams. We prefer to hear our dwellings talk to us."

"Yes, "Kiana concurred, "The Romans beat the life out of the Goddess-given materials to build their empire. They never give thanks or ask permission of the spirits within, so the only spirits in the stone are the spirits of the men who slaved to extract it from the earth, with their sweat and blood. And often their lives. Those brave souls taught me a big lesson, "she murmured gently, "they gifted me their wisdom as I lay in the Temple of Diana, tormented at the loss of my daughter. We are the Creators. We have the power. It is as simple as that!"

"*Giese!*" Dagrun replied, then breaking into a spasm of coughing that spewed blood again, as she collapsed in terrible pain.

"Shall I get your daughter?" Kiana asked, forcing her legs to move and failing.

"*Na*," Dagrun gasped, "Not just yet. I have a favour to ask of you. Please gift my daughter the wisdom of Zoroaster, the Ab-Zohr. Be with her after my passing. She has much to learn from you. It will be needed in times to come."

"It will be my honour, Cwèn of the Wihtwara," Kiana bowed her head, knowing these were the last few days for the Queen, and her tribute was sincere.

"Now," said Dagrun, turning her head to see her companion in full light, "It would be a great honour for me to hear your story." Dagrun sank back, the effort of speaking was becoming too much for her. Yet she knew this woman's story was so important for her to hold and carry to *Neorxenawang*.

And so, Kiana described her journey, miraculous and dangerous, heart-breaking and joyous, along the famed Silk Road. A soft and gentle smile settled on the gaunt features of the Cwèn. Her eyes became wide, pupils enlarged and far seeing. She was being transported to a far wider horizon and a different world from the one she had grown up in. Kiana left nothing out, as Sunni began to sink in the sky, splashing her multi-coloured hues across the solar to bathe Dagrun in gentle light.

But when Kiana described the arrival to Pessinus, the nadir of the sacred feminine, and the sacking of the Temple to Cybele by the Romans, Dagrun shifted suddenly, sat bolt upright, spine rigid and hands clenched.

"*Forsyngod ðíefð*" the Cwèn of Wihtland roared. Her guttural sounds came across as a croak, the veins in her skeletal neck bulging and throbbing. She saw the look of horror pass across Kiana's face, who understood not a word.

Dagrun changed her Suevii tongue for Latin, "*malum. Parce mihi .... Furtum. Cares Suevii lingua. quod si furto ablatum fuerit Cybele dominam, ex quovis nomine appellamus, Roma capta est, horret me.*"

"Evil Theft. Forgive me…. You lack the Suevii tongue. That the precious gift from Cybele should be stolen, taken to Rome, horrifies me." Dagrun fell back onto her pillows, her body so frail and small, they almost engulfed her.

"*Giese*," Kiana replied, as she had learnt that Suevii word, and received a warm smile from Dagrun.

"We left Pessinus weary and sad," she continued, "And wanting very badly to reach Byzantium, the Golden City on the sea. Tamina had not experienced the expanse of water in her life. I was anxious for her to see it. In the event, she fell in love with it. The sea birds flew about her low and calling. She is a maiden of the waters for sure! When I saw the flags honouring Hecate, which is Cybele, Diana and Nerthus, our Divine Mother, I shed thankful tears. We all felt a release from the pain of many years, trapped and enslaved.

"Achaikos, although his soul had been fragmented by the Fall, dictated by Abrasax as the final teaching, had come home, and he found true joy."

"We do not have this "Fall" you speak of," Dagrun said quietly, reflectively, "In our spirit world, we travel on the river of Wyrd, there is no "up" or "down." Is it because your journey is marked by the stars? The planets in the Cosmos, as you call it?"

"Achaikos knows," Kiana replied, smiling at the thought of him, "I believe we would have remained in Byzantium had it not been for the damned Romans and the persecution of those followers of the new faith."

"What new faith?" Dagrun interrupted sharply, "Do you speak of Christians? They speak of only one god. And Jesus Christ is the son of this god. All other Gods and Goddesses are full of sin and must be abandoned!"

"Yes, it is true," Kiana spoke back sharply, her emotions rising, "We witnessed terrible torture and the ritual killing of entire Christian families, before a blood-thirsty audience of Romans. They were asked to recant their faith and perform a ritual sacrifice to Roman gods in front of this baying crowd! It will remain with me all my life. And Tamina also.

"Achaikos felt sure these Decian persecutions would soon lead to other faith-ways like ours being targeted, as Zoroaster is the human embodiment of Ahura Mazda, who abhors sacrifice."

"We would be next."

"Oh! Queen Sumaya, it is being written in blood!" Dagrun cried, exhausted and in great pain. She sought to continue, "It is they who will be torturing and killing us! The Christians will be the end of us all! I have seen it, and there is absolutely nothing to be done. Now I understand. It is the Romans at the heart of everything that is evil!"

"My work here is done. I will do better in Wyrd."

Kiana pulled herself up, and with every nerve shuddering in pain, she walked over to Dagrun, and in holding her hand, feeling the parchment skin only barely keeping her bones together, she leaned forward, kissing her forehead, slowly, lovingly, tears falling upon Dagrun's cheeks, melting into her grey hair.

With the most supreme effort, Dagrun forced her eyes to meet Kiana, they had turned dull and milky, she was beginning to see very little.

"You are the most ancient spirit, Sumaya. You are as ancient as the pink marble that spoke so clearly to you. Take your story to our leaning stone. It will hear you."

"I received a vision of our end, Dagrun," Kiana blurted out, "I was shown the destruction of Berandinzium Villam, and the murder of Achaikos and Vrittakos. At the bloody hands of the Christians, in all their damn finery carrying weapons of death! I cannot tell Achaikos and it is a boulder sitting between us!"

"Then take that to the *Sāwol Stān* also. Then tell Achaikos to put his hand on the stone. He will either receive the vision, or he will not. It is meant."

Dagrun wheezed a laboured breath and looked at Kiana beseechingly.

"My family, dear one, I need them with me now."

"And teach Lāfa all you know, please!"

"You are the most eloquent of Queens, dear Dagrun," Kiana whispered, "Your deep heart and brave mind are open to all higher spirits, yet now, you are being called to Wyrd, where your power will divest most adequately for the future. You are leaving us before your time, age-old bones you will never know until the next time. I am humbled in your presence and so very honoured to meet you now. I will stay here on Wihtland. I will be close to your daughter. Never fear."

Kiana stepped away, keeping her gaze on the queen, never blinking, and only allowed the tears to fall as she quietly closed the door.

As the family sombrely made their way upward to Dagrun's Solar, Kiana heard the main door scrape open. Her heart jumped as Tamina and Achaikos made their way over and simply engulfed her in their arms. So much had been stripped away by events out of their control. Their souls were raw. And only the comfort of each other warmed the cold chill that gripped the very air in this Warinni mead Hall.

A long gasp escaped, and Kiana whispered on its dying breath, "These are her last moments, and I feel as if I have known her all my life! It is unjust!"

"Dear heart, Kiana," Achaikos held her face up to stare deeply into her soul, "We must walk so quietly, speak very gently and pour our love to her family, as Queen Dagrun will be doing over the coming days. Calm strength, Queen Sumaya!"

... ...

Lãfa knelt by her mother's bed, consumed almost entirely by her Will not to be engulfed with bone-shaking sorrow. She watched, her gentle tears falling on the parchment skin of her mother's hand, while Lãfa held it to her lips, willing her to stay for just a few moments more. Suddenly she felt her baby move and gasped softly. She opened her mouth to tell her, but the words died on her lips, unspoken, unheard.

Dagrun knew. She smiled so faintly, it could have been taken for a grimace of pain, but she slowly led her hand to the heron wing lying on her chest and patted it softly.

"*Fran mín Ealdmōdor, und nūðã æt þu, mín dohtor. Þæt Hragra is þín. Frætwa Hiè wielle. Gifu Hiè æt þin dohtor nūðã in þín bulga.*"

"From my dear Grandmother, and now to you, my daughter, the Heron is yours. Treasure her well. Gift her to your daughter now growing in your belly."

Lãfa released a small cry of astonishment. Dagrun really did smile, her spirit reaching her eyes for one more time, as she turned to her own *Mōdor*, reaching for her hand. And her *Fæder* standing to her side quelling his tears and hiding in his beard, as men do.

"*Ðoncian þu,*" she whispered. And then her gaze became far, very far. A beautiful smile grew on her serene and pain-free face.

"*Eileifer!*" she exclaimed. And then she left. Life disappeared from those stunning eyes. Dagrun Wahl was gone.

... ...

BOOK FOUR

Chapter 47

Mithra

Vrittakos and his family retired quietly, unobtrusively, from the *Deaō-gerihte*, with Achaikos, leaving the Warinni family to mourn. This was no place for them to remain. They were visitors. Vrittakos was relieved, for news had arrived via messenger from Villam Regis, that Postumus would be arriving on Wihtland within the next moon. Venitouta had left reluctantly, for she had had a deep relationship with Dagrun. Kiana had been asked to stay. Dagrun's dying wish was for her to support Lāfa.

Venitouta's parting comment as she slipped into her private *cubiculum*, "the hardest thing, beyond all knowing, is the deep empty hole left for a mother losing her child before herself! What of poor Gudrun, may I ask? What life is left for her now?" She closed the heavy curtain, locking herself away for her own mourning, feeling alternately angry and profoundly useless.

Aia too felt bereft. Her closeness and growing love for Eastmund settled in her heart like a lead ball. She too sought her privacy within Berandinzium Villam.

The men, then, were left to themselves and talk soon reverberated around Postumus, his acolytes, and most certainly the deep suspicion both men held towards Honoratianus, "The Shade".

"Whatever doubts we may harbour towards the Usurper," Vrittakos stated, leaving little doubt that there were many oscillating around the German "grunt," "they pale into insignificance when looking at the maleficence of Honoratianus. He squeezes my heart into a tight ball within seconds of being in his energy!"

"Ditto," Achaikos replied, thinking momentarily about Hecate. In her most terrifying aspect, she was less chilling than this cold monster, "I fear our acting skills will fall like so much muslin at our feet. He will see past them."

"So, he sees our nakedness! We think he is a *venenatus spuo* and many people would be agreeing with that," he continued, slapping his thigh in irritation, "I'm sure he is immune. He knows he is a total arsehole. What matters is we protect Eyvindr? He is vulnerable."

"Agreed," said Vrittakos, whose love for his "*libertus*" was akin to fatherhood, "Postumus will be rubbing shoulders with Eyvindr. They are both being initiated into the fourth level, Leo and at Iuppiter igne villam.

"A case of Mithraic equality. Slave and Emperor together!"

"We must prepare him fully," he stated, "Let us bring him here as soon as possible." The men sat huddled around the glowing brazier, the afternoon winter light fading rapidly, as Sunni seemingly had given up the struggle to warm the Earth and sank gratefully into the underworld. The logs from the brazier momentarily sparked, swirling upward to dance briefly with the growing shadows. Vrittakos' *tablinum* was without doubt, the warmest room in the villam. The great heating of the hypocaust was being saved for the imperial visit. Finding extra fuel was a heavy task for all the villams required maximum heating. It was not just the long ceremonies dedicated to their sun God Mithras, but there would be sacred meals, and Mithrasmas to be fully celebrated. Their divine God was born in December.

Both men sunk into their own thoughts. The faintest culinary smells reached them from the *culina* but neither man felt inclined to shift from their *birrus Brittannicus*. The thick wool insulating them completely. Vrittakos stirred.

"I am very concerned for the spiritual steadfastness of Eyvindr," he stated, leaning forward to stir up the glowing logs, now collapsing into a near-white heap, "he is of two minds, two hearts, yet only the one soul. He tells me he is walking in two worlds. Yet he has no notion, no idea whatever of the stricture, the sheer torment that will be inflicted upon him for this level of Leo. It is of Fire, Achaikos, pure fire I tell you!"

Achaikos stared at his friend aghast.

"Are you really, truly, telling me that you, YOU are a devotee of Mithras?"

Vrittakos shifted heavily in his chair, planting both hands squarely on his knees, learnt forward to stare Achaikos in his face, defiant, daring a rebuke to follow.

" Ναι, γιε του Αμπράραξ. Ποιος είσαι εσύ που θα με κρίνεις? Yes, you son of Abrasax. Who are you to dare judge me!?"

Achaikos immediately put his hands together in supplication.

"I apologise, my friend," he replied, "Only the most supreme God can do that. I am only shocked as you have always given little credence to the Roman bull-slayer god."

"Well, oh wise old man, you may have a gaping hole in your knowledge. Your wisdom shows some holes my friend."

Vrittakos chuckled softly to himself, eying Achaikos with consummate fondness, his eyes shining with affection.

He leaned forward to hold Achaikos by his arm. "I am a devotee of the original Eastern god Mithra, my friend," Vrittakos announced, "To be clear, there was a catastrophic spiritual event, aeons past, a devastating soul-quake born from visioning of a Magi, or two. It left humanity in the eastern world, reeling, soulless and helpless. Mithras the bull-slayer was born from that devastation. Mithraism is now quintessentially Roman. But I cannot give my heart or soul to it, I'm afraid. And I am equally afraid for Eyvindr, because I don't feel he can either.

"What will be required of him now, is complete and total adherence to the creed. He will be shown secret esoteric knowledge. It will literally forbid him to falter or remove himself. He will become an adept in every way!"

"And just to be clear, again. I am only at the Corvus level. The first initiation, though still sworn to secrecy. That is fine with me. I watch, I listen, and I learn from all the ceremonies that have taken place here at Berandinzium Villam. This is the final Mithræum, by the way, the level of Pater. I have watched initiates move through the stages. How do you think I could oversee and organise all this on Wihtland?"

"And by Eyvindr's side will be the posturing Postumus," Achaikos added, "A wily Emperor with a vicious side-kick. Eyvindr will need to cloak himself fully with protective layers. *Drýcræft*, he calls it."

Indeed," Vrittakos nodded balefully, "come friend let us fill our bellies, if not our souls." They both shuffled out, not shedding their *birrus*', but gripping the woollen folds even tighter as the blast of winter air hit them from the open *exedra* whose wilting plants echoed the men's own frailty.

"Abraxas' Eyes," growled Achaikos, "My Fall cannot get much lower! I hate this god-forsaken hinterland of a piss-pot country!"

... ...

Chapter 48

Sophia Invictus

Kiana straightened out from her foetal position, rubbing her frozen feet to bring some blood to them. She had been given an alcove, with a shuttered window, and a reasonably sized bed with several sheepskins, but this did not help. It was bitterly cold. Neither did the noises, now gaining strength, of Lãfa and Arkyn making love in the cold night. Kiana felt robbed of her sleep. She was missing Achaikos very acutely as their climax was recorded in sighs and cries. So, she began a long liturgy of prayer to Zoroaster. She succumbed to sleep halfway through the Avesta, her last thoughts of accomplishment that she had remembered so much of it.

The morning brought frozen limbs and glued eyes. Pulling one eye open to see the lovers leaning, yes by Hecate, leaning out of the large window, shutters thrown back, ushering in a truly wicked wind. Kiana decided she loathed Britannia deeply, and Wihtland in particular. She had also decided that the Warinni were not human. Their giant bodies were an astonishment to her. Kiana was of the slightest build, so she came to their elbows at best and was cricking her neck daily just to communicate with them.

But she had made a promise to the dying queen and she would fulfil it. She just wished Dagrun had passed in the Spring!

Lãfa turned to see Kiana, stiff with cold, trying to wrap sheepskins around herself.

"*Oh, gecwèman forgefūs. Sãreg þu are frèorg!* Please forgive us. Sorry, you are frozen!" Lãfa paced over to her frozen companion and hugged her tightly, eclipsing Kiana, leaving her fighting for breath.

"Here, please use my cloak," Lãfa commanded, as she wrapped Kiana up like a chrysalis with just nose and mouth available to take air. "Sit by the fire." The fire was now embers giving off the mere promise of small heat.

"Arkyn, my love, please can you shout for a servant to build up the fire and bring some food too!"

"*Đinen, þin cwèn has níed fram þu*" Arkyn bellowed in baritone, smiling to himself as hurried footfalls from clogged feet rattled up the oaken stairs. Arkyn was every inch a Wōden figure, muscular, tall and elegant with the same copper brown locks of the young Wotan. Lãfa adored him and so did most of the Mead Hall inhabitants, from servants to villans and equerries. Arkyn very naturally commanded respect.

But for Kiana, he held pure intrigue. She failed to get the measure of this man. For her intuition told her he was far too good-looking for his own good. But her attention was pulled towards Lãfa. She was the reason for her stay in this horrendously cold hall. Her first thought was to give them lessons in hypocaust building. Yet it would fall on deaf ears, she thought, for they just do not seem to feel any cold.

They sat silently for a while, staring at the *Đinen* as she knelt building up a tall pyramid of kindling, then throwing on hot ember coals she kept tied to her waist in a thick beaten copper pouch. She was a fire keeper, and before Kiana could voice her first thoughts, a small fire was crackling and being built upon.

"Dear lady, how are you today?" Kiana asked circumspectly, taking the oblique route.

"Far warmer than you, it would seem, Queen Sumaya. Your "Silk Road" body is not attuned to our cold climate."

Lãfa smiled apologetically, "You are here to teach me," she stated, getting straight to the point. "It was my Mōdor's last wish I should learn about the Eastern religions. They fascinated her I know, but there is a powerful reason behind the request. She saw into the future; she was an adept. For me and my children," Lãfa caressed her burgeoning belly, "The future my Mōdor saw will be chaotic at best, catastrophic at worst."

"I have witnessed this also," Kiana broke in, holding Lãfa's hand in hers, "and I spoke to your Mōdor about it. Her visioning and mine correspond in a confirming and yes, terrible way."

Both held to their thoughts for a while. Three young girls entered, their clogs throwing up detritus from the impacted earth floor, not yet strewn with dried herbs. The *Deaō-gerihte* had suspended time. Kiana felt Dagrun's spirit enter the void. She knew Lãfa felt her presence also. The three serving girls had brought food. Steaming bowls of *Kornmjölsgot* and warmed gritty bread broken into hunks for dipping.

Kiana's stomach revolted at the sight and the aroma. She silently spoke harshly to herself, "It's winter, it is all they have, eat it!" She found Britannia food not just alien but almost indigestible.

The youngest servant girl was charged with building the fire. She placed log upon log onto the now sparking and lively fire. It was placed in the centre of the solar, a rectangular box of hardened oak timbers lined with darkened copper. The billows of smoke created from the fire-building, snaked and wafted up to the smoke-hole in the roof.

The heat became pleasurable and Kiana took the heat of the porridge into her starving body and soon felt infinitely better.

"When I made that incredibly arrogant decision to run away from my royal home in Sogdia, my designated life as a Royal queen-in-waiting," Kiana began her discourse gently, staring into the flames, as if to see her own father there looking out to her, " I was living with pure faith at my side. Knowing absolutely nothing of the torments this life-choice would bring to me. Yet, the sheer heights of life-learning were granted to me also. And my beautiful daughter. Yet, I lost her to an evil man for many years. And those years are lost, Lãfa. Gone. We can only rebuild from shattered remnants and with a love so strong, so sacred, a better life is born.

"We are, us women, all of us, Sophia Invictus. The Great Feminine creative soul of our world. Our ancient forefathers knew this wisdom and strived to nurture and guard it well. And against the evil Ahriman all Zoroastrians live good thoughts, good deeds and right action. When I entered the Zoroastrian Temple of the Eternal Flame in Bukhara, I had to prove myself worthy to the Magi there. He was distant and incorruptible. I was a young rebel of a wayward girl. So, I prayed, constantly. As I cleaned the Τουαλέτες. He saw my soul and gave me a chance. He did not return me to my palace.

"This action has led me here, to you, with your *Mōdor* at your side now," Kiana leant forward to hold Lāfa's hand as tears gently fell to water the *Kornmjölsgot* that lay on her lap.

"Lāfa, can I ask you," Kiana continued, aware that Dagrun was sending intense energy towards her. What needed to be shared was important to her, "Does your faith believe in returning souls to live another life, a new life?"

Lāfa, looking down at her porridge so intensely, Kiana thought she might be looking for the answer within the thick mass of vegetables and barley.

"*Nã*," came the quiet reply, almost a whisper.

"Your *Mōdor* is here with you now. She has not died. Her spirit lives on. And she wants you to know this very much."

Lāfa suddenly raised her head, eyes glistening with fresh tears. She was looking beyond herself, her solar, trying to "see" her *Mōdor*. She looked down at her bulging belly.

"Ahh," she suddenly expelled a deep sigh, "I can feel a weight on my belly! Just like my *Mōdor* did at the very end. She knew I was pregnant, without me saying a word!"

"*Giese!*" Kiana replied with the only Suevii word she had learnt, "She is saying to you, "please know I am and will be close to you." Her soul has entered your daughter. Please to call your new child, Dagrun. She will be as powerful in *drycræft* as your mother was! It will be needed in the future time."

For the first time since the *Deaō-gerihte* Lāfa smiled, her body relaxed, the extreme tension that had overtaken her, left with the spiralling smoke, snaking upwards to the smoke hole and beyond. And with release came a cry of joy.

"The quickening," she exclaimed, "I felt her move, my little Dagrun, a sweet butterfly skittered across my belly."

"Cybele be praised," Kiana exclaimed, reaching over to place her hand on Lãfa, to feel the new life that had suddenly sprung into action. And to hear the quiet chuckle of Dagrun Wahl, settling into her role as guardian, invisible in the apparent world, but apparent to those with sight.

"Your dear *Mōdor* taught you the wisdom of the stones," Kiana leant back in her high-backed chair settling in, hugging her sheep blanket, to share the arcane wisdom, slowly, gently and one piece at a time.

"In our world, in the ancient times when Gods were busy making the world and its firmament, us mortals looked up to the heavens. We barely saw the earth as a living Goddess, the way you do...Until Zoroaster, the messenger God from Ahura Mazda taught us to worship the earth equally. He is the God I follow, Lãfa.

"And the word firmament is encoded. Like a *drycræft* in your language. We have three gods who live there in the firmament, the heavens. These new Christians have borrowed from our faith to name theirs, Father, Son and Holy Ghost. It happens. The Romans are masters at stealing from others to make their own version of reality!

"Abrasax, this God is the most ancient. He has dominion over the 360 interconnecting heavens, and is within us also, as we have 360 bones to our physical body connecting us, divinely so, to those heavens. With him is Sophia, the creator Goddess of all.

"Lãfa, beautiful woman, one important lesson that was given to me, on my journey from the East to be here with you, is whatever name we give to our Goddess, whatever power we may place upon her to do our will, the pure essence of Her is within us, immutable, incorruptible. And it is to that we must join, always.

"I worshipped Hecate, another name for Sophia, in my cruellest times, I called upon Her in her dark aspect to help me, to sustain me in anger, against the cruelty laid upon me from my master.

"It proved enough. But when I was freed, she became Diana, the goddess of love, or the Roman Venus. When we entered the magnificent Pessinus, she became Cybele, the whole city is dedicated to Her.

"And here, on Wihtland, she is Nerthus."

Lãfa sat, half turned in her chair. Her hand laid upon her unborn daughter, transfixed, with barely a blink of her eyes, soaking in Kiana's words, the images playing across her mind.

"How was it discovered, learnt, that there are 360 worlds in this *drycræft* firmament, and we have 360 bones in our physical body?" Lãfa asked, as she looked down, stroking her baby, and the miracle of creation came upon her in a murmured gasp of astonishment.

"Ahh," replied Kiana gently, reaching back to her treasured memories in the East. They wrenched her heart sideways, and she had to pull herself back to this cold wretched place. Was this really her punishment?

"Ancient scholars, generation upon generation studied the mysteries, both spiritual and mundane, in the Agoras across the eastern world. Scrolls upon scrolls have been written in many languages for us to learn from. Our scholarly ancestors left a supremely deep knowledge and wisdom of the arcane laws, the path of our major planets, how they interact with us. The libraries of the east are a testament to humanity's skill."

"So, what of our Mother Earth?" Lãfa insisted, "where is all the knowledge of our Runes, our futhark, færies and tree spirits? Are they kept in your famous libraries?"

"That I cannot answer," Kiana replied, shaking her head, "It may be so now, as we meet with other cultures like yours. When I visited the Agora, as a young child, I would say not." Kiana felt a strong poking in her left shoulder, knowing full well Dagrun was requesting focus.

"Umm, shall we get back to our Ancient Ones? Ahura Mazda and Mithra sit side by side almost. They are twin sun Gods, Gods of the light. Zoroaster became the Avatar, or messenger on earth for Ahura Mazda. The eternal flame is kept alive for him. And Zoroaster is akin to your nature Gods and Goddesses, as he protects Mother Earth.

"Yet it is with Mithra that the confusion, the spiritual devastation occurred and led to a "freezing" of the soul. Our lives are governed, led by the Gods' telling and we always believe their wisdom to be inviolate. Well that wisdom was sorely challenged many moons ago."

Kiana paused to collect her thoughts. She needed to create a joining of the eastern and western religions. Dagrun was showing her the leaning stone, which she had never visited, but knew this was of importance. Suddenly a realisation sped to the front of her mind. She saw in all its beauty, the treasure stone cast down from heavens, from Cybele to her people in Pessinus.

"Lãfa, your *Mōdor* showed you the teachings and *drycræft* of the stones. She is asking you to connect with the leaning stone again, before it becomes defamed, spoilt."

"*Hwæt!*" Lãfa cried, horrified at the thought.

"Your *Mōdor* sees all," Kiana replied, "she is so much more powerful now, Lãfa. She is trying to reach you. You will find each other again at the leaning stone.

"It is the power of the stone that connects us all. It is the recorder of events and lives in our apparent world. It holds ancient wisdom from past teachers and wise men. And our Ancestors believed stone to be truly sacred.

"Our god Ahura Mazda created the heavens from stone. Stones fell as great gifts to our earth for people to hold as precious, like the stone gifted from Cybele herself. They built a temple around it in Pessinus. To have a sacred stone here on Wihtland makes this island sacred. It is why the damned Romans are here to exploit it. They created Mithras the bull-slayer from our gentle and kind god Mithra.

"They created a reason. Some learned Magi had visions which showed the heavens, the milky way, as changeable, not made of stone at all! And this brought spiritual chaos to the minds and hearts of many people in the East. To overcome this, they made

Mithras as a bull slayer, the bloodshed in the constellation of Taurus the Bull, thus making a pathway to eternal life for humanity."

"Magi?" Lãfa questioned, "Is that your name for our *Halíg Monna?"*

"Holy man," Kiana offered, "Yes I mean *Gíese"*

They both sat silently, watching the fire spark, then dwindle to glowing, creating intricate fire-reading shapes. They both became entranced with the playful fire-spirits. It was myopic and Kiana felt her lids close into sleep. She gratefully succumbed, her body needing repair. Lãfa stayed awake. She stared into the fire, committing this new knowledge to memory and to her soul, for deep within her heart, she knew it held the key for her to be ever closer to her *Mõdor.*

Kiana suddenly shifted her body, and the sheepskin cover fell to the floor. Her eyes sprang open wide, training from her warrior days, instinct kicking in. She looked over to Lãfa, who was staring at her in surprise.

"Do you have *thermæ balneæ*?" she asked softly, seeing Lãfa's confused expression, "Hot baths."

"*Nã,*" she replied, slightly stiffening in response to the request. "We do not want *ãwuht* from the Romans. Not a thing. We walk the other way! They are hurting and ruining our *Folde Mõdor.* Why in Nerthus' name should we want to copy them?"

"Indeed no," Kiana agreed, "But you must know my blood is so different from yours. You Warinni giants, you just don't feel this cold, do you?"

"The men are down at the *Dūn botms* now, breaking the ice to gather water for heating. And you are right. We do not feel the cold." Lãfa replied, smiling apologetically.

Kiana heaved herself upright, gathering her now third skin about her.

"I need to go and warm my blood and my bones before I freeze to death. I am so sorry. I will return. We need to visit your leaning *Hãlig Stãn* as soon as this weather breaks."

"*Iuppiter igne Villam* is close, just beyond the line of trees past *Lãfa Dũn*. Eyvindr will be there," Lãfa smiled at hearing her name spoken, given by her *Fæder*, Eileifer. She never tired of hearing it. Remembering the day, with Sunni blessing them in full light, the overpowering perfume of the yellow gorse flowers, and her *Mõdor* and *Fæder* each holding her up as they swung her, chanting the name, so she may never forget. She never did.

Lãfa leant forward to build up the flagging fire, as if the growing heat might keep this wise woman here, with her. She so badly needed this link to her *Mõdor*.

Kiana turned to look back. Lãfa had a glow about her, and it was not just from the fire's glow. This was much more. An ephemeral white light surrounded her entire body. And she knew Dagrun Wahl had come, to guard her daughter, to protect her and her granddaughter until the birthing. She would not leave for Neorxenawang until then. She had chosen to be earth-bound. Kiana suddenly felt tears rise. The instincts of a mother transcend death. She pledged silently to Dagrun Wahl that she would do all in her power to gift Lãfa with the "sight".

"Lãfa," she called out, "There is no death, my dear. Your mother is saying, "there is just a change of energy.""

... ...

Kiana found Eyvindr, scroll and stylus in hand, scribbling notes in some frustration. Cæna and Cahal stood patiently behind him, hands behind their backs, waiting for the inevitable explosion. Eyvindr had morphed into Aelius, the Roman manager. The boys had got used to this transformation more than Eyvindr ever had. They found it hilarious. Kiana swore she saw Cæna's shoulders shake, and Cahal had sucked in his cheeks.

They were all standing at the entrance to the Mithræum plainly seeing half-finished frescoes and a shabby plinth supporting the God in all his sculpted finery.

"Genae oculique Iunonis iniquae? Quid video tamen ineptitudinem, vel inertiam, malis operibus. Postume, quid ego video? Et furor meus super hoc habent verbero? Et si non vult non facit? Ut me ad artifices et nunc est artifex?

"By Juno's eyeballs! What do I see but incompetence, laziness, bad workmanship? What will Postumus see? He will have a whipping frenzy over this! And if he does not, I will!

Get me the craftsmen and artists NOW!"

Kiana stood back watching Eyvindr struggle with himself. All was not well. She stepped quietly forward to whisper in Cahal's ear,

"Hey, son of Eyvindr, please take me to see Vrittakos before I change into the dark aspect of Hecate Herself and blow you all away!"

Cahal let out a supressed guffaw and pulled Kiana with him, away from the drama, leaving Cæna to deal with it.

Kiana padded as softly as she could, along the *ala*, still wearing the bathing sandals that clacked with every footfall. She observed the recent décor. So recent the whole interior smelt damp. The frescoes, all brightly painted held pigment that was still drying, and she resisted the urge to put her finger to the idolised paintings of nymphs in erotic postures.

All this, for the errant usurper, Postumus.

After much searching around *Iuppiter igne Villam*, she discovered Vrittakos in the *culina*. By any measure the warmest room in the whole villa. He was no man's fool.

"Kiana, my dear!" he exclaimed, leaping up from his seat, wiping his mouth with the back of his hand, then down his woollen tunica, swallowing hard on a large lump of meat. He smelt of damp wool and mutton. Kiana had become very fond of this ebullient Greek for she knew him to be utterly loyal and honest. Rare qualities in these times most certainly.

"And to what do we owe the pleasure, my dear," he asked, as he leant over for more mutton, "please do take some hot food. Have you warmed up enough now? The hall at *Lãfa Dūn* is only habitable in summer. These Warinni are a hardy people."

"Yes, thank you. The *Balneæ* was steamy and hot. Very welcoming to these frozen bones," Kiana replied, relaxing for the first time in these turbulent days in Britannia. To add to it, Achaikos had been rather indifferent towards her, more distant than she had ever known. There were raging waters surging beneath that calm Magi exterior. But her attention and purpose of meeting with Vrittakos, was for Eyvindr.

"Vrittakos," she turned to hold his gaze, "You are, at your own admission, the guardian of Eyvindr, are you not?"

"Φυσικά, απ ' την καρδιά μου, είναι σαν γιος μου!

"Absolutely, from my heart, he is like a son to me!"

"Then you must assist him now," Kiana continued, "he is tearing his soul in two! The pretence of being *Romanesque* is wearing thin. He is not happy in his skin, Vrittakos. He is about to commit wholly and completely to the strictures and total obedience of the God Mithras.

"The level of Leo, as you know, gifts hidden knowledge, high magic to the initiate. They become Magi. You are Corvus and have seen, as you serve and observe, quietly taking it all in!"

Vrittakos arched his back at this, "And how may I ask does a female come to know the secrets of the Mithræum?"

"I am a high priestess to Ahura Mazda," Kiana replied, shifting in her seat as her special privileges were known to very few, "and as Ahura Mazda sits with Mithra, in our world, some of the teachings were given to me in trust.

"I tell you," she went on insisting Vrittakos listened, "Eyvindr is struggling. His soul-deep love for the Earth, for Nerthus, is being weakened, in his eyes, by the commitment to forever look heavenward, to live in the cosmos, the Milky Way which is our path of renewal and redemption."

Vrittakos remained silent looking to the ground, shuffling his sandals in the compacted dirt of the *culina*. The earth, he thought, the life of Eyvindr, pulled away to walk in two worlds as a lost soul might.

"Why could he remain at peace in the Nymphus grade?" Vrittakos replied heatedly, "It is the sacred choir he enjoyed. He is a natural performer and the gentle reflective nature of the rituals suited him entirely. As close to Nerthus as a Mithras initiate could get, in my opinion!" He shook his head, grey matted curls bouncing.

"Because he is showing his love for you in the only way he can," Kiana retorted, forcefully, "do you think this love you hold so dear is one-sided?

"Do you think it is just duty that Eyvindr will force himself to stand beside the *venenatus spuo* that is Postumus? And how vulnerable it will be for him. Honoratianus, "The Shade" will see through his façade. It will end badly," Kiana stated.

"Eyvindr's dark history will follow him into the Mithræum," Vrittakos muttered, almost to himself, "I will take him aside, today."

"At least pull him out of his management duties," Kiana replied, smoothing out her full-weight woollen tunica and wrapping more warm layers of *stola* around her, "He is driving everyone crazy! And his son is choking up with laughter because his *fæder* is being ludicrous! Tell him to visit the Ancestor circle. Dagrun is waiting to console him."

"*Dagrun!*" Vrittakos cried, "but we have only just finished cremating her!"

"She is still with us, old man," Kiana laughed, "you know there is no death. And tell Eyvindr that also, from me!"

As Kiana turned to leave, she turned, reflectively, looking strangely at Vrittakos, "You know Mithras and this Christ could be twins. Both were born on the same day and both are honoured in ritual in very similar ways. Their stories overlap. We humans make of our Gods what we will! Tell Eyvindr to go with his heart."

… … … … … … … … …

Chapter 49

Postumus et al.

Postumus stood, *birrus Britannicus* billowing in the gusty wind that had brought them all in racing time to the landing stage at *Point Aegypti*. He absorbed all aspects, eying the large villam a few metres away in critical fashion. Principally because no one had come to greet their Emperor. Not a single islander. The party of eager and nervous initiates were disembarking in a cackle of mannish wisecracks. Their cloaks flapped noisily in the winter wind. The freezing numbness of the snow had gone, leaving sludge and rivulets of dirty snow everywhere.

Postumus reached up and rammed his crown further into his bushy hair.

"*Et canetis buccina!* Sound the horn!" he bellowed. Muffled cries came from the *trireme* as the long, heavy *buccina* was lifted to frozen lips. By the third blow, even the landing stage vibrated with a deep resonance. Postumus and Honoratianus fixed intense stares at the villam, as figures began to emerge, scurrying like worker-ants disturbed from sleep.

Vrittakos with Octavious, who had elected to join the host group, both strode out of the opulent entrance to formally greet the Emperor. Vrittakos nearly reached the sludge with his greying locks as he bowed deeply to Postumus.

"Our deepest apologies to you, Emperor Postumus, pontifex Maximus. We have prepared everything for your visit. All is ready. We did not imagine the winds would bring you here so very fast!"

"Shame on you, Vrittakos!" Honoratianus sniped, "you! A seasoned islander surrounded by the sea cannot commune with Neptune to discover his will!"

Postumus let out a long chuckle. "Come, I am in good cheer. And am I not looking at an impressive façade for a such a little island!"

Sol rex villam was built in dedication to the older Egyptian Sun God, ancestor to Mithras himself. It was indeed impressive as they walked casually towards the front entrance, guarded by two tall grey marble statues of Anubis, twinned and regal. Postumus brushed a hairy hand along the box trees, sculpted and immaculate. He stopped at two effigies in trimmed green leaves of the two Anubis statues, and nodded in appreciation.

As they stepped inside, they all shed their cloaks, now soaked to knee level, to waiting slaves who vanished noiselessly into the depths of the villa. Octavious, who held the highest Mithraic level of Pater immediately stepped forward to take charge of the group of men. They were all different degrees of initiation, and his role was to guide them, instruct and support them in the forthcoming days of travel, ceremony and celebration.

Vrittakos, joined by Achaikos, Censorinus and Libertus, guided the Emperor, with his detestable "shadow", away from the main group towards the state apartments along the northern *ala*. All these *cubiculums* looked out to sea.

Postumus settled his ample body in the chair closest to the brazier, dislodging the cumbersome *carbatinæ*, to reveal hairy, podgy feet that stank of weeks-old grime.

"Once a soldier, always a soldier," Achaikos thought.

"I understand you have a Briton native, a *Romanesque* awaiting the death and rebirth of Leo, like myself," Postumus said to no one in particular, gazing into the hot coals of the brazier.

Vrittakos' heart missed two beats before he felt his voice return.

"Yes, we do, my adopted son." He said, for the first time in anyone's hearing. It felt wonderful, a warm glow reaching his old heart. "He is solely responsible for the décor you see around you. A talented young man."

"I wish to meet him. Now if you please," Postumus reached for a stuffed date and a cup of red wine.

Vrittakos swished out of the *cubiculum*, his hardened leather sandals impacting on the mosaiced floor. He hadn't noticed the décor. Hadn't taken in the artistry bestowed on this showpiece villam until now. Eyvindr had superb skill. The interior was a wonderful blend of colours, favoured by the Pharaohs. The vibrant blue oscillated everywhere interfacing with gold and shots of earth red.

Just that combination of hues gave the whole villam a rich tone, coupled with the simple mosaic-patterned floors and *ala*. Vrittakos made a mental note to find Eyvindr's source for those pigments.

He found Eyvindr, as Aelius, fringe battened down tight on his forehead, in with the group of initiates. Octavious was hovering like a mother hen with her clutch.

"Postumus wishes to see Aelius," Vrittakos stated, the tension in his voice so apparent, Octavious nearly squealed with apprehension.

Aelius walked over on hearing his name, and looked from one worried face to the other, catching the intention without another word being spoken.

Ita sit! So be it, "he said, resignation sounding in his voice, thinking how it would always come to this. His fate was determined the day he knocked the general into next week and furthermore inflicted serious injury to the centurion, Gallus.

Aelius bowed low and stayed there until Postumus spoke. He was after all not quite a *libertus*, still a slave.

"My compliments to you, *Romanesque*, your skill is apparent and very welcoming," Postumus turned as he spoke and motioned for Aelius to rise. "Tell me, where did you learn your skill? For a native, it is impressive"

"In Cantwara and here at Berandinzium Villam, Emperor Augustus," Aelius replied, holding his breath, waiting for the rebuttal that was sure to come. It didn't.

"You are an émigré, then?" Postumus went on, "Not a Durotrige. Are you a Suevii?"

"*Giese,*" Aelius replied in his native tongue, before his brain could halt him.

"HaH!!!" exclaimed Postumus, speaking in his native tongue, "*Đonne wè are cynn, þu und Ic! Und Ic blíðemod und giefan mín lèaf æt Gewadan wiþ mè in þæt Mithræum.*"

The twin expressions of Vrittakos and Octavious, holding open-mouthed astonishment, and were frozen in a moment of time that stood still.

"And I know your history, young man," Postumus continuing, now smiling broadly, showing cracked and broken teeth from years of misuse and much hand-to-hand fighting, "You were never a penis-sucker, or a bumboy and you proved it, twice. My army is riddled with all it. Like a plague of locusts. No women you see."

Aelius audibly expelled a breath of relief.

"I will issue your *libertus* papers before I leave. You will be a free man, Aelius. You have my word on it."

... ...

Chapter 50

"We humans make of our Gods what we will!
Go with your heart."

The following day dawned with Sunni gifting some warmth to the winter's morning. The line of covered wagons, four in all, had been made ready days before, but saw a flurry of slaves freshening up the interiors, plumping up cushions and laying heated bricks underneath. Equerries fussed over their mounts. All were stallions of pure pedigree. They were journeying to the far south of Vecta. The vineyard and the home of Bacchus.

Aelius had been a temporary overseer for the improvements to the run-down *villam*. And a new authoritative figure had emerged to join him and beat some sense into the lackadaisical staff of the place. Too much wine being consumed, was the verdict. It was banned and one hundred lashes kept the workers sober.

And now he stood, quite aimlessly looking on, from the porch entrance, hugging his *birrus* about him, against the prevailing gusts that carried a punch to the gut, despite Sunni's embrace.

The young men destined for their first initiation huddled together by the waiting wagon, oxen already harnessed up, kicking mud and softly bellowing vaporous steam. Octavious as Pater and guardian, who was meant to oversee their journey with last-minute preparations, walked past them, much to their astonishment and then annoyance. He made straight for Aelius.

"Young man, you will come with me," Octavious ordered sharply, supporting Aelius with a firm grip on his elbow.

"Have you communed with your near Ancestor Dagrun lately?"

Aelius turned sharply, with an accusing expression that plainly said, what business is it of yours?!

"*Giese*," he replied after a pause, "we are in accord, in principle. But it will not reach to my heart, let alone my soul. She knows this. She remains close."

Both men clipped their speech through clamped lips. The cold was returning with a vengeance. They climbed into the stately wagon, fitted out for an emperor. Postumus had absented himself in favour of a hot brazier where he could roast his hairy knees to second-degree burns.

Octavious slammed the heavy wooden door shut and settled into the warming cushions.

"You refuse to open your soul to Mithra because you fear betrayal of your goddess Nerthus and all you hold dear," Octavious stated, pinning Aelius with an ice-hard stare as cold as the winter outside, and which denied any reply.

"Listen and do not interrupt me in any way," he continued, "I am breaking strict protocol. I am giving you the initiation instructions for Leo ahead of your time. Then, and only then, when you have assimilated all into your heart, you are free to choose. Deny or accept. Each must be done willingly."

The wagon suddenly lurched forward into a gyrating motion of heavy wheels hitting deep ruts, the curtains swaying, and the wagon groaning. They were on their way. It would take several hours and Octavious knew those hours to be precious for Aelius.

"In this Mithraic level of Leo, you will experience your death, Aelius. Make no assumptions about it, enter with no expectations whatsoever, and submit willingly. Your death, if done courageously, will engender your rebirth. Again, make no assumptions about how that will occur.

"You will endure the extremes of heat and then of cold. It is the end of your world. *Ragnarök* in your spiritual way. You will be as *Wōden* hanging from *Yggdrasil*, the Tree of Life.

"You see, your faith-way is not so different from our own. The Romans have adapted, stolen, changed whatever they feel. But essentially, we are all interconnected to the great God of all creation.

"Your rebirth, just like that of *Wōden,* will entrust you with magic. Pure ancient alchemy our ancestors have kept intact. You will see the cosmos as never before. You will understand the relationships of our planets to us, because we humans have sacred knowledge embedded into our very being."

Aelius suddenly felt a heavy pressure on his shoulder, looking round, seeing no one there. He knew absolutely that his sister was with him. He began to relax and be more open to what Octavious was teaching him.

"Firstly, I have decided to share the gnostic secrets now being given to your niece, Lãfa by the Zoroastrian priestess, Kiana, on the behest of Dagrun herself. They are very important and may help you to decide.

"Our Eastern ancestors always looked to the heavens, the stars and constellations, named them, came to revere them. Your northern ancestors, by contrast looked to the earth, as mother and guardian to humanity. Your Gods and Goddesses have an earthly connection. Except of course for Sunni and Mōnã.

"Now, Aelius, more than ever, it has become necessary to seek a union with both heaven and earth. And it is the Romans who are to blame for this present crisis.

"I am Roman by birth and blood, and I am ashamed. Their carnage to the earth and disrespect stretches back to the time of the original Gods who, on seeing the damage, called down Avatars to represent them and become teachers and leaders.

"Zoroaster, the young god from Ahura Mazda is one such, and a powerful message he brings to care with compassion, the waters of our earth. Kiana is his disciple. The eternal flame is his very presence, and in constant attendance by worshippers. It is never extinguished.

"We now turn our attention to the crux of your dilemma, Aelius. The God Mithras, the bull-slayer.

Aelius lurched forward to glare into the impassive face of the Pater, Octavious, who, on his own admission had just slated the Romans openly.

"With respect, Pater," Aelius retorted icily, "My name is Eyvindr. I am a Warinni of the Wihtwara peoples. I was taken prisoner, made a slave, forced to work in terrible conditions. I have been whipped, beaten and attacked! I want my *Libertus*, in written script on a scroll with signature and seal! That is *my* dilemma, sir." Eyvindr smashed back against the wooden side of the wagon, which groaned almost as loud as he did. He winced and put a cushion against his back, still tender against any kind of attack. He stared silently out to the meandering countryside. The oxen had settled into a snail's pace. There was no escape.

"So," Octavious shot back without a second's delay, leaning forward to get Aelius's attention, "You are a performer. It is your natural trait, is it not? And you are exceptionally good at it, so I've been informed. That being so, why did you not remain at *Sacrum Nymphus, chorum Villam* with the choir, singing and in the quiet refection of the Nymphus grade of initiation? I would like to know the truthful answer before I can discuss any more with you!"

Eyvindr continued to stare out over his beloved Wihtland, tall trees forging a union in dance with the ferocious wind. And that wind spoke to him in a truth he could not deny.

"Pure anger," he replied, at last looking at his mentor, "Intense, incurable fury."

"So, do you intend bringing this fury with you to the Mithræum on your initiation day? Are you planning to attack Postumus with your thunderbolt or your sacred key?"

"What thunderbolt, what sacred key?" Eyvindr shot back.

"That would be seriously jeopardizing your *Libertus*," Octavious continued, ignoring Aelius's outburst, "seeing as Postumus has promised, literally given his word, that you will be a freeman by this time next week!

"Be contained young man, patience has its rewards.

"Do you wish me to continue, Aelius," Octavious asked, insisting on using his Roman name, "Trust me, this is truly your last lap around the Hippodrome."

"*Giese, gecwèman*," Aelius replied quietly in his native tongue, then returning to Latin, "*Etian commodo.*"

"I will explain the birth of Mithras, and his growth to become a Sun god. He now sits with Sol, in an alliance, they are twinned by consent. Never a more powerful union has ever taken place before or since.

"Humanity believed to its very soul that the heavens were created by Ahura Mazda, who sits with Abrasax and Sophia as co-creators of the heavens and of earth. And that he made the constellations and the milky way of stone, immutable, ever-permanent stone.

"The stones that fell to earth from the night-sky were proof and seen as gifts to humanity from the gods. How else could such a miracle be?

"One day, this whole belief came crashing down around the ears and souls of many people in the East. Magi, several of them, all had the same visions, independent of each other. They were shown moving constellations, shifting in the night sky. The equinoxes that heralded these stars moved also and were not permanent at all.

"Belief became fluid as a result. Disbelief became prevalent and the inevitable encroachment of the angry spirit, Angra Mainyu, into people's consciousness. Hostility grew among the peaceful tribes of the East."

Octavious paused for a moment, looking deep into Aelius, to see if his soul was shifting. An impassive face stared back. Not hostile, just listening.

"There can be no war, no hostility in your soul, Aelius. It gives Ahriman, the devil, free reign and dominion in your heart otherwise."

Aelius turned to gaze out to the countryside, swathes of bare trees buffeted by the angry wind. It was his choice entirely. To succumb to it or quell it with his own will. He turned to Octavious and rewarded with him with a smile, one that reached his eyes. Octavious let an audible sigh of relief escape into the warm air of the wagon. He had not realised just how tense he was. "How many troublesome initiates have I tutored, he thought, and why is this one so damn important?"

"Good," he said, "let us continue. Mithra, the eastern god was born out of a stone. So, it was seen that he came from the Gods.

He had a union with the stones, like your Nerthus and the War-inni, being guardian of the stones. There is a unity there with the Sun god, is there not, Aelius?"

Aelius looked shocked, then nodded in agreement.

"Now we are making progress," Octavious thought.

"Mithra even shot an arrow into a sacred stone and it gushed forth with life-giving water. "When the sacred stone weeps" Aelius, I believe is in your teachings is it not?"

Another approving nod, though Aelius elected not to comment. He had been instructed to listen and since his outburst, he chose to do just that.

"So, Mithra was transmuted into Mithras the bull-slayer, a Roman construct. But it served the purpose of focusing many people to the idea of sacrifice and the rewards therein. Why a bull? The constellation of Taurus sits at the one end of the Milky way, that represented the celestial pathway of all souls. Souls being born, came in through the sign of Cancer and left through the sign of Capricorn. So, to give the blood of the bull to the heavens in sacrifice made a river and a road to eternity for all humanity."

"Our river of Wyrd. It is similar," murmured Aelius reflectively.

"Yes, I concur," Octavious replied, "now here is a fascinating addition to this discussion. Mithras was born on December 25st, witnessed by shepherds, and honoured with Magi presence, men carrying incense and gold. Is that not like this new Christ and his birthing? There were also other Avatars making their presence felt in the East. Paul of Tarsus became known as the Pagan Christ. A veritable melting pot of new ideas and visions.

"We will be celebrating the birth of Mithras on his day, with the sacred meal at Berandinzium Villam."

Octavious drew in a deep breath, for he had chosen to keep the white-bull sacrifice at the sacred leaning stone, a secret. "Just let him get his *Libertus*," he thought, regrettably knowing full well the torment Eyvindr would suffer for all his Wihtwara people, on that day.

"I have decided to give you, in advance of your initiation, the sacred magick to ensure your communion with the Gods. This is for you alone. My reasoning is this.

"The golden-scarab beetle, Aelius. It has chosen Wihtland to mate, create life. It comes each year, does it not, to your famed Ceofodūn? Why? Because the island is sacred. The constellation of Cygnus, the swan settles on your horizon. What a gift! The Dragon line, along which all the Mithræum villams are built in honour of the magical energy that holds this island amongst the most powerful on earth.

"And you are its guardian. You have seven days from now as the moon is dark, to complete the task.

"Take the sun-scarab beetle, which has twelve rays and make it fall into a deep turquoise cup, at a time when the moon is invisible. Put it in together with the seed of the lotometra, and honey, and after grinding it, prepare a cake. And at once you will see the scarab moving forward and eating and when it has consumed it, it immediately dies. Pick it up and throw it into a glass vessel of excellent rose oil; as much as you wish, and spreading sacred sand in a pure manner, set the vessel on it, and say the formula over the vessel for seven days, while the sun is in mid heaven:

"I have consecrated you, that your essence may be useful to me, to Aelius alone, *IE IA E EE OY EIA,* that you may prove useful to me alone. For I am *PHOR PHORA PHOS PHOTIZAAS, PHOR PHJOR OPHOTHEI XAAS*

"On the seventh day, pick up the scarab and bury it with Myrrh and wine and fine linen; and put it away in a flourishing bean field. Then after you have entertained and feasted together, put away, in a pure manner, the ointment for the immortalization. If you want to show this to someone else, take the juice of the herb called "kentritis," and smear it, along with rose oil, over the eyes of the one you wish: and he will see clearly that will amaze you. I have not found a greater spell than this in the world. Ask the god for what you want, and he will give it to you!"

"Now presentation before the great God is like this: obtaining the herb, kentritis, at the conjunction of the sun and moon occurring in the Lion, take the juice and after mixing it with honey and myrrh, write on a leaf of the persea tree, box will also be good, the eight-letter formula:

I EE OO IAI

"Keeping yourself pure three days before, set out early in the morning toward the East, and lick off the leaf while showing it to the Sun, and he, Sol/Mithras, will listen to you attentively. Begin to consecrate this at the divine new moon in the Lion."

Octavious handed a leather bag, tied tightly, to Aelius, who took it gingerly, still feeling completely overwhelmed by the depth of these sacred instructions.

"You say, for me alone," he said, "Does this exclude Postumus?"

"Absolutely!" Octavious replied quickly, "And you must not feel bound to share it with him, should he ask. I have decided to mentor him. I was going to leave him to his own devices. But no! I want to see you a freed man, Aelius. Postumus needs great assistance just to progress down the aisle of the Mithræum. His soul is fractured by his own greed for power. This will visit him upon his spiritual death. Be sure of that. How he responds and emerges from the trial is quite crucial to your future wellbeing."

Aelius leaned forward to grasp his mentor, arm to arm, in a mark of respect, then settled back to see they had progressed along the Roman path to scale the heights of the dūn, showing at last the roof tops of *Mercuri vulpes corvum videt villam*.

… … … … … … … … …

Chapter 51

Mercuri vulpes corvum videt villam
Mercury's raven villam

The young men had arrived at the raven villam. Seven new initiates in all, given leave to wear Persian-style trousers in honour of Mithra, several layers of close-woven woollen undergarments and a thicker tunica tied at the waist. Their *birrus Britannicus* billowed in the gusty west-wind. Their hobnailed *calceas* made a sludgy mess of the furrowed lane between the sleeping vines.

There were no vine workers to gawp and stare. The Warinni and the Durotrige were safely ensconced at home, hugging fires and cooking stews. The only welcome for these men was the biting island wind.

Despite their clothing, they stood in a huddle, hopping and cursing in Latin until an overseer emerged to guide them to the *atrium*, where Octavious and Aelius stood together, looking most severe.

"*Receperint Mercurio villam vulpes corvum videt. Corax Mille tui initiation incipit nunc*

Welcome to Mercury's raven villam. Your initiation to Corax begins now." Octavious generated a booming voice of total authority.

"There is to be total silence from now," he bellowed, "you will not talk to your companion, even if he is your closest friend!

"Remove negative thoughts, lustful thoughts and jealous thoughts from your mind, think only of the eternal Light of Mithras and that the God is looking down upon you all!"

There were speculative nods amongst several of the young men, just boys really, in years. The remainder, of which Aelius made a strong mental note, looked shocked and shifted uneasily. Uncomfortable with the coming ceremony.

"You will all follow me," he said, hoping to sound as authoritative as the Pater, "the Mithræum is a cave two *míllia* from here." Aelius walked out, and felt a needle of anger on his back, burrowing into his spine. One of these boys is an antagonist, he thought, but which one? The winding path down to the beach was worn clear by the salt-workers, whose days never ended. It was the one product the Romans paid good *denarii* for. The youth trundled along behind Aelius, in serpent style. The beach was windblown, the sand wet from a tide just receding. The strong west wind brought floating sprays of foam to land on the boys. The sea was roiling, the surf bubbling with energy, its whiteness almost blinding in the midday sun.

The cave was hidden and almost indistinguishable within the rock face. A mere sliver of an opening that a man could squeeze through sideways. Corax was designed for young soldiers. Octavious was already inside, in ritual clothes and a fire blazing at the end of a makeshift aisle. Benches either side were of rough-hewn wood. And the frescoes, freshly painted, smelt of pigment and egg white. Crude in their application, they nonetheless honoured the constellations, and the zodiac. Mithras with Sol stood as sculptures on plinths, gazing at each other with regal expression, either side of the fire. But several of the youth were intensely unimpressed and showed it. Aelius made a slight nod towards the difficult group and Octavious picked it up.

"Initiates be seated," Octavious called, "the ceremony begins.

"Mithras O great God of Light with Sol, Sun God, look upon these new initiates with kindness and give them strength to pursue the Divine practice to reach attainment." The pater reached inside a bag to extract incense and herbs and threw them on the fire.

"Now stand initiates", he commanded "and come forth each in turn to receive the rewards of your diligence and humility.

"Coracem *sub tutela Mercurii laborasti His datum suum nosse. Vos accepit certamen contra tenebras apud te et suscitabuntur lacerantes te, et in luce, in doctrina moralis ex humilitate*

"Corax, under the tutelage of Mercury, you have laboured well to understand these lessons given to you. You have accepted the struggle against darkness in yourself, to awaken to the Light within you, by the moral lesson of humility"

Octavious reached over to take a caduceus, delicately crafted and painted, the serpents twinned and circling up the wooden stem. It was received with humility, head bowed, by the first initiate, who had excelled on the battlefield by caring for his injured friend. The cup followed, which he held in his left land. Now the raven mask appeared, beak protruding from layers of feathers fixed onto hardened papyrus lacquer, the bird-features shaped and moulded.

The boy held his head down, as Octavious placed it carefully to entirely eclipse his face and hair.

"*Mercuri vulpes corvum videt propinquam praecinit; salutant!*

Mercury's raven is born. Salute!"

The young men, waiting their turn banged the benches in a raucous salute. Egos now suitably inflated, the energy within the cave expanded and became vibrantly masculine. They strode forward now, each in turn to receive their honouring. Aelius stood to one side assisting Octavious in placing the totems within the gaze of the God.

And it was then, in a pure second of intense awareness, that his heart froze. Looking at him, with a hatred so intense, sending a knife to his heart, stood his tormentor, Gallus. Those pale ice-blue eyes were boring into his soul. Aelius felt his knees crumple. Recognition met with confusion. It could not possibly *be* him! Yet there he was. Could Gallus have a twin?

He was next to last. He stood and strode forward, the same easy, almost graceful walk, those shoulders, one higher, in that arrogant pose. His head was bowed and the long lashes hiding his intent, made Aelius's heart palpitate. He felt Octavious stiffen slightly. He hoped he had not given any fear away.

At last, the final initiate accepted his honouring and the ceremony ended. Aelius watched as they filed out, squeezing through the rock slit with all their impediments causing raucous laughter and rude jokes. The tension wafted away with the sun-white receding surf. Sol and Mithras wrapped their new adherents to them.

Aelius stood immobile, the frozen expression giving nothing away, and yet everything.

"What is troubling you?" Octavious peered into those inscrutable eyes.

"Nothing, no it is nothing Octavious," Aelius replied, giving him as warm a smile as he could manage.

"Good, my young friend. You did well, very well.

"I relieve you of all your duties, Aelius. Go and meditate, learn, assimilate. Come back to me in a week hence. You are required to attend your current level of Miles along with Postumus. Then, we will see you become the adept you truly deserve in Leo."

Aelius walked away from his friend and mentor, out onto the beach, striding away from all of them, head bowed. He was unaware of the solitary figure shadowing his movements. The sand dulled all footfalls. The afternoon sun painted long shadows, as she slipped closer to the horizon.

The salt workers had left for a warm *hūs* and warmer stew. The salt ponds now abandoned, held an eerie feel. The wind ruffling the surface of the newly laid saltwater created a sound. Yet the firmer ponds that lay still, with deep salt-layers, were ominous.

Aelius suddenly felt a rush of wind behind him, and the blow to the back of his head brought swirling lights, intense white and then red breaking into his vision, before disappearing. The overwhelming pain entered his fading consciousness as pure torture. Then, blackness entered from the side and grew, welcoming him to a respite.

His first awareness that he was not indeed totally dead, came with a mouthful of wet, gritty salt, as he tried to breathe, he choked hard on more salt entering his mouth and sliding down his burning throat. His attacker was forcing his head beneath the thick pond of salt. Pure survival instinct kicked in with empowered muscles beating the air and his assailant. It continued relentlessly until Aelius weakened and he felt life slipping away from him.

As suddenly as he was struck, he was yanked out of the broiling mess. His attacker held Aelius by his tunica, as he heaved fresh air into his burning lungs. Then, he was dumped onto the ground, writhing in an agony not felt since the brutal attack on him by Gallus in the mausoleum.

"This is but a taste of things to come," came a deep voice full of fury, "I will avenge my brother. I will enjoy hearing you die!"

So! He is the twin of the brute Gallus, Aelius thought as he struggled to his knees. The disappearing shadow of the younger version of the sadist gave him little comfort. He dragged himself to his feet and made a striding, loping run up the pathway before anyone saw him and the dishevelled mess he was in. He desperately needed to hide. And the only place left to him was home. His real home. The Warinni village in Sudmōr.

... ...

Of course, all mothers know their own son's deepest agonies. It was not long before Gudrun teased the story from her son over warming barley stew and much love and tenderness from her and Folkvarthr. As for the son, Eyvindr felt Aelius slip away easily into the night. His twin was leaving, and for good. Like the dark shadow of that other "twin" it could not live in this *hūs*.

Eyvindr became easy in his own skin. The only jarring to this was the inevitable honouring ceremony, the respect he held for Vrittakos and above all the sharing of his decision with not just his step-father but his wife and family.

The following days mingled into each other, he was aware only of Mōnā's path, of Sunni and the planets he was linked to. Eyvindr made his magick, all according to Sacred Law. He did not intend to fall short on any level, knowing now, that he was separate and apart from it all, yet able to honour Mithras sincerely because he had stood back.

He visited Lāfa and Kiana and shared his feeling with them. Kiana was impressed. She told him he had expanded his vision, increased his wisdom all before he was given the hidden secret key to the cosmos!

Lastly, on the eve of his return to *Martiæ militibus villam*, Eyvindr walked in fading sunlight, to the Ancestor stone circle. Here, and only here, could he speak with Dagrun Wahl. Lāfa had given him the heron wing. He sat on the cold earth holding it before him. Sending silent prayers and waiting for *Ealdmōdor,* his beloved sister to come.

It was not until the crescent moon was shining high in the night sky, did the heron wing begin to flutter and tremble. Eyvindr hardly noticed, he was frozen solid. The night had become bitterly cold. A hazy white glow spread along the wing and surrounded him with a gentle warmth. With only pure thoughts conveyed, *Ealdmōdor* spoke; -

"*Mín ælfscíenu ellenrōf brōðor.*

"*Húmeta fæst þu āgan Geweorðan Eyvindr. Sōð wè are brōðor und sweostor!*

"*Ic am þurh þín healf hwæþer þín cunnan hit or ne. Wè bā faran midde burna in þæt èa fram Wyrd.*

"*Þu agan becuman hãm æt last...wítega, ðeorl und ǽnlic in þín geāscian.*

"*Mǽran!*

"*Þu āgan Nerthus und Mithras þín wynstra und þín swiðra.*

"My beautiful, courageous brother.

"How stubborn you have become Eyvindr. Truly we are brother and sister!

"I am by your side, always, whether you know it or not. We both travel mid-stream in the river of Wyrd.

"You have come home at last... a wise man stronger and unique in your learning. Celebrate!

"You have Nerthus and Mithras on your left and on your right."

Eyvindr felt warmth and profound love encircle him. He did not want to move. His eyelids drooped and he fell asleep. The first hint of dawn saw him wake up. He was not quite frozen yet was truly happy for the first times in years.

... ...

Chapter 52

Martiæ militibus Villam
Soldier of Mars Villam

Martiæ militibus villam was quite beautiful, pre-dawn, Eyvindr decided, head cocked to one side judging the surroundings, neat box trees, small and compact leading to the modest *Atrium*. The Mithræum was equally very modest. There was only one fresco painted on the end wall, above the altar. It illustrated the complex iconography surrounding Mithras, who, kneeling against the bull, its head pulled back, ready to feel the slash of the knife. It was Taurus, giving its life for humanity.

Or so the Romans would have us believe, Eyvindr thought. He shook his head and smiled, pushing that rebellious thought away. Eyvindr entered the Mithræum, memories flooding back of his initiation, which for him was so very difficult. He had only just returned from the punishments meted out by Gallus in Cantium. His life was fragile, emotions burning within him. His only escape was to bury himself into the training for this degree. And now like an evil spectre, it had returned to haunt him. He stared down at his right wrist which still bore the branding, remembering the intense pain, the sound of sizzling flesh and the smell.

He scanned the images of Scorpio, Canis minor, the dog, Hydra, the snake, Leo, the lion, Crator, the mixing bowl, the star spika and the wheat ear, surrounding Mithras and the bull, each carrying a wisdom and a teaching for the initiates.

And he had learnt, done his research well. He knew he was ready. The villam stood in the peaceful valley, close to *Iuppiter igne villam*, where in a short three days' time, he would be standing, buff-naked, waiting for his trial to begin. Eyvindr shook his head some more and sent a prayer to Nerthus to uphold him, to be the hidden strength for him. He found the old oak that had given him so much solace and care at his own initiation to Mars. He sat against the knarled bark now, gyrating his back against the friendly ridges, massaging away the tension and pain that was always present since the lashes had destroyed his skin.

He heard voices, getting louder, more raucous and defamatory of imperial Rome, and the senate. It was highly political, and it came as no surprise to see the famous flame-haired usurper Emperor right in the middle of the gaggle of older men. These were not youths. And Postumus was not dressed as an Emperor, nor did he act like one. Mithras equalled all men. Eyvindr felt a movement beside him, turning to see Octavious join him by the oak tree.

"I am having severe doubts about the efficacy of Postumus' spiritual focus ever reaching the desired level of worship," Octavious stated in a clipped tone, "Observing him now I am seeing his own end. His ego rules!"

"*Giese*," Eyvindr replied," Sir, I have created the magick, as you requested. All is in readiness. Can I ask, who will have the honour of going first, down the aisle for our initiation?" he nodded his head towards Postumus.

"Protocol requests Postumus defer to the younger, the slave, the more unfortunate. But unfortunely, knowing this Emperor's unpredictability, who knows, Aelius?"

"And may I suggest you keep your native tongue still, until we have a completion, young sir?

"Come let us get this particular ritual completed. You will be the server of totems and Postumus will bear the branding iron."

"Do any of these men know what is about happen?" Eyvindr asked.

"No! "he replied. "The *fraters* do not."

… … … … … … … … …

"*Nabarze, Nabarze, Nabarze!*" came the loud incantations to Mithras and the Gods. They were calling spiritual power to enter the tiny Mithræum. The door was bolted shut, and darkness prevailed, broken only by the two sconces holding a wavering light and the glow of the brazier standing alone and imposing by the *præsepia*. Postumus stood immobile by its side, and Eyvindr, placed to Octavius's left, chanted with passion, eyes closed, head raised to the heavens.

"*Et liberasti nos vivifici sanguinis effusione æternitatis.*

"And us have you saved by shedding the eternity-giving blood."

Eyvindr opened his eyes briefly, chanting with a wide smile, as he nodded to his stepfather, Vrittakos, who had come as a Corvus to assist in the aftermath of the branding.

"*Nama, Nama Nama, Mithras, deus genitor rupe natus.*

"Holy Mithras, the God born from the rock."

The chanting continued until the resonance vibrated around the Mithræum. Each *frater* in turn, came forward to receive the laurel wreath, which they ceremoniously flicked off with their hand. Eyvindr picked up the deposed crown and listened while the devotee proclaimed Mithras alone to be victorious. It was then placed on his shoulder.

Vrittakos deftly moved forward to hold and support the *frater* as his right hand was extended towards the brazier, with Postumus jiggling the branding iron in the white-hot coals, a look of amused detachment on his face. Vrittakos' face went into an intense scowl.

The man began to struggle, the chanting faltered as all realised what was about to happen to all of them.

"*Nabarze, Nabarze, Nabarze,*" Octavious bellowed.

The iron struck flesh, sizzling white agony was expressed in high-pitched screams, as Vrittakos held the *frater* up with an arm lock round his chest, as his legs sagged from under him. He was led away, as another man took his place by the *præsepia*.

And so, it continued, seemingly for eternity itself. Mithras was honoured, the bruised egos limping away to be fed with amphorae of island wine, bluster and bawdy jokes both drowning the pain.

Eyvindr felt utterly wasted and empty. He chose to wander home alone, following Sunni in her path to the underworld and waiting for Mōnā to appear to soothe his shattered emotions. This devotion to Mithras held no uplift for him, without the honouring of mother Earth, it was quite meaningless. He told Vrittakos he needed time alone in preparation, but the quizzical look that came upon his stepfather's face, begged the truth to be told. And it would, after the next trial.

Eyvindr found himself walking towards the leaning stone, *Halíg Stān*, up high, wind swirling around him, kindly taking all the negative feelings with it. Here, he felt completely free and at one with Nerthus.

Here was his home, his spirit and his soul dwelt here. Eyvindr sat down and gently cried and cried while the *Halíg Stān* wept with him.

… … … … … … … …

Chapter 53

Iuppiter igne Villam
Fire of Jupiter Villam

Eyvindr had checked and double-checked the arrangements and final fitting-out of the Mithræum at Jupiter Villam. He spent time looking over the intricate arrangement of pipes and heat vents attached to the "the tomb of death" as it was affectionately named. His own safe passage depended upon it. Satisfied, he left to make the meeting with Vrittakos and Octavious in that final cross-examination of intention and dedication. He had failed to notice the passing shadow of a figure skirt around the back of the Mithræum.

And now, as the day presented clear skies and crisp sunny air, the usurper Emperor, Postumus and the slave stood side by side, both dressed identically in the attire of a soldier of Mars, as if preparing for battle. The hardened-leather kilt and jerkin under armour would soon be ceremoniously thrown-off and discarded leaving the two men totally naked battling the cold, instead of a bloodthirsty enemy.

Both looked ahead, silently expelling clouds of breath that evaporated in the chilly air.

Suddenly without preamble, Postumus turned to Eyvindr, grinning widely. He lifted his right hand and turned it to show the slave his identical branding.

"We are equal under Mithras, slave, you and I."

He dipped into a fold in his tunica and pulled out a newly minted gold coin that had his portrait blazoned on it.

"That being so, what say we toss this coin, for sport, to see who will go first? My head has it. I'm freezing my balls off here!" Eyvindr looked at him askance, then nodded. What did he care? Protocol had declared the slave go first. The emperor with or without clothes was an arrogant.... usurper, Eyvindr smiled inwardly. The coin flew heavenward and landed on his hairy wrist, a gleaming eye shining out.

"Ahh!" he exclaimed, fisting the coin in triumph, "Apologies slave, you will have to freeze for longer."

A *buccina* sounded twice. The door of the Mithræum slowly opened to welcome the initiates inside. This atrium was hardly warmer than outside and very dark. Two slaves deftly removed the heavy military clothing from both men. Silently and with heads bowed, these slaves made both the Emperor and the slave as nude as a new-born babe.

Except Postumus looked akin to very hairy ginger gorilla, while Eyvindr, being the Warinni he was, had all the attributes of a giant. The deep scars rippled on his bare back as he shifted and quietly cursed. The *buccina* heralded the start of the ceremony, in a haunting long-drawn-out resonance that reached the soul and brought more bumps to the chilled skin of the waiting initiates.

Both men entered the interior of the Mithræum together equal under the God's searching eyes, but it was Postumus who, with a single glance back to Eyvindr, strode forward, buff-naked and head held high. Eyvindr was awarded the itchy warmth of a *birrus Britannicus*, as he sat at the rear, watching. All eyes were on the Emperor as he stood facing Octavious, who was wearing all the ritual clothing of the eastern God Mithra. He looked resplendent, but the look of surprise turning to anger, marred the effect. Postumus electing to be first, had arrogantly broken protocol held in place for generations.

Octavious coughed hard to dispel his feelings and taking a deep breath began the invocation.

"*Nabarze, Nabarze, Nabarze,*" he intoned, echoed by the reply from the crowded celebrants squeezed onto the aisle seats.

"*Nama, Nama, Nama, Mithras, dues genitor rupe natus.*

Postumus grew in stature as the power grew, his back now ramrod straight, the light from the nearby sconce flickered across his back in a dance in tune to the chant.

"Mithras, we offer our supplicant, Postumus," Octavious had turned to face the bull-slayer God, "With good thoughts, good words, and good deeds lying dormant in his soul, we offer Postumus up to you, to experience his death, like the death of the world, to be reborn and cleansed of all sin."

The Nabarze chant reached a crescendo on these powerful words of initiation, as Postumus was led, by Vrittakos to the left, behind a screen hiding the "tomb of death." He faltered momentarily, then straightened to walk behind the screen.

There came a horrifying scream, staccato words flung into the dark air, "NO, *ut autem non est tibi. Et secundum esse videatur. Tunc nequissimus malarum depopulator est intelligendum sit mori!*

"NO, it must not be you. You were meant to be second. The vile despoiler was meant to die!"

A scuffle and grunts followed, as an unwitnessed fight ensued behind the screen. Postumus could be heard swearing in Suevii, and a crunch of fist upon bone followed. A limping and hunched figure loped out from the "tomb of death" holding his side, hair and face bloodied. He sped up the aisle, and cranking the door open just enough to disappear, he fled the Mithræum. But not before casting a steel-blue glare of pure hatred towards Eyvindr, whose mouth just sprang open in frozen shock.

Octavious appeared and boomed out to dispel the look of shock on all the celebrants' faces.

"The ceremony of Leo has been defiled. It is suspended, upon thorough investigation. Please leave!"

The furious voice of Emperor Postumus could be heard shouting at Honoratianus, "*Et inveniam illum, Da mihi bastardis!* Find him! Bring the bastard to me!"

The celebrants eased off the aisle benches and slowly began to file out, heads bowed, but several turned to give Eyvindr dark questioning looks that left him wanting so badly to disappear into his *birrus Brittannicus*. And it answered his last pleading question to the Nornir; Urdhr, Verhandi and Skuld, about his spiritual destiny. They had surely answered him, in their own inimitable way.

Eyvindr sat alone, hugging the *birrus,* eyes closed. Octavious and Vrittakos came to sit quietly beside the Warinni. Eyvindr was feeling so completely damned if he did and equally damned if he did not!

"If you so wish it, beloved friend," Octavious declared softly, "We will be honoured to bring you to your rebirth, at your own calling. Privately, with only trusted companions near you."

"*Giese,*" came the whispered reply, "I will honour you, Vrittakos, my *gradus a patre* and you Octavious, *Pater Sacrorum,* and then I am done!"

... ...

Chapter 54

Faran midde burna on þæt èo fram Wyrd
Travelling midstream in the river of Wyrd

Postumus did not, as was expected, leave the island. He made for Berandinzium Villam, and stayed there, in the modest guest quarters, and to the intense irritation of Venitouta, who found him distasteful on many levels. He also expected his entourage and personal guards to be housed, and they complained incessantly about the meagre hospitalities.

Honoratianus and his private army of henchmen, were called over from Villam Regis to conduct the swift apprehension of the blue-eyed attacker. It did not take long. All the harbours and ports were manned within hours. The distinctive features could not be hidden from acquisitive eyes.

He was taken trying to board a small *sæ naca* stolen from an unsuspecting Durotrige fisherman. He was questioned, and not kindly by the "shade" himself, so the truth came gushing forward with much of his blood, pooled on the floor before him. Postumus had ordered his life be spared. The ingenuity of the lad was commendable. Pipes leading to the incarcerating tub had been cleverly tampered with to inject scalding heat first, with nuggets of white-hot coals, causing fatal damage, to be followed by ice-cold water that simply continued until death by drowning was achieved.

Postumus had use for such talent, but it would come at a high price. This young lad's life was forfeit on many counts should he err just a small way from being a mindless slave to Postumus and his "shade".

Censorinus and Libertus arrived suddenly from Villam Regis, to add to this mix, but were encouraged to move forthwith, to Heliodromus Villam. It was high on the ridge and would more suit their skills and temperament. It was stately and sunny. Even more situated thus to welcome the sun God Sol into the villam.

And all this flurry of visitors signalled the most important event in the Mithraism calendar, celebrating the birth of Mithras on 25th December.

Three days prior to this celebration, Eyvindr stood once again, buff-naked before the Pater, with Vrittakos as assistant to undergo his death and rebirth into the Mithraic cult. There were no other witnesses, and it was in total secrecy. Eyvindr had brought the sacred herbs and honey. He waited in silence. Patiently and at some peace, having reconciled the differences, he would honour, if only for this day, the wonder that was Mithras.

"Aelius," Octavious began, solemnly giving his Roman title for the last time, "you have chosen to undergo your death and rebirth. Are you prepared?

"I am," came the reply.

"Your trial therefore commences with meeting the end times, the conflagration of terrible cold around the world, Sol, hiding and turning his face away for three full years. Followed by intense heat and destruction by fire. Are you prepared?"

"I am," Aelius re-iterated. And then slowly but clearly, he began his invocation to Mithras.

" First-origin of my origin, AEEIOYO, first beginning of my beginning," Aelius sounded the spirit of wind ,fire, PPP SSS PHR, " spirit of spirit, the first of the spirit in me, MMM, fire given by god to my mixture of the mixture in me, the first of the fire in me, EY EIA EE, water of water, the first of the water in me, OOO AAA EEE, earthy substance, the first of the earthy substance in me, YE YOE, my complete body, I Aelius, named Eyvindr Wahl, whose mother is Gudrun Wahl of the Warinni, my complete body, which was formed by a noble arm and an incorruptible right hand in the world without light yet radiant, without soul and yet alive with soul, YEI AYI EYOIE: now if it be your will, METERTA PHOTH YEREZATH, give me over to immortal birth and , following that, to my underlying nature, so that, after the present need which is pressing me exceedingly, I may gaze upon the immortal, beginning with the immortal spirit, ANCHREPHRENESOYPHIRIGCH, with the immortal water, ERONOYI PARAKOYNETH, with the most steadfast air, EIOAE PSENABOTH, that I may be born again in thought, KRAOCHRAX R OIM ENARCHOMAI, and the sacred spirit may breathe in me, NECHTHEN APOTOY NECHTHIN ARPI ETH, so that I may wonder at the sacred fire, KYPHE, that I may gaze upon the unfathomable, awesome water of the dawn, NYO THESE ECHO OYCHIECHOA, and the vivifying, and encircling æther may hear me, ARNOMETHPH, for today I am about to behold, with immortal eyes - I, born mortal from mortal womb, but transformed by tremendous power and an incorruptible right hand, and with immortal spirit, the immortal Aion and master of the fiery diadems - I, sanctified through holy consecrations, while there subsists in me, holy, for a short time, my human soul-might, which I will again receive after the present bitter and relentless necessity which is pressing down on me

"I, Aelius, named Eyvindr Wahl, whose mother is Gudrun Wahl of the Warinni according to the immutable decree of god, EYE YIA EEI AO EIAY IYA IEO. Since it is impossible for me, born mortal, to rise with the golden brightnesses of the immortal brilliance, OEY AEO EYA EOE YAE IAE, stand, O perishable nature of mortals, and at once me safe and sound after the inexorable and pressing need."

Eyvindr stood statuesque, his body rigid with tension. Octavious was watching closely as his celebrant transformed before him. His eyes had become opalescent, pupils enlarged yet unseeing. Eyvindr spoke out the final words to this initial invocation, his voice resonating around the Mithræum.

"For I am the son! PSYCHON DEMOY PROCHO PROA. I am MACHHARPHN MOY PROPSYCHON PROE!"

Octavious wasted no more than a second in guiding Eyvindr forward, Vrittakos moving forward to support his adopted son, in readiness for the walk to the chamber.

"Draw in breath from the rays," he commanded, "drawing up three times as much as you can, and you will see yourself being lifted up and ascending to the height so that you seem to be in mid-air."

Eyvindr's lungs expanded as he drew in air, and spiritual rays, his feet lifting slightly off the ground.

"You will hear nothing, either of man or of any other living thing," Octavious continued, "nor in that hour, will you see anything of mortal affairs on earth, but rather you will see all immortal things. For in that hour, you will see the divine order of the skies, the presiding gods rising into heaven."

Octavious took hold of Eyvindr, unseeing as he had become. Slowly putting one foot before the other, Vrittakos supporting his left side, they guided him towards the iron tank, hidden from view. They supported him fully as he was lifted to descend inside, hunched into a foetal position, his head bowed into his chest. The lid was carefully put in place. Eyvindr had become effectively buried.

Silence. As the water, ice cold, could be heard gushing in, they expected a cry of shock from inside the tomb. Nothing. Pure silence. It was in that moment that *Pater Sacrorum* knew beyond doubt that his initiate had indeed reached a heavenly space. He knew because he had reached it many years ago. Without any warning an intense sadness engulfed him. His head bent, he shook momentarily before gathering his wits about him.

The twisted, decadent affairs of Romans had been a destructive experience of pure betrayal for this pure spirit named Eyvindr Wahl. And there was absolutely nothing Octavious could do but watch this beautiful man leave and disappear from his life. He turned to see Vrittakos watching him, the same look of intense sorrow etched into his craggy Greek features. They silently mourned together as their celebrant was being presented to Mithras.

Suddenly, a clear but muted voice came from within and brought them both back to the guardianship of Eyvindr, here in the Now.

"Give ear to me, I, Aelius named Eyvindr Wahl, whose mother is Gudrun Wahl of the Warinni, O Lord, you who have bound together with your breath, the fiery bars of the fourfold root, O Fire-walker, PENTITEROYNI, Light-maker, SEMESILAM, Fire-breather, PSYRINPHEY, Fire-feeler, IOA, Light-breather, OAI, Fire-delighter, ELOYRE, beautiful Light, AZAI, Aion, ACHBA, Light-Master, PEPPER PREPEMPIPI, Fire-Body, PHNOYENIOCH, Light -Giver, Fire-Sower, AREI EIKITA, Fire-Driver, GALLABALBA, Light-Forcer, AIO, Fire-Whirler ,PYRICHIBOOSEIA, Light-Mover, SANCHEROB, Thunder - Shaker, IE OE IPEIO, Glory-Light, BEEGENETEE, Light-Increaser, SOYSINEPHEIN, Fire-Light-Maintainer, SOYSINEPHI ARENBARAZEI MARMARENTEY, Star-Tamer, open for me PROPROPHEGGE EMTHEIRE MORIOMOTYREPHILBA."

Eyvindr, with due diligence had honoured all the Fire and Light deities that created the Eternal flame. The guardians of the Fire, keeping it alive and sentient. For the heat was upon him now, and he was at his limit of endurance.

Silence prevailed. Octavious became anxious. Suddenly, out of that silence came a choked voice, shrieking at staccato level, fighting for air that did not burn his lungs.

"I invoke the immortal names, living and honoured, which never pass into mortal nature and are not declared in articulate speech by human tongue or mortal sound,

"EEO OEEO IOO OE EEO OE IOO OEEE OEE IE EO OO OE IOE OE OOE IEO OE IEEO EE IO OE IOE OEO EOE OEO OIE OIE EO OI III EOE OYE EOOEE EO EIA AEA EEA EEEE EEE EEE IEO EEO OEEEOE EEO EYO OE EIO EO OE EE OOO YIOE" The fading note on a choking breath slipped to nothing, and a profound silence prevailed.

"GET HIM OUT!" screamed Vrittakos, "Just get him out, NOW!"

They both heaved the lid away, leaving gravity to take it to the floor. Billows of scalding steam escaped and completely enveloped them. They searched and found the limp body of Eyvindr, unresponsive and heavy to shift. They heaved his head and shoulders up into clean air, and saw his lungs explode into action, as Eyvindr heaved his first breath as a reborn soul. They laid him on the floor as he gasped for more air, then vomited widely over his naked body. Vrittakos took to cleaning him up, lovingly, muttering words of compassion to his son, and tributes to his bravery. Octavious went to arrange the clothes marking Eyvindr's success in reaching the acclaimed level of Leo. And as he stood allowing Octavious to dress him in the silk tunica, which felt cooling on his reddened and scorched skin, the outer toga of white silk with red borders, signifying his union with the Sun god, Eyvindr slowly came back to himself. His eyes focused on the altar, holding the thunderbolt, sistrum and Fire shovel. Eyvindr's focus settled on the keys, for he knew they represented the balance between heaven and earth. He needed them and he felt he deserved them above all else.

Octavious carefully handed all the sacred items to Eyvindr, pinning the thunderbolt to his chest with a secure gold pin. Eyvindr's last dedication came as the sun began to settle in the late afternoon sky.

"Hail, O seven Fates of Heaven, O noble and good virgins, O sacred ones and companions of MINIMIRROPHOR, O most holy guardians of the four pillars!

> Hail to you, the first, CHREPSENTHAES!
> Hail to you, the second MENESCHEES!
> Hail to you, the third, MECHRAN!
> Hail to you, the fourth, ARARMACHES
> Hail to you, the fifth! ECHOMMIE
> Hail to you, the sixth! TICHNONDAES!
> Hail to you, the seventh, EROY ROMBRIES!

"Hail, O guardians of the pivot, O sacred and brave youths, who turn and one command the revolving vault of heaven, who send out thunder and lightning and jolts of earthquakes and thunderbolts against the nations of impious people, but to me, who am pious and god-fearing, you send health and soundness of body, acuteness of hearing and seeing, and calmness in the present good hours of this day,

Hail to, the first, AIERONTH!
Hail to you, the second, MERCHEIMERO!
Hail to you, the third, ACHRICHIOYR!
Hail to you, the fourth, MESARGILTO!
Hail to you, the fifth, CHICHROALITHO!
Hail to you, the sixth, ERMICHHATHOPS!
Hail to, the seventh, EORASICHE!"

"O Lord, while being born again, I am passing away. While growing and having grown, I am dying, while being born from a life-generating birth, I am passing on, released to death, as you have founded, as you have decreed, and have established the mystery. I am PHEROYRA MIORYI."

Eyvindr expelled a long and precious breath. His work was so nearly done, and in the heightened energy, so secret and unmolested with diverse other energies, he truly felt alive and re-born. Octavious handed him the large bay leaf upon which he had written I EE OO IAI consecrating it by turning to the East. He dipped it in the honey and herb mixture and ceremoniously licked it on his tongue. Keeping his words true and pure. Octavious came forward to rub his hand with the sacred herbs to keep his actions pure and true, then on his forehead to stay negative thoughts from here on in.

"Congratulations, Eyvindr Wahl of the Warinni, you are now an adept, worthy and true," Octavious boomed loud in relief and some happiness that the job had been completed well. He came forward to hug Eyvindr not in Roman way, but the Warinni way and Vrittakos joined them. They remained together for some while.

Octavious led the way out as protocol demanded. The chink of amber light grew into a sunburst of oranges and crimson, as the door widened. Eyvindr was momentarily blinded by the strong hues bathing his body in stunning light. And that was how his Warinni family first saw him as he emerged from the "tomb of death".

They were all gathered, each one to honour him. And Eyvindr let out a cry of sheer joy. He was swamped by his family, lost within love, his wife and children amongst them. Cahal and Blãth-nat, Aia and Kenward, Lãfa and Arkyn. Eystein, Folkvarthr and Gudrun. But most urgently of all were the tears he quietly shed into the strong and capable shoulder of his wife Aife, whom he felt he had abandoned on this wildest of sacred journeys.

Octavious and Vrittakos quietly began to withdraw. Eyvindr momentarily broke free from his family and came over to the two men.

Putting his hand on Vrittakos' arm he said with compassion, "I shall come to the celebration of Mithras' birth, have no fear, I will come!"

Then he walked away with his family to Sudmōr.

... ...

Chapter 55

White Sacrilege.

The pure white heifer stamped her hoof in panic, snorting steam wildly as she was restrained from following her young off-spring. Her still-full udders shaking as the slave yanked even harder to restrain her. She knew. The young white bull did not. Her panic bled quickly to the other heifers in the stock yard, who began to jump and shift uneasily.

"*Cavet optimum sacris fortior.* Young blood is best, far more powerful at the sacrifice," muttered the older slave, long in tooth and cynical with life altogether.

As Sunni was rising in the early dawn morning, in a cloudless and strikingly blue sky, she was promising a hint of warm on the day of the Sun God's birth. Her first rays created a glow on the pure white hide of the bull. In this Roman world of mindless bar-barity, it was normal. No thought given to prayer in taking a young life. The mind set closed to compassion.

Miles away at his family *hūs* in Sudmōr, Eyvindr was rising to give his own welcome to the day. A prayer to Nerthus, as he knelt close to the cold earth, and to Sunni for gifting another day, with gratitude to Mōnā for illuminating the night and protecting the dormant ones. The official invitation to the grand celebration of Mithras' birth at Berandinzium Villam lay unopened on the rough-hewn oak table. He did not welcome it. His family were ex-tremely nervous of it and he wished in the morning prayer for divine intervention to forestall the Wahls from attending.

Folkvarthr stood quietly in the shadows cast by the *hūs*, watch-ing his son in his private torment.

"*Mín bearn,*" he said softly into the dawn air, "*Ic āgan nā drèogan swā mōdelíc fram þu ealswā ðā þu came úyt āht-lice und gefyllan fram þæt ã-fandung wíþ þes Dryhten Mithras.*

Hwæt cearu þu nú?

"My son, I have never felt so proud of you as when you came out, triumphant and fulfilled from the trial with this God Mithras.

"What troubles you now?"

Eyvindr pressed both his hands into the earth balling it with his fists. He threw both clods, hard into the misty dawn, hearing them thud uselessly on the ground yonder. He twisted round to face his *fæder,* looking up in deep anguish,

"Those clods are all I am to the Romans. Just that. Pieces of dirt! It is all I and my family will ever be to them! They take your soul, *Fæder*, and they crush it, slowly, with great attention to the pain they are inflicting. And when they see your spirit is still alive, they invent more ways to kill you!

"I have been diligent and obedient in every way I can. Yet still their evil worms its way into my life and tries to destroy me! I am done *fæder*. My second father, Vrittakos, who is not even Roman, is all I have in this Roman world that I respect and care for. But even he is not powerful enough to keep them away.

"I have prayed for my *libertus* to be in my hand for many years, a freedman at last, always promised, but never given. Now, when it is finally within my grasp, it means nothing. Nothing!

"It is being offered to me by a callous murderer of young men, a usurper Emperor who will himself be murdered!" Eyvindr wiped his hands and got up to stand with his *Fæder* in the shadows of the *hūs*.

"*Fæder*," he began warily, softly, looking to see how Folkvarthr was reacting, and he saw sorrow growing across his rugged, lined features. There was not much to see of his eyes, as aging skin and wrinkles had covered so much. Yet those piercing eyes still shone out and broke Eyvindr's heart.

"I'm leaving, *Fæder*," Eyvindr said simply, "Aife has begged for us to leave, to reunite with the Durotrige in Frescewætr Ealond, then to settle in Ytene Weald. We will take the girls but will give Cahal and Blãthnat their will to choose."

Folkvarthr turned away, to hide his face, saying gruffly, "Do not tell your *Mōdor* until this day is done. And then wait some more!" As he walked away towards the white augury meadow, the sun caught the tears streaming down his face.

... ...

Eyvindr walked before his wife and the Warinni family, dressed in the ceremonial toga of a Leo adept, and as he neared the waiting group of guests, who were almost standing to attention as this new adept's arrival, Vrittakos to the fore, his attention was caught by the venomous glare of Honoratianus standing beside his Emperor. Postumus wore a glittering array of gold, saffron and purple, which spoke eloquently of the fact that he had been robbed of the rightful attire of a Leo adept.

Eyvindr sighed deeply, almost too tired of the charade to care. But Vrittakos held genuine admiration and respect for his adopted son and stepped forward to arm clasp his son then hug him heartily. He then moved to welcome all the Warinni host and brought Venitouta forward to care for the women, whilst the men followed the guardian of this sacred villam through to the main *ala*, where a table was set with scrolls to be awarded. Amongst them was the *libertus* for Eyvindr. This annual event set before the celebration and sacred meal in honour of the God Mithras' birth was usually overseen by Vrittakos. So rare was the appearance of an Emperor on Vecta, a huge tree had been erected in the *ala* festooned with votive cones dedicated to the Leo level and Mithras. They had been imported from Gaul and beyond to mimic the décor at the Palatine hill in Rome itself.

Everyone was unusually tense. This pleased Postumus who delighted in tension and the manipulation of it. The main hall was crowded now, with Romans from all walks of life, many from Britannia who had travelled on choppy waters to get here. The wharf held many small boats and some larger ones.

There were exactly thirteen scrolls and thirteen hermetic 13-pointed star bracteates waiting for new owners. Eyvindr, realising instantly that this was not just a *libertus* event, but a sacred honouring to Mithras on his birthday, he scanned around the audience to find men he knew, attired in ceremonial clothes and holding their amulets close to their chest.

Aetius, the young man from *Sacrum Nymphus Villam*, holding his mirror and lamp, self-reflection in service to Mithras. Eyvindr had never known he was a slave. Similarly, Aquilinus, who lived at *Persici luna villam*, yet was a known Corax initiate. There were strangers too, from across the water, all waiting patiently and in anticipation of their precious freedom scroll.

Postumus wasted no time in preamble. He was anxious to leave this island and seriously intended never to return! Though he was enjoying being bathed in the adulation of a benefactor gifting his subjects. He wore his finery in excess to mask his soldier's physique and his golden laurel crown to disguise his sinister ways.

"Salutem laetaque Romano marte Britannus et Romanicae." He bellowed, holding a bejewelled hand out to his subjects, *"Hodie unius magnorum celebrationem ad Deum Mithrae dei gloriam ut nos beneficentia nihil lux et potentia magni libertus XIII, et apud homines ad libertatem* tredecim *eternitas. Nos in gloriam nostram prandium sacris, in sacris modo pluribus reparant et taurum animarum in caelum.*

"Greetings and welcome Roman, Romanesque and Briton.

"Today is one of great celebration to our God Mithras, God of Light and Beneficence

"We honour him to the great power of 13 and in *libertus* to thirteen men in freedom earnt.

"We honour him in our sacred meal, the bull sacrificed to replenish the sacred way of souls in the heavens."

Postumus picked up the first scroll and scanning the list before him bellowed out to a nervous recipient, "Aetius, slave to Antoninus Appius, you have attained your *Libertus*, you are free to go." Aetius jumped forward with a joyous grin, taking the scroll and slapping his chest in salute, he was awarded the 13-pointed star.

"Aquilinus, slave to Marcus Lucretius, you are free to go" And so, with the order of *libertus* before him, Postumus worked down the list. Eyvindr's mind began to wander, then suddenly sprang back into the present

"Aelius, slave to Vrittakos Eluskonios, your freedom has been well earnt. You have achieved *libertus*."

Eyvindr felt a sudden glow, a warmth spreading into his heart, as he realised this was the very last time he would answer to that false Roman name. He walked forward, aware that Vrittakos, his adopted father, was looking intently at him, knowing this was a great release for him, a burden lifted and pride too, at the relentless diligence and courage Eyvindr had shown to reach this moment.

Eyvindr kept his gaze on Postumus, who stared back, masking his feeling in true Roman style. Giving nothing away, the usurper Emperor handed the scroll to Eyvindr. He then reached for the 13-pointed star bracteate, leaning forward to personally pin it to his chest.

"Aelius," he growled low, grinning as the name hit Eyvindr hard, "You are chosen, as your rank of Leo dictates, to perform the sacrifice this noontide. You *will* draw the knife. And if you resist, I *will* hunt you down!" Eyvindr stood bolt upright, frozen to the spot, then slowly but surely, as protocol dictated, he took the required steps back, facing his Emperor. And his gaze never wavered, the anger and resentment shot through to Postumus, who smirked and declared loudly,

"Ego *hodie Britannia ad sissam, qua proficiscerentur. Omnem Galliam legiones ero custos. Et ponam solium meum in Capitolio Treverum Augusti. Ave Dei Mithrae insistimus.*

"I will be departing Britannia today at high tide. I will be guarding Gaul with all legions. I will establish my capitol in Augustus Treverum. Hail to our mighty god Mithras."

And with that, he turned and walked away.

... ...

Eyvindr hardly felt the claps on his scarred back, from his family, his friends. He rocked back and forth in a daze. Only his *Mōdor* knew something was very wrong. Gudrun eased herself through the men and took her son by the elbow and led him aside.

"What did that *Ǽttren wyrm* say to you Eyvindr?" Gudrun stared deeply into her son's eyes, finding a tortured soul looking back at her.

"He has bribed me, *Mōdor*," he replied, "I must perform the bull sacrifice in but two hours' time, and if I do not, he will hunt me down.

"He knows my weakness, you see. He has seen my soul is in conflict, still, and that I have chosen to walk from Mithras to find some peace. It is not the celebration of this god, *Mōdor*, it is the venal way men abuse his wonder. That *Ǽttren wyrm* is playing with my soul again!"

Gudrun wrapped her arms about Eyvindr, holding him tight, as if he might shatter.

"I know you are leaving us, *mín weorð bearn*," she whispered in his ear, "It is what you must do. But remember where we are, and we will hold you in our hearts forever!"

Eyvindr felt her unclasp and move from him. Gudrun Wahl's whole body shook with her will to contain her soul's devastation. As tears welled up in her eyes, she turned and walked away, head bowed, shaking. Folkvarthr followed, supporting his wife, leaving Berandinzium Villa, never to return.

"Aelius!" came a shrill call from the young Corax initiate, "the stallions are ready, the wagons also. We must leave to process to the sacrifice. I am to give you this." He handed Eyvindr a gladius, sharpened and gleaming. Eyvindr shot his head upwards, silently pleading to Nerthus for strength and courage.

Octavious and Vrittakos joined him, and they strode out of the *ala*, Sunni hitting their faces with welcome warmth. The air was crisp, the stallions whinnying to go. Eyvindr's ceremonial toga was entirely inadequate, Vrittakos handed him a thick *birrus*. Wrapping up so only his face was visible, and that carried a worried frown that got deeper as they followed the Emperor's party ahead of them.

Suddenly, instead of making for *Iuppiter igne Villam* where the herd of cattle were penned, they veered right to scale the rise of *Ceofodūn* to traverse the *dracona line* to where? Eyvindr thought wildly.

Just as he was about to ask why, both older men spurred their mounts to ride wildly on. They were expert horsemen, and it took all Eyvindr's skill to catch up with them. It was only when the distant sighting of the *Halíg Stãn* came into view, an unspeakable horror slithered into Eyvindr's mind, and he howled until his throat broke.

Vrittakos and Octavious wheeled about and galloped to join him.

"Come" they shouted, "we are ahead of the party, "We do not have much time!"

When they reached the sacred and hallowed ground of the Wihtwara, an obscene and terrible sight met them. The upright and gentle female companion to the *Halíg Stãn* had been brutally pushed over to lay forever in front of the tall ancestor, as a prelude to the bloody sacrifice about to take place there.

The Romans had desecrated their most sacred of all places on Wihtland. It was the Wihtwara's by right and the Romans had callously defiled it!

"*Na, Na, NA!*" screamed Eyvindr, as he vaulted off his stallion and sunk to the ground, beating his fists on the cold, compacted earth. He looked up at the bleating noise and let forth a tortured scream. Before him stood the youngest, most beautiful sacred white he had ever seen. The young bull looked at him in all innocence.

"They are going to sacrifice a sacred white!" Eyvindr shouted. "Here at our most precious of sacred places. They are beyond evil. And they KNOW exactly what they are doing!"

Octavious looked to the horizon and saw the approaching party. They were not taking their time to be sure. Eyvindr had but minutes to affect his escape.

Vrittakos hurried over to unleash the bull and handed the rope to Eyvindr.

"GO, now!" Vrittakos commanded, "Leave this island by nightfall and you may have a chance. *Ytene Weald* will guard you. Send word when you are safe, and I will bring your family to you. The Durotrige will welcome you.

"You are my son, Eyvindr and you will always have a place in my heart. Farewell, GO!"

"Put the bull before me," Eyvindr suddenly shouted, "I will not make it otherwise."

They heaved the sacred white up and it settled after furious flurries with its limbs that were roped to the sides. Eyvindr gave one last loving look to his adopted father and sped away.

He made straight for *Iuppiter Villam*. Untying the calf, he heard its' mother calling before he even saw her. A joyous reunion lifted his heart as he knelt by the willow that grew on these wet-lands. Underneath lay peat, and he dug ferociously to find the dense soil. Whereupon he lay, with no prayers spoken or other-wise, the libertus scroll and the 13-pointed star bracteate.

He had absolutely no need for either. As he laid the soil to bury them, the false name, Aelius, truly went down with them forever.

··· ··· ··· ··· ··· ··· ··· ··· ···

BOOK FIVE

PROLOGUE

Aleen's joints scraped mercilessly giving her a silent scream to hold in as she slowly sat down on the stone seat, warmed by the afternoon summer sun that fanned in golden rays onto the fields around the villam. Oh! she was getting old.

"My body is ready for rest" she thought, knowing this next winter would be her last. But then she quietly marvelled at her length of years on this beautiful island called Wihtland: a hard life in a warm climate grants more years, she was sure of it. She loved her Isle. It was her home from birth and all she had known. Her mother and sometimes her father had done all the travelling, and Aleen smiled remembering the torch-lit nights when they returned from their trips to feed her hungry imagination with visions of places and people across the water.

"Beatha," she called out to her daughter, who was ambling back from the adjacent field, holding under her arm a ceramic bowl full of equina beans for their supper.

"Maybe you will stir those beans for me tonight. My bones are crying. I'm stuck on this seat till sundown."

Without looking up, Beatha replied with a sideways grin that showed her dimpled cheeks and nodded. She was her beautiful girl, thought Aleen. And so convivial, good natured and close to nature. "So very like my mother," she decided, nodding in memory of her. Agrona, meaning warrior woman in Durotrige but

Drusilla as she was called in Roman, was every inch a warrior. "She had to be," thought Aleen, thinking back to that time when all of life stopped and became a screaming, shrieking cry to every Goddess my mother could name. "Now she is resting with them," though Beatha, "Nantosuelta, Brigantia," she whispered slowly looking into the dying sun," Sulis, Sulis, life-giver and granter of the curse, answer our prayer to end the Roman. Give them up to Agrona and Andarta. We are our own people in our owned land, yet we are not yet free"

... ...

Chapter 56

Berandinzium Villam 294 A.D.

I heaved the last sack of equina beans onto the cart, the sun glinting through on this hot September afternoon. The sack was old, like me, and some spilled out onto the ridged earth, baked dry by a long summer and no rain for days. "Let them sprout new shoots by here," I thought, to the Awen, a gift. A testament to the long drudgery of this. By the Goddess, but I'm feeling old, but I am in my sixth month of pregnancy and not a young maiden anymore. If I were Roman, I would be slithering across the slimy marble of the bath house, to sink into the cool water, and just stay there. My greedy Roman mind birthing new adornments, copper with garnets brought from Byzantium and made by my talented son, Aonghus now an apprentice *drycræft* metal-forger at the foundry only a bow's length away from here.

"He must be watering the copper with his own sweat," I mumbled aloud.

"What is that whisper Liberta?" Aodhan my husband smiled as he packed the sacks at the back, all these ready for the waiting ship close by. He always used that word, whisper. I am charged with casting nature spells, magic at season's height and many evocations to our Goddess and Gods. I mostly do these under muttered breath for we live amongst Romans, even though now, they are from some part of Gaul and hear said have become some form of Pagan.

My name is Agrona, meaning warrior woman, my father naming me amidst battle. He must have thought warring was a way of all life, and I had to have the Gods' blessing with a warrior woman's name. But life changes as the seasons and we found ourselves this island. The rest of our tribe live on the mainland, still warring, so I believe, with the Romans.

This part of the island belongs to the Wihtwara, we Durotrige are close neighbours, and the Regni on the small island over the causeway. Some are still owned as slaves to the Romans, but we are not. We are freedmen, *manumissio*, Aodhan and me. That is why he delights in calling me Liberta.

We run Berandinzium Villam and all the industry around it for the old Greeks, Vrittakos and Achaikos, who are venerable and generous in their dotage. They have allowed us to take some profits from it. We work hard, harder than when we were slaves. This sacred island Wihtland is overflowing with riches. And the Romans saw this as soon as they landed. Much salt is made, for salt is a precious material indeed. Without it we human would suffer greatly. Ours is taken by ship to nearly everywhere and much coin is made. Piles of it.

Wine is made by the amphorae, shiploads of this because Romans do not know what fresh water means. They drink just wine.

Then there are the metal foundries and the clay cookware makers. Our pots leave this island to go to lands over the wide sea. We get our cookware from the Durotrige and those living in Ytene, the large forest. They are beautiful and we treasure these.

The owners of the Villam receive altogether more beautiful cookware. And ornaments also from Byzantium and the Franks. That is what we are going to collect this hot afternoon. The Romans take, and then they take some more, for we do not get to use these beautiful objects. But still, I must stop this carping, for we lead a better life than some, a good life amongst these Romans. Some are bad, some evil, but not these people. They treat us with respect and for that we are grateful and send prayers to the Goddess in thanks.

"After we have finished this loading, I will go down to the foundry with fresh water for Aonghus," I replied, "He will be wilting in this heat."

"No," Aodhan stated, "I will go wife. You will sit and stir the beans. I need to meet with our sons, for there is a storm brewing over by the Yaverland and we must be ready to meet it."

"What is this," I asked," It is the first I have heard! If you are planning a defence against the Belgic, and I believe I am not far wrong, then I must be a part of the talking for I need to protect you with a call to our Gods."

These wanderers from across the water were a wasp in our hair, and sometimes their sting meant a period of painful recovery. I think they are from far yonder still, up in the Welsh mountains where they lived in deep forests. Now they travelled away from the Roman battalions to hide in Ytene Weald across our water. They are Silures that mingle among the Belgic. They are said to be head-hunters and are not to be taken lightly.

"Breathe easy, Agrona. It is not the head-hunters who threaten us. Rumour is spreading of rebellion and it is the Romans who have a nest of wasps in their helmets!" Aodhan replied, smiling warmly, "It is but a whisper of sword drawn from the hilt. We are meeting to prevent it rather than spill blood. But I will bring our sons to you this evening and we will all talk of a way through."

I leant over to kiss him on the forehead, for he was a wise man and I loved him as much now in our long years together, as I did when we first met as slaves, Felix, and Drusilla. The Roman chose our names, and he said they came from this Christian's book some Romans worship, but he had never seen it. Bah! I believe only what I see and feel. The Nature's spirits and power within the land itself. Our mother earth and mother sun, Sulis I can see every day. What need of a book written by men about just one god no-one has seen? These Roman minds are soaked in wine!

… … … … … … … … …

The old reliable ox we had to pull the wagon, lumbered along to the wharf, a route it knew so well, the deep troughs mostly avoided, and nothing spilled. The men working the cargo off the low-hulled boat had already piled the goods onto the wharf for us to load onto the wagon and take back to the villam. Some amphorae were destined for the emporium, built recently as a commercial warehouse for the many goods that arrived from over the wide sea. We had given ourselves some time to spare, and I eagerly wandered over to see inside the emporium, to view the wonders from afar.

The emporium was a huge building. It towered over the boats, making them seem too small for its hungry jaws to swallow all those goods. It was forever hungry for more too. My son had been released from the hot hell of the foundry to help build this monster of a building. He learnt wood carving and joinery and some mortar-making and slab-building. The Romans used stone and wood together. They knew carpentry and my son became knowledgeable. He also got healthier this last summer. His skin glowed and he got firm muscles that had hitherto been hiding!

The smell of the spices just overwhelmed my senses. I could not distinguish one from the other, but it was intoxicating. These spices were magical to me and I knew they had power. We had several kinds at the Villam, and I learnt their nature, and some could be used for healing and magic. I was looking so intently at the beautiful markings on the pottery vases that held the spices that I almost missed the huddle of men in the shadows, to the left of the main holding space. And that is how I came to be drawn into the peril.

My child, my happy accident, was now moving in my womb, blessed by the Goddess, for the many times in twilight I had laid the magic pouch at Her blessing place and called for my baby's health to be strong.

And now something far from blessed was taking place in the shadows, in whispers and the waving arms of men intent on mischief.

I did not break into that energy they were making. And I would not have been thanked if I had. So, I made my way out into the sun. I took a deep breath and looked up. "Sulis" I breathed quietly, "protect us! Andraste sink their ships. We cannot be overcome by yet another sea of bloodshed."

My life had been one of peace, my sons had grown into wisdom that is birthed from peace. Yet they were men and men wage war.

I went over to start piling the sea goods onto our wagon, now empty of bean sacks that were destined for the Roman soldiers on the mainland. They had demanded so much of our harvest, more than usual.

"Well met," came a voice behind me, "I see you are stocking up for the villam."

I turned to see my dear brother. His face was in shadow against the sun, but his smile shone. I hugged him sideways, my baby already making a good embrace impossible.

"Hah," he said happily, "I see I am going to be an Uncle very soon. Have you magicked the day?"

"Now even I do not hold such power, Barra! But I have asked to be shown and I know it will be full moon when my waters break. It will be a daughter. And she will be fair of face."

"Well," he retorted, "that would be an obvious thing as your beauty is well-known hereabouts."

"Bah! You are sounding like a woman-flatterer!" I scolded smiling at the compliment.

Well Barra was all those things and more, yet he had never found a wife. He preferred to taste and run!

"Tell me, dear brother," I turned towards the emporium, "have you had wind of war. Rebellion is on the breath of my sons over there in the shadows. What new kind of will is being born here?"

"Ah, yes sister," Barra's face lost its cheery charm, becoming overcast with a deep worry. "'Tis so. I fear there is plotting, and a massive rebellion being grown on the mainland. When did you last take to the water and visit Britannia? We are cut off here on the island and lose much news. The rebellion is getting stronger by the day and the Romans are massing their army and their fleet. The tribes have been united for some time now. But the Romans are fighting amongst themselves more than ever before! The tribes are discussing independence from the Rome itself, or so I hear."

"Blessed Agrona," I cried, putting my hand to my face, "what will become of us now?"

"The Caesar will feed us all to their beasts. They will rip us, all of us, to pieces," Barra stated with a certainty born of knowledge.

A cold frozen hand gripped at my stomach and I almost bent double. I clutched my unborn and wished I could flee, hide in my secret magical glade, and stay there.

From that moment my life and the lives of all I held dear, changed forever. We would never recapture the golden time we enjoyed then. And I don't believe we appreciated it enough then. Only in remembering did it take on the golden glow of the better times.

... ...

I held my silence close to my chest, breathing heavily, taking in some beautiful spice to calm my nerves, as my husband and sons helped heave the over-laden wagon back to the villam. It was carrying precious pottery from Byzantium and amphorae of wine. We had to use a less well-trodden path, as absolutely nothing could be damaged on our return to the villam. Our wages would be slender indeed if there were breakages.

We took a route by the water, following the causeway that had supporting wood and piles rammed into the marshy ground. This was fairly level, nearly to the beachhead where we veered off right to tack our way back to the villam, amidst rushes and moss. A slim trackway had been forged over-time and it was soft. I enjoyed this route much more than the commercial roadway. Wonderful smells drifted up, from tansy, vettivert and trefoil. Bees hovered over late summer flowers. And best of all the magical Yaverland dragonfly would flit past, settling on a rush-head. We Durotrige hold this magic within us: the story told by our forefathers, certainly my own grandfather, in hushed silence over a warm fire and flickering shadows.

In time before the Romans came, and when this island was of two islands, and at war with each other, when blood split turned the river red and families were broken beyond repair, there came a truce. Enough was enough. The killing had to end. The Battle of Two Champions was announced, to be held near the river Yar. The priest and high commander of Yar would fight with his equal from our side, Wiht.

And so, it came, that famous evening. They both held their magical staffs before them. Each wearing their ceremonial dress. The evening sun cast long shadows as they met in combat. A loud crash of hardened wood met the ears of those watching. Many calls and cheers erupted from the gathered crowd. The battle to end all wars carried on for what seemed like forever. Each man returning from a last devastating wound made by the enormous staffs they carried. Their blood flowed into each other's as the battle continued. Twilight foreshadowed an ending. Both commanders were now just shadows fighting in the dark.

Suddenly there was an enormous crash that silenced the calls of the watchers. From one staff came a glittering flight of tiny lights that flew as one into the night sky. The priest from Yar lay still on the ground. He was finished and his magical staff that held magical energy was broken in two.

The priest from Wiht island came over and knelt to put his hand on the forehead of the vanquished, saying, "Fear not, brave one, your spirit has forever entered the realm of the Ancestors and is borne into this world by the beautiful Yaverland dragonflies you see before you. They will be adorning the River Yar for ever more. Your Spirit will live amongst the living for ever more. You have brought peace to this land." And so, it was.

… … … … … … … … …

Chapter 57

Roma crevit ex tenui principio se habet cum sua magni-

tudine est oppressae.

Rome has grown since its humble beginnings that it is

now overwhelmed by its own greatness.

(Titus Livius 59 BC-17AD)

I found Faustina sitting on the pool's edge, swinging her feet gently in the warm water, her fingers finding the figs on a plate beside her. Absently chewing at the delicious fruit, squinting into the bright sunlight that filtered through the elaborately decorated window-glass just installed at great expense by her grandfather, Vrittakos, and from Byzantium, at her demand. She was wearing only her *indutus tunica* of the sheerest, finest cloth. She entered the warm water for her daily swim. The tiles were greasy with old oil and I nearly slipped with my cloth sandals. Suddenly she lifted the tunica over her shoulders and enter the water, submerging down to the floor of the intricately tiled bath. The sun glinted through the window and played a colourful dance on the tiles through the ripples of water left in her wake. A blue-tinted mosaic of Neptune, Goddess of the sea, rippled indolently as she swam. Around the edge was a multi-coloured patterned mosaic where she now flipped in the water and glided underwater.

"Oh, my Sulis," I muttered quietly, "This young person is the most pampered, indolent creature that I have had to bend my back to!"

She is the daughter of Lucretia and Bricius. Lucretia is a Romano/ Gaullist who was born into wealth and holds all the purse strings here.

Bricius is a Romano/ Greek, son of Vrittakos, with wealth-making coursing through his blood. He came into our lives when

Vrittakos, now entering an incredible ninth decade in years, became too infirm to keep the Villam in decent working order. He is no Roman lover, if truth be told, but between them they weave as intricate a dance around the Romans as the ripples in the pool I am now staring at. They are clever, they are astute, and most importantly, especially Brice, as he likes to be called, treats us all equally fairly. He has my respect. He also sees within himself the burning flame of justice, the triumph of good over evil. So much so, the mosaic of Orpheus adorns the front corridor of the villa. I believe he has seen much in the Roman world that has turned his stomach and his heart against the Romans.

And my quiet, simmering fear is that they will one day trip up in this dance of theirs.

And suffering will surely arrive at this villam of plenty. I thought back to earlier in the day, when my sons and husband were talking about a great threat that might suck us into a turgid marshland that could drown us all.

"Agrona," Faustina called in her perpetually shrill voice, which shot me back to the present moment, "I need a linen shawl and my *tunica* and fetch my *strophium*."

I shuffled over to her and reached for the tunica.

"NO," She screeched. "I need a linen shawl, look over there!"

Shuffling on an oily floor is comical and demeaning. I turned halfway to see her clearly grinning at my discomfort.

"Oh, the little wretch!" I thought. Having retrieved the shawl, I went back to hold it out so she may elegantly step out of the bath and I wrapped it around her. I was furious at her for I believe she knew a fall this late in my pregnancy might induce my baby too early.

"My *strophium*," she announced, "is in my room. Get it." Faustina was only just into womanhood, the barest growth of her breasts from the flat-chested girl of a few months gone. But she had persuaded her mother that her courses had started, therefore she must be adorned in a *strophium*. And what a luxurious garment arrived from the emporium, especially made in Gaul. Of the twelve rooms that surrounded the main reception area, Faustina's room was the farthest from the bathhouse. And there were stairs to climb.

So, I trudged off to get her precious *strophium*, feeling as if I had slipped back to those dark slave-years of my childhood.

On entering her room, there were precious silk hangings draped at different angles to catch their intricate design with the passing of the sun. The shutters were always open, and the breeze caught the drapes swinging them in a slow indolent dance, a rhythm of delicate light. I stopped for a moment and marvelled at the sheer cleverness of design.

"Out of my world," I thought," Her mother is a clever woman. Whoever wins Faustina's hand, will have all the luxury he might desire....and all the spoilt manipulating ways Faustina has learnt from her mother too!"

Lucretia, being a wealthy Romano/ Gaullist, was brought up in Southern Gaul, where life was easy, warm and full of the grapes that made her father's fortune. The Romans could not get enough quantities of it. Amphorae of this wine sat at every table, drinking water was unheard of and not to be trusted either. Pestilence carried by dirty rivers was still a recent memory not to be re-visited.

Her chest, locked in her room, was full of coin. Byzantine gold, Breton silver and everything in between. But it did not get opened very often, except when more coin arrived from sales overseas or from trade with the tribes over the water. She was as tight as a bow tendon and would barter rather than pass coin over. This hidden wealth, if she but knew it, would leave her grasp in a sudden irrevocable way.

... ...

Chapter 58

The Burning

The *Trireme* slid silently, with the just faintest lapping of water against the wharf's aged timber. It had been travelling so very low in the tidal waters. It carried the feared scorpion giant sling, constructed with solid oak beams. The *Tormentum* was its name given by the four *scorpionarius* praetorians manning it. Added to that was the heavy pile of fireballs they had all spent building, during the hours on the crossing, rounding in the cement moulds. The weather had favoured them in this clandestine mission ordered by Maximian himself. Emperor Diocletian had declared himself Brittannicus Maximus, and Maximian wanted to curry favour in eradicating the troublesome usurpers in Britannia.

The Villam Regis Cogidvbni was one of the favoured hiding places for the Usurper clique, who felt the replica of Caesar's palace on the Palatine hill, a rather fitting place to congregate. Maximian who had the coined the phrase "That Despicable Clique" to describe the usurpers, wanted it destroyed, along with their hide-outs on Vecta. He had commissioned this special elite band of praetorians, all with consummate skills to destroy the Villam and all within. It was covert, nocturnal and there were to be absolutely no survivors.

Aetius Septimius, the *optio*-in-charge, whispered in a hiss, between clenched teeth, "Drusus, Lucius, get the wheels of the Tormentum covered and tied securely! There must be no sound as we roll it out."

The praetorians nodded and worked in silence wrapping thick wool around the solid oak wheels. That completed, they heaved and cursed in silence, until the machine was level with the wide gangplank. They eased it down until it reached the wharf's compacted earth. The fire balls, each exuding a terrible stench of bitumen, quick lime and resin were placed into carriers, two a man, on a wooden shoulder harness. The *Sagittarii* clutched their long bows and fire arrows before them. Longinus Octavius cursed quietly at the overwhelming load and received a smash into the base of his spine by *optio*, Faustus Silvanus.

"*Propter mandatum assume fatuus vobis, et aliud sentire Vox flagelli meus proximus!*" Shut up you fool, else you will feel the crack of my whip next!" Silence reigned, even their breathing was reduced to silent exhalations.

Two shadowy figures suddenly appeared on the wharf, hunched and moving forward swiftly. Aetius pulled his gladius out, silently without a scrape, as he had oiled it copiously on the *Trireme*. A signal whistle from one of the figures eased his sword arm as he replaced the gladius carefully in its sheath. As they drew close, Aetius saw the blood dripping from Norbanus' gladius, who held both his arms up in a shoulder shrug "How many?" came the hissed question.

"Two Britons, watchmen, I think. We made sure there were no more. There will be no alarm called," Fabius stated, nodding his head. They all knew they had just a few hours to complete the mission. Their escape back to the waiting *trireme* would be fraught. They all knew that. So, they made good their progress towards the wood that had been reconnoitred by the *exploratores*.

Fabius and Norbanus had been challenged by the Britons, as they were treading and marking the *passus* needed to securely place the Tormentum and be within reach of the Villam Regis. And it would be hidden within the first trees. Young oaks. The Britons had neither time to shout a warning or even pray to their God, as both Fabius and Norbanus, veterans in clandestine missions, had slit their throats across, dragging their twitching bodies to be dumped under tree cover. Fabius thought he heard one call out to his mother, and looking at the twitching eyes, realised they were both so very young, hardly more than fifteen summers. His heart clenched for the briefest moment. And his soul shrank that one bit more.

Now, they were heaving the *Tormentum* into place, in between two oaks, whose leaves made adequate cover. The *Sagittarii* were in place, fire-arrows poised, tense within the grip of the gut and the bow's centre. And these archers were forward by several *passus*, in a line facing the Villam Regis, waiting. The night was young, the moon, barely a sliver and there was even a ground mist growing leaving the *Sagittarii* almost invisible save for the tips of their longbows.

The *Tormentum* creaked as the first firebomb was placed in the metal sling, as if dormant muscles were suddenly springing into action. Drusus, a hefty broad-beamed Roman tested the thick ropes holding all the parts together, peering in to see any frayed edges. Any weak parts, under the enormous pull back of the forward thrust, could see the whole *Tormentum* just crumble like play sticks in a child's game. The wooden arm rose obliquely to its highest, the range needed to hit the target. The concussion felt would be at its most extreme and they had eight fireballs to propel. It had been agreed if the machine broke, they would abort and leave it there.

A steady glow appeared suddenly within the shadowed trees. Lucius Duccius brought the hammer down hard on the pole bolt, which scudded out onto the grass and a tremendous whoosh arose as the fireball was expelled, singeing the leaves and bark as it flew high, a tail of flame flaying in the night air, hitting the roof of Villam Regis. As soon as the trajectory was assured, the Tormentum was then moved a few degrees, the second fireball was lit, placed and ejected in a matter of a few minutes. The kickback shook the oak trees that were its cover.

The screams of women and shouts from the men inside the stricken villam could now clearly be heard. The second fireball hit. Shadowy figures could now be clearly seen running from the palace.

The *Sagittarii* stood, clearly seen against the growing flames as poised shadows in the night, taking aim to hit their targets. The flaming arrows arced into the darkness, the screams now shrill and terrifying, as bodies hit the ground burning in agony.

The brutal onslaught continued and continued, though in time for fifteen minutes only. And it became clear to the praetorians that this mission was a success. The Villam Regis was ablaze. The last expulsion from the *Tormentum* had seen several beams crack. Now spent, Aetius Septimus made the quick decision to leave, run with all speed back to the *Trireme* and set sail. He gave the retreat call and was gratified to see the swift downing of the long bows and the shadowy figures join him in the wood.

There was no challenge to them as they sped back to the wharf. The *Trireme* was just a speck on the night sky when the first survivors reached the water's edge, sinking to their blackened knees, screaming abuse to an empty sea and a moonless night.

... ...

The first fireball hit the roofing just above the *oeci*. Shingles shattered and cascaded down onto the fine mosaic floor, raising the dust which came to meet the fireball as it hit the head of Apollo, smashing the tesserae into shards. The two slave women cleaning there did not stand a chance. Their body parts were hurled across the *ala*, whereupon Agrippa Aquila, who had come to chide them on their laziness was hurled away and hit the wall, to land in a heap by the entrance to the exedra. It saved her life.

The terrible screaming of people joined the battering explosions of the next fire ball and those following. The silken drapes, chosen for their luxury had flames licking upwards to claim the busts of Goddesses perched above them. All the *lectus* and *cathedra supinas* were victims to the flames. The plants shrivelled and bent down to a blackened dust. The heat became intense. The screams of the trapped and dying echoed relentlessly into the night. The body parts of the slaves blackened, and became unknown, anonymous and forgotten in the surge to find life.

Agrippa suddenly opened her lungs and brought back life to herself. Smoke-ridden and toxic, it was still oxygen. She moved her bruised limbs. Her head was excruciatingly painful, white lights flickered before her eyes. Slowly vision returned and she pulled herself upright, looking for escape. The *exedra* promised her life, and she took it, making striding, lurching steps towards the open sky. Agrippa Aquilla gave not one thought to the safety of her children, and even less to her husband, Albanus, as she strode away from Villam Regis Cogidvbni, towards a life Hades himself had created.

... ...

Aquilla's children and her husband Albanus, were all in the state apartments along the east wing, when the third fireball made a direct hit. Aurelius and Crispus were seated with other men around the gambling table. Usurpers took delight in breaking Roman laws. And the stakes could not have been higher. Aurelius had just forfeited his best stallion to an intolerable jerk of a centurion, and Crispus was gaining his own ground. They had stopped gambling and were looking at each other, expecting the next man to take the lead when that third fireball negated any negotiation. It reverberated through several rooms, sending chips and knuckle bones asunder.

"Window NOW!" shrieked Aurelius, as he leapt up to dive out of the adequately large window, shattering the green glass in his exit. The rest followed, all escaping the carnage with a few cuts and bruises to arms and legs.

Balbus Decimus, the youngest son, was knocked hard against the wall of his *cubiculum* as the other wall crumbled under the impact of the fireball that made a direct hit to the state rooms of Albanus Antonius Cogidubnus. Balbus lay unconscious for several minutes, finally grabbing the smoke-filled air to revive himself. And it was then that he made the mad dash to save his pater. He soaked a woollen cape in the fountain outside and ran towards his father's *cubiculum* dodging the flames fanned by a wind that had sprung up. He shouted again and again, although it was a smoke-damaged throat that croaked out in alarm. He saw a crumpled form lying amid a roaring loud fire that was engulfing his father. He lunged forward but was beaten back by the flames.

Covering himself even tighter in the dripping cloak, he tried again, this time reaching Albanus, reaching down to take his arms to drag him away. The cloak fell. His arms caught fire. He saw beyond a doubt that his father had died.

"Pater, I always loved you. Know that I always loved you!" he screamed as his throat burned. Balbus turned and faced a wall of fire now licking ferociously up the wall, eclipsing the doorway from which he had entered. Suddenly a figure loomed there with outstretched hand. "Take it," the figure cried, "NOW!" Balbus lurched forward and held the offered hand, screaming in pain as the flames took him. The slave who had saved Balbus, reached in the burning room to retrieve the cloak and swamped Balbus' body damping down the flames until just smoke escaped the crumpled heap before him.

"You are being favoured by the Gods," the slave whispered as he gently stroked the stricken form of Balbus, now third in line to the Cogidubnus Briton Kingship, "Never feel guilt. You tried all you could."

The slave helped Balbus reach the other survivors, and they huddled together on the wharf, silently, in their own private pain and for some, in pure hell. Help reached them by dawn. Healers arrived from the nearby *ceasterwic* plying healing ointment and bandages to those badly burnt. Balbus was one such. They were taken in covered wagons to the village where they were fed and cared for. It was some days before the messenger arrived from Carausius with coins for the *ceasterwic* and clothes for the royals who were to make fast to Berandinzium Villam on Vecta, to hide until events calmed down. Even timid Balbus knew this to be an outright lie. Everything was going to get so much worse.

... ...

Chapter 59

294 A.D

Vrittakos, leaning heavily on the oak table, his aging face subsumed in wrinkles, and his arms, exposed, showing a mountainous range of raised purple veins, growled through congestion of his airways, "The survivors of the burning have almost reached us. They plead sanctuary and we will accord them that privilege."

"Granted," came the murmured replies from the men cloistered in the small *tablinum* that was becoming stuffy and airless. Summer was at its height and gave weight to the extraordinary carnage of the exquisite Regis Cogidvbni Villam.

"And who exactly is coming?" asked Achaikos, whose mind was as sharp as a gladius, but whose body was crippled. He was almost entirely in pain, save for the ointments and potions created by Kiana and Lãfa, between them, formidable healing Wítig cwèns.

"The three remaining sons of Cogidubnus," replied Bricius, "Orders from Carausius himself, who has retreated to Lundinuim. Leaving Allectus to marshal legions in preparation for the invasion from Maximian. May his soul rot in Hades!"

"This island home is a Goddess-created hiding-place for people." Vrittakos growled, his eyes eclipsed completely in a Greek wide grin." We must offer our thanks to Nerthus."

"I have heard that the sons are itching to repay this outrage with the scattered entrails and guts of any Roman that comes in their path!" Bricius added with a salutary nodding of his head, as if the deed was already done. "The wonder of the Villam Regis is mostly destroyed and along with it the legitimacy of native rule in Britannia."

Silence fell upon the men as they pondered the enormity of the loss. Each had spent days of exquisite luxury there, in the *oeci*, the large ornate baths and superb *cubiculum*.

"Word has it that Maximian sent a force of legionnaires to set fire to the villam. To destabilize the hold the Britons have here." Bricius continued, seemingly knowing a great deal about the event. He had a network of messengers and spies that defied that stretch of water completely.

"No doubt the brothers' Cogidubnus will add more to this turgid mix," Vrittakos growled, as he heaved himself up from the chair, signalling that the meeting was at an end. The men all shuffled out of the *tablinum*, the doom-laden energy sitting heavy on their old shoulders.

Achaikos saw Kiana standing in the shadow of the high plinth displaying the Augustus Claudius in a beneficent pose. She was holding the astringent and potent herb potions for his twice-daily punishments. He grimaced, as she smiled and crooked her head. "Oh, how does she defy the aging process that bedevils me!" he thought for the thousandth count, and in the same moment sending silent gratitude to Hecate.

"The worry upon you is making you look haggard, old man!" she remarked, taking his arm gently and leading him away to her *cubiculum* that had become an apothecary, stacked to the ceiling with herbs, mortar and pestles. Achaikos's face relaxed, as he always softened in her presence. Their love had become inviolable, unassailable and simply sacred. She had gifted him a healthy son, Alexios, now a young man who understood and could speak fluently, three languages, Assyrian, Greek and Suevii, but who struggled with Latin, as he had grown to dislike the Romans entirely. He had a kinship with Eastmund of the Wihtwara, who was married to Aia, Vrittakos' daughter. Alexios' kinship sprang from the deep spiritual connection he had to the white augury horses of the Warinni. Now that Bricius had travelled to Wihtland to become overseer to Berandinzium Villam, Alexios felt a freedom to become his own man, and it had led him to the white auguries and Eastmund, who, now in his mature years, welcomed the support.

Those wonderful creatures, spoilt and pampered as they were, were a great handful. Vrittakos held a deep union with the Warinni, and let his son go, on the promise that he would visit his old father regularly.

"And who will it be, beloved, that I will have administer to?" Kiana asked, as she applied the turgidly smelly herb mixed in goose grease to the taut muscles of his shoulders. He sagged visibly, being brought back to the terrible present from a perfect vision of Alexios riding the great white stallion across swaying grass in full-summer sunlight, towards a glistening sea. He growled, a low deep guttural rumble as Kiana's kneading had found a stricture and dealt with it as only she knew how!

"The Cogidubnus family, the three brothers and their mother, have escaped the fire," Achaikos growled through the pain. "Old Albanus perished," he stated without emotion. He looked up, but Kiana did not halt her massage. "Under the orders of Carausius, they are to remain here in secrecy and your care. Albanus and Carausius were very close and masterminded many an insurgence against the Romans. An invasion is imminent. Maximian is taking his orders direct from Diocletian. I believe the latest victory for Carausius and Albanus came on the battlefield in fury over Diocletian's assumption of the title Brittannicus Maximus! That is the title belonging to the Briton King. Bricius knows more, he has spies everywhere it seems."

"He is his father's son," Kiana murmured, "we need to be very clever and swift in response if needs be."

"I believe this is a time to call on the Goddess for assistance," Achaikos remarked, "Wítig Cwèns will be needed."

"I will travel to Lãfadūn," Kiana stated simply, "And bring Agrona along. This *drýcræft* will be needing the Goddess power of three." Kiana continued pulling Achaikos' muscles into alignment. It was the only way to ensure a decent night's sleep for him. But a seeping cold ice flow was spreading into Kiana's bones and her heart, freezing her gut in fear. The timing of her vision, all those years ago in Byzantium, was approaching, relentless and unchanged. She wanted to scream. And to run. To save them from the destruction of their lives together and all they held dear.

She had chosen to stay here on this small exquisite island. It had wrapped its green tentacles around her and had almost promised her immortality. Almost....

... ...

Tamina knelt before the badly burnt form of Balbus Decimus. He had been wrapped carefully in a silk sheet, which was now clinging to patches of burnt skin deftly treated with herbs by Lãfa. He had arrived off the *cnearr* that had come to their rescue, shaking. He now had beads of sweat building on his brow, presaging a fever taking hold. He was in trauma and had become mute. He had always found talking painful for his stutter had never really left him. Balbus was an abused child now grown to a fractured adult. Tamina was instantly drawn to him.

"Why?" Kiana asked herself, "Does my daughter always open her heart to the ugly ones, the disfigured." An image of the one-eyed Andreas pushed itself to the forefront of her mind, and she deftly shunted it away. Tamina had stayed true to him. She had never even taken a lover. Maybe this was about to change. Achaikos had sent Andreas off into the wilderness of the Silk Road nearly thirty summers ago. He must be lost to her by now.

Tamina was now gently stroking the silent Balbus, talking gently to him, questions, that might make him answer. He looked deeply on her gaze, "I, I, can n ot reeee...mmember." he stuttered, "I I pass....ed ooout!" Tears filled her eyes and she looked away. But held his hand all the while.

Meanwhile in the *tablinum*, there was much talk. Voices of the men overlaid each other in a flurry of descriptive. The older brothers were relieving themselves of shared pain.

"There was no warning, no messages from our spies. None!" exclaimed Crispus, who had minor burns and injuries from the flight away from Villam Regis. A sprained ankle from scaling the high wall and landing badly and a disjointed shoulder, both now bandaged. He wiped a grimy hand over his face and hiding it in wild curly hair, began to shudder, gasping as tears began to flow.

"Pater did not escape," he spluttered, "he was burnt, blackened, unrecognisable."

"We were near the west *exedra*," Aurelius growled in the bass voice so like his poor Pater, Albanus, "We both saw the fireballs hurl over the night sky. I can still hear the swish of flames and thuds as they hit our home, our palace! And the legionnaires sent fire-arrows to build up the flames."

"Did you not try to rescue your pater?" Vrittakos asked quietly, as both men's gaze drifted to the mosaiced floor. He knew the answer but felt compelled to ask it anyway. Albanus was of their blood, no matter how bad a father he truly was.

"It was too quick," Crispus answered eventually, "The fire just spread everywhere. We could never have reached him, and I had no idea where he was in the palace!"

"Balbus tried to rescue him," Vrittakos stated, now eying both men directly, "and he has the burns to prove it. Yet he cannot speak."

Both brothers were silenced. Suddenly Crispus blurted out, like a strangled goat, "He was not my real pater anyway! And I have been beaten cruelly because of it!"

"And I have spent most of my youth being trained by Postumus," Aurelius added, "Who was his real father!"

Vrittakos held up both his hands in submission to the two young men. They were the product of a different time, a usurper Emperor and a grasping over-ambitious father. A Briton/ Romanesque who believed his was a divine right to rule his kingdom. Postumus had met his violent end in an assassination by his own soldiers, now a hallmark of a poisonous reign.

Bricius entered the *tablinum*, brushing off dirt from his *tunica*. He had been travelling back with messages and news of the assault on Villam Regis.

"It was an elite force", he began, settling himself heavily on the nearest *supina*, "Equites and praetorians who boarded a *trireme* in Gaul, along with a monstrous-looking catapult, many long bows with big arrows fitted with tallow for burning. Upon landing at Noviomagvs Regnorvm, absolutely in the dark moon, they travelled with this thing, and equipment to a nearby wood, constructing the sling there. They murdered anyone who came too close. They found two young boys with their throats cut. No warnings ever came through to the palace. And when the firing was complete, they disappeared into the night, like shadows of Hades himself!"

"And now Berandinzium Villam had become once again a refuge for fugitives from Rome's anger and a glaring direct target", Bricius continued, looking over to Vrittakos, "And of the mother, Agrippa Aquilla, that wild-eagle woman, who has wrought more than enough damage on her children? Well, Venitouta, you dear wife, has spirited her away to her apartments. A role, you Vrittakos, would not envy her for one second. Between the huge dichotomy of her dark roiling spirit sinking into more blackness and her new Christian sanctimonious speeches, you could fear for your wife's sanity."

So, Vrittakos made his way along the winged corridor to her apartments, on a kind rescue mission, leaving the young brothers to simmer in their guilt.

"Apollo, Juno, Diana," he exclaimed, looking heavenward, "What an unholy mess we find ourselves embroiled in. Can we ask for a rescue too?"

... ...

Chapter 60

Drycræft

I saw Kiana, high priestess from the Villam before she saw me. I was down by the quayside, at the Emporium, a daily chore, now that the season was in full flow and we had *cnearr* and *skiff* arriving almost on top of each other. Dust and pollen danced together as footfalls and breeze orchestrated the swirl. Sunni was at her most brilliant, her rays highlighting the dust's dance. I did not know Kiana that well. I was wary of her. Her spirit was quite foreign to mine. Her focus high, up with the oldest Gods, and stars, planets and milky way, as she called the heavens.

I was unpacking a wooden box with many layers of straw, that had travelled along the Silk Road to us. An absolute marvel! Exquisite and expensive pottery was cradled within. Sunni caught the stunning blues and gold of a small urn so intricate it took my breath from me. I set it carefully aside as I knew this was from the priestess's homeland. Kiana was so preoccupied with picking some vetch and honeysuckle, she did not see me until she was almost abreast with me, as I held this urn before me and offered it up.

"Oh, ahh!" she exclaimed, holding her arms full length, "Ευλογημένη Εκάτη! Νόμιζα ότι δεν θα ξανάβλεπα ποτέ την Σογτιανή τέχνη.

"Blessed Hecate! I thought I may never see Sogdian art ever again!" She turned it slowly around, her eyes dazzled and wide open. Her smile was so fetching as she touched this part of the design and another, caught up in a time long past, I saw tears well up in her dark-brown eyes and I held her hand as she placed it back on the trestle table. Her full black hair, with only a spattering of grey strands, fell about her face, covering intense emotion as she shook herself free and turned to me, her expression now one of alarm and yes, even fear!

"Agrona, I have come to give you a warning," Kiana stared at me in an intense way I had not witnessed before, "Dark and terrible times are upon us here on Wihtland. The evil Roman legacy is about to be played out here! Be under no illusion, we will not be spared, even as this island may be sacred, and seen as such by the Caesars. Their depravity will be turned against them and we will be caught up as if we, ourselves are in the circus with the lions. As victims, slaughtered, in front of the eyes of the Gods, looking on with thumbs down, we will be brought down!"

I had never seen her so upended, so scared, she, who was the warrior from Persia, who had fought herself clear of many an enemy. I had listened to the stories and marvelled at her courage.

"When this time comes, Agrona," she continued, looking straight into my soul, "You must leave and return to your tribe, the Durotrige. They will be your safety and your calm. Believe me! I will send word!"

"But for now, Wihtland is offering up her magick, her secrecy and *drýcræft*, for we, *wítega cwèns* are being asked to conjure up high magick in the defence of our men, the rightful rulers of Britannia. The Despicable Clique need our powers."

I drew in a deep breath before answering, "I can feel the dark energy billowing up around this island," I replied, "We need to counter it with our own. I hear the royal survivors are here, at Berandinzium Villam. They are very vulnerable."

"Indeed," countered Kiana, "I have come to take you to Lãfadūn. There is little time to waste. The invasion of Britannia is imminent. We need to know exactly when this will be."

I hesitated. I have always been a solitary, with my own powers kept close. I had made a vow never to dilute, it leads to diminishment often. I was taught by my Ancestors, the Mights. I never needed to divulge any wisdom to anyone else.

Kiana saw my reluctance. "I beg you, please do this!" she implored, holding my arm in a grip that hurt me. I struggled free and turned away. "I will ask!" I replied, walking from her, leaving her standing there looking aghast at my retreating back.

Mōnã was full, beaming her gentle light onto the Earth Mother as I reached my sacred place, hidden on the high down, overlooking Berandinzium Villam. The moonlight refracted the white lime walls and made the villam shine. Ghostly and silent, this night was to call my Ancestors to me. And to us. This is holy ground. The only place where the two ancient male and female energies conjoin in eternal embrace. The heartbeat of Wihtland lies here. I had been praying and felt nothing except the gentle breeze on my face. I asked again, for the ancestors of Mōnã and Lugh to show themselves and speak.

"Hynafiaid a alwaf i ti. Yr ydym yn wynebu perygl dirfawr yma. Helpwch ni i ddiogelu ac arbed y tir hwn a'i bobl rhag y Rhufeiniaid.

"Ancestors I call to you. We are facing grave danger here. Please help us protect and save this land and its people from the Romans."

I sat with head bowed. A rustling of the tall grasses around me increased until a blowing wind came, and I jerked my head up. There was a shimmering form before me, not solid or even recognizable, but the voice was distinct, and all around me.

"Daughter, we hear you. You must not stand alone, nor should you feel frightened to share your power. Nor should you feel so important that you are above those who have asked for your help. Join them! At the time of the next full moon, conjure up a mighty mist, a fog. Lugh will assist you all. It will not be the only time. You will know.

"The Sogdian princess is right. The wheel is turning, and it cannot be stopped. It is left for all to endure, with right thinking, right action and pure thought. To survive, if the Fates decree it and bring Light to all left in the Wake."

I sank to the ground, needing to be smothered by the earth, the grasses, now still. All was quiet and I stayed there till dawn crept up upon me, and Sunni kissed my cold cheeks with her warmth.

… … … … … … … … …

My husband, Aodhan was waiting for me, by the door of our *hūs*, wearing an expression that bounced from intense anger to worry. On seeing me dishevelled and cheeks still wet with tears, he dropped and lost all anger, coming up to hug me tightly, whispering words of calm and endearment. He is my anchor and my rock. He smelt of cow and forged metal. And I felt totally safe. I explained all to him as Sunni rose in the sky to promise yet another sweltering day. We shared the dread and it made it bearable. Courage made possible by the power of love. We are simple peasant folk and I felt nervous at the prospect of mixing with royals, highborn and suchlike.

"Remember this," Aodhan stated, looking me square in the face, "they do not need your culinary skills, great though they are, nor your needlecraft and weaving! They need your *drycræft*, and it is truly formidable."

And so, together we walked with purpose to the villam, stepping up to the wheel of fortune as it slowly rotated.

A slave girl took us immediately to the *cubiculum* where Achaikos was resting on a *lectus* stretched on his belly, head towards us, eyes tight shut, moaning in some pain, as Kiana massaged his shoulders quite aggressively. She turned and stopped immediately, getting up to greet us, bringing with her an atrocious odour of curative herbs in goose grease.

"Ahh, beloved Juno," Achaikos rumbled deep in his throat, "You have heard my prayers. My heartfelt thanks to you both, Agrona, Aodhan. My torture is ended...for today at least." He smiled at Kiana, blowing her a kiss. Kiana bent over the washbowl on a golden plinth, nodding to the girl for more fresh water. She cleaned her hands and arms for several minutes, then rubbed perfumed oil to rid herself of any trace of the pungent mix. She half-turned to eye her husband,

"This is but a prelude, old man, for this evening's session!" She turned to face us, giving me a wonderful smile, and bowed elegantly.

"I am honoured you came," she said sincerely as I felt her eyes bore through me to reach my heart, "and so very relieved. We need to reach Lãfadūn with all speed. Do you ride?"

"Whenever I am able," I replied quickly, meaning to add that was rarely indeed. But I was forestalled by her taking my hand and leading me away. She turned to face Aodhan, "This is women's work, and I would be so very grateful if you would take my husband for his daily walk."

"Huh!" came the outburst from Achaikos, "Patronise me woman at your peril!"

"I look forward to it," Kianna bounced back, smiling.

"Aodhan, take me to the *culina*, if you please." Achaikos commanded, "There we shall sit and play knuckles for a considerable time. I wager highly, I warn you, over amphorae and sweet meats."

Kiana strode forward shaking her head. The horses were waiting for us. A piebald gelding was led to me. He looked placid enough and as I mounted up, I felt his energy meet mine. I patted and ruffled his mane. I told him he was handsome, and he shook his head in complete agreement. We cantered off round the open field next to the villam, breaking into a gallop along the stone road, then up the *dūn* along its rim. It was sheer freedom and it was glorious. I forgot our real purpose and lived in the moment. Sunni was dancing her brilliant colours before us, shadows flicking past as we galloped past the trees of Lukely Broc. Lãfadūn soon came into view, with the great mead hall perched at its highest point. The gorse bushes cascading down to the rippling water at the *botms*, shimmering their brilliant yellow and as we passed the glorious pungent aroma of their flowers. I took a heady breath in.

As we dismounted and two boys took our horses away, Lãfa came to greet us. I barely knew her, but her energy was so strong, and her eyes emitted that special gaze of the adept. It runs deep into you and you realise your soul is being met as well as the physical body present. She was a Warinni giantess. So tall I was looking up to her. Her hair was copper brown with many streaks of grey. "We are of the same age," I thought as she came to hand-clasp me in the Suevii greeting. Kiana and Lãfa simply hugged, tight and for a long embrace. Theirs was a deep relationship born from years of sharing, mourning and celebrating in a spiritual bond. Lãfa led us to the main hall, high-roofed and oak-pillared. I met the spirits-of-ages-past and they almost overwhelmed me. I had to take a breath and request they withdraw, so eager were they to be part of this *drycræft*. I had no doubt the Mights themselves would be present, so terrible the prospect this future held for us all.

The spirits-of-the-fetch animals carved into the oak pillars, some encrusted, and ancient, gave their greeting to me. We were not alone here.

"Come and sit for some dinner," Lãfa signalled to the servant girl to bring plates of food for us. We sat facing each other, deep in our own thoughts, as we eat in silence. Mead began to loosen our tongues, as our brains began to grip the grim reality.

"My daughter will be here presently, "Lãfa stated, "She has spent two twilights seeking help from the Ancestors."

"You will know after this day, what and when you must do the conjuring." Kiana replied, fingering her food pensively.

"You do not intend to be part of this?" I asked, not feeling I had a right to even ask.

"No," Kiana replied, "I have a different path to travel. My way is not this. Even though I am Zoroastrian and sacredly linked to the waters of this world, my dominion is also in the heavens. This *drycræft*, as you call it, is of the Earth. It is to Nerthus, Lugh and Mõnã you call, and you will be answered, believe me." I looked at her intently. Did she know? I knew now why I had been given this answer from my Ancestors.

Suddenly the giant oaken door at the end of the hall, began screeching and was dragged open. There before us stood a giant-ess. She was an absolute replica of Lãfa, her mother, save for the sharp blue-grey eyes. She had the same chestnut brown hair cascading down to her waist. Her wide smile reached those piercing eyes and her face dimpled with that smile. She was extraordinarily beautiful.

"Hello *dohtor*," her mother called out, "Come sit with us. We need your wisdom. My *dohtor* has returned from the Ancestor stones in Sudmōr." Lãfa turned to me,

"Agrona, meet my *dohtor*, Dagrun Wahl of the Warinni!"

Dagrun sat down opposite me and stared straight into my soul. Her eyes held mine. Unwavering and intense. Then she nodded.

"So, you too have been given the wisdom of our Ancestors," she stated quietly, "Is this not so?"

"The next full moon will augur the invasion from Roman ships carrying thousands of Centurions," I stated, as I had been told, marvelling quietly just how she knew.

"We need to hold the sacred Trinity in all we do from now on," she stated. Her words came clipped and brokered no dissension. "We need to call the Nornia to our left and our right and behind us. We need to call on the Mights to be around us. And most of all, our *Eall Fǽder* Wōden, to bring the *Galdercrǽft* to us. It must hold *Hagalaz* and *Nauðiz* as the primal forces."

"We need to call on Mōnã too," I suggested, "I made my call at the burial mound of our oldest Ancestors. The mound above Berandinzium Villam. The Nerthus and Wōden energy meet and embrace there, going deep into the earth for their communion. I was given that Mōnã will embrace the *drýcræft* in union with Lugh, so the clouds will roil, and the winds blow viciously."

"*Gíese, Gíese, þes is gōd!*" Dagrun exclaimed, smiling and bringing her hands up palms outstretched." We have but ten twilights to prepare. And from now, nothing must interfere. All must be set aside, mundane or otherwise. Are we in accord?"

"*Gíese*," we echoed together.

… … … … … … … …

Chapter 61

Galdercræft Sege

If some stranger had entered our *hūs*, they would have witnessed an obdurate, pre-occupied and even morose *wíf* who was calling for a good beating. But Aodhan knew precisely what I was doing and smiled, caressed and kissed me when he felt I needed calm and support. I had visited the burial mound of our Ancestors twice more in the hidden twilights, very late, coming back near dawn. He never questioned me, just made sure my belly was full. We had changed roles and for me it was a miracle before my very eyes!

I was calling in Mōnã, who was ripening. On the Rune sounds, I made a cascading song, lilting and quite beautiful I felt. Her power was coming ever stronger each night. The Moon song was with Laguz, all the three fates in the rushing waters were invited to join, in the high-trill sounds L. My tongue was moving at high speed, and I literally left this earth. I sang to Wunjō, sapphire-blue and sap-green bringing me back to earth. And I fleetingly saw the iridescent shining white of *Ealdmōdor* Mōnã as she appeared, arms outstretched towards me, before she faded. I knew then that we were being heard.

The following morning, I saw the striding figure of Kiana appear by the tall beech, her dark eyebrows furrowed, lashes guarding her eyes. She was deeply worried, and I felt her energy hurtling towards me. I swiftly put up a guard in protection. I was so open in these days of preparation. She held out her hand to catch mine, and without explanation took me with her, as I darted a quick glance to Aodhan, who shrugged and nodded, as he got on with the chores.

"We must make swift this journey to Everelant Ealond. This is Druid domain and we must ask permission to create this *galder-cræft*." She spoke in bursts as we hurtled along the well-trodden path, a short cut to the villam. My bare legs were getting scratched as we cut through the pinto bean field, freshly cut, with drying stalks at knee height.

"You can speak the Druid language," Kianna stated, half turning towards me, "There is an old, very ancient Druid I'm told, from whom we must get approval. We are to create a storm, Agrona. A big mighty Runic tempest that will halt Maximian. His ships will flounder."

"Where?" I asked, suspecting we must be on the highest ground for this.

"On the high cliff, above the Druid cave." Kiana replied, giving no more or less than I needed to know.

Dagrun was waiting near the stable yard, holding the horses, patting her mount. He was an enormous stallion, frisky and impatient. I guessed she was an expert horsewoman. He was infecting the other horse, so she pulled his head toward her, and whispered long and low. He settled quite remarkably to stand as quietly as my docile piebald, whom I quite loved. I would like to think it was mutual. And as we neared, I did see him frisk his head towards me and neigh a gentle greeting. Tied on the horses were leather bags full of gifts, provisions, herbs and medicines, for the Druid. He was alone. He was a hermit. The tide was low, so we were able to gallop over the causeway to Everelant. We hobbled our mounts within reach of lush grass and set off on foot to climb over the rocks to the Druid cave. Inside was dark, dank and quite cold. The tidal reach at its height kept this cave dripping in sea water and the only dry area was a stone platform where I saw a huddled figure busy making fire. Sparks flew, as his ageing crooked hands worked relentlessly with the wooden pole resting in the well-used dent of identical wood underneath. We watched in silence, as the sparks lit the kindling and he tenderly placed it in the round of small twigs, nurturing it until the flames could take the larger wood waiting in a pile.

He became aware of us as his attention moved away from the fire. His face was completely hidden under a cowl so large, only shadow could be seen of his face. He groaned low as he stood and wrenched his aging limbs into place. The shadow inspected us, in silence. Suddenly a loud gasp came from him, as he pushed his cowl away to show his face suffused with intense joy,

"Brigid, duwies sanctaidd. Ai ysbryd yw hwn, arswyd? Rhaid i'm llygaid fod yn fy twyllo. Damaethun!"

"What is he saying?" Dagrun turned to me.

"He is saying he is seeing a ghost and that his eyes are deceiving him. He is calling you by your name, Dagrun!"

"He must have known my *Ealdmōdor!*" Dagrun cried, breaking into her beautiful smile, as she nodded towards him in acknowledgment. "She often told me the story of when she and Eyvindr travelled to the Druid cave in Frescewætr Ealond. How wonderful," she enthused, "Tell him, Agrona, please!" So, I shared the news with him, and that he was seeing the granddaughter of Dagrun Wahl, now her namesake and so very like her!

He began to walk forward, still shaking his head, a skull with many blue veins and a few wisps of hair. Tears were coursing from puffed lids as he held out his bony hands to take Dagrun's in his.

"Roeddwn i'n fachgen ifanc bryd hynny. Rhoddodd ein offeiriad uchel ei ganiatâd. Derbynnir eich Teyrnas am byth gennym. Y mae fy nghalon yn gorlifo i'ch gweled chwi, yn brydferth Damaethun."

Dagrun looked towards me.

"He is saying, he was a younger man then. His heart is overflowing to see you. And that the Druid will always honour your tribe."

Very slowly and with great tenderness, Dagrun, a giant as she was, reached down to fold her arms tenderly around this most ancient of beings. And she stayed until he was calm.

"Please tell him that he will not be alone any longer. I will visit, often."

I explained, and a toothless smile spread across his face, concertinaing the wrinkles into a mass that hid his eyes altogether.

"*Dyna a wnaeth eich nain. Sawl gwaith.*" He cackled low as his shoulders shook a little.

"He is saying that is what your grandmother did. Many times!"

I presented him with the provisions and food, and we ate quietly around his fire, which was growing strong, warming our bones. I told him our mission and as much back story as I could translate. I was rusty, even in my mother tongue. I watched as his face lost all the joy and clouded over with anxiety and some anger.

"*Byddaf yn eich cynorthwyo.* I will assist you" Was all he said and pointed to a rattle that lay on a higher shelf above us. The skulls of many ravens hung from oakwood. And I knew exactly who he would be calling. We stayed until the tide made us leave.

"*Byddwn yn cwrdd eto mewn dwy twmi.* We will meet again in two twilights" he called after us.

… … … … … … … … …

Chapter 62

The Nornia, the Mights & the Witeg Cwèn Trinity
"As above, So Below"

The full moon shone with a brilliance, oscillating energy outwards, and upon us, as we stood in a line, facing her on the cliff edge. Three women, linked by hand and heart, souls quivering in expectation and the sheer power we were about to release. We were the Nornia on earth. We were the sacred trinity.

The Ancient One stood a spear length away, in the background, calling in *Eall Fæder* as only he could, with raven rattle's steady beat which never faltered. We each felt *Eall Fæder* come, a torrent of male energy in deep violet, Ansuz swirling around him, blast past us, out to sea, pulling us dangerously forward towards the edge of the cliff. Steadying, we began our own calling in. We each had our own runic spirit to invite in. Together they would unite in *galdercræft,* and the work would begin. We called it *Seiðr,* ancient. The most powerful magick of all.

I reached my sound pitch for Laguz, the trill echoing out to sea and meeting the waves. They danced back as the spirit caught each one and made them grow.

Lãfa sought the high "T" sound, trilling then dipping low to call in Teiwaz. The Mights of this Rune were inviting Lugh and Thor bringing combat in the skies.

And then to Dagrun, standing to her full height, in silhouette on the inky-dark blustery headland, her voice rose to a screech, bursting her throat vessels to carry the sound far away. It was Nauðiz, the black rune, she sought, the most violent and unpredictable. The one that nearly killed Wōden when he hung from Yggdrasil. Only she could withstand the force of this energy. *Eald Mōdor's* blood was coursing through her veins.

We brought all these energies together until our lungs ached. Then Dagrun raised her arm. The signal. We stopped. The silence was met with a growing sound without, far away. We waited. Then we called to the Nornia, with our hearts outstretched, in our mouths.

Urdhr, Verhandi, Skuld, Rūnar, Radha, Rètt Rãdh!

We watched almost without breathing. Every movement of the clouds, the beating of the waves. That distant noise was still present. But nothing was changing within our horizon. We sank to our knees, exhausted and anxious. Was this all for nothing? Was that distant sound, the Roman ships, hundreds of them beating a course for our land? We watched as Mōnã slid inexorably towards her earthly home. We all lay down, neither wanting to leave but wishing we could. I think we dozed for a short while.

Then, suddenly the strongest gust of wind nearly blew us from the cliff edge. As it swirled around, I heard the runic sounds in unison whistle past us, and looking at one another, we cried and jumped up. Before us was a roiling sea and tempestuous sky. Thor graced us with a thunderbolt that shook the earth. The rain came in torrents as the sea and the wind met to create gigantic waves that stretched as far as I could see. The Ancient One came to us, we huddled together giving thanks to the Gods and Goddess, to the Mights and their Runes.

We had halted the Roman invasion of Britannia.

… … … … … … … … …

Chapter 63

The Calm before the Storm

Vrittakos sat hunched over his desk in the *tablinum*, sweating profusely, and fingering the many messages from across the water, Lundinuim mostly, where Carausius and Allectus bathed in the glory of a victory without much Briton-blood spilt over Roman *carbatinæ*. The dispatches, some as scrolls with official wax seals, in one pile, which made Vrittakos mutter "καταραμένα ψέματα, damn lies!" under his breath. The other was a larger pile, grubby vellum squares with scratched messages from Bricius' many spies. Now they told another story.

For several months, Carausius had been frenetically minting his face on all coins cast, entertaining visions of legitimacy and official recognition. Three leather pouches had just arrived.

"Achaikos, here, look at these!" Vrittakos wheezed, "They arrived just this morning." He fumbled clumsily with the tight knotted leather thong. Achaikos looked on. Both suffered from painful swollen joints. "Ahh! The joy of decrepit old-age," he grumbled, at last releasing the glittering coinage over the walnut table. The high-quality silver glistened in the hot mid-day sun. The embossing was immaculate and of such a high standard, they shouted "Augusti" to anyone who traded with them.

"Look at this!" Achaikos exclaimed, holding one up to the light, "PAX AVGG, the peace of three Augusti! Incredible!"

"He's lining himself up alongside Diocletian and Maximian!" Vrittakos replied, shaking his wizened old head. "And see this! It says here," as he rotated the large coin around, "Restitutor Brittanniæ, Restorer of Britain."

"According to this one he is Genius Brittanniæ! Spirit of Britain, my backside!" Achaikos chipped in.

"And this...Expectate veni, Come long-awaited one!"

"And this," Vrittakos said loudly, flapping a piece of vellum, scrunched and worn as it was, holding very troubling news, "This is what Rome thinks of Carausius and Allectus. Both Maximian and Diocletian are incensed, furious and determined to put an end to usurper rule in Britannia and Gaul."

Both men sat in silence for several minutes, fingering the coins, muttering expletives under their breath. The plethora of coded letters underneath the image, like VICTOR CARAVSI AVG, the victory of Carausius Augustus, and PACATOR ORBIS Peace bringer of the world, made Greek swear-words reverberate around the villam. It all spelt out terrible trouble for everyone in Britannia, Wihtland and Berandinzium Villam.

"We will all get sucked into the battle," Vrittakos groaned softly, "And it will come."

"When Carausius came to the villam, what three years gone, what did you feel, what did you think of him, old friend?" Achaikos asked, smiling gently, thinking of those times past when peace reigned, and crops flourished.

"He came for the boys, the young men, did he not," Vrittakos answered, "Balbus was just about walking again. Terrible disfigurement for the poor lad."

"Oh!" Achaikos interrupted, "I was relieved he left. Tamina was in the process of losing her heart to the lad. Not a good choice!"

"The hairs on the back of my neck stood up in the company of Carausius, that charismatic, arrogant facsimile of the dreaded Nero!" Vrittakos replied, spitting out each word, "He is the master of illusion. He is also the master of propaganda and has the peasants eating out of his hand. If he said it was necessary for everyone to jump off the cliff...they would!"

Vrittakos held yet another message from Bricius' spy network, "And here is word that Agrippa is in Lundinuim. She has lost all her Christian devotions completely and become a regular visitor to the Temple of Bacchus in Lundinuim!"

He held another message, this time royal and official, "Carausius is marshalling support in Gaul. He is even pulling the

Christian emigres into service for Britannia. They are on the increase now you know," Vrittakos lent forward to examine Achaikos' reaction. "They are moving West. These Christians are creating larger groups in Gaul and elsewhere. Diocletian has an evil turn of mind and is on a full Christian purge. I'm hearing reports of terrible executions, forced repentance of faith. The worm will turn, Achaikos."

Achaikos remained silent for a while. Memories suddenly flooded back of trauma, screams and terror in Byzantium when Tamina and Kianna were trapped in the baying crowd of citizens wanting bloodletting to be inflicted on Christian families refusing to recant their religion.

"We came upon a community of disparate groups, Christian families in exile," Achaikos began, staring into space, in remembrance of a sudden fear, and the need to escape, "We had been travelling for many months. My boat had been left in a safe harbour, anchored in Aqullela. I had planned a slower journey, stopping to explore. To give both my women the chance to see more of their world, denied them for so long. But it was not meant to be. The plague stopped us from exploring the land. We kept to sea and only moored to bring food and water aboard. Kianna insisted on only taking the freshest of water on board, from clear bubbling streams. Never from the city. She believed that was how the plague travelled, in the water. It is her Zoroastrian wisdom that saved us, I do believe that.

"It was about ten miles outside of Aqullela that we came upon this community, with small villams, a meeting house, plots of land for growing. We needed refreshment, provisions, and poor Tamina was quite unwell. We were scared it might be the plague, but she passed the time when all signs would prove it. Turns out she was suffering her moon time.

"These Christians, they welcome you at first. Though wary of us, I believe their doctrine insists on welcoming strangers as the Nazarene did. They eat communally in this meeting house, turned dining-area. There were several professional people, two doctors, several academics and teachers. We were told Christians were on the increase everywhere and I believed them. Yet the power of the undercurrents, the tensions with us was getting stronger. We sat with them, they served us a dinner, a vegetable stew of artichoke and onions with herbs to flavour and barley to thicken it.

Suddenly this teacher spoke up, "So you must be Greek Christians, then?" I felt both Kiana and Tamina's backs arch up and felt the retort on their lips. I banged my hand down on Kiana's hand to stop her reply. "No, we are not," I said plainly, without adding any further explanation.

"Where are you heading?" he then asked.

"Britannia," I replied, "To my colleague and friend on Vecta, the Isle of Wihtland."

"That is a pagan stronghold!" he almost shrieked at us.

"Then you must attend our meeting after dinner is served," he replied in a sharp way. We could not refuse. The dinner plates were removed by women who were part of the community. I did not witness any slaves there. People began to file in sitting on the floor, on mats or leaning against a wall.

And then this tall, charismatic man entered and walked to the front.

"Greetings Mikael, son of Paul," everyone spoke at once, not in unison.

"Welcome friends and followers of Christ. Good Christian people. We Live!" he raised his hand in praise, and so everyone followed suit. "Our enemies will not sit at our table! Our lord is protecting us from evil pagans who are polluting our God-given world.

"They must be made to repent! Only those who serve our Lord will enter the gates of Heaven. So many of our loved ones have suffered terribly at the hands of the pagans whose vile idolatrous gods command them to kill.

"NOW we are the ones to kill the heathens!"

The teacher who had asked the question of us, suddenly stood up and pointed and accusing finger towards Kiana.

"So, what are you? Pagan!"

"I could not stop her this time, Vrittakos. She is such a diminutive size. The baying crowd were leaning in to stare and accuse before she opened her mouth."

"I am from Sogdia," she said loudly. It really reverberated around the room and challenged the speaker, "I am a Zoroastrian High Priestess. My God is Ahura Mazda and he is a wise and gentle god."

There was a stunned silence for just a few seconds, then all hell broke loose!

"Kill the pagans! Kill the pagans!" came shouts across the room. The scraping of swords from sheaths could be heard and we were not too close to the door and escape. Kiana had neglected to tell them, that she was a trained martial arts warrior. Before I could count to ten, she had three men on the floor panting for breath and unable to move. The screams from the baying Christians had reached a ferment and crescendo. Kiana had laid a path to the door, and we took it. Scrambling over prone bodies, we ran together as fast as we could. They chased us to the boundary of their land, then stopped.

"We did not venture further into Belgica. Instead we took the longer route following the Germania border where no Christians would even consider entering and where the plague was lessened. It was damnably cold though!"

"The worm is turning my old friend," Vrittakos said, as he poured more wine to refresh dry-throats after so much talk, "And it will devour everyone in its path, no matter if their spirituality be pure and their hearts open."

"The Warinni *Ealdmōdor* told Kiana to take me to the *Halíg Stãn*, their standing stone," Achaikos spoke after some silence pondering this dark future that was presenting itself, "She told me to just put my hand to the stone. I did."

Achaikos halted. His throat choked. He took more wine determined to share the vision that was now his. His spine creaked as he leant forward to take his soul companion by both hands, holding them tight. Vrittakos looked questioningly at him, frowning.

"What are you about to share with me, old friend?" he asked quietly.

"We must be prepared and hold all our courage in both hands over our heart," he replied, eyes glistening in the sudden swamping of emotion he had kept at bay for so long a time.

"There will come a time, very soon, at nightfall, when we will meet our adversaries on our own land. They are coming to us, Vrittakos and the wheel is about to make its final turn. It has been written. We will make our mark in the stars, my friend. Our Gods and Goddesses will surround us. Have no fear." They sat, their gaze upon each other never wavering for an unknown time. Souls meeting, hearts strengthening. Sharing, always sharing.

… … … … … … … … …

Chapter 64

296AD

I sat hunched over the bowl of pinto beans, fingering them nervously, checking for maggots, as Aodhan shared the terrible news he had got from Alexios, who had stood silently listening behind the partition to Vrittakos' tablinum.

"They are coming again, Agrona! This time Constantius is amassing a huge fleet to massacre us all! Diocletian is hell-bent on purging all usurpers and those very usurpers are coming here to hide their ships and mount a surprise attack.

"*Wíf*, you must gather again in the Trinity to command the *galdercræft seiðr*. Stop them Agrona," he pleaded, bloodshot eyes staring wildly at me, from a sleepless night and torment. I knew this was the horror Kiana had held inward for so many years. How she could never seem at ease with the wonderful gift the Fates had given her in coming here all those years ago. She knew this ending well enough. And just as her image came into my mind, I felt her energy, strident and intense, approach our humble *hūs*.

Her hair was loose, flaying out in the gusts of wind on this autumn morning. Her eyes, too, were bloodshot from tears of rage, fear, hopelessness? With her hands, fists clenched, she marched towards me. She stopped suddenly and took a breath, sagging, looking to the ground. Fighting to find the right words. She looked up, eyes drilling into my soul.

"*Wíteg Cwèn*," she began, honouring me in a rare way, "Whatever supreme efforts and *Seiðr* we call up in two twilights' time, we may fail. But if we do nothing, I believe our souls, whether here on our Earth mother, or in Neorxenawang, will cry for the want of trying!

"Our old men are busy pretending. But that is acceptable for the moment, for there, hope still lies. The youth, however, are churning. Alexios would gladly take up arms today but is resigned to skulking around corners to gain news. He will share any news with us. The messengers of Bricius have agreed to come to him first. They are giddy with coming to and fro!"

Kiana took a deep breath and came to sit with me, taking the pinto bowl from my iron grip. My hands had locked, white knuckled and blue-veined; they had gone quite numb. She took them gently and rubbed life back into them.

"We are older women, you and I, Agrona. Cynical and wizened. I know you can sense my pain and why. I do not even have to spell it out to you. But you do not know the full extent of it. And why should you? You will be spared. But dear Dagrun, now she is young and passionate, and her power is fuelled by that passion. I have hidden my vision from her. She must not know of it. She is our engine. Our powerhouse. And the old Druid, both. You are cynical enough to know it is expedient, don't you?"

I nodded, silently, half-turning to see her face, eclipsed in dangling, raven hair. I was curious to know, but dread overtook me, seeing the torment she had carried, now facing its unremitting glare.

"Now!" She turned, giving me a weak smile, "I am going to Lukely Broc to sink my face in clear, cold water to scare my nightmare face away, and visit Lãfadūn. Will you come with me?" she asked, squeezing my hand. I thought for a moment.

"I think not," I decided, "I fear my face will give too much away." Aodhan nodded, "'Tis true." He said smiling at me. Kiana raised her tired body up. Turning to smile back at me, she strode off again, skimming around our giant beech tree that always shielded us from wind and rain and whose ancient bark we called Nerthus' tapestry.

... ...

It was late evening when we both looked up from our stew, Aodhan reaching for his *birrus* as we heard the canter of hooves. It was already blowing a gale outside, and I wondered if Dagrun and the old Druid had already done their *Seiðr*. Bricius' messenger leapt off his mount, Aodhan leading the tall stallion to a dry roof, straw-bed and food. He was lathered to near exhaustion, so Aodhan remained to wipe him down. The messenger came in and bowed his greetings.

"Please sit and have food with us," I said, laying out a bowl and bringing the hanging-pot from the fire to the table.

"I bring very urgent news, *cwèn*, He looked harried. His eyes held a frozen look of sheer panic.

"Food first, I will not have otherwise," I commanded. Before he reached for the wooden spoon, he delved into his large leather satchel, producing one large scroll, officially stamped with the seal of Allectus. And several vellums, folded notes from spies in the field. We sat in silence, as the poor man devoured the stew and asked for more. He was wiping bread round the second empty bowl when Aodhan returned and saw the messages strewn on the table.

"Who are we welcoming in our home?" Aodhan asked politely.

"Messenger of Bricius," came the reply, "That is all you should be knowing." He reached for the scroll and produced a thin-bladed knife. "Heat that up will you," he commanded, handing it Aodhan. I just sat and watched, fear, tingling, reaching my spine and throttling my guts.

"The messages from the spies tell me that Constantius Chlorus is leading this assault, with two fleets of *Trireme*, amounting to thousands of centurions. He intends a massacre. Believe me, rivers will flow blood red!

"He is one evil bastard. You should be fearing him above all others. They say he is crafty, and that he runs with the foxes and chases with the hounds."

He took the knife and melted the underside of the seal, opening the scroll. He gasped, swearing quietly under his breath.

"Allectus is commanding the safety of Wihtland as a base for all his fleet. He is coming on the dawn tide with many vessels of Frankish warriors. Half of his army will be on those boats. The other half in Lundinuim." He took the knife again, softening the wax and resealing it as if no one had seen it.

"I must go!" he suddenly cried, gathering all the messages back into the leather satchel, giving us a brief nod of thanks, reaching for the door.

"If I were you, I would run!" he said and disappeared into the darkness.

We sat in shock, numbed and silent. Then panic overcame me.

"I must go, my love," I stated, "I must get Kiana and meet Dagrun, now, this night. It is the land mist we must call up. To hide them and confuse the Roman fleet!" He handed me his *birrus* against the cold and I rushed out, not even a hug afforded this night.

… … … … … … … … …

We stood looking out to sea, at the high point, before the *Halíg Stãn*, creating the sacred sounds to call in our Gods and Goddesses. There had been no preparation, just the swift decision to be here, to ask the Ancients, the Mights to coat our beloved island in a mist, to save all our souls. We believed it completely. Dagrun was empowered, and we followed her lead. We lost our earthly connections in the chanting and soon our souls were above us and beyond us. We called to the Mights to bring the rune of Wunjō to hail Nerthus and Lugh, air and earth co-joined in a harmony of balance. Above all we needed stillness, no rush of air. We entered that stillness in silence and wonder, as this place was known for Lugh to come crashing in.

In that silence, Dagrun broke in a piercingly high shriek, for the Mights to bring in the runes, Hæg and Isax, to chill the air. I was chanting to Mōnã, as ever to raise the warm waters, to chill in the cold still air. Lãfa joined with me. We saw the sea mist rising.

Heartened, we sang until our throats ached and we sank to the green earth and prayed, hands spread before the *Halíg stãn*, for deliverance, peace and safety once more. It was just before Sunni rose from her sleep that we awoke for we had dozed, yet again. Soft cries of astonishment died in the still, dense foggy air. From our high point, we saw a blanket of mist had covered the low ground. And we saw also, the tip end of many masts, ships laying still and hidden. The fog was growing as we made our way home, to wait, and pray for another victory.

... ...

Chapter 65

"The Worm is Turning"

Aodhan and I sat in muted, ghastly silence at the horrifying message delivered to us from Alexios, who had chosen to run straight here before facing his pater and uncle, let alone his mother. Bricius' spy had already fled from the island.

"Your fog achieved nothing!" Alexios stated, accusingly, "Yes my mater told me! All it did was grant Allectus and his Frankish army more time before getting slaughtered!" I gasped and held my hands together so tightly, white knuckles showed. I began to sway, trying to block out the rest of his tirade.

"Asclepiodotus, a Prætorian commanded by Constantius himself, landed his ships in Clausentum and gave the order to burn them all! There would be no retreat. They just lay in wait for Allectus to show up. The Frankish army ran to Calleva Atrebatum and were surrounded. Allectus, the coward, tried to become a peasant and stripped himself of all regalia. He was beaten to death," Alexios stated, devoid of feeling.

"Then, Constantius arrived to massacre every single Briton and Frankish soldier left in Lundinuim. I am told there were no survivors. I am also told he is on his way here. We have very little time left."

"To do what!" Aodhan shouted in horror.

"To wreak his own revenge on this pagan island, which harboured usurpers. Bricius' messenger told me he is travelling with a group of these Christians and a group of his elite Prætorian guard!"

"Oh! Oh, Lugh defend us!" Aodhan muttered, slamming his fists on the table, sending wooden plates and spoons clattering to the floor. He expression was full of numb horror, as his gaze darted to and fro, trying to bring rational thought forward. I was too numb to move or think anything, let alone act.

"I must go and be with my family!" Alexios cried, jumping up and heading for the door. He turned before leaving, "Thank you for all that you tried to do. May your Gods protect you. We will not meet again!" I turned to see him run from us, *birrus* flapping about him in the wind, seemingly attacking all he represented. I gulped to swallow a scream, then buried my head in arms to silently weep.

... ...

Alexios stood rooted to the floor of his parent's *cubiculum,* eyes like rounded-orbs and a mouth moving silently, like a stranded koi fish, "You mean to tell me you have known about this catastrophe for years! And neglected to share this with me, your son!" He glared at Kiana, to whom he was closest, holding his hand out in supplication.

Kiana gave him a full-stare back, gentle and full of compassion, "I did not want to give you the weight of it all these years. We wanted you to grow free and strong. And there never seemed to be a right time."

"So, this is the right time is it?" Alexios shouted back, "With just a few hours to gather my wits and things I treasure, before we all run for the first sailing away from here. This is my *home!*" Alexios shuddered to a halt, then broke into tears. Kiana leapt forward to surround him in her arms and held him tightly, their tears mingling and falling to trembling shoulders, they remained for some time until the grief eased.

Tamina was crying gently, trembling as she held on even tighter to her beloved pater. Achaikos had been a true father to her. Suddenly, images of her real brute of a father, his bloated drowned body in the dirty water of the Orientis, hit her and she hugged Achaikos even tighter. Their life was being broken into fragments, like shattered tesserae.

Achaikos turned to look up to his daughter, mature, sure of her way in life, and he nodded imperceptibly, "You must go with your mama and your brother back to your true home, to Sogdia, to Samarkand." Tamina bent back to stare at him in horror.

"Noooo!" she cried, realising just what he was saying, "You must stay with us pater! We will find somewhere here. Go to the Wihtwara, the Durotrige! They will take us and protect us. Go to Ytene Weald where Eyvindr lives."

Both Kiana and Alexios had cried out in protest. Kiana, now completely hysterical sank to her knees before Achaikos, pleading with him to stay with her. He gently laid his hands on her shoulders.

"My beautiful Sogdian princess, look at me, *look at me!*" Achaikos demanded, "You know in your heart and your ancient soul, that you would be going back to your real home. You have known it all along! Now it is time my love. You have many years left, and your children, have many more.

"I am far too old to make the journey back, Kiana," Achaikos said, whose eyes were swimming, as he stroked her hair gently, "you know this. And," he paused, gathering strength, "Vrittakos has told me he will not leave. He will not abandon his temple, his villam, to thugs and religious terrorists. He will go down fighting, as will I, at his side."

"But you have both lived for nearly ninety seasons," Kiana shrieked, "What fighting and defending can you do!"

"We will be fighting in our own way until the last breath, as well you know," Achaikos came back with determination in his voice.

"Go! My family, go now and prepare. The horses are waiting."
"GO!"

… … … … … … … … …

The night had fallen too fast on us. I had placed a tallow light outside for Aodhan to see well enough to pack the horses. And it was in that flickering glow, that I saw the tall elegant shadow of

Dagrun leaning forward to stare intently at the beech tree's bark, just at eye level. She then came running forward to us.

"This is it!" she cried, standing tall and rigid staring wildly at me, "this is the beginning of the end for my people, our way of life, our faith and spirituality. It is NOW!"

"What have seen, Dagrun?" I cried.

"My *Ealdmōdor* was always telling me as I grew, to watch for the beech tree rune. She said, when she was a watcher for Wōden, the Nornia told her how important this sign would be. To tell her children and her children's children. It is this." She drew the rune on the dirt floor, with her finger, large and unmistakable.

þ

"It is the Rune of unstoppable change. The Rune of the Nornia, the Fates. There is nothing we can do to change this!"

"Dagrun, Constantius is nearly upon us," I replied, catching her arm, "he is coming with some Christians in tow. And Prætorian guards. Why is he bringing Christians here?"

"To make Achaikos and Vrittakos recant and deny their ancient religions, of course!" Dagrun replied, "I have had the visions of my *Ealdmōdor* given to me to carry. So, I will know when it happens. It will be now, believe me. And if they refuse, they will be slaughtered."

"Oh! blessed Nerthus, that is evil!" I cried, trying to keep from screaming, "Aodhan and I have decided to stay for as long as we can. To be witness. Will you join us?"

"*Giese*," came the short reply, "We need to be in very dark clothes and black our faces and hands."

We made good our camouflage, and as Mōnã was in hiding, she blessed us too. We made our way to Berandinzium Villam, finding a thick and tall box-tree to shelter and hide behind. The villam was all alight, every sconce flaming with the strongest beeswax. Done deliberately to create a beautiful sight and one I committed to memory. There was so much light I immediately recognized Kiana, Tamina and Alexios jump onto their mounts and gallop from their home. It was heart-breaking to see the two ancients, courageous men both, hold onto each other for support, as their old hearts must be breaking. Then I gasped in horror as I saw the willowy figure of Venitouta join them. Oh Nerthus, please no! I thought. I looked over to Dagrun. She shook her head and looked down to the earth, praying.

That terrible night wore on, in silence. Our patience stretched yet our hope stayed alive, believing we would witness no more than a few rooks cawing and fighting over a meal. I saw three horses with riders stationed on the *dūn* ridge, looking down on the villam. Kiana and her children.

Then that sound of Roman footfalls and metal jangling that can never be erased from memory. Fear shot through us all. Dagrun sprang alert, her eyes everywhere. They were coming. We all looked to the entrance of the villam. With hearts stuck in our throats, we watched as the small army of Praetorians, shields and gladius in battle readiness, marched into the sacred grounds of Berandinzium Villam, the temple of Abrasax, Mithras and Ahura Mazda. Their helmets with full regalia swayed as they marched, with only their eyes showing. There is nothing more terrifying than a Prætorian army, every sinew itching to maim and kill. Their souls long-gone, these soldiers held no honour.

They stopped as they came abreast of us. We held our breath. But they were as iron statues, facing forward to the *vestibulum*. I glanced over to Dagrun, and I knew by her expression that she was calculating the odds of attack and rescue. And they were fruitless and stupid. We had committed ourselves to absolute silence, so I fixed her with my strongest stare and shook my head. Her best gift to them was to become *scōp*. To keep the memory alive of these courageous Greeks. There were about fifty of these monster Praetorians. What a ridiculous sight, I thought. Fifty Praetorian elites against three very old people.

Then suddenly they parted to create a path, along which came a very tall, granite-featured Roman, with acutely staring eyes, now glaring with brows deeply furrowed. He wore a toga with the purple trim. And he carried a huge weighted scroll, with wooden ends, tassels decorating it, which swayed as he walked forward.

"Constantius Chlorus!" I hissed. I had been told he favoured the Christians by Bricius' spy, and I had declined to believe him, until now. For with him came four men in priestly robes, stark white, and wearing this Jesus cross, large and wooden. They stood by Constantius, not behind him.

"*Custodes Villam Berandinzium. Facite vobis notum, NUNC.* Keepers of Berandinzium Villa. Make yourselves known to us. NOW!" Constantius bellowed, his voice shriller than his bodyweight suggested. Silence, with only the sconce flames hissing and flickering in the night. Then, as if pulled by an invisible pulley, the two ancient men came out of the shadow of the *vestibulum.* Supporting each other, they limped towards the western Emperor.

"Well, well," Achaikos growled, "If it isn't young Constantius before us! My, how you have grown, young sir, since we met last. How many years is it now? I am glad the plague did not claim you." Achaikos crooked his head to one side, questioning, but alert and keenly watching the changes in attitude of Constantius. Confusion, he thought. He does not remember us at all. He continued,

"My wife saved your life, I remember. In saving the usurper Postumus from a very bloody killing, she saved all of us at Villam Regis, so I recall. She quite took to you, as a lad, by the way. Have you come to thank us?"

Constantius frowned, took a pace backwards, as his Christian cohorts stared at him. Then remembrance dawned, his stance wavered, as he fingered the scroll, looking hard at it. He heaved a breath and looked up, teeth bared, body quivering. Achaikos knew they were lost from that second onwards and so did I. I gripped Aodhan's hand, squeezing so hard, for courage to witness the next minutes.

Constantius' tirade began.

"Pagan devil worshippers! You have harboured and protected usurpers, the despicable clique! Your sacred island with the devil god Mithras will not save you now. This pimple on the backside of Britannia is the home of the devil. We are about to purge you. Allectus came to hide here. You protected him. Your witches blew up a storm and made our ships flounder! Do you really think we did not know about this!

"There is nothing you can say to us except one thing," he turned to the Christians now hanging on his every word. Constantius held up the scroll, which momentarily caught the light.

"*RENUNTIO, RENUNTIO, paganus vias tuas nunc RENUNTIO.*

"RECANT, RECANT, RECANT your pagan ways NOW!" The Christian priests held up their large wooden crosses, taut, in front of them, willing the old men to submit. "Bring your souls to the Light of our Lord," they chanted.

"The word of Jesus Christ and our lord his Father is the only way, the only religion that can be accepted now. There can be no other!" Constantius cried.

"His mistress Helene, that little child, I remember, schooled intensely to Christianity by fervent Agrippa, had succeeded in turning him," Vrittakos thought. He saw Constantius' look deepen, alarmingly. War-fever, blood-fever was taking him over. His eyes, glazed from too much killing in Lundinuim, stared in deep hatred, as he took steps towards the old men, gladius scraping from its hilt. Vrittakos knew it was just precious seconds now.

Suddenly, he became aware of soft footfalls behind him. Venitouta appeared beside him, smiling, shoulders squared, her expression determined and calm. She stepped in front of her husband and spoke directly to Constantius.

"If you have come to murder my husband, you will have to do it through me!" she stated clearly, "And what does your so-called religion say about murdering a defenceless old woman, in cold blood?" Constantius froze, took a step back and seemed to deflate, air being sucked from his body. Venitouta had succeeded on putting this fanatical man on the back foot.

"We will not deny our most ancient Gods, not to you or anyone!" Venitouta replied loudly, clearly, so all could hear, "They are far more venerated, powerful and compassionate than this so-called Jesus Christ, who is Mithras by another name! Abrasax sees down on us all. Ahura Mazda cares for our Earth. Do you?

"You Romans! All you can do is steal our most precious God-given gems sent from the heavens, place them in Rome and think they will serve you there! The jewel of our Goddess Cybele lies not in Pessinus but in Rome! We pagans are the true guardians, not you! We do not deny any God, as we are all together as One! Why must you think you are exclusive? It is true madness and you are mad!" Venitouta stopped and looked squarely into the eyes of Constantius, receiving pure vitriolic hatred in return.

"Look at these," he pulled a leather-pouch from his belt and scattered them before the Greeks, jangling on the ground, they shimmered golden in the light. He bent to pick one up and thrust it towards Venitouta, who repelled her head backwards, "Look, this is my victory over all usurpers and pagans. I have won!

"*Redditor lucis æternæ*, Restorer of the Eternal Light. Recant now!" he screamed

"Never!" came the united chorus of the Greeks. Venitouta reached back to grab her husband's hand, as Constantius growled and pulling the aged-women's hair back to expose her throat, dug his gladius deep in and swiped it across Venitouta's throat. Her mouth opened and blood began to pour out, as it flowed from her, she crumpled to the ground, twitching and gurgling words that Vrittakos could not hear. He howled long and low. Achaikos cried,

"Abrasax be with us now. My soul is whole, I am yours. Protect my family!"

"Kill them now!" ordered Constantius and destroy this villam until nothing is left!"

The Prætorians charged the old men, fifty soldiers to two hunched figures, but their gladius swung and hit them again and again. It was obscene butchery. I looked up to the *dūn* ridge. There was no one there. The family had gone.

… … … … … … … … …

We ran from the killing, Dagrun lurching and choking on her tears. We took the horses and galloped away, to Lãfadūn and safety. We sank ourselves into strong mead, medicine of the spirit. I could not sleep, just remain in that neutral space of feeling nothing.

… … … … … … … … …

The three mutilated bodies had been left. Just left for the flies to skim over. We needed to bury those bodies, before we could even begin to salvage all we could from the villam, which was very little. They had destroyed so much and torched what was left. We wrapped the bodies in white muslin tied close. I looked up and suddenly saw Kiana with Alexios stride towards us. Her eyes were bloodshot, and her face still stained with many tears. But she was strong.

"We have come to reclaim Achaikos," she choked on his name, and Dagrun just broke away and hugged her, as they both cried, shoulders heaving, and loving words spoken through rents of tears.

"We are taking my father back to his home. We have barrels of salt gifted to us by the Durotrige. He is not to be buried here," Alexios stated, "We have a ship waiting by the wharf."

Without more words spoken, we carefully laid the body over my sweet piebald and walked to the wharf. Our last words were softly gifted, and our last sighting of the Greeks was a wave from them all as they sailed away.

As we walked back, Aodhan jangled something in his pocket. What's that?" I asked.

"Oh, I retrieved those bloody medals. I think I will melt them down. I will make much better use of such fine metal."

"Oh, and what will that be?" I replied, curiously handling one that had no blood on it.

"I will caste a new medal I think," Aodhan smiled, "A powerful talisman, much older and loved by all Pagans who know their Mysteries and respect their Gods and Goddesses.

"The thirteen-pointed star!"

EPILOGUE

Kiana turned towards Tamina, her son sitting beside her on the stallion gifted to him by Eyvindr. She was shielding his eyes. For the love of Hecate, he is only 15 years old, she screamed inwardly.

"Tamina my love. It is time. WE are going home."

... ...

The journey to Samarkand was long, arduous but focused. Mother and daughter knew exactly where they were going. For the son, it was an extraordinary adventure. For Tamina, too, it was unknown. She had no knowledge of her heritage.

As they entered the palace of the Sogdian king, and her father, all eyes suddenly turned heavenwards. Kiana, old as she was, felt tears stream down her face. She could no longer control the ages-old emotion from surfacing and finding expression at last. The gold on the columns glittered in her vision as she cried. The unique light blue of her people and of Zoroaster melted into the intricate design. The two colours entwined in a geometry she had forgotten. It grew up the dizzying heights of the dome. The pure gold of its epicentre shone, no matter how dull the day may be.

And in that huge room, her father lay, on the imperial bed, propped up by tasselled pillows. He looked miniscule and very old. She remembered only the youth of him. The height. She had been so small as a girl.

A cry of recognition came from his dry lips.

"Sumaya, my Sumaya! daughter, oh my god, blessed Ahura Mazda, you have heard my prayers!" he uttered with so much joy in his voice

Kiana collapsed into his outstretched arms.

"Papa." Was all could she say. They remained entwined for a long time, silent, unable to find words, for they were inadequate to cover the years of heart-breaking loss.

At last, Kiana reached her hand to Tamina and her son.

"Papa, here is your Granddaughter and Grandson.

The king of Sogdia's hand shook, as he held it out,

"My children, my blessed children" was all he could say over and again. This was beyond his wildest dreams and prayers. More, much more than he hoped for.

Suddenly, from across the room, came a thunderous crash, as platters and goblets hit the marbled floor. And leaning against the nearest column for support, tears streaming from his one good eye, and his mouth trying to make words, but none arriving, stood Andreas.

Tamina let out a cry so profound. The king, looking shocked, twisted his pained neck to see his granddaughter speed into the arms of her lover.

The passion, the love and joy being born in that royal palace, entwined in a spiral growing upwards to the epicentre of the sacred dome, and made all the Gods and Goddesses rejoice.

... ...

"And now my daughter, you must tell this old father everything of your life and leave nothing out!"

"Well," Kiana paused, "there was once this rebellious, arrogant young fool of a girl, who was stupid enough to think her palace home was too small for her. It took three score years to find out how wrong she was!" ....

... ...

AFTERWORD

The synod of Nicaea created a powerbase for the Roman Catholic Christian church. In 303A.D. the highest levels of men within the church, discussed and argued on one major sticking point: Was Jesus Christ ever a human soul, as the early Gnostic Christians, the Essenes always professed he was?

These powerbrokers created a new and permanent version with Christ forever sitting at the right hand of God the father. A trinity was also created of Father, Son and Holy Ghost. Roman Catholicism was born. Edicts were passed and made law.

All who believed and shared the early Gnostic teachings were at first rebuked and then reviled. Gnosticism was trampled underfoot and made heretical. The mystical, compassionate and beautiful Nag Hammedi Codex was buried in the Essene caves, protected from Catholic hands. Gnostics were herded and jostled under the euphemistically large umbrella of Paganism.

The purges and destruction of paganism throughout the Roman Empire began and were born from a deep-festering wound inflicted on the early Christians in sustained and horrendous torture by three despotic Roman Emperors. Nero created a public spectacle of the torture of Christians. It became a signature in times to come. Christianity was viewed as a weird cult. Monotheism was a strange concept for many Pagans, who revered and worshipped many Gods and Goddesses. Archaeological finds in Pompeii, for example, show many figurines of gods and goddesses as personnel amulets. The sacred relationship was almost intimate and personal. Their persona very real. So, the exclusivity of a one-god worship may have seemed alien to many Romans.

The well-documented Decian persecutions of Christians in the middle of the 3rd century was followed by even more harsh acts of public torture in Diocletian's reign as Emperor. These three despotic Emperors effectively laid a curse on humanity of religious fundamentalism and reprisal. It has echoed across the centuries, and that curse we battle with to this very day.

Christianity became something of a groundswell movement in the 3rd century due to several overlapping events. Plague, earthquake, climatic upheaval and rebellion.

It is the lot of the Gods to get blamed with anger, and retribution towards humanity was often attributed to them. Fickle humanity turned to newer gods to worship. Heavenly Father, Son and Holy Ghost offered forgiveness, compassion and above all, exclusivity. A rewritten bible, by the men of Nicaea, forerunner to the St. James' version, negated the feminine principle, and the worship of Mother Earth. This edict put humanity above and beyond all nature.

These faceless bishops and clerics of the holy Roman Catholic Church placed another curse on humanity: the total suppression of the Feminine principle, the very heartbeat of our earth. This relentless suppression of the Feminine into every nook and cranny of societies, histories and education has diminished humanity by negating and making inferior half of our humanity, degrading and debasing women and Mother Earth herself. The insidious Madonna or whore label was created at this time and glued to womankind to endure for centuries. These Roman Catholic men degraded and humiliated Mary Magdalene by making her a whore, when she was in truth (Nag Hammedi) the respected partner to Jesus Christ working alongside him.

And we are now, in the last millennium of all, trying desperately to save our planet home from extinction, honouring the Earth Mother after so very long.

… … … … … … … … …

Emperor Constantine, son of Constantius, declared in an edict that Christianity was the official religion throughout the Empire. He also declared in the same edict, religious tolerance. Paganism and Christianity co-existed for a while under this edict, but the festering wound in many a Christian psyche to the torture and death within so many families, rose up in retaliation.

The worm had turned.

... ...

Hypatia

Hypatia was born in 320A.D in Alexandria, Egypt. She became renowned as a great teacher and a wise councillor. The rich pagan Alexandrian library had been destroyed before her lifetime, but she became an expert in mathematics, philosophy and astronomy. She was a prominent thinker in the Neoplatonic School in Alexandria. She was deeply pagan but was very tolerant towards Christians, and she taught many Christians within her school. She became very popular and justifiably earned an impeccable reputation as a wise councillor. Socrates of Constantinople, a contemporary of Hypatia describes her thus:

"There was a woman at Alexandria named Hypatia, daughter of the philosopher Theon, who made such attainments in literature and science, as to far surpass all the philosophers of her own time. Having succeeded to the school of Plato and Plotinus, she explained the principles of philosophy to her auditors, many of whom came from a distance to receive her instructions. On account of the self-possession and ease of manner which she had acquired in consequence of the cultivation of her mind, she not infrequently appeared in public in the presence of the magistrates. Neither did she feel abashed in going to an assembly of men. For all men on account of her extraordinary dignity and virtue, admired her the more."

These should have continued to be halcyon days for all at the Alexandrian Agora. But there appeared on the scene Cyril, the bishop of Alexandria, a power-hungry fundamentalist Roman Catholic who closed all the synagogues and expelled all the Jews from the city. A terrible feud sprang up between Orestes the Roman prefect to Alexandria and a close colleague and friend to Hypatia.

Cyril and his allies then began a sustained campaign to denounce and undermine Hypatia. It reached a crescendo of hateful "spin" rhetoric from a Coptic bishop John of Nikou:

"And in those days, there appeared in Alexandria a female philosopher, a pagan named Hypatia, and she was always devoted to magic, astrolabes and instruments of music, and she beguiled many people through her Satanic wiles. And the Prefect of the city, Orestes, honoured her exceedingly, for, she beguiled him through her magic. And he ceased attending church as had been his custom...And he not only did this, but he drew many believers to her, and he himself received the unbelievers at his house."

In March 415A.D. a posse of Cyril's henchmen, the parabalani, (fundamentalist Christian yobs) attacked Hypatia's carriage on her way home. They dragged her into a building known as the Kaisarion, a former pagan temple and centre of the Roman imperial religion that had been converted into a Christian church.

There, they stripped Hypatia naked and murdered her using ostraca, oyster shells. They also cut out her eyeballs. They tore her body into pieces and dragged her mangled limbs through the town to a place called Cinarion, where they set them on fire in the traditional Alexandrian manner of cremation of the vilest criminals, symbolically purifying the city of any taint!

Hypatia's murder shocked the entire Roman Empire. It shocked the world. And it shocks us still.

Hypatia: Your illumination shines ever strong, ever brilliant and is never dimmed. Blessed be to you.

... ...

AUTHOR'S NOTE

Berandinzium Villam is a work of fiction. The second historical work, in the Wihtwara Trilogy, based on several years of deep research, using both archaeological evidence and ancient spiritual codex.

The "deep core" of the story, or the "essence of intent" is to underpin the birth of the genocide in 686 A.D. that wiped out the Wihtwara. The focus of the final book in the Wihtwara trilogy.

In delving into our ancient history, it brought me to the stark realization that the dark Roman soul placed a curse on Humanity by glorifying in punitive reprisals on religious minorities. This "essence of intent" was sown and watered. We are still living with that poisoned plant to this day.

My close friend, Merry, and diligent proof-reader offered a title descriptive of Berandinzium Villam. "It is the knot that ties the other two books together."

... ...

The story, which begins in Wihtland, nevertheless took me to surprising and amazing places. I followed the trail with faith. It took me to the Silk Road, and though I have not travelled along its hallowed path in this lifetime, some ancient memory stirred in me. The ancient city of Antioch was on a major fault line and experienced earthquakes of varying magnitudes. But as a fiction writer, I took some artistic licence here, to fully describe an earthquake in Antioch around 259AD, which did not happen at that time. It provided an exciting backdrop to develop the characters in the story. I apologise to any purists in historical accuracy at all costs. Apart from harrowing dialogue, the sheer joy of capturing at least some of its wonders along the Silk Road, will stay with me, and I hope you, the reader will find some lasting reward in reading it.

The Romans gave us straight roads. It was their consummate skill coupled with obsessive tendencies that opened the Silk Road to the Western world. The trade routes were incredible, both over land and sea. And it was not just exquisite goods and artefacts that found their way to western shores. Eastern culture and more importantly, Eastern religions arrived with the goods.

When I learnt that Byzantine treasures and goods from Antioch had found their way to Wihtland, my excitement grew. The Silk Road had even reached Britannia! It is now accepted that the migration of the Suevii from their homelands in the Cimbric Peninsular to Britannia was much earlier than history has told us and that they were established in Britannia and Wihtland at the time of the Romans.

They would have handled and known the Byzantine treasures. They may have been curious and searched for more, finding the sacred and spiritual meanings of Eastern religions. The ancient wisdom from the Silk Road became accessible.

I hold a hitherto unspoken yet tantalizing idea, that the seven Roman Villas occupying the ridge known as the Dragon Line on Wihtland were also used as temples, or Mithraeums, to their god Mithras. Mithraeums were essentially small and mostly underground. Caves were sometimes used to serve as a makeshift temple. There are exactly seven levels of initiation into the faith way of Mithras. And there are, to date, seven villas on Wihtland, Gurnard making an eighth and a possible hospitality villa.

I literally held my breath on this one essential idea. The book stalled. I did not feel I had enough evidence to even entertain the storyline I knew was pivotal to the book.

Then, one day, a piece of archaeological work literally plopped into my inbox. Excavations at Clatterford Villa, Isle of Wight. I owe a debt of gratitude to Malcom Lyne and his team, whose pivotal work at Clatterford exposed and named votive remains and hermetic artefacts definitively showing Eastern religions were indeed practised at the villa and on Wihtland.

"Pines cones are known to be associated with the mystery religions, especially those devoted to the deities of Bacchus and

Mithras. The pinecones found at Clatterford villa were used as symbols of immortality. It is known that imported whole pine-cones were used as votive offerings in temples. It has been suggested that black shiny materials, such as jet and shale are linked to eastern mystery religions that became popular in the 3rd century A.D." (Excavations at Clatterford Roman Villa, Isle of Wight, by Malcolm Lyne and the Hampshire Archaeological Group.)

The thirteen-pointed star braecleat, which I have placed at the beginning of each book in this story, is a hermetic artefact of great importance, because it is so ancient and magical. We have been tricked into falsely believing the number thirteen is bad. The Roman Catholic Church has long tendrils, yet thirteen was the number of people in the original Nazarene Last Supper. And thirteen was also the number I have mentioned in the sacred meal celebrated on Mithras' birthday date of 25th December.

In the occult science of numerology, it is said, "He who understands the number 13 will be given power and dominion." So, in relation to countries and empires, it is no accident that the USA has grabbed the mystic and given this magical number 13 to their flag, with 13 stars, and 13 stripes. On the dollar bill there are 13 steps on the pyramid of the Great Seal. The motto above, Annuit Coeptis has 13 letters. The official birthdate of the United States of America is July the Fourth, containing 13 letters. And so on...

But I believe the significance of this number 13, for our Ancestors was placed heavenwards and astrologically understood. The Romans revered the Sun god, Mithras, or Mithra in his Eastern lineage. The Sun conjoins with the great star of Sirius, whose longitude is 13 degrees Cancer. Sirius is the first-magnitude star that is 40 times brighter than the Sun and is the star that rules all African people. It was venerated in ancient Egypt from time immemorial and was held with great reverence by the ancient Egyptians because it rose heliacally with the Sun at dawn, during the inundation of the life-giving waters to the River Nile.

And even more so, looking to our Pagan roots, we celebrate the solstices and equinoxes governed by the passage of our Moon in 13 weeks x4 which gives us our number of weeks in the year.

And lastly, if there were left any doubts to the sacredness of the number 13 in our lives as human beings, the thirteenth letter of the alphabet is M, which finds its roots in the 13th letter of the Hebrew alphabet, "mem"(meaning Mother) and is the ancient Phoenician word for water. The Egyptian word for water is "moo." M is the most sacred of all the letters, for it symbolizes water, where all life begins.

... ...

East meets West
For the many, not the Few

From the sheer number of archaeological finds on the Isle of Wight and along the Southern coast, of artefacts, coinage and goods from the Eastern countries, there is compelling evidence that the Romans opened the Silk Road for trade to reach the most far-flung places in its Empire. Britannia was considered a hinterland, cold, damp and uncomfortable to live in. Yet, it was mineral rich, so they "soldiered on!"

With that very broad spectrum of human behaviour, from quintessentially very brutal to spiritually uplifting and magnificent, there lies the everyday clashes of will and intent to then experience compassionate understanding and renewal. So, after the seaxes, gladius and bosses were laid down, the Romans, Suevii, (Wihtwara) and Britons went about the business of getting along, as Homo sapiens have this intense herding instinct, living together is as paramount as the sun rising each day!

It was this great divergence of cultural and spiritual focus between the Romans and Wihtwara that gave me huge research material. It was a wonderful learning curve. I hope this is shared well with you, the reader, as it gave me many moments of wonder to experience, albeit 2nd hand, the ancient rituals of Zoroaster, unearthed ancient codex of Mithras, and the sheer magnificence of Abrasax, who made our world with seven laughters!

And how did these ancient Gods and Goddesses of the East interact with the Pagan Wihtwara, with Nerthus and Wōden? From the evidence I found, there was an accord. The Romans had already called Wōden, Mercurius and they, being a very acquisitive race had borrowed the Celtic Goddess Sulis and co-joined her with Minerva. There appeared little or no tensions within this ancient Pagan world to their Gods and Goddesses joining. And I got the real feeling of Multifaith naturally occurring.

In fact, there must have been a learning curve taking place within spiritual communities as aspects of the Eastern knowledge, the stars and astrology were new. Similarly, the deep understanding of the Earth mysteries could be shared too. This placed humanity at its rightful place at the junction of the Infinity 8, between Heaven and Earth. "As above, so below".

The reverse side of the Roman coin, however, offers up a brutality that is extreme and breath-taking. The near total militarization of a whole culture spreading world-wide impacted so much on daily life, resulting in embedded trauma for many people.

The main character, Eyvindr, a Warinni and brother to Dagrun Wahl, battled with his trauma throughout the story, and how this impacted on his spiritual life. In such an emasculated world, the only recourse, I felt, was to bring in the Nornia, the Three Fates, in an imaginary *galdercræft* spell-working to seal the Fate of Rome. Such is the role of a fiction writer, and it felt very good!

... ...

The Villams

Berandinzium Villam, (Brading Villa) holds the focus of this work. And here again, there were hiccups in the research. The villa holds a very special place in the heart of any archaeologist interested in exquisite mosaics. Brading Villa has some very thought-provoking examples, linked to artistry from Antioch, in the first place, and mysterious in true-origin-of-meaning. The cockerel-headed man has defied a definitive explanation. Added to that the remains of a very large cockerel at the entrance of the Atrium led me to think about a Gaullist influence etc. (The ancient Gaul revered the cockerel) And it led me up several alleyways. Again, the book stalled.

My husband, and very best buddy, who is a marvel with internet research, showed me an illustration of the god Abrasax. His cockerel head and serpent legs just clinched it for us. His arms outstretched holding a whip and sun globe was an accurate facsimile of the partly destroyed mosaic at Brading Villa. This mosaic is missing a head, and what is being held in outstretched arms. But the serpent legs are the same as Abrasax. Coupled with the cockerel headed man in another mosaic, we joined up the dots. I have created the lead characters of Berandinzium Villam as Greek/Romans, who revered the ancient religions and created a hidden temple within the villa.

(Excerpt from Roman Wight by Malcolm Lyne: -
Ceremony Ritual and religion.
Perhaps the most unusual evidence of religious practises comes from Brading Villa. The Bacchus mosaic in the south-east corner of the final 3rd c. building has a curious panel depicting a cock-headed man standing at the foot of a flight of steps leading up to a temple. To the left of this temple are two gryphons walking left and right. Recent excavations in the courtyard immediately to the east of this room, uncovered a pit containing the skeletons of two cockerels.

One of the symbols used by Gnostic sects on amulets is that of a fowl-headed man with snakes for limbs. We lack details about Gnostic rites and ceremonies as most of their writings were burnt as heretical by the early Church Fathers. It does seem very possible that Gnostic rites of a Pagan nature were practised by the inhabitants of Brading Villa during the 3rd century.)

There are varying degrees of villa-remains on the island. Newport Villa is worth a visit but Combley saw much of its finds spirited away to the mainland. And that, sadly, is the story for much of the island archaeology. Most of the villas I have created elsewhere on the island have not had extensive excavations except for Clatterford Villa, where Malcolm Lyne and his group excavated to find those exceptional votive cones, and the thirteen-pointed breacleats that are real clues to eastern mystery religions being present on Wihtland.

In some instances, there is very little remaining to excavate. Yet the ghost of them remains, and I have tried to give them life.

Imagine if you will, the Roman elites and Caesars travelling to Britannia, to a replica of Caesar's palace in Rome, Villam Regis Cogidvbni (Fishbourne Palace) close to the south coast, a mere short trip to Vectis, where seven villas reside to offer all seven initiations to Mithras. It would be like taking the waters in Bath!

It behoves me to say, at this point, if fictional inspiration fills the yawning vacuum in our knowledge of our Ancestors, be they Roman or Native, and based on the best research available, then it holds a relevance and I have done my job. But to reiterate it is still fiction!

Villam Regis, (Fishbourne Palace) is in a league all its own. Built as a replica to Caesars's palace on the Antonine hill in Rome, it is stunningly beautiful, restored and well cared for. Some of this huge Villa was destroyed by fire during the troubled 3rd century, when usurpers and would-be western Emperors fought and vied for supremacy. Challenging the might of Rome itself. And in that historical fact lay the opportunity to explore the cause of that fire. I researched to find an elite force of Prætorians, skilled in covert warfare. I would compare them to our SAS. It is within the bounds of possibility that Emperor Constantius commissioned these elites to break the powerbase of the Usurpers, before the invasion could take place.

Berandinzium Villam was similarly destroyed in the late 3rd century, as was Newport Villa (Persici luna Villam) and I have given these events relevance to each other. They became the climax to the book, punitive retribution from Rome for daring to rebel. And there is yet an additional retribution meted out to the Greek/Romans at Brading Villa, that echoes the fate of Hypatia. It exposes the very first stirrings of the purge on Paganism.

This is an excerpt from Roman Wight by Malcolm Lyne: -

"Brading Villa provides a clearer picture of the abandonment of the Villa around 300A.D. Disarticulated human remains from the villa house and evidence for burning, suggest the possibility of a violent event leading to its abandonment."

... ...

The Characters,
Real and Fictional.

I have included some real characters into the plot of Berandinzium Villam, as very fortuitously, they really did appear in Britannia at the right time and added weight to the usurper challenge in western Europe.

I practised some artistic license in building their characters to assist in the plot.

Postumus was a usurper, who declared himself Emperor and came to Britannia in 260A.D. to revel in his sudden glory. In his murky rise to power, he murdered (or ordered the murder) of the son of Emperor Gallienus. It was the mark of a promising usurper to murder someone on the way up. Or, better still, get his soldiers to do it! The power broking and political chicanery takes place at Fishbourne Palace, with Roman elites arriving to curry favours or stab people in the back. The governor of Britannia superior makes a brief appearance, Titus Desticius Juba and a more prominent Roman who does interact with the characters, Octavious Sabinus, governor of Britannia Inferior, whose headquarters were in York (Eboracum). He brings the young Constantius to Villam Regis to protect him from the Cyprian plague just rearing its head in the western reaches of built-up cities.

This is purely a fictional element to the story, but it created an opportunity for Constantius to meet and relate to Helena, who was also sent away from the plague that was devastating her part of the Eastern world. It allowed a sub-plot to grow. Agrippa, the wife of Albanus moulded the young Helena into a devout Christian. Helena became the driving force behind her son Constantine. He created monotheism throughout the Empire. Christianity became the exclusive religion throughout the Western world and set the scene for the obliteration of Paganism.

In addition, I need to add a historical footprint of my own. I have, for story context and plot plausibility, added some artistic licence to the storyline. Both the destruction of Villam Regis,

(Fishbourne Palace) and Berandinzium Villam (Brading Villa) were given by archaeological carbon dating to occur sometime apart from each other, although both occurred well within the usurper rebellions within the troubled Empire of the 3rd century. The Palace was burnt in 280AD approximately and Malcolm Lyne dates the destruction of Brading Villa and Newport Villa to approximately 303AD. The need to bring these events closer together, and to impress upon you, the reader, that no reason was given for their destruction, gave me a fictional opportunity to intensify the story's plot. The Greek main characters, Achaikos, Vrittakos and Venitouta were aging as the story jumped from 260AD to 294AD.

They had reached their nineties, a rare old age in these early days, but not impossible as the wealthy Greek diet was very good.

It was a punitive attack by the Roman Empire, on those "Despicable Clique" usurpers.

To add a postscript to this section, Postumus was assassinated by his own soldiers several years later. The fictional element is Constantius (who was known to be a Christian sympathizer) becomes the fundamentalist Christian who murders the Greek/Romans and torches Brading Villa. On the factual side, however, he did take part in the genocide of Allectus' army in Lundinuim, and when he died suddenly in York it is said no-one would go near his body. He had a nickname: Constantius Chlorus, "Constantius the Pale".

… … … … … … … … …

The sections with the Wihtwara and the Warinni were a joy to write. Writing and speaking O/E was like coming home. I felt it necessary to include Latin phraseology, Assyrian quotes and Welsh to honour those people of different tribes and races: characters though they may be, with their own language being spoken, they became much more authentic. It has underpinned the now known fact that multiculturalism we herald today as a 21st century phenomenon was accepted and flourishing in the 3rd century. I found Latin difficult to get to grips with. Greek was just fun to see their alphabet spill onto the page like a tapestry. Welsh, as the nearest language, to honour the Durotrige, who I gave much more flesh to, and created characters I would want to expand even more. The old Druid is immortal.

And Dagrun Wahl. She came back as a Spirit, because I simply could not have her exit. And her ethereal presence gave some weight to the story.

Eyvindr is the male "spine" of the story. He is the Warinni who suffers most at the hand of the Romans. He is a "marked" man if ever there was one. His trauma is carried nobly. And his courage is enormous. But the blows dealt to his spiritual life is the focus, for much of the story. He truly walks in two worlds, and he honours both to the very end. But it is his heart that speaks finally and the acknowledgment that the twisted ways of the Roman mind will be the end of them. The three Fates win. But it costs him his family and his home.

The female "spine" of the story is Kiana. She carries the spiritual wisdom of the East, of Persia. Her character just grew effortlessly, becoming the conduit to learn the wonders and extraordinary power of Zoroaster, the first environmental God!

Achaikos, the "fallen" priest became wonderfully human as the journey progressed. And learning the ancient depth and wisdom of Abrasax, the real magick in the codex was truly enhancing. And I hope, like myself, it has piqued your interest to learn more. The bibliography will give you much reading material.

And speaking of Codex: the Mithras papyrus that lives in the Paris museum and is now printed for us to assimilate, offered up a truly unique insight into the depth of reverence expected and practised by initiates of Mithras in the ancient days.

It taught me the reverence of human sound, vocalization to call to the higher Spirits. It taught me the sharpness of mind and memory to access in full, this alliteration and invocation. My goodness they did these things seriously then with knobs on!!!!

The passage with Aelius/Eyvindr passionately invoking the Fire Gods from the Mithras liturgy will remain one of the most powerful descriptive to grace the pages of the Wihtwara trilogy.

Finally, it has been asked on occasion, why the Suevii and Britons did not, upon the exit of the Roman civilization from their land, keep up, improve the infrastructure, which was, by our standards far superior to theirs.

"Ne'er the twain shall meet" answers that.

They watched as the Romans tortured their Earth Mother. Gave not one prayer to the land spirits, the earth spirits. Nerthus was not respected. They were militarized to an intense degree. Testosterone ruled their lives. The Feminine principle was absent. Compassion had little place for expression.

But above all, there was no love for the land. No deep closeness to the Earth and therefore no peace. The Suevii simply did not want to copy them in any way.

And here we are, trying at this late hour to save our Earth Mother, wanting from a deep-soul depth, the very life the Suevii won back from the Romans.

Lest we forget!

Bletsunga Beorhte. Jan Harper Whale. 2019

... ...

Latin Glossary

Ala...reception room
Atrium...
entrance with pillars
Avunculus...
Uncle on mother's side
Avus...Grandfather
Ballistæ...fireballs
Birrus Britannicus...
British winter cloak
Buccina...Horn
Calceas...
hobnailed closed boots
Capite velato...head veil
Cardo Maximus...
pillared main avenue
Cathedra supinas...
chaise longue
*Colonia Claudia Ara
Agrippinensium*...
German city of Cologne
Cornu...Tuba
Cubiculum...bedroom
Cubitum...
length of 1½ Roman feet
Culina...kitchen
Denarius...

higher Roman currency
Diadem...crown of kings
Diamones...demons
Divas Diva Sacrarium...
Sanctuary of the Gods
Donna Dia...
Roman Goddess
Exploratores...
military explorers
Formosus...beautiful
Frater...Mithraic' brothers
Gesoriacum...Boulogne
Gradus...2½ Roman feet
Hōræ Arum...
Goddess of the seasons
Hospes cubiculum...
guest bedroom
Hydraulis...Greek organ-
type musical instrument
Impluvium...pool
Impossibilis...Impossible
Indutus...Underwear
Ita est...yes!
Justa Facere...Honourable
mausoleum burial
Legatus Legionis...

Commander of a legion
Lúna...
Roman Moon Goddess
Lunula...
female adolescent talisman

Lycium barbarum...
box trees
Magnificus...magnificent
Maius rite of Ver...
May rite of Spring
Manumissio...
slave's freedom
Mesa...main street
Míllia...1 mile
Minerva...
Roman Goddess of the Arts
Mitra...turban
Morpheus...God of dreams
Novem annus...9 years
Nymphæum...
indoor water feature
Opus cæmentium...
Roman cement
Palanquin...
sedan travelling chair
Passus...
pace 5 roman feet (1.48m)
Pater Sacrorum...
Father of Fathers
Patruus...
Uncle mother's side
Pattilum...spade
Peditatus...foot soldier
Per omnis Hades...
By all Hades!

Peripteros...
Temple to Cybele
peristylium...garden
Pertinax...
Governor of Britannia
Petasus...
wide brimmed travelling hat
Pila...cape
Pileus Libertus...
hat only worn by Freedmen
Point Ægypti...Egypt Point
Popinas...public house
Præsepia...Altar
Problemata...problem
Prohibeo...Halt!
Religio Licita...
Religious high Status
Sagittarii...archers
Saxum Demulceo Villam...
Lulling stone Villa
Scabellums...
foot musical instrument
Scapha...boat
Seconda...24 seconds
Servus...slaves
Sestertii...Roman currency
Soccus...felt slippers
Sol Rex Villam...
Sun God villa
Stade...607 feet
Stadion...Roman mile
Stolæ...over shawl
Subligaculum...day bedroom
Subligaria...underpants
Superstitio...A religious cult
Tablinum...reception room

Tali game...
knuckle bones (5 jacks)
Testudo...
military turtle formation
The Stephane...
female triangular crown
*Thermæ Balneæ...*hot baths
Toga Prætexta...
Vestal Virgin Toga
Tormentum onager...
giant sling
*Triclinium...*office

Trireme...
Roman ship 3 banks of oars
Tu cumulus excrementum...
you pile of excrement!
Tunica...
simple over garment
*Uncia...*inch (24.67mm)
Venenatus spuo...
Poisonous spit!
Virgo et Mater...
girl and her Mother

... ...

Anglo-Saxon Glossary

Adlian síclian...become sick
Ãðum...sister's husband
Æðele...high born noble
Æðeling...prince
Æðelu...noble family
Ægishjãlmar...helm of awe
Ælf...elves
Ælf gescot...elf shot
Ælfscyne...elf-fair
Ælfsiden...
apparition, nightmare
Ælscienu...beautiful
Æmta...quiet
Ãlfablõt...elf-blessing
Ãrtèas...dishonourable
Attorlaðe...betony
Bæc bord...larboard
Bèahgifa...ring-giver
Bèam...wooden ship
Bebod...decree
Belene...henbane
Beorht stãn...bright stone
Brim...sea
Brimfugol...sea bird
Brõðor...brother
Burgstede...city (m)
Buriel...bury
Byrg...to bury

Byrgels...Burial place
Cealcstãn...limestone
Ceaster...city (f)
Ceasterwic...women's village
Cenningstãn...
touching stone
Ceorl...husband
Cnearr...small ship
Cnèomagas...kinsmen
Cõlian...become cold
Cwèn...Queen
cwèn...wife
Cýððu...native land
Cynecynn...royal family
Cynedõm...kingdom
Cyng...king
Cynn...family
Dæg...day
Dæg weorþung...celebration
Deaõ...death
Deaõ-gerihte...death rite
Ðèodcyning...
king over a nation
Dèore brõðor...dear brother
Ðinen...servant
Dohtor...daughter
Ðoncian þu...thank you
Ðoncian þu mín drihten...

Thank you, my lord,

Drímeolce Cwèn...
May queen
Drímeolce intrepettan...
May dance
Đrítig...thirty
Đrūh...coffin
Drýcræftig...
magically skilled
Drymãnn...magician
Dūnælfen...mountain elves
Ealdorðegn...chief thane
Ealdorman...earl
Èalond...island
Èam...uncle Maternal
Eard...homeland
Eatenas...giant kin
Èðel...family's land
Fæðe...father's sister
Fæder...father
Fædera...father's brother
Fæderansuni...Cousin
Feferfuge...feverfew
Fille...thyme
Finule...fennel
Flot...Sea
Fōdhèrun...
the stretched one
Forðgeorn lytling...
Impetuous child
Foregísl...hostage
Forlidennes...Shipwreck
Forstoppian...stop
Forwrègan...
wrongly accused
Friþ-spott...vigil
Fylgia... "Fetch" animals

Galdrastafur...
binding runes
Gangern...shit house
Gebroðor...
oath-sworn brothers
Gebūr...farmer
Gecwèman...please
Geðèode...nation
Gefreoge...tradition
Gehwilian...
become poisonous
Gerihte...rite
Gesib...Kinsman
Godcund...sacred
Hãlig mōnaþ...September
Hãlig stãn...sacred stones
Hãlig wielle...Sacred well
Hèaburg...capitol
Hèahfæder...patriarch
Hèahwita...high councillor
Heorð Cyng...hearth king
Hlýda...march
Hū...hut
Hūs...house
Hwata...soothsayer
Hymlic...hemlock
Ieldran...parents
Kornmjölsgot...
barley porridge
Lãcnung...medicine house
Læringmæden...
female pupil
Lèasung...liar
Lenctenmōnaþ...
spring month
Leof frèond...dear friend
Lèogere...liar
Ljðð leoð...spell song

Londlèod...native people
Lytel spere...little spear
Mæden...girl maiden

Mædmōnaþ...
meadow month
Mægðe...mayweed
Medowyrt...meadowsweet
Menniscnes...humanity
Mín frèogan...my love
Modrigensunu...Aunt
Morðor...murder
Mucgwyrt...Mugwort
Næhfædras...
close Ancestors
Nefene...Nephew
Nefene...niece
Neja...nephew
Neorxenawang...
Nerthus meadow
Neorxenawang...
Spiritual home
Nigon mōnaþ...
9 month's pregnancy
Nigt-gala...night singer
Niht...night
Onflyge...flying venom
Orcneas...zombies
Ordœðung...Start breathing!
Popina...local wine bar
Pypelian...become pimply
Rihthand...right-hand
Rōmãnisc...roman
Rōmwèalas...Romans
Sãcerde...priestess
Sǽ...Sea, Ocean
Sǽ genga...sea-going vessel
Sǽ naca...sea vessel

Sǽl lida...sea farer
Særima...coast
Sãwol...spirit/soul
Scip...Ship
Sciprap...ship's rope
Scōp...storyteller
Seax...domestic dagger
Seiðr...feminine magic
Slæn wyrhta drymãnn...
blacksmith
Smiððe...smithy
Soctunga...succubus
Spakōna...high priestess
Spíwãn...vomit
Stefn...ship's stern
Stiðe...nettle
Stune...lamb's cress
Sumor...summer
Sweostor...sister
Swustersuna...sister's son
Þearu...copse
Tunstede...men's village
Utiseta...
shamanic vision quest
Völva...high priestess
Vördhlokkur...Warlock
Wacian...prayer vigil
Wælspere skaldcræft...
sacred spear
Wæterfæsten...
camp by water
Wæterœlfadl...
water-elf disease
Warlocan...wizard
Wealte...ring
Wegbrade...Plantain
Wergulu...crab-apple
Wice...week

Widwe...widow
Wíscwèn...wise woman
Wita-wítega...wise-man
Woruld scamu...
public disgrace
Wranga...ship's hold
Wryd rapas...
magical weaving
Wuduelfen...woodland elves

Wudufæsten...
camp by woods
Wuduwosan...
wild spirits of the wood
Wuldortanas...
rods of wonder
Wynstra...left
Wyrt-hūs...herb-house
Ýðfaru...sea journey

... ...

Bibliography

The Fate of Rome: Climate, Disease, and the end of an Empire...Kyle Harper

The Germany and the Agricola of Tacitus

Life in a Roman villa...Brenda Williams

Roman Wight...Malcolm Lyne

Martin Henig.... Gnostic interpretation of the Brading mosaics.

Abrasax, beyond good and evil...Michael Faust

The Book of Abrasax...Michael Cecchetelli

The Mysteries of Mithras...Charles River Editors

Roman Britain...Henry Freeman

Mithras, Mysteries and Initiation Rediscovered...D. Jason Cooper

Hampshire Field club Archaeological society

Excavations at Clatterford Roman villa - Isle of Wight

(Peter Busby, Dominque de Moulins, Malcolm Lyne, Sean Phillips and Rob Scaife)

Web links: -

Wikipedia: -

Zoroastrianism

Zoroastrian Creed

Zoroastrian Calendar

The Gathas

The Avesta and Ab-Zohr Yasna service

Sogdia

Abrasax

Papyri Graecae Magicae:

The Mithras Liturgy

First Council of Nicaea

The True meaning of the number 13

Lulling stone Villa

... ...

Printed in Great Britain
by Amazon

72802799R00312